By Robert Ludlum

The Bourne Sanction (*with Eric Van Lustbader*)
The Bourne Betrayal (*with Eric Van Lustbader*)
The Bancroft Strategy
The Ambler Warning
The Bourne Legacy (*with Eric Van Lustbader*)
The Tristan Betrayal
The Janson Directive
The Sigma Protocol
The Prometheus Deception
The Matarese Countdown
The Cry of the Halidon
The Apocalypse Watch
The Road to Omaha
The Scorpio Illusion
The Bourne Ultimatum
The Icarus Agenda
The Bourne Supremacy
The Aquitaine Progression
The Parsifal Mosaic
The Bourne Identity
The Matarese Circle
The Gemini Contenders
The Holcroft Covenant
The Chancellor Manuscript
The Road to Gandolfo
The Rhinemann Exchange
Trevayne
The Matlock Paper
The Osterman Weekend
The Scarlatti Inheritance

THE COVERT-ONE NOVELS
The Altman Code (*with Gayle Lynds*)
The Paris Option (*with Gayle Lynds*)
The Cassandra Compact (*with Philip Shelby*)
The Hades Factor (*with Gayle Lynds*)
The Lazarus Vendetta (*with Patrick Larkin*)
The Moscow Vector (*with Patrick Larkin*)
The Arctic Event (*with James Cobb*)

Also by Philip Shelby

Days of Drums
Last Rights
Gate Keeper

ROBERT LUDLUM'S
THE CASSANDRA COMPACT
A COVERT-ONE NOVEL

Series created by Robert Ludlum
Written by Philip Shelby

An Orion paperback

First published in Great Britain in 2001
by HarperCollins*Publishers*
This paperback edition published in 2005
by Orion Books Ltd,
Orion House, 5 Upper St Martin's Lane,
London WC2H 9EA

An Hachette Livre UK company

A CIP catalogue record for this book is available
from the British Library.

Printed and bound in Great Britain by
Clays Ltd, St Ives plc

The Orion Publishing Group's policy is to use papers that
are natural, renewable and recyclable products and
made from wood grown in sustainable forests. The logging
and manufacturing processes are expected to conform to
the environmental regulations of the country of origin.

www.orionbooks.co.uk

THE
CASSANDRA
COMPACT

1

The caretaker stirred when he heard the crunch of tyres on gravel. There was barely any light left in the sky, and he had just made coffee and was reluctant to get up. But his curiosity got the better of him. Visitors to Alexandria seldom ventured into the cemetery at Ivy Hill; the historic town on the Potomac had a brace of other, more colourful attractions and amusements to offer the living. As for the locals, not many came out on a weekday; fewer still on a late afternoon when the April rains lashed the sky.

Peering through his gatehouse window, the caretaker saw a man get out of an ordinary-looking sedan. *Government?* He guessed that his visitor was in his early forties, tall and very fit. Dressed for the weather, he had on a waterproof jacket, dark pants, and workman's boots.

The caretaker watched the way the man stepped away from the car and looked around, taking in his surroundings. *Not government – military.* He opened the door and came out under the overhang, observing how his visitor stood there, gazing through the gates of the cemetery, oblivious to the rain matting his dark hair.

Maybe this is his first trip back here, the caretaker thought. They were all hesitant their first time, loath to enter a place associated with pain, grief, and loss. He looked at the man's left hand and saw no ring. *A widower?* He tried to remember if a young woman had been interred recently.

'Hello.'

The voice startled the caretaker. It was gentle for such a big man, and soft, as if he'd thrown the salutation like a ventriloquist.

'Howdy. If you're fixin' to visit, I got an umbrella I can let you have.'

'I'd appreciate that, thank you,' the man said, but he didn't move.

The caretaker reached around the corner into a stand made from an old watering can. He gripped the handle of the umbrella and stepped towards the man, taking in his visitor's high-planed face and startling navy blue eyes.

'Name's Barnes. I'm the caretaker. If you tell me who you're visiting, I can save you wandering around in this mess.'

'Sophia Russell.'

'Russell, you say? Doesn't ring a bell. Let me look it up. Won't take but a minute.'

'Don't bother. I can find my way.'

'I still gotta have you sign the visitors' book.'

The man unfurled the umbrella. 'Jon Smith. Dr Jon Smith. I know where to find her. Thank you.'

The caretaker thought he detected a break in the man's voice. He raised his arm, about to call after him, but the man was already walking away, his strides long and smooth, like a soldier's, until he disappeared into the grey sheets of rain.

The caretaker stared after him. Something cold and sharp danced along his spine, made him shudder. Stepping back into the gatehouse, he closed the door and bolted it firmly.

From his desk, he removed the visitors' ledger, opened it to today's date, and carefully entered both the man's

2

name and the time he had arrived. Then, on impulse, he turned to the back of the ledger, where the interred were listed in alphabetical order.

Russell . . . Sophia Russell. Here she is: row 17, plot 12. Put into the ground . . . exactly one year ago!

Among the three mourners who'd signed the register was Jon Smith, MD.

So why didn't you bring flowers?

Smith was grateful for the rain as he walked along the road that wended its way through Ivy Hill. It was like a shroud, strung across memories that still had the power to cut and burn, memories that had been his omnipresent companions this past year, whispering to him in the night, mocking his tears, forcing him to relive that terrible moment over and over again.

He sees the cold white room in the hospital at the United States Army Medical Research Institute for Infectious Diseases in Frederick, Maryland. He is watching Sophia, his love, his wife-to-be, writhing under the oxygen tent, gasping for breath. He stands, only inches away, yet powerless to help her. His screams at the medical staff echo off the walls and return to mock him. They don't know what's wrong with her. They, too, are powerless.

Suddenly she cries out – a sound Smith still hears in his nightmares, and prays never to hear again. Her spine, bent like a bow, arches to an impossible angle; sweat pours off her as if to rid her body of the toxin. Her face is bright with fever. For an instant she is frozen like that. Then she collapses. Blood pours out of her nose and throat. From deep within comes the death rattle, followed by a gentle sigh, as her soul, free at last, escapes its tortured confines . . .

Smith shivered and looked around quickly. He didn't

realize that he had stopped walking. The rain continued to drum on the umbrella, but it seemed to fall in slow motion. He thought he could hear every drop as it spattered off the nylon.

He wasn't sure how long he stood there, like an abandoned, forgotten statue, or what finally made him take a step. He didn't know how he came to be on the path that led to her grave or how he found himself standing in front of it.

SOPHIA RUSSELL
NOW IN THE SHELTER OF THE LORD

Smith leaned forward and ran his fingertips across the smooth top of the pink-and-white granite head-stone.

'I should have come more often, I know,' he whispered. 'But I couldn't bring myself to do it. I thought that if I came here, I would have to admit that I've lost you forever. I couldn't do that . . . until now.

'"The Hades Project." That's what they called it, Sophia, the terror that took you away from me. You never saw the faces of the men who were involved; God spared you that. But I want you to know that they have paid for their crimes.

'I had my taste of revenge, my darling, and I believed that it would bring me peace. But it did not. For months I have been asking myself how I might earn that serenity; in the end, the answer was always the same.'

From his jacket pocket, Smith took out a small jeweller's box. Opening the lid, he stared at a six-carat, marquis-cut diamond in a platinum setting that he had picked out at Van Cleef & Arpel in London. It was the wedding ring he had intended to slip on

4

the finger of the woman who would have become his wife.

Smith crouched and pushed the ring into the soft earth at the base of the headstone.

'I love you, Sophia. I will always love you. Your heart is still the light of my life. But it is time for me to move on. I don't know where I'll go or how I'll get there. But I must go.'

Smith brought his fingertips to his lips, then touched the cold stone.

'May God bless you and look after you always.'

He picked up the umbrella and took a step back, staring at the headstone as though imprinting its image in his mind for all time. Then he heard the soft football behind him and turned around fast.

The woman holding the black umbrella was in her mid-thirties, tall, with brilliant red hair pulled back in a ponytail. A spray of freckles dotted her nose and high cheekbones. Her eyes, green like reef waters, widened when she saw Smith.

'Jon? Jon Smith?'

'Megan . . . ?'

Megan Olson walked up quickly, took Smith's arm and squeezed it.

'Is it really you? My God, it's been . . .'

'A long time.'

Megan looked past him at Sophia's grave. 'I'm so sorry, Jon. I didn't know that anyone would be here. I didn't mean to intrude.'

'It's all right. I did what I came to do.'

'I guess we're both here for the same reason,' she said softly.

She drew him under the shelter of a massive oak and looked at him keenly. The lines and creases on his face

5

were deeper than she remembered, and there was a host of new ones. She could only imagine the kind of year Jon Smith had endured.

'I'm sorry for your loss, Jon,' she said. 'I wish I could have told you that sooner.' She hesitated. 'I wish I had been here when you needed someone.'

'I tried calling but you were away,' he replied. 'The job . . .'

Megan nodded ruefully. 'I was away,' she said vaguely.

Sophia Russell and Megan Olson had both grown up in Santa Barbara, had gone to school there, then on to UCLA. After college, their paths had diverged. Sophia had gone to complete her Ph.D. in cell and molecular biology and had joined USAMRIID. After receiving her master's in biochemistry, Megan had accepted a position at the National Institutes of Health. But after only a three-year tenure she had switched to the medical research division of the World Health Organization. Sophia had received postcards from all over the world and had pasted them in a scrapbook as a way to keep track of her globe-trotting friend. Now, without warning, Megan was back.

'NASA,' Megan said, answering Smith's unspoken question. 'I got tired of the Gypsy life, applied to the space-shuttle candidate school, and was accepted. Now I'm first alternate on the next space mission.'

Smith couldn't hide his amazement. 'Sophia always said she never knew what to expect from you. Congratulations.'

Megan smiled wanly. 'Thanks. I guess none of us knows what we can expect. Are you still with the army, at USAMRIID?'

'I'm at loose ends,' Smith replied. It wasn't the whole

truth but close enough. He changed the subject. 'Are you going to be in Washington for a while? Might give us a chance to catch up.'

Megan shook her head. 'I'd love to. But I have to go back to Houston tonight. But I *don't* want to lose touch with you, Jon. Are you still living out in Thurmont?'

'No, I sold the place. Too many memories.'

On the back of a card he jotted down his address in Bethesda, along with a phone number that he was actually listed under.

Handing her the card, he said, 'Don't be a stranger.'

'I won't,' Megan replied. 'Look after yourself, Jon.'

'You too. It was good to see you, Megan. Good luck on the mission.'

She watched him walk out of the overhang and disappear into the drizzle.

'I'm at loose ends . . .'

Megan had never thought of Smith as a man without purpose or direction. She was still wondering about his cryptic comment as she walked over to Sophia's grave, the rain drumming on her umbrella.

2

The Pentagon employs over twenty-three thousand workers – military and civilian – housing them in a unique structure that covers almost four million square feet. Anyone looking for security, anonymity, and access to both the world's most sophisticated communications plus the power centres of Washington could not ask for a more perfect venue.

The Leased Facilities Division occupies a tiny portion of the offices in the Pentagon's E block. As its name implies, Leased Facilities oversees the procurement, management, and security of buildings and land for the military, everything from storage warehouses in St Louis to vast tracts of Nevada desert for an air force testing ground. Given the decidedly unglamorous nature of its work, the men and women in the division are more civilian than military in character. They arrive at the offices at nine o'clock in the morning, put in a dutiful day's work, and leave at five. World events that might keep their colleagues at their desks for days on end have no impact on them. Most of them like it that way.

Nathaniel Fredrick Klein liked it too – but for altogether different reasons. Klein's office was at the very end of a hall, tucked between doors that were marked ELEC-TRICAL ROOM and MAINTENANCE. Except there were no such service rooms behind those doors and their locks could not be opened even with the most sophisticated key card. That space was part of Klein's secret suite.

There was no nameplate on Klein's door, only an internal Pentagon designation: 2E377. If asked, the few coworkers who'd actually seen him would describe a man in his early sixties, medium height, unprepossessing except for his rather long nose and wireframed glasses. They might recall his conservative and somewhat rumpled suits, perhaps the way he would smile briefly when passed in the hall. They might have heard that Klein was sometimes called before the joint chiefs or a congressional committee. But that would be in keeping with his seniority. They might also know that he was vested with the responsibility of checking the properties the Pentagon leased or had an interest in throughout the world. That would account for the fact that one seldom saw him at all. In fact it was sometimes difficult to say who or what Nathaniel Klein really was.

At eight o'clock in the evening, Klein was still behind his desk in the modest office that was identical to all the others in the wing. He had added a few personal touches: framed prints depicting the world as imagined by sixteenth-century cartographers; an old-fashioned pedestal-mounted globe; and a large, framed photograph of the earth taken from the space shuttle.

Although very few people were aware of it, Klein's affinity for things global was a direct reflection of his real mandate: to serve as the eyes and ears of the president. From this nondescript office Klein ran a loosely knit organization known as Covert-One. Conceived by the president after the horror known as the Hades Project, Covert-One was designed to be the chief executive's early warning system and secret response option.

Because Covert-One worked outside the usual military-intelligence bureaucracy and well away from the scrutiny of Congress, it had no formal organization or headquarters. Instead of accredited operatives, Klein recruited men and women whom he called 'mobile ciphers' – individuals who were acknowledged experts in their fields yet who, through circumstances or dispositions, found themselves outside the mainstream of society. Most – but certainly not all – had some military background, were holders of numerous citations and awards, but had chafed under structured command, and so had elected to leave their respective services. Others came from the civilian world: former investigators – state and federal; linguists who were fluent in a dozen languages; doctors who had travelled the world and were accustomed to the harshest conditions. The very best, like Colonel Jon Smith, bridged the two worlds.

They also possessed one factor that disqualified so many Klein looked at: their lives were strictly their own. They had little or no family, few encumbrances, and a professional reputation that would stand up to the closest scrutiny. These were invaluable assets for an individual sent in harm's way thousands of miles from home.

Klein closed the folder on the report he had been reading, removed his glasses, and rubbed his weary eyes. He was looking forward to going home, being greeted by his cocker spaniel, Buck, and enjoying a finger of single-malt scotch followed by whatever dinner his housekeeper had left in the oven. He was about to get up when the connecting door to the next room opened.

'Nathaniel?'

The speaker was a trim woman a few years younger than Klein, with bright robin's eyes and greying blond hair done in a French twist. She wore a conservative

10

blue business suit accented by a string of pearls and a filigree gold bracelet.

'I thought you'd gone home, Maggie.'

Maggie Templeton, who'd been Klein's assistant for the ten years he had worked at the National Security Agency, arched her neatly sculptured brows.

'When was the last time I left before you did? Good thing I didn't, too. You'd better have a look at this.'

Klein followed Maggie into the next room, which was really one large computer station. Three monitors were lined up side by side, along with a host of servers and storage units, all driven by the government's most advanced software. Klein stood back and admired the dexterity and proficiency with which Maggie worked her keyboard. It was like watching a virtuoso performance by a concert pianist.

Besides the president, Maggie Templeton was the only person familiar with the entire workings of Covert-One. Knowing he would need a skilled and trusted right hand, Klein had insisted on Maggie's being involved from the get-go. Besides having worked for him at the NSA, she had better than twenty years experience as a senior CIA administrator. But most important to Klein, she was family. Maggie's sister, Judith, had been Klein's wife, taken by cancer years ago. Maggie too had had her share of tragedy: her husband, a CIA covert operative, had never returned from a mission abroad. As fate would have it, Maggie and Klein were the only family each had.

Finished on the keyboard, Maggie tapped on the screen with an elegantly manicured fingernail.

VECTOR SIX.

The two words pulsed in the centre of the screen like a blinking traffic light at an empty intersection in a country town. Klein felt the hairs on his forearms push against his shirtsleeves. He knew exactly who Vector Six was; he could see his face as clearly as if the man were standing next to him. Vector Six: the code name, if it ever appeared, was to be construed by Klein as a panic signal.

'Shall I pull up the message?' Maggie asked quietly.

'Please . . .'

She touched a series of keys and the encrypted message of letters, symbols, and numbers shot up on the screen. She then repeated the process with different keys to activate the decryption software. Seconds later, the message appeared in clear text:

> *Dîner – prix fixe – 8 euro*
> *Spécialité: Fruits de mer*
> *Spécialité du bar: Bellini*
> *Fermé entre 14–16 heures*

Even if a third party somehow managed to decode the message, this menu of a nameless French restaurant was both innocuous and misleading. Klein had set up the simple code the last time he had met Vector Six face to face. Its meaning had nothing to do with Gallic cuisine. It was the call of last resort, a plea for immediate extraction.

Klein didn't hesitate. 'Please reply as follows: *Reservations pour deux.*'

Maggie's fingers flew over the keys, tapping out the secure response. The single sentence bounced off two military satellites before being sent back to earth. Klein didn't know where Vector Six was at that moment, but as long as he had access to the laptop Klein had given him, he could download and decrypt the reply.

Come on! Talk to me!

Klein checked the time stamp on the message: The message was less than two minutes old.

A reply flashed across the screen: *Reservations confirmées.*

Klein exhaled as the screen faded to black. Vector Six would not stay on-line any longer than was absolutely necessary. Contact had been established, an itinerary proposed, accepted, and verified. Vector Six would not use this channel of communications again.

As Maggie shut down the link, Klein sat down in the only other chair in the room, wondering what extraordinary circumstances had prompted Vector Six to contact him.

Unlike the CIA and other intelligence agencies, Covert-One did not run a string of foreign agents. Nonetheless, Klein had a handful of contacts abroad. Some had been cultivated during his days at the NSA; others were the results of chance meetings that had blossomed into a relationship based on both trust and mutual self-interest.

They were a diverse group: a doctor in Egypt whose patients included most of the country's ruling elite; a computer entrepreneur in New Delhi who provided his skills and equipment to his government; a banker in Malaysia adept at moving, hiding, or ferreting out offshore funds anywhere in the world. None of these people knew each other. They had nothing in common beyond their friendship with Klein and the computer notebook he had given each one of them. They accepted Klein as a midlevel bureaucrat but knew that secretly he was much more than that. And they agreed to serve as his eyes and ears not only out of friendship and belief in what he represented, but because they trusted him to help them if, for any reason, their

13

respective homelands suddenly became a dangerous place for them.

Vector Six was one of the handful.

'Nate?'

Klein glanced at Maggie.

'Who gets the call?' she asked.

Good question . . .

Klein always used his Pentagon ID when travelling abroad. If he was going to meet a contact, he made sure it would be in a public place, at a secure location. Official functions at a U.S. embassy were the best choices. But Vector Six was nowhere near an embassy. He was on the run.

'Smith,' Klein said at last. 'Get him on the line, please, Maggie.'

Smith was dreaming of Sophia when the insistent beep of the telephone intruded. He was watching the two of them sitting on a riverbank, in the shadows of immense triangular structures. In the distance was a great city. The air was hot, filled with the attar of roses and of Sophia. *Cairo . . .* They were at the pyramids of Giza, outside Cairo.

The secure line . . .

Smith sat up fast on the couch where he had fallen asleep, fully dressed, after coming home from the cemetery. Beyond the windows streaked with rain, the wind moaned as it drove heavy clouds across the sky. A former combat internist and battlefield surgeon, Smith had developed the gift of waking up fully alert. That ability had served him well during his time at USAMRIID, where sleep was often snatched between long, gruelling hours of work. It served him well now.

Smith checked the time at the bottom right-hand corner of the monitor: almost nine o'clock. He had been asleep for two hours. Emotionally spent, his mind still filled with images of Sophia, he had driven himself home, heated up some soup, then stretched out on the couch and listened to the rain churn overhead. He had not intended to fall asleep, but was grateful that he done so. Only one man could call him on that particular line. Whatever message he had could signal the beginning of a day of infinite hours.

'Good evening, Mr Klein.'

'Good evening to you too, Jon. I hope I'm not disturbing your dinner.'

'No, sir. I ate earlier on.'

'In that case, how soon can you get out to Andrews Air Force base?'

Smith took a deep breath. Klein usually had a calm, businesslike demeanor. Smith had seldom found him curt or abrupt.

Which means there's trouble – and it's closing fast.

'About forty-five minutes, sir.'

'Good. And Jon? Pack for a few days.'

Smith stared at the dead phone in his hand. 'Yes, sir.'

Smith's drill was so ingrained that he was hardly aware of going through the motions. Three minutes for a shower and shave; two minutes to dress; two more to double-check and add a few things to the ready bag in the walk-in closet. On his way out, he set the security system for the house; once he had the sedan out in the driveway, he armed the garage using the remote.

The rain made the ride to Andrews Air Force base longer than usual. Smith avoided the main entry and turned in at the supply gate. A poncho-covered guard examined his laminated ID, checked his name against those on the list of approved personnel, and waved him through.

Smith had flown out of Andrews often enough to know his way around. He had no trouble finding the hangar housing the fleet of executive jets that, most times, ferried around the brass. He parked in a designated area well away from the aircraft taxi lanes, grabbed his ready bag from the trunk, and splashed his way into the immense hangar.

'Good evening, Jon,' Klein said. 'Crappy night. It'll probably get worse.'

Smith set down his bag. 'Yes, sir. But only for the navy.'

The age-old joke didn't get a grin out of Klein this time.

'I'm sorry to have dragged you out on a night like this. Something's come up. Walk with me.'

Smith looked around as he followed Klein to the coffee station. There were four Gulfstream jets in the hangar, but no maintenance personnel. Smith guessed that Klein had ordered them out to ensure privacy.

'They're fuelling a bird with long-range tanks,' Klein said, glancing at his watch. 'Should be ready in ten minutes.'

He handed Smith a Styrofoam cup filled with steaming black coffee, then looked at him carefully.

'Jon, this is an extraction. That's the reason for the rush.'

And the need for a mobile cipher.

Given his army background, Smith was familiar with the terms 'extraction,' as Klein had used it. It meant getting someone or something out of a place or a situation as quickly and quietly as possible – usually under duress and on a tight schedule.

But Smith also knew that there were specialists – military and civilian – who handled this kind of work.

When he said as much, Klein replied, 'There are certain considerations in this case. I don't want to involve any other agencies – at least not yet. Also, I know this individual – and so do you.'

Smith started. 'Excuse me, sir?'

'The man you are going to meet and bring out is Yuri Danko.'

'Danko . . .'

In his mind's eye Smith saw a bearlike man, a few years older than he, with a gentle moon face pockmarked by childhood acne. Yuri Danko, the son of a Dobnets coal miner, born with a defective leg, had gone on to become a full colonel in the Russian army's Medical Intelligence Division.

Smith couldn't shake his surprise. Smith knew that before signing the security agreement that had made him part of Covert-One, Klein had put his entire life under a microscope. That meant Klein was aware that Smith knew Danko. But never in all the briefings had Klein ever hinted that *he* had a relationship with the Russian.

'Is Danko part of –?'

'Covert-One? No. And you are not to mention the fact that you are. As far as Danko is concerned, I'm sending a friendly face to bring him out. That's all.'

Smith doubted that. There was always more to Klein than met the eye. But one thing he was sure of: Klein would never place an operative in harm's way by not telling him everything he needed to know.

'The last time Danko and I met,' Klein was saying,

'we established a simple code that would be used only in an emergency scenario. The code was a menu. The price – 8 euros – indicates the date, April 8, two days from now. One, if we're working on European time.

'The specialty is seafood, which stands for the way Danko will be coming: by sea. The Bellini is a cocktail that was first made in Harry's Bar in Venice. The hours that the restaurant is closed, between two and four in the afternoon, is the time the contact is supposed to be at the rendezvous point.' Klein paused. 'It's a simple but very effective code. Even if the encryption was compromised and the message intercepted, it would be impossible to make sense of the menu.'

'If Danko isn't due in for another twenty-four hours at least, why hit the panic button?' Smith asked.

'Because Danko hit it first,' Klein replied, his concern obvious. 'He might get to Venice ahead of schedule; he might run late. If it's the former, I don't want him twisting in the wind.'

Smith nodded as he sipped his coffee. 'Understood. Now, for the sixty-four-thousand-dollar question: What made Danko jackrabbit?'

'Only he'll be able to tell us his reasons. And believe me, I want to know them. Danko is in a unique position. He would never have compromised it . . .'

Smith raised an eyebrow. 'Unless?'

'Unless *he* was on the verge of being compromised.' Klein put down his coffee. 'I can't say for sure, Jon, but I think Danko is carrying information. If so, it means he thinks I need to have it.'

Klein glanced over Smith's shoulder at an air police sergeant who entered the hangar.

'The aircraft's ready for takeoff, sir,' the sergeant announced smartly.

Klein touched Smith's elbow and they walked to the doors.

'Go to Venice,' he said softly. 'Pick up Danko and find out what he has. Find out fast.'

'I will. Sir, there's something I'll need in Venice.'

Smith needn't have lowered his voice as they stepped outside. The drumbeat of the rain drowned out his words. Only Klein's nod indicated that Smith was talking at all.

3

In Catholic Europe, Easter week is a time of pilgrimages and reunions. Business and schools close their doors, trains and hotels are overbooked, and the denizens of the Old World's landmark cities brace themselves for an onslaught of strangers.

In Italy, Venice is one of the most popular destinations for those seeking to combine the sacred and the profane. The Serenissima is a rich tapestry of churches and cathedrals, enough to satisfy the spiritual needs of even the most devoted pilgrim. Yet it is also a thousand-year-old playground whose narrow streets and cobblestone alleys shelter enterprises catering to a whole spectrum of earthly appetites.

At precisely one forty-five in the afternoon, just as he'd done the past two days, Smith threaded through the rows of tables set out in front of the Florian Café on the Piazza San Marco. He always chose the same table, close to a small, raised platform upon which stood a grand piano. The pianist would arrive in a few minutes, and punctually on the hour, notes written by Mozart or Bach would dance above the chatter and footsteps of the hundreds of tourists who crowded the square.

The server who had waited on Smith the last two days hurried over to his customer. The American – he could only be that, given his accented Italian – was a good customer; that is to say, one who didn't recognize bad service and so tipped generously anyway. Judging by the smart charcoal-grey suit and hand-tooled shoes, the waiter took Smith for a prosperous business executive who, having concluded his transactions, was enjoying a few days' sightseeing at his company's expense.

Smith smiled at the waiter, ordered his usual caffe latte and prosciutto affumicatio sandwich, and flipped open the day's edition of *The International Herald Tribune* to the business section.

His late-afternoon snack arrived just as the pianist struck the opening chords of a Bach variation. Smith dropped two sugar cubes into his coffee and took his time stirring. As he opened his newspaper, he scanned the open area between his table and the Doge's Palace.

Most anytime, St Mark's, with its inevitable crowds, was the perfect place to pick up a running man. But the runner was a day late. He wondered if Yuri Danko had even made it out of Russia at all.

Smith had been with USAMRIID when he had first met Danko, his counterpart in the Russian army's Medical Intelligence Division. The venue was the palatial Victoria-Jungfrau Grand Hotel near Berne. There, representatives of the two countries came together in an informal setting to brief one another on the progress of the gradual shutdown of their respective bioweapons programmes. The meetings were an adjunct to the formal verifications made by international inspectors.

Smith had never been in the business of recruiting agents. But, like every other member of the U.S. team, he had been thoroughly briefed by CIA counterintelligence officers as to how the other side might make its approaches and overtures. During the first few days of the conference, Smith found himself partnered with Danko. Always careful, he nonetheless took a liking to the tall, burly Russian. Danko did not hide the fact that he was a patriot. But, as he told Smith, his work was important to him because he did not want his children to live with the possibility of some madman unleashing a bioweapon for terror or revenge.

Smith was very much aware that such a scenario was not only possible but a grave likelihood. Russia was in the throes of change, crisis, and uncertainty. Meanwhile, it still had an enormous stockpile of bioweapons stored in rusting containers under the halfhearted supervision of researchers, scientists, and military personnel who, more often than not, weren't paid enough to feed their families. For these men, the temptation to sell a little something on the side could be overwhelming.

Smith and Danko started to meet outside the conference's regular hours. By the time the parties were ready to return to their respective countries, the two men had forged a friendship based on mutual respect and trust.

Over the next two years, they met again – in St Petersburg, Atlanta, Paris, and Hong Kong – each time under the auspices of a formal conference. But on each occasion, Smith noticed that Danko was more and more troubled. Although he eschewed alcohol, he would sometimes ramble on about the duplicity of his military masters. Russia, he hinted, was violating its agreements with the United States and the world. While it was making a good show of reducing its bioweapons programmes, advance research had actually accelerated. Worst of all, Russian scientists and technicians were disappearing only to surface in China, India, and Iraq, where there was high demand and unlimited funds for their skills.

Smith was a keen student of human nature. At the end of one of Danko's tortured confessions, he'd said: 'I will work with you on this, Yuri. If that's what you want.'

Danko's reaction was akin to that of a penitent who has finally been cleansed of his burden of sin. He agreed to provide Smith with information he thought the United States should have. There were only two caveats: he would deal only with Smith, not with anyone from the U.S. intelligence community; second, he wanted Smith's word that Smith would look after his family in the event that anything happened to him.

'Nothing's going to happen to you, Yuri,' Smith had said at the time. 'You'll die in your own bed, surrounded by your grandchildren.'

Observing the crowds streaming out of the Doge's Palace, Smith reflected on these words. At the time, he had meant them sincerely. But now, with Danko twenty-four hours late, they tasted like ashes in his mouth.

But you never once mentioned Klein, Smith thought. *That you already had a contact in the United States. Why, Yuri? Is Klein your ace in the hole?*

New arrivals were coming in by gondola and launch that tied up at the wharves in front of the lions of St Mark's. More exited by the majestic basilica, glassy-eyed from the landmark's overwhelming grandeur, Smith watched them all – the young couples holding hands, the fathers and mothers herding their children, the tour groups clustered around guides who shouted above the din in a dozen different languages. He held his newspaper at eye level, but his gaze roamed ceaselessly above the masthead, scanning faces, trying to find that special one.

Where are you? What did you find that was so terrible you had to compromise your secrets and risk your life to bring it out?

The questions gnawed at Smith. Since Danko had

23

severed all contact, there were no answers to be had. According to Klein, the Russian would be coming across war-scarred Yugoslavia, hiding in and moving through the chaos and misery of that region until he reached the coast. There he would find a ship to ferry him across the Adriatic to Venice.

Just get here and you'll be safe.

The Gulfstream was on standby at Venice's Marco Polo Airport; a fast launch was moored at the dock next to the Palazzo delle Prigioni on the Rio di Palazzo. Smith could have Danko on the boat within three minutes of spotting him. They would be airborne an hour later.

Where are you?

Smith was reaching for his coffee when something drifted across his peripheral vision: a heavyset man skirting the edge of a tour group. Maybe a part of it, maybe not. He wore a weatherproof nylon jacket and a golfer's cap; a thick beard and large wraparound sunglasses concealed his face. But there was something about him.

Smith continued to watch, then saw it – a slight limp in the left leg. Yuri Danko had been born with a left leg one inch shorter than his right. Even a custom-made platform shoe could not fully disguise the limp.

Smith shifted in his chair and adjusted his newspaper so that he could follow Danko's movements. The Russian was using the tour group very effectively, drifting alongside, close enough to be mistaken for belonging, not so close as to get the leader's attention.

Slowly, the group turned away from the basilica and headed in the direction of the Doge's Palace. In less than a minute it was abreast the outer row of tables and chairs of the Florian Café. A few tourists broke away from the group, heading for the small snack bar

24

next to the café next door. Smith did not stir as they passed his table, chattering to one another. Only when Danko was passing by did he look up.

'No one's using this chair.'

Smith watched as Danko turned, clearly recognizing Smith's voice.

'*Jon?*'

'It's me, Yuri. Go on, sit down.'

The Russian slipped into the chair, bewilderment etched across his face.

'But Mr Klein . . . He sent *you?* Do you work –?'

'Not here, Yuri. And yes, I came to bring you over.'

Shaking his head, Danko flagged a passing waiter and ordered coffee. He tapped out a cigarette and lit it. Smith noticed that not even the beard could hide how gaunt Danko's face had become. His fingers trembled as he worked to light the cigarette.

'I still can't believe it's you . . .'

'Yuri –'

'It's all right, Jon. I wasn't followed. I'm clean.' Danko leaned back in his chair and stared at the pianist. 'Wonderful, isn't it? The music, I mean.'

Smith leaned forward. 'Are you all right?'

Danko nodded. 'I am now. Getting here wasn't easy, but –'

Danko broke off as the waiter brought his coffee. 'It was very difficult in Yugoslavia. The Serbs are a paranoid bunch. I was carrying a Ukrainian passport but even that was closely checked.'

Smith was straining to still the hundreds of questions swirling in his mind, trying to focus on what had to be done next.

'Is there anything you want to tell me, or give me – right now?'

Danko appeared not to have heard him. His attention was on a pair of carabinieri – Italian militiamen – who were walking slowly among the tourists, their submachine guns slung across their chests.

'Lots of police,' he murmured.

'It's the holidays,' Smith replied. 'They always add extra patrols. Yuri . . .'

'I have something to tell Mr Klein, Jon,' Danko leaned across the table. 'What they're going to do – I never would have believed it. It's insanity!'

'*What* are they going to do?' Smith demanded, trying to control his tone. 'Who's *they*?'

Danko looked around nervously. 'Have you made the arrangements? Can you get me away from here?'

'We can leave right now.'

As Smith dipped into his pocket for his billfold, he noticed the two carabinieri moving between the café tables. One laughed as though the other had made a joke, then motioned in the direction of the sand-wich bar.

Smith counted out some lire, placed the bills under a plate, and was about to push back his chair when the universe exploded.

'*Jon!*'

Danko's scream was cut short by the brutal sound of automatic weapons fired at point-blank range. After passing the table, the two carabinieri had whirled around, guns blazing. Death spat from the two barrels, riddling Danko's body, the force of the bullets slamming him into the back of his chair, then flinging it over.

Smith had barely enough time to register the carnage before he threw himself in the direction of the small grandstand. Bullets stitched the stone and wood around him. The pianist made the fatal mistake of trying to stand up; a fusillade cut him in half. Seconds seemed to move as though trapped in honey. Smith could not believe that the killers were taking so much time, working with deadly impunity. What he did know was that the grand piano, its glossy black frame and white keys horribly splintered, was saving his life, absorbing burst after burst of military-grade bullets.

The killers were professionals; they knew when they had run out of time. Dropping their weapons, they crouched behind an over-turned table and ripped off their military jackets. Underneath, they wore grey and tan windbreakers. From the pockets, they pulled out fishermen's caps. Using the bystanders' panic as cover, they broke and raced towards the Florian Café. As they burst through the front doors, one of them yelled: '*Assassini!* They are killing everyone! For the love of God, call the *polizia!*'

Smith raised his head just in time to see the killers plunge into the screaming crowd of café patrons. He looked back at Danko, lying on his back, his chest shredded. A low animal growl rose in Smith's throat as he leaped off the grandstand and elbowed his way into the café. The herd swept him away to the service doors and into the alley at the back. Gasping, Smith looked frantically in both directions. On the left, he caught a glimpse of grey jackets disappearing around a corner.

The killers knew the area very well. They cut down two twisting alleys, then reached a narrow canal where a gondola was tied to a pier post. One jumped in and grabbed the oar, the other slipped the rope. In seconds they were moving down the canal.

The killer who was oaring paused to light a cigarette. 'A simple enough day's work,' he said to his partner. 'For twenty thousand American dollars, it was almost

27

too simple,' the second replied. 'But we should have killed the other one too. The Swiss gnome was very specific: the target and any contact with him.'

'*Basta!* We fulfilled the contract. If the Swiss gnome wants –'

His words were cut off by the oarsman's exclamation. 'The devil's own!'

The second gunman twisted around in the direction his friend was pointing. His mouth fell open at the sight of the victim's partner pounding down the walkway alongside the canal.

'Shoot the *figlio di putana*!' he screamed.

The oarsman brought out a large-calibre handgun. 'With pleasure.'

Smith saw the oarsman's arm come up, saw the pistol waver as the gondola rocked. He realized the insanity of what he was doing, chasing armed killers without so much as knife to protect himself. But the image of Danko kept his legs churning. Less than thirty feet and closing, because the oarsman could not steady himself to take the shot.

Twenty feet.

'Tommaso –'

The oarsman, Tommaso, wished that his partner would shut up. He could see the demented one closing in, but what did it matter? Obviously he had no weapon, otherwise he would have used it by now.

Then he saw something else, partially exposed beneath the floor planks of the gondola: a hint of a battery and multicoloured wires . . . the kind he himself had used often enough.

Tommaso's scream was cut off by the explosion and the fireball that consumed the gondola, heaving it thirty feet into the air. For an instant, there was nothing but black, acrid smoke. Hurled against the brick wall of a glass factory, Smith saw nothing after the flash, but he smelled the burning wood and blackened flesh as they began to rain down from the sky.

Amid the terror and fearful uncertainty that gripped the square, one man, hidden behind the pillar supporting one of the granite lions of St Mark's, remained calm. At first glance, he appeared to be in his early fifties. But possibly it was the moustache and goatee that made him look older. He wore a French-cut sports coat in window-pane check with a yellow rosette in the lapel. A paisley cravat was nestled against his throat. To the casual observer, he appeared a dandy, perhaps a tenured academic or a genteel retiree.

Except that he moved very quickly. Even as the echoes of gunfire caromed around the piazza, he was already heading in the direction of the fleeing gunmen. A choice had to be made: follow them and the American who was in pursuit, or go to the wounded man. He didn't hesitate.

'*Dottore!* Let me pass! I'm a doctor!'

Cowering tourists responded instantly to his perfect Italian. In seconds, he was kneeling by the bullet-ridden body of Yuri Danko. One glance told him that Danko was beyond anyone's help except perhaps God's. Still, he pressed two fingers to the man's throat as though feeling for a pulse. At the same time, his other hand was busy inside Danko's jacket.

People were beginning to stand up, look around. Look at him. Some were moving his way. As shell-shocked as they were, they would still ask questions that he would rather avoid.

'You there!' the doctor said sharply, addressing a young man who looked like a college student. 'Get over here and help me.' He grabbed the student and forced him to hold Danko's hand. 'Now squeeze . . . I said squeeze!'

'But he's dead!' the student protested.

'Idiot!' the doctor snapped. 'He's still alive. But he will die if he doesn't feel any human contact!'

'But you –'

'I must get help. You stay here!'

The doctor pushed his way through the crowd gathering around the slain men. He was not concerned about the eyes that darted to meet his. Most witnesses were notoriously unreliable under the best of circumstances. Under these conditions, not a single person would be able to describe him accurately.

The first hee-haw of police Klaxons reached him. Within minutes, the entire square would be overrun by carabinieri and cordoned off. Potential witnesses would be rounded up; the interrogations would go on for days. The doctor could ill afford to be caught in the dragnet.

Without seeming to, he moved swiftly to the Bridge of Sighs, crossed it, went past the stalls where hawkers peddled souvenirs and T-shirts, and slipped into the lobby of the Danieli Hotel.

'Good afternoon, *Herr Doktor* Humboldt,' the concierge said.

'A good day to you,' replied the man who was neither a doctor nor Humboldt. To the few who needed to know, his name was Peter Howell.

Howell wasn't surprised that word of the massacre hadn't yet reached the august oasis of the Danieli. Very little of the outside world was permitted to penetrate this fourteenth-century palace built for the Doge Dandolo.

Howell turned left into the magnificent living room and headed for the small bar in the corner. He ordered a brandy and, when the bartender's back was to him, closed his eyes for an instant. Howell had seen his share of dead men, had initiated and been on the receiving end of extreme violence. But the cold, stark killing in St Mark's still managed to sicken him.

He drank half the brandy in a single swallow. When the liquor hit his bloodstream and he felt himself relax, he reached into his coat pocket.

Decades had passed since Howell had been taught the pick-pocket's skill. Feeling Danko's notepaper between his fingers, he was glad to see that he hadn't lost his touch.

He read the sentence once, then a second time. In spite of knowing better, he had hoped that something on the page would give a clue as to why Danko had been slaughtered. And who might be responsible. But none of the words made any sense except one: *Bioaparat.*

Howell refolded the page and tucked it away. He drained the remains of his brandy and signalled the bartender for a refill.

'Is everything all right, *signore?*' the bartender asked solicitously as he served up the drink.

'Yes, thank you.'

'If there's anything you need, please don't hesitate to ask.'

The bartender retreated before Howell's icy gaze.

There's nothing you can help me with, old boy. You're not the one I need.

When Smith opened his eyes, he was startled to see grotesque faces gazing down at him. As he pulled himself back, he discovered that he was slumped in the recess of a doorway to a mask and costume shop. Slowly, he staggered to his feet, instinctively checking for injuries. Nothing was broken, but his face stung. He passed a hand across his cheek and his fingers came away bloody.

At least I'm alive.

He couldn't say that about the killers who had tried to flee in the gondola. The explosion that had caused the craft to disintegrate had also taken its occupants' identities to eternity. Even if the police corralled eye-witnesses, they would be worthless: professional killers were often masters of disguise.

It was the thought of police that got Smith moving. Because of the holidays, all the shops along the canal were closed. There were no people around. But the telltale sound of the police launch Klaxon was growing louder. The authorities couldn't have helped but connect the massacre at St Mark's with the explosion in the canal. Witnesses would tell them that the assassins had run in that direction.

Where they'll find me . . . The same witnesses will connect me to Danko.

The police would want to know about Smith's relationship to the dead man, why they had met, and what they had talked about. They would seize on the fact that Smith belonged to the American military and the interrogation would become even more intense. Yet, in the end, Smith could tell them nothing that would explain the massacre.

Smith steadied himself, wiped his face as best he could, and brushed off his suit. He took a few tentative steps, then walked as quickly as he could to the end of the sidewalk. There, he crossed a bridge and slipped into the shadows of a boarded-up *sequero*, a gondola construction yard. Half a block up, he entered a small church, drifted among the shadows, and emerged through another set of doors. Several minutes later, he was on the promenade next to the Grand Canal, lost among the throngs that moved ceaselessly along the waterfront.

St Mark's Square was cordoned off by the time Smith reached it. Grim-faced carabinieri, submachine guns held at port arms, created a human barrier between the granite lions. Europeans, particularly Italians, were well versed in what to do in the aftermath of what was clearly a terrorist attack: they looked straight ahead and kept on moving past the scene. So did Smith.

He crossed the Bridge of Sighs, passed through the revolving doors of the Danieli Hotel, and made straight for the men's washroom. He splashed cold water on his face, then little by little slowed his breathing. He looked in the mirror above the sinks but saw only Danko's body, jerking as the bullets struck it. He heard the screams of passersby, the shouts of the killers as they spotted him racing towards them. Then the terrible explosion that had vaporized them . . .

All this in a city that was one of the safest in Europe. What in God's name had Danko brought with him that would merit destruction?

Smith took a few more moments, then left the washroom. The lounge was empty except for Peter Howell, tucked away at a table behind a tall marble pillar. Without a word, Smith picked up the brandy balloon and drained its contents. Howell seemed to understand.

'I was beginning to wonder what happened to you. You took off after those bastards, didn't you?'

'The killers had a gondola waiting,' Smith replied. 'I

think that their plan was to fade into the landscape. Nobody looks twice at a gondola.'

'Except?'

'Except whoever hired them to kill Danko didn't trust them to keep their mouths shut. The gondola was rigged with C-twelve attached to a timer.'

'Made for quite the bang. I could hear it all the way back in the square.'

Smith leaned forward. 'Danko?'

'They made no mistake about him,' Howell replied. 'I'm sorry, Jon. I got there as fast as I could, but –'

'You did what I brought you over to do – to cover me while I got Danko out. There's nothing more you could have done. Danko told me he was clean and I believed him. He was edgy, but not because he thought he was being followed. It was something else. Did you find anything?'

Howell handed over the single piece of paper that looked like it had been torn out of a cheap notebook. He looked at Smith steadily.

'What?' Smith asked.

'I didn't mean to peek,' Howell said. 'And my Russian is a bit rusty. All the same one word leaped out at me.' He paused. 'You had *no* idea what Danko might bring out with him?'

Smith scanned the handwritten text. He picked out that one word as quickly as Peter Howell had: *Bioaparat*. Russia's centre for bioweapons research, design, and manufacture. Danko had often spoken of it, but as far as Smith knew, his work had never taken him there. *Or had it?* Could he have been rotated through Bioaparat? Had he discovered something so terrible that the only way to get it out was to carry it out himself?

Howell was studying Smith's reaction. 'Scares the

bloody hell out of me too. Anything you'd care to share with me, Jon?'

Smith looked across at the taciturn Englishman. Peter Howell had spent a lifetime of service in the British military and intelligence worlds, first with the Special Air Service, then with MI6. A lethal chameleon whose exploits always went unheralded, he had 'retired' from his profession but had never left it altogether. The need for men with Howell's expertise was always there, and those who required it – governments or individuals – knew how to find him. Howell could afford to pick and choose his assignments but he had one ironclad rule: the needs of his friends came first. He had been instrumental in helping Smith run down the instigators of the Hades Project. He hadn't hesitated to leave his retreat in the High Sierra in California when Smith had asked him to cover his back in Venice.

Sometimes Smith bridled under the constraints Klein had put on him as a mobile cipher. For example, he couldn't tell Howell anything about Covert-One – that it existed or that he was a part of it. He had no doubt that Peter had his suspicions. But being the professional he was he kept them to himself.

'This could be something very big, Peter,' Smith said quietly. 'I have to get back to the States but I also need to know about those two killers – who they were and, as important, who they were working for.'

Howell regarded Smith thoughtfully. 'Like I said. Even the remotest reference to Bioaparat is enough to keep me awake at nights. I have a few friends in Venice. Let me see what I can find out.' He paused. 'Your friend, Danko – did he have family?'

Smith recalled the photo of a pretty, dark-haired woman and a child that Danko had once shown him.

'Yes, he did.'

'Then go do what you must. I know how to get hold of you if need be. And just in case – here's the address outside of Washington I use occasionally. It has all the bells and whistles. Never know when you might need the privacy.'

4

The new NASA training facility on the outskirts of Houston consisted of, among other things, four giant hangars, each the size of a football field. Air force police patrolled the outermost perimeter; inside the Cyclone fence, motion sensors and cameras augmented surveillance.

The building designated G-3 housed a full mock-up of the latest generation of the space shuttle. Built along the lines of a commercial flight simulator used to train pilots, it provided the shuttle crew with the hands-on experience that they would carry with them into space.

Megan Olson was in the long tunnel that led from the shuttle's mid-deck to the back of the payload bay. Dressed in baggy blue pants and a loose cotton shirt, she floated in the partial-gravity environment as gently as a falling feather.

A voice crackled in her headset: 'You look like you're having way too much fun in there.'

Megan gripped one of the rubber handles embedded in the tunnel wall and twisted around to face the camera that was tracking her progress. Her red hair, pulled back in a ponytail, floated in front of her and she brushed it aside.

'This is my favourite part of the whole experience,' she laughed. 'It's like scuba diving – without the fish.'

Megan floated to a monitor where she saw the face

of Dr Dylan Reed, head of NASA's biomedical research programme.

'The lab doors will open in ten seconds,' Reed cautioned her.

'On my way.'

Megan worked her way down at a forty-five-degree angle to the circular hatch door. Just as she touched the handle, she heard the hiss of compressed air releasing the cylinder bolts. She pushed on the door and it swung away smoothly.

'I'm in.'

She settled herself on the specially lined floor and felt the soles of her booties grip the Velcro-type material. Now she was stable. She closed the door, then punched in a code on the alphanumeric pad. The door bolts shot home.

She turned and faced the space lab's work area, divided into a dozen modules. Each was the size of a broom closet; each was designed for a different function or experiment. Carefully, she walked down the centre aisle, barely wide enough to accommodate her shoulders, past the Critical Point Facility and the SPE (Space Physiology Experiment), and up to her station, the Biorack.

Like the other stations, the Biorack was encased in titanium housing that resembled a large air-conditioning duct, four feet wide, seven feet high, with the top two feet tilted towards the user at a thirty-degree angle. This design was necessary since the entire lab was encased in a large cylinder.

'Today, we have a Chinese menu,' Reed said cheerfully. 'Choose one from column A, and one from column B.'

Megan stationed herself in front of the Biorack and

flipped the power switch. The uppermost module, the freezer, was the first to hum to life. Then, working down, the cooler, incubator A, the Glovebox, and incubator B, all came on. She checked the access and control panel, then finally, at knee-level, the power plant. The Biorack, or Bernie, as the unit had been nicknamed, was functioning flawlessly.

Megan checked the LCD readouts of the experiments to be performed. As Reed had joked, it was a Chinese menu of options.

'I think I'll go with the flu, then add a little spice – Legionnaires' disease.'

Reed chuckled. 'Sounds fine. I'll start the clock as soon as you're in the Glovebox.'

The Glovebox was a shoebox-size unit that protruded ten inches from the Biorack. Modelled on the much larger containment units found in most labs, it was totally secure. But unlike its earthbound cousins, this box had been designed to be operated in microgravity. This allowed Megan and her fellow scientists to study organisms in a way not possible in any other setting.

She fitted her hands into thick rubber gloves that extended into the box. The seals between the gloves and the box were two inches of solid rubber, metal, and Keflex – a thick, virtually unbreakable glass. Even if a spill occurred, it would be contained within the box.

Good thing, too, she thought, given that she was handling Legionnaires' disease.

Although the gloves appeared thick and ungainly, they were actually quite sensitive. Megan touched the control screen located inside the box and gently pressed a three-digit combination. Almost instantly, one of the fifty panels – no bigger than compartments for compact disks – slid forward. Instead of a CD nestled in the recess, there was a circular glass tray, three inches in diameter, a quarter inch deep. Even without the microscope, Megan saw the greenish grey liquid inside: Legionnaires' disease.

Both her scientific training and her specialized work in biochemistry had instilled in her a profound respect for the cultures that she handled. Even under the most secure conditions, she never forgot what it was she was holding. Very carefully, she set down the glass tray on the pad. Then she removed the cover, exposing the bacteria.

Reed's voice drifted through her headset: 'The clock's running. Remember, in partial gravity you only have thirty minutes for each of the experiments. On the shuttle you'll be able to take your time.'

Megan was grateful for his professionalism. Reed never distracted his scientists by speaking to them in the course of an experiment. Once she had opened the sample, she was on her own.

Megan brought forward the microscope fixed to the top of the shoebox and took a deep breath. She stared at the specimen. She had worked with Legionnaires' disease before; it was like looking at an old friend.

'Okay, fella,' she said out loud. 'Let's see if you can get it up when you don't weigh so much.'

She touched the button that activated the video recorder and went to work.

Two hours later, Megan Olson floated from the Spacelab back to the mid-deck, which housed the sleep stations, food lockers, washrooms, and storage lockers. From there, she climbed the ladder to the flight deck, deserted now, and manoeuvred her way to the inter-com.

'Okay, guys. Let me out.'

She steadied herself as the air pressure inside the mock-up was equalized. After half a day of partial weightlessness, her body felt extremely heavy. It was a sensation she had never quite gotten used to. She had to reassure herself that she weighed a perfect 118 pounds, almost all of it highly toned muscle.

When the pressure was correct, the cockpit hatch swung open. The air-conditioned breeze that hit her as she stepped out made her clothes stick to her skin. Her first thought after a training session was always the same: *Thank God I can have a real shower*. Onboard the mock-up, she had practised taking towel baths.

You'll settle for towel baths if you get to go at all, she reminded herself.

'You did very well in there.'

Dylan Reed, a tall, distinguished-looking man in his late forties, greeted Megan as she came out.

'Do we have a printout of the results?' she asked.

'The computers are crunching as we speak.'

'This is the third test we've run with Legionnaires'. I'll bet you dinner at Sherlock's that these results will be the same as the other two: Legionnaires' multiplies ferociously, even in the small adjustment to gravity that we've been able to make. Imagine when we can run the experiments in microgravity conditions.'

'Do you really think I would bet against you?' Reed laughed.

Megan followed him across the platform to the eleva-tor that took them to ground level. When she got out, she paused and looked back at the mock-up, majestic under the blaze of a thousand lights.

'I'll bet that's the way she looks in space,' she said softly.

'One day, you'll take a space walk and see for yourself,' Reed assured her.

Megan's voice dropped. 'One day . . .'

As one of the alternate crewmembers, Megan knew that her chance of going on the next mission, scheduled to leave in seven days, was slim to none. Reed's group of scientists were in top condition. One of them would literally have to break a leg in order for her to move into the slot.

'The space walk can wait,' Megan said as they walked towards the trainees' quarters. 'What I need right now is a hot shower.'

'I almost forgot,' Reed said. 'There's someone here whom I think you know.'

She frowned. 'I wasn't expecting anyone.'

'It's Jon Smith. He arrived a little while ago.'

Two hours after the Gulfstream had gone wheels-up from Venice's Marco Polo Airport, the pilot came into the cabin with a message for Smith.

'Any reply, sir?' he asked his passenger.

Smith shook his head. 'No.'

'The routing change from Andrews to Houston will give us another two hours of flight time. You can get some sleep if you want.'

Smith thanked the pilot, then forced himself to eat some cold cuts and fruit from the galley. The message from Klein had been succinct. Given the bloody events in Venice and the nature of the material Danko had brought out with him, Klein wanted a face-to-face briefing. He also wanted to be close to the president, who was visiting Houston as a show of support for the space programme, in case Smith's information had to be brought to the chief executive's attention immediately.

After finishing his snack, Smith prepared his briefing for Klein. He also mapped out what he thought had to be done next and honed his arguments. Before he knew it, the jet was winging over the Gulf of Mexico on its final approach to the NASA airfield.

As he saw the vast facility come into view, Smith suddenly remembered Megan Olson. The thought of her brought a welcome smile to his lips.

The pilot taxied the craft to the security area where Air Force One was parked. Smith descended the steps and was met by an armed air police sergeant who drove him to the visitors' centre. In the distance Smith saw the grandstands, packed with NASA employees listening to the president's address. He very much doubted that Klein would be anywhere near the centre of attention.

The sergeant showed him into a small office well away from the main exhibits. The place was barren except for a government-issue desk and several chairs. Klein closed the state-of-the-art laptop he had been working on and came to Smith.

'Thank God you're alive, Jon.'

'Thank you, sir. Believe me, I share your sentiment.'

Klein never failed to surprise him. Just when Smith thought that the head of Covert-One had ice water in his veins, Klein would demonstrate genuine concern for the mobile cipher he had sent in harm's way.

'The president will be leaving in less than an hour, Jon,' Klein informed him. 'Tell me what happened so that I can determine whether or not to brief him.'

When he noticed Smith glancing around the room,

he added, 'The Secret Service swept the room for bugs. You may speak freely.'

Smith detailed, minute by minute, what had happened from the moment he had spotted Danko at St Mark's Square. He noted how Klein flinched when Smith described the shooting. When he mentioned Bioaparat, Klein was clearly shocked.

'Did Danko tell you anything before he died?' Klein demanded.

'He didn't get the chance. But he was carrying this.' He handed Klein the page with Danko's handwriting.

Bioaparat cannot go from Stage One to Stage Two. It is not a matter of money, but of inadequate facilities. Still, rumours persist that Stage Two will be completed, though not here. A courier is to leave Bioaparat no later than 4/9 with the cargo.

Klein glanced at Smith. 'Who's the courier? Is it a man or a woman? Who does he work for? This is maddeningly inconclusive! And what are Stages One and Two?'

'They generally refer to viruses, sir,' Smith replied, then added, 'I'd also like to know what the courier is bringing out. And where he's headed.'

Klein went to the window, which had an excellent view of a fuel depot. 'It doesn't make any sense. Why would Danko run if this was all he had?'

'Exactly the question I've been asking myself, sir. Consider this possibility: Danko comes across information about the courier while he's rotating through Bioaparat. He starts investigating – and ends up digging deeper than he should have. He makes someone suspicious and has to make a run for it. But he doesn't have a

44

chance – or doesn't dare – to put down anything else he might have learned. If Danko ever discovered the courier's identity, payload, or destination, that information died with him.'

'I can't believe that he died for nothing,' Klein said softly.

'I *won't* believe that,' Smith said vehemently. 'I think that Danko was anxious to get to us because whatever's headed out of Russia is coming our way.'

'Are you saying that someone is bringing a Russian bioweapon into this country?' Klein demanded.

'Given the circumstances, I'd say it's a strong possibility. What else could have frightened Danko so badly?'

Klein pinched the bridge of his nose. 'If that's the case – or even the suspicion – I have to alert the president. Steps need to be taken.' He paused. 'The problem is, how do we protect ourselves when we don't know what to look for? Danko didn't leave us any clues.'

Something in Klein's words jogged Smith. 'That might not be true, sir. May I?' He gestured at the Dell computer sitting on the desk.

Smith logged on to USAMRIID and wended his way through the numerous security checkpoints until he reached the library, the world's biggest, most comprehensive compendium on biowarfare. He entered Stage One and Stage Two and asked the computer to bring up the names of all the viruses that had two distinct development levels.

The machine offered him thirteen choices. Smith then instructed the computer to check those thirteen against viruses that Bioaparat was known to have developed, manufactured, and stockpiled.

'Could be Marburg or Ebola,' Klein said, looking over

his shoulder. 'Some of the most lethal bugs in the world.'

'Stage Two implies reconfiguration, gene splicing, or some other form of alternation,' Smith told him. 'Marburg, Ebola, and others can't be 'developed' per se. They exist in nature – and, of course, in the bioweapons labs. With them, it's more a case of designing effective battlefield delivery systems.'

Suddenly Smith gasped. 'But this . . . this can be tampered with. We know that the Russians were playing with it for years, trying to alter it to produce a more virulent strain. They were supposed to have shut down those labs, but . . .'

Klein was listening, but his eyes were locked on the screen where black letters blinked like death's-heads against a white background: SMALLPOX.

Virus is derived from the Latin word for poison. Viruses are so minuscule that their existence was unknown until the late nineteenth century, when Dmitri Ivanovsky, a Russian microbiologist, stumbled across them while investigating an outbreak of disease in tobacco plants.

Smallpox belongs to the pox family of viruses. Its earliest recorded history dates back to China in 1122 B.C. Since then, it has changed the course of human history, decimating the populations of eighteenth-century Europe and the native peoples of the Americas.

Variola major attacks the respiratory system. After an incubation period of five to ten days, the disease brings on high fever, vomiting, headaches, and stiffness of the joints. After a week, a rash appears, localized at first, then spreading throughout the body and causing blisters. Scabs appear, fall away, and leave scars that serve as incubation beds for a fresh assault. Death can come within two to three weeks or, in the case of the red or the black pox, in a matter of days.

It wasn't until 1796 that a medical assault was mounted on the virus. A British doctor, Edward Jenner, discovered that milkmaids who had contracted a mild form of the pox virus from cows seemed immune to smallpox. Taking samples of a milkmaid's lesions, Jenner inoculated a young boy who subsequently survived the epidemic. Jenner named his discovery *vaccinia* – vaccine.

The last known case of the disease was reported and treated in Somalia in 1977. By May 1980, the World Health Organization had declared smallpox vanquished. The Organization also ordered the cessation of immunization programmes, since there was no tangible need to subject people to even the slightest risk associated with vaccination.

By the end of the 1980s, only two stockpiles of *Variola major* remained on earth: at the Centres for Disease Control in Atlanta, and at the Ivanovsky Institute of Virology in Moscow. In the case of the latter, the virus was subsequently moved to Bioaparat, located near the town of Vladimir, 350 kilometres southeast of Moscow.

Under an international treaty signed by both the United States and Russia, the samples were to be preserved in highly secure laboratories subject to international inspection. None of the samples could be used for any kind of experiment without the World Health Organization monitors being present.

That, at least, was the theory.

'In theory, monitors were supposed to be present,' Smith said. He glanced at Klein. 'You and I know better.'

Klein snorted. 'The Russians gave the WHO bureaucrats some song and dance about updated facilities at Vladimir and the fools let them move the smallpox. What they never realized was that the Russians showed them only the parts of Bioaparat that they wanted them to see.'

This was true. Through defectors and on-site sources, the United States had, over the years, managed to piece together a solid composite of what was really taking place at the Bioaparat complex. The international inspectors had seen only the tip of the iceberg – the variola storage facilities, which were subsequently approved. But there were other buildings, disguised as seed and fertilizer laboratories, that remained hidden from the world. Klein had enough evidence to bring before the WHO and demand that Bioaparat be completely opened up. But politics was an issue. The current administration did not wish to antagonize Russia, which was threatening to revert to communist rule. Also, a number of the WHO inspectors were not inclined to take American-produced evidence at face value. Nor could their discretion be relied on. American intelligence agencies feared for the lives of those who had furnished him with the information, believing that if the Russians knew what information the West had, they could walk back the cat and discover who had passed it on.

'I have no choice,' Klein said grimly. 'I must tell the president.'

'Which could make it a government-to-government situation,' Smith pointed out. 'Then the question becomes:

do we trust the Russians enough to go after the leak and the courier? We don't know whom we're dealing with at Bioaparat, how senior he is, or who gave him his marching orders. It's possible that this isn't some rogue scientist or researcher looking to make a quick buck by delivering a package to New York City. This could travel all the way up to the Kremlin.'

'You're saying that if the president were to speak to the Russian prime minister we might be tipping our hand – to the wrong people. I agree – but give me an alternative.'

It took Smith three minutes to lay out the contingency plan he had come up with during the flight. He noticed Klein's sceptical expression and was prepared to argue, but Klein surprised him.

'I agree. It's the only course of action we can take immediately – and that has a chance of success. But I'll tell you this: the president won't give us much time. If you don't get results fast he'll have no choice but to come down hard on the Russians.'

Smith took a deep breath. 'Give me two days. I'll check in every twelve hours. If I miss a signal by more than sixty minutes, assume that I won't be calling in at all.'

Klein shook his head. 'That's a hell of a gamble, Jon. I don't like sending men in on a wing and a prayer.'

'A prayer is all we have right now, sir,' Smith said sombrely. 'There's something else you might want to tell him. We stopped manufacturing smallpox vaccine years ago. Right now, all we have are a hundred thousand inoculations – at USAMRIID, strictly for military use. We couldn't inoculate even a fraction of our population.' He paused. 'There's even a lousier scenario: if someone is stealing smallpox because they *can't* do Stage Two development in Russia, they're bringing it here because they *can* – something's already waiting for the courier on this end. If that's the case, and the object is not only to create a mutant strain but to disperse it in this country, then we're defenceless. We could manufacture all the vaccine in the world, but none of it would be effective against a new strain of variola.'

Klein's eyes locked on Smith. His voice was low and harsh.

'Go and find out what kind of hell the Russians are letting loose. Find out fast!'

5

Megan's heels echoed smartly off the polished concrete floor as she walked through the giant hangar and into daylight. Although she'd been in Houston for almost two months, she still wasn't used to its climate. It was April but already the air was humid. She was glad her training wouldn't extend into the summer.

Sandwiched between buildings G-3 and G-4 was the new visitors' centre. Megan walked past the flotilla of NASA buses, which ferried guests from the main gates into the compound, and entered the atrium-style lobby. Suspended from the overhead girders was a half-size mock-up of the shuttle. Slipping around groups of schoolchildren who were staring wide-eyed at the mock-up, she headed for the security desk. Visitors to NASA, as well as their destinations within the facility, were logged into a computer. Megan was wondering where she would find Jon Smith when she caught a glimpse of him walking beneath the mock-up.

'Jon!'

Smith was startled to hear his name, but his frown turned into a smile when he saw Megan.

'Megan . . . How wonderful to see you again.'

Megan came up to him and took his arm. 'You look like a man on a mission – all so serious. Don't tell me you weren't even going to look me up.'

Smith hesitated. His thoughts *had* wandered to Megan

51

Olson but nothing had prepared him for actually running into her.

'I wouldn't have known where to begin to look for you,' he replied truthfully.

'And you being such a resourceful man,' Megan teased him. 'What *are* you doing down here? Did you come in with the president's party?'

'Hardly. I had a meeting, something that came up at the last minute.'

'Uh-huh. And now you're galloping off. Do you at least have time for a drink or a cup of coffee?'

Although he was anxious to get back to Washington, Smith decided he didn't want to raise any suspicions, especially since Megan seemed to have accepted his vague explanation for his presence at NASA.

'I'd love a drink,' he said, then added, 'You seemed to be looking for me – or am I imagining things?'

'I was,' Megan replied, leading them towards the elevators. 'Actually, a friend of yours, Dylan Reed, mentioned that he'd heard you were on-site.'

'Dylan . . . I see.'

'Where do you know him from?'

'Dylan and I worked together when NASA and USAMRIID were retooling the biochem programme for the shuttle. That was a while back. I haven't seen him since.'

Which begs the question: how the hell would Reed or anyone else know that I was here?

Since the air space around NASA was restricted, the Gulfstream pilot would have filed a crew/passenger manifest with the NASA controllers, who would have passed it on to security. But that information should have remained confidential – unless someone was monitoring flight arrivals.

Megan slid a card key into the slot of the glass-enclosed elevator that went up to the private dining room. Upstairs, she and Smith walked past the dining room's floor-to-ceiling windows that offered a panoramic view of the centre's air-training facilities. Megan couldn't help but smile when she saw a KC-135, a converted aerial tanker, lumber down the runway.

'Fond memories?' Smith asked her.

Megan laughed. 'Only in retrospect. That one-thirty-five has been especially modified to pretest various experiments and equipment for the low gravity of shuttle flights. It climbs steeply until its acceleration reaches two Gs, then freefalls, creating a weightless environment for twenty or thirty seconds. When I took my first ride, I had no idea how greatly reduced gravity stresses the body's internal systems.' She grinned. 'That's when I discovered why the one-thirty-five has onboard a generous supply of emesis bags.'

'And why they call it the Vomit Comet,' Smith added.

Megan was surprised. 'Have you ever ridden in that thing?' she asked.

'Wouldn't dream of it.'

They took a table by the window. Megan ordered a beer but Smith, about to get back in the air, chose orange juice. When their drinks arrived, he raised his glass.

'May you reach the stars.'

Megan met his glance. 'I hope so.'

'I *know* so.'

Smith and Megan glanced up to find Dr Dylan Reed standing by their table.

'Jon, it's good to see you again. I was waiting for someone on another flight when I saw your name on the arrivals roster.'

Smith returned Reed's strong handshake and invited him to pull up a chair.

'Are you still with USAMRIID?' Reed asked.

'Still attached. And you've been down here for what, three years?'

'Four.'

'Are you onboard the next mission?'

Reed grinned. 'Couldn't keep me away. I've become a shuttle junkie.'

Smith raised his glass again. 'To a safe, successful flight.'

After the toast, Reed turned to Megan. 'You never told me how you two met.'

Megan's smile faded. 'Sophia Russell was a childhood friend of mine.'

'Sorry,' Reed apologized. 'I heard about Sophia's death, Jon. I'm very sorry.'

Smith listened as Reed and Megan discussed the morning's exercise in the mock-up, noting the affectionate way Reed treated her. Smith wondered if there was something more than just a professional relationship between them.

Even if there is, it's none of my business.

Smith felt heat at the back of his neck. Casually, he shifted so that he could see the entire room in the reflection of the windows. Standing by the hostess's station was a slightly overweight man of medium height, in his early forties. His head was completely shaved, the scalp shiny beneath the lights. Even from this distance, Smith could tell that the man was staring directly at him, his mouth open slightly.

I don't know you, so why are you so interested in me?

'Dylan?'

Smith gestured in the direction of the hostess's station. His motion made the watcher duck, unsuccessfully.

'Are you expecting someone?'

Reed glanced around. 'Right. That's Adam Treloar, the mission's chief medical officer.' He waved. 'Adam!'

Smith watched as Treloar approached reluctantly, like a child dragging his feet to the dinner table.

'Adam, meet Dr Jon Smith, with USAMRIID,' Reed said.

'My pleasure,' Smith said.

'Yes, nice to meet you,' Treloar mumbled, betraying the remnants of a British accent.

'Have we met before?' Smith inquired pleasantly.

He wondered why the polite question would make Treloar's egg-shaped eyes bulge.

'Oh, I don't think so. I would have remembered.' Hastily, Treloar turned to Reed. 'We have to go over the crew's last physical. And I *must* make that meeting with Stone.'

Reed shook his head. 'Things get a little hectic as we approach launch date,' he apologized to Smith. 'I'm afraid you'll have to excuse me. Jon, it was great to see you. Let's not leave it so long, okay?'

'Definitely.'

'Megan, I'll see you at three o'clock in the biolab.'

Smith watched the two men take a booth at the far end of the room.

'Treloar's a little strange,' he commented. *Especially since he wanted to discuss physical exams but wasn't carrying any medical files.*

'Yes, he is,' Megan agreed. 'As a doctor, Adam's one of the best. Dylan stole him from Bauer-Zermatt. But he is eccentric.'

Smith shrugged. 'Tell me about Dylan. What's he like to work with? I remember that he was a by-the-numbers kind of guy.'

'If you mean he's really focused, that's true. But he always challenges me, makes me think harder, do better.'

'I'm glad you found someone like that to work with.' He glanced at his watch. 'I have to get going.'

Megan rose with him. 'Me, too.'

When they stepped out of the elevator on the main floor, she touched his arm. 'It was good to see you again, Jon.'

'You, too, Megan. The next time you get to Washington, the drinks are on me.'

She grinned. 'I'll take you up on that.'

'Don't stare at them!'

Adam Treloar jerked his head, startled by the harshness of Reed's command. He could not believe how Reed, with an easy smile on his face, could be so cold.

Using his peripheral vision, Treloar watched as Jon Smith and Megan Olson made their way to the elevator. He heard a soft *ping* when the car arrived and finally let out his breath. Reaching for a napkin, he dabbed his face and crown.

'Do you know who Smith is?' he demanded hoarsely.

'As a matter of fact I do,' Reed replied calmly. 'I've known him for years.'

He pressed his back against the banquette, anything to get further from the sour odour that seemed to follow Treloar wherever he went. Reed didn't care that his gesture was so obviously rude; he had never made a secret of the contempt he felt for the shuttle mission's chief medical officer.

'If you know who he is, then tell me what he's doing

here,' Treloar demanded. 'He was the one with Danko in Venice!'

Reed's hand shot out like a cobra, seizing Treloar's left wrist, his powerful grip squeezing the delicate nerves. Treloar rolled his eyes and his mouth fell open as he gasped.

'What do you know about Venice?' Reed demanded softly.

'I . . . overheard you talking about it!' Treloar managed to say.

'Then forget that I ever did, do you understand?' he said in his silky voice. 'Venice is not your concern. Neither is Smith.'

He released Treloar's wrist and was pleased by the residual pain he saw in the medical officer's eyes.

'It just seems too much of a coincidence that first, Smith was in Venice, now he's here,' Treloar said.

'Believe me, Smith knows nothing. He *has* nothing. Danko was dealt with before he could say anything. And there's a simple explanation as to why he was in Venice. Danko and Smith knew each other from international conferences. Obviously they were friends. When Danko decided to bolt, Smith was the man he decided he could trust. Nothing more complicated or sinister than that.'

'Then it's safe for me to travel?'

'Very safe,' Reed assured him. 'In fact, why don't we have another drink and go over the arrangements.'

Peter Howell let several hours go by before he left the Danieli Hotel and threaded his way to the Rio del San Moise, where the assassins had gone to their fiery deaths. As he anticipated, there was only a handful of carabinieri patrolling the perimeter to ensure that no tourists wandered into the roped-off crime scene.

The man he expected to see there was examining the charred remains of the assassins' gondola. Behind him, divers continued to scour the canal for more evidence.

A carabinieri blocked Howell's path.

'I wish to speak with Inspector Dionetti,' the Englishman said in fluent Italian.

Howell waited as the policeman walked up to the short, trim man, thoughtfully stroking his goatee while he examined a piece of blackened wood.

Marco Dionetti, an inspector in the Polizia Statale, looked up and blinked when he recognized Howell. He stripped off his rubber gloves, brushed imaginary lint off the lapels of his hand-tailored suit, then came to Howell and embraced in the Italian fashion.

'Pietro! A pleasure to see you again.' Dionetti looked Howell up and down. 'At least I hope it will be pleasant.'

'It's good to see you too, Marco.'

During the golden age of terrorism in the mid-1980s, Peter Howell, on loan from the SAS, had worked with high-level Italian policemen on kidnappings involving British citizens. One of the men he had come to admire and respect was a soft-spoken but tough-as-nails aristocrat by the name of Marco Dionetti, then a rising star in the Statale. Over the years, he and Howell had kept in touch. Howell had a standing invitation to stay at Dionetti's ancestral palazzo whenever he was in Venice.

'So here you are in the Serenissima but you have not called on me, much less allowed me to be your host,' Dionetti chided him. 'Where are you staying? *I Danieli*, I'll wager.'

'My apologies, Marco,' Howell replied. 'I just arrived yesterday and things have been a little hectic.'

Dionetti looked behind him at the wreckage strewn on the embankment. 'Hectic? Of course, the classic British understatement. May I be so bold as to ask whether you know anything about this outrage?'

'You may. And I'll be happy to tell you. But not here.'

Dionetti let out a sharp whistle. Almost instantly a blue-and-white police launch purred up to the steps leading from the embankment to the water.

'We can talk on the way,' Dionetti said.

'On the way to where?'

'Really, Pietro! We are going to the Questura. It would be bad manners for me to expect you to answer my questions if I do not answer yours.'

Howell followed the inspector to the stern of the craft. Both men waited until the boat had cleared the Rio del San Moise and throttled out into the Grand Canal.

'Tell me, Pietro,' the inspector said over the rumble of the diesels. 'What do you know of that little horror that erupted in our fair city?'

'I'm not running an operation,' Howell assured him. 'But the incident involved a friend of mine.'

'And did your friend happen to be the mysterious gentleman at the Piazza San Marco?' Dionetti asked. 'The one seen with the shooting victim? The one who chased after the killers, then disappeared?'

'The same.'

Dionetti sighed theatrically. 'Tell me this has nothing to do with terrorism, Pietro.'

'It doesn't.'

'We found a Ukrainian passport on the victim, but

little else. He looked like he had had a hard journey. Should Italy be concerned as to why he came here?'

'Italy needn't be concerned. He was only passing through.'

Dionetti stared at the traffic on the river, the water taxis and water buses, the garbage scows and the elegant gondolas bobbing in the wakes of the larger vessels. The Grand Canal was the main artery of his beloved Venezia, and he felt its pulse keenly.

'I do not want trouble, Pietro,' he said.

'Then help me,' Howell replied. 'I'll see to it that trouble leaves.' He paused. 'Did you find enough to identify the killers and how they were murdered?'

'A bomb,' Dionetti said flatly. 'More powerful than need be. Someone wanted to obliterate them. However, if that was their intention, they failed. We found enough for identification – assuming those two were in our records. We shall see shortly.'

The launch slowed as it reached the Rio di Ca Gazoni, then rumbled slowly into the dock in front of the Questura, the Polizia Statale headquarters.

Dionetti led them past the armed guards stationed outside the seventeenth-century palazzo.

'Once the home of a proud family,' Dionetti said over his shoulder. 'Repossessed for back taxes. When the government took it over, it became a fancy police station.' He shook his head.

Howell followed him down a wide corridor into a room that looked like it had once been a formal drawing room. Beyond the windows was a garden, lying fallow.

Dionetti went around his desk and tapped on the computer keyboard. A printer whirred to life.

'The Rocca brothers – Tommaso and Luigi,' he said, handing Howell the printouts.

Howell contemplated the photographs of two very tough-looking men in their late twenties. 'Sicilians?'

'Exactly. Mercenaries. We have long suspected that they were responsible for the shooting of a federal prosecutor in Palermo and a judge in Rome.'

'How expensive were they?'

'Very. Why do you ask?'

'Because only someone with both money and connections would have hired men like them. These are professionals. They do not need to advertise.'

'But why kill a Ukrainian peasant – if in fact he was that?'

'I don't know,' Howell replied truthfully. 'But I need to find out. Do you have any idea where they were based?'

'Palermo. Their birthplace.'

Howell nodded. 'What about the explosives?'

Dionetti returned to the computer.

'Yes ... the preliminary report from the forensics laboratory indicates that it was C-twelve, about half a kilo's worth.'

Howell looked at him sharply. 'C-twelve? You're sure?'

Dionetti shrugged. 'You may recall that our laboratory has very high standards, Pietro. I would accept their conclusion at face value.'

'So would I,' Howell replied thoughtfully.

But how had the killer of the two Sicilians gotten hold of the U.S. Army's latest explosives?

Marco Dionetti's home was a sixteenth-century, four-storey limestone palazzo that fronted the Grand Canal a stone's throw away from the Accademia. In the grand dining room, dominated by a fireplace sculpted by Moretta, the stern faces of Dionetti's ancestors gazed down from portraits painted by Renaissance masters.

Peter Howell finished his last bite of *seppioline* and sat back as an elderly servant removed his plate.

'My compliments to Maria. The cuttlefish was excellent – just as I remembered it.'

'I'll be sure to tell her,' Dionetti replied as a tray of *bussolai* was presented. He picked up one of the cinnamon-flavoured biscuits and nibbled thoughtfully.

'Pietro, I understand your need for discretion. But I too have masters I must answer to. Is there nothing you can tell me about the Ukrainian?'

'My job was simply to cover the contact,' Howell replied. 'There was no indication that there would be bloodshed.'

Dionetti steepled his fingers. 'I suppose I could make a case that the Rocca brothers had a contract and carried it out on the wrong individual, that the man seen fleeing from the piazza was the intended victim.'

'That may not explain why the Roccas were blown up,' Howell pointed out.

Dionetti dismissed the possibility with a wave of his fingers. 'The brothers had many enemies. Who's to say whether one of them finally managed to settle a score?'

Howell finished his coffee. 'If you can put that spin on it, Pietro, I would. Now, I don't want to seem the ungracious guest but I must make that flight to Palermo.'

'My launch is at your disposal,' Dionetti said, accompanying Howell down the centre hall. 'I will contact you if there are any further developments. Promise me that when your business is finished you will stop by on your way home. We will go to La Fenice.'

Howell smiled. 'I would enjoy that very much. Thank you for all your help, Marco.'

Dionetti watched the Englishman step over the gunwale and raised his hand as the launch slipped into the Grand Canal. Only when he was absolutely certain that Howell couldn't see him did his friendly expression dissolve.

'You should have told me more, old friend,' he said softly. 'Maybe I could have kept you alive.'

6

Eight thousand miles to the west, on the Hawaiian island of Oahu, Pearl Harbour lay placid under the hot, tropical sun. Overlooking the harbour were the navy's administrative buildings and the command-and-control headquarters. This morning, the Nimitz Building was off-limits to everyone except authorized personnel. Armed Shore Patrol units were stationed both inside and out, in the long, cool corridors and in front of the closed doors to the briefing room.

The briefing room was the size of a gymnasium and could easily accommodate three hundred people. Today there were only thirty, all seated in the first few rows before the podium. The need for heavy security was reflected in the medals and ribbons that decorated the uniforms of those in attendance. Representing every branch of the armed services, they were the senior officers of the Pacific theatre, responsible for perceiving and eliminating any threat from the shores of San Diego to the Strait of Taiwan in Southeast Asia. Each was a battle-tested combat veteran who had seen more than his share of conflict. None had any patience with politicians or theorists, which is to say they did not suffer fools gladly. They relied on their own expertise and instincts and respected only those who had proven themselves in the field. That was why all eyes were riveted on the figure at the podium, General Frank Richardson, veteran of Vietnam and the Gulf War, and a dozen other sorties that the American people had all but forgotten about. But not these men. To them, Richardson, as the army representative on the joint chiefs of staff, was a true warrior. When he had something to say, everyone listened.

Richardson gripped the lectern with both hands. A tall, well-fleshed man, he was as solid now as he had been during his gridiron days at West Point. With his iron-grey hair cut *en brosse*, cold, green eyes, and firm jaw, he was a public relation's man's dream pitchman. Except that Richardson detested virtually everyone who hadn't bled for his country.

'Gentlemen, let's summarize,' Richardson said, gazing over his audience. 'It's not the Russians who worry me. Most time it's hard to know who's running that damned country – the politicians or the *mafiya*. You can't tell the players without a scorecard.'

Richardson paused to savour the laughter brought on by his little joke.

'But while Mother Russia is in the toilet,' he continued, 'the same can't be said about the Chinese. Past administrations were so eager to get into bed with them that they never saw through to Beijing's true intentions. We sold them our most advanced computer and satellite technology without realizing that they had already infiltrated our major nuclear development and production facilities. Los Alamos was a one-stop Wal-Mart for those guys.

'I keep telling this administration – as I did the previous one – that China cannot be contained by nuclear force alone.'

Richardson shifted his gaze to the back of the room. A sandy-haired man in his early forties, dressed in civilian attire, was leaning against the wall, his arms crossed over his chest. The general caught the civilian's almost imperceptible nod and changed gears on the fly.

'But neither can the Chinese hope to challenge us by playing the nuclear card. The nut is that they have an option: chemical-biological warfare. Slide a bug into one of our major population centres and into our command-and-control systems and presto! – instant chaos. With complete plausible deniability on their part.

'Therefore, it is imperative, gentlemen, that in your patrols, your oversight and intelligence sorties, you gather as much information as possible on China's bioweapons programme. The battles of the next war will not be won or lost in the field or on the seas – at least at first. They will be waged in the laboratories, where the enemy is measured in the trillions of battalions and can be mounted on the head of a pin. Only when we know where those battalions are created, nourished, sustained, and deployed from can you dispatch your resources to eliminate them.'

Richardson paused. 'I thank you for your time and attention, gentlemen.'

The man in the back did not participate in the outpouring of applause. He did not stir when others in the audience surrounded the general, congratulating him, peppering him with questions. Anthony Price, deputy director of the National Security Agency, always reserved his comments for the private moment.

As the officers dispersed, Richardson made his way to Price, who was thinking just how much the general resembled a preening rooster.

'God, I love these guys! You can smell the stink of war on them.'

'What I smell is that you almost blew it, Frank,' Price replied dryly. 'If I hadn't caught your attention, you would have laid it out for them chapter and verse.'

Richardson shot him a withering look. 'Give me some credit, will you?' He pushed open the door. 'Come on. We're running late.'

They stepped out into the peerless blue day and walked swiftly along the gravel path that curved around the auditorium.

'One day, Tony, the politicians will have to get it,' Richardson said grimly. 'Running this country through public opinion polls is killing us. Mention that you want to stockpile anthrax or Ebola and watch your numbers sink. That's bullshit!'

'Old news, Frank,' Price replied. 'You might recall that our biggest problem is verification. Both we and the Russians agreed to have our biochem stockpiles monitored by international inspectors. Our labs, research and manufacturing facilities, the delivery systems – everything was out in the open. So the politicians don't have to "get" anything. As far as they're concerned, bioweapons are a dead issue.'

'Except when they come back to bite them on the ass,' Richardson said caustically. 'Then they'll be screaming, "Where are ours?"'

'And you'll be able to tell them, won't you?' Price replied. 'With a little help from the good doctor Bauer.'

'Thank Christ for guys like him,' Richardson said through clenched teeth.

Behind the auditorium was a small, circular landing pad. A commercial Jet Ranger helicopter with civilian markings sat waiting, the rotors spinning lazily. When the pilot saw his passengers, he began to warm up the turbos.

Price was about to duck into the passenger compartment when Richardson stopped him.

'This business in Venice,' he said over the growing whine of the engines. 'Did we take it on the chin?'

Price shook his head. 'The hit came down as arranged. But there was an unexpected development. I'm expecting an update shortly.'

Richardson grunted and followed Price into the cabin, strapping himself into his seat. As much as he respected Bauer and Price, they were still civilians. Only a soldier knew that there were always unexpected developments.

The sight of the Big Island from two thousand feet never failed to stir Richardson. In the distance was the lush Kona Coast, with its grand hotels moored like great ocean liners along the seaside. Farther inland were the black plains of hardened lava, as foreboding as the lunar landscape. In the centre of what appeared to be sheer desolation was the fountainhead of life: the Kilauea volcano, its crater glowing red from the magma seething deep within the earth's core. The volcano was quiet now, but Richardson had seen it during eruptions. Creation, the formation of the newest place on the planet, was a sight that he had never forgotten.

As the helicopter swung along the edge of the lava field, what had once been Fort Howard came into view. Occupying several thousand acres between the lava field and the ocean, it had been the army's premier medical research facility, specializing in cures for tropical diseases, including leprosy. Several years ago, Richardson had set the wheels in motion to have the base decommissioned. He had found himself an opportunistic senator from Hawaii and, with a little behind-the-scenes help, had gotten the politician's pork-barrel project through Congress: a brand-new medical facility on Oahu. As a quid pro quo, the senator, who was on the Armed Forces Appropriations Committee, had rubber-stamped Richardson's request that Fort Howard be mothballed and sold off to private enterprise.

Richardson had already had a buyer waiting in the wings: the biochemical firm Bauer-Zermatt A.G., headquartered in Zurich. After two hundred thousand shares of company stock had been deposited into the senator's safe-deposit box, the politician saw to it that no other bids for the base were acceptable to his committee.

Richardson spoke to the pilot over the headset: 'Swing over the compound.'

The helicopter banked, giving the general a panoramic view of the area below. Even from this height, he could tell that the perimeter fence was new and strong – a ten-foot-tall Cyclone fence topped with razor wire. What looked like military personnel manned the four guard posts. The Humvees parked at each post heightened the effect.

The compound itself was startlingly empty. The Quonset supply huts, barracks, and warehouses stood baking under the tropical sun, with no activity around them. Only the old command building, repainted, with a few Jeeps parked nearby, looked as though it was being used. The overall effect was perfect: a mothballed military installation, still off-limits to everyone except a few locals who serviced the skeleton staff working there.

The effect was extremely deceptive. In truth, what had once been Fort Howard now lay three stories beneath the earth.

'We're cleared to land, General,' the pilot informed him.

Richardson took a last glance out the window and saw a toylike figure tracking the helicopter's flight.

'Take us down,' he replied.

He was a short, muscular man in his early sixties, with swept-back silver hair and a carefully trimmed goatee. He stood with his feet apart, his back ramrod straight, hands clasped at the small of his back – an officer of wars past.

Dr Karl Bauer watched the helicopter drift down, flutter above the grassy landing area, then settle. He knew that his visitors would have hard questions for him. As the rotors wound down, he carefully reviewed just how much he would tell them. *Herr Doktor* did not take kindly to having to provide explanations or apologies.

For over a hundred years, the company founded by Bauer's great-grandfather had been at the forefront of chemical and biological technology. Bauer-Zermatt A.G. held a myriad of patents that, to this day, were a revenue-producing stream. Its scientists and researchers had developed pills and potions that remained household staples; at the same time they had brought to market esoteric drugs that had won the company international humanitarian awards.

But for all the medicines and vaccines it distributed to healthcare workers in the Third World, Bauer-Zermatt had a dark side that its well-paid spinmeisters and glossy brochures never alluded to. During World War I, the company had developed a particularly noxious form of mustard gas that was responsible for the slow deaths of thousands of Allied soldiers. A quarter century later, it supplied German companies with certain chemicals that were then combined to subsequently create the gas used in the death chambers throughout Eastern Europe. The firm had also closely monitored the ungodly experiments of Dr Josef Mengele and other Nazi physicians. At the end of the war, while other perpetrators and accomplices were rounded and hanged, Bauer-Zermatt retreated behind the Swiss cloak of anonymity while quietly extrapolating on Nazi medical research. As for Bauer-Zermatt's owners and principal officers, they disclaimed any knowledge of what might have been done with the corporation's products once they'd left the alpine borders.

In the second half of the twentieth century, Dr Karl Bauer had not only kept the family firm in the forefront of legitimate pharmaceutical research, but had also broadened its secret programme of developing biochemical weapons. Like a locust, Bauer went where the fields were most fertile: Gadhafi's Libya, Hussein's Iraq, the tribal dictatorships of Africa, and the nepotism-infested regimes of Southeast Asia. He brought with him the best scientists and the most modern equipment; in return, he was showered with largesse that was transferred by computer keystroke into the vaults beneath Zurich.

At the same time, Bauer maintained and upgraded his contacts with the military in both the United States and Russia. A prescient student of the global political condition, he had foreseen the breakup of the Soviet Union and the inevitable decline of the new Russia struggling to adopt democracy. Where the twin streams of Russian desperation and American ascendancy met, Bauer fished.

Bauer stepped forward to greet his visitors. 'Gentlemen.'

The three men shook hands, then fell in step to the two-storey, Colonial-style command building. On both sides of the gracious, wood-panelled lobby were the offices of Bauer's hand-picked staff, who looked after the administrative duties of the facility. Farther along were the cubbyholes where the scientists' assistants toiled, inputting data from the laboratory experiments. At the very back were two elevators. One was hidden behind a door that could be opened only with a key card. Built by Hitachi, it was a high-speed unit that linked the subterranean labs with the command building. The second elevator was a beautiful brass birdcage. The three men got in, and in a few seconds were in Bauer's private office, which occupied the entire second floor.

The office might have belonged to a colonial governor from the nineteenth century. Antique Oriental rugs graced polished hardwood floors; mahogany bookcases and South Pacific art filled the walls. Bauer's massive partner's desk stood in front of floor-to-ceiling windows that overlooked the entire compound and the ocean below the cliffs, straight across to the black lava fields in the distance.

'You've made a few improvements since the last time I was here,' Richardson commented dryly.

'Later, I will take you to the staff and quarters and recreation area,' Bauer replied. 'Life here is not unlike on an oil rig: my people have leave only once a month, and then only for three days. The amenities I provide are well worth the expenditure.'

'These furloughs,' Richardson said. 'Do you let your people go off by themselves?'

Bauer laughed softly. 'Not likely, general. We book them into an exclusive resort. The security is there, but they're never aware of it.'

'From one gilded cage to another,' Price remarked.

Bauer shrugged. 'I've had no complaints.'

'Given what you pay them, I'm not surprised,' Price said.

Bauer stepped over to a well-stocked liquor cart. 'Can I offer you a drink?'

Both Richardson and Price chose the fresh pineapple juice over ice and crushed fruit. Bauer stayed with his usual mineral water.

After the others were seated, Bauer took his place behind his desk.

'Gentlemen, let me recapitulate. The project that we have devoted five years of our lives to is almost ready to bear fruit. As you know, during the Clinton administration, smallpox, which was to have been destroyed in 1999, had been granted a reprieve. Currently, there are two consignments left in the world: one is in the Center for Communicable Diseases in Atlanta, part of the CDC; the other is in central Russia, at Bioaparat. Our entire plan rested on the ability to procure a sample of the smallpox virus. Efforts to get such a sample from the CDC had proved futile; the security was simply too stringent. However, such was not the case at Bioaparat.

'Given the Russians' dire need for hard currency, I was able to make certain arrangements. I am pleased to tell you that within days, a courier carrying a sample of the virus will be leaving Russia.'

'Are your Russians guaranteeing delivery?' Richardson asked.

'Of course. In the unlikely event that the courier fails to rendezvous with our people, the second half of the payment will not be released.' Bauer paused, polishing his sharp, small teeth with his tongue. 'There will also be other, more far-reaching, consequences. I can assure you that the Russians are very much aware of this.'

'But there's a problem, isn't there?' Richardson said bluntly. 'Venice.'

Bauer did not reply. Instead, he slipped a disc into

73

a DVD player. The monitor went from blue to jagged images, then to a startlingly clear picture of St Mark's Square.

'This footage was caught by an Italian journalist who was enjoying the day with his family,' Bauer explained.

'Does anyone else have it?' Price asked at once.

'No. My people got to the journalist immediately. Not only will he never have to spend a cent on his children's education, he can retire – which, in fact, he has.'

Bauer pointed to the screen. 'The man on the right is Yuri Danko, a high-ranking officer in the medical division of Russia's security service.'

'And that's Jon Smith, on the left,' Price added. He looked at Richardson. 'Frank and I know Smith from his involvement in the Hades Project. Before that, he was with USAMRIID. Rumour had it he was close to someone in the Russian Medical Intelligence Division. NSA wanted in, but Smith refused to share. He claimed that he had no such source.'

'Now you see his source: Danko,' Bauer continued. 'A month ago, I began receiving reports that Danko was sniffing around Bioaparat as part of his security rotation. As the day approached for our courier to depart, Danko bolted. But he was in such a hurry to get out that he became sloppy. The Russians discovered that he was on the run and passed that information to me.'

'At which point you arranged for the triggermen,' Richardson said. 'You should have paid for better talent.'

'The executioners were top grade,' Bauer said coldly. 'I had used them before and the results had always been satisfactory.'

'Not this time.'

'It would have been better to get Danko while he was

still in Eastern Europe,' Bauer admitted. 'However, that was not an option. He was moving too quickly, covering his tracks very well. Venice was our best chance. When my people reported seeing Danko with a contact, I knew immediately that this man would have to be disposed of as well.'

'But he wasn't,' Price said.

'A mistake that will be rectified,' Bauer replied. 'At the time we had no idea who Danko would contact. The key thing is that Danko, who was last stationed at Bioaparat, is dead. Whatever he knew died with him.'

'Unless he managed to tell Smith,' Richardson cut in.

'Study the footage,' Bauer suggested. 'Check the time.'

He played back the disc. Richardson and Price stared intently at the screen. The carnage at St Mark's lasted only seconds.

'Play it again,' Price said.

This time, the two men concentrated on Danko's actual meeting with Smith. Richardson had produced a stopwatch and was timing the brief encounter as he focused on Danko's hands. Nothing passed between the Russian and Smith.

'You're right,' Price said at last. 'Danko comes up, sits down, orders a coffee, he and Smith talk . . .'

Bauer pulled out two copies of a transcript and handed one to each man. 'I had a lip-reader prepare this. Small talk is all it was. Nothing more.'

Richardson scanned the page. 'Looks like you were right: Danko didn't have a chance to say anything. But you can be sure that Smith won't fold up his tent and disappear into the night. He's going to dig hard and deep.' The general paused. 'Who knows what other contacts he has in the Russian military.'

'I realize that,' Bauer replied. 'Believe me, I do not intend to underestimate Dr Jon Smith. That is part of the reason I asked you here, so that we can decide how to proceed with him.'

Price, who had been using the remote control to jog the images on the screen, froze a particular frame.

'This guy here, the Good Samaritan. He looks familiar.'

'According to my sources, he identified himself as an Italian doctor.'

'Did the police interview him?'

'No. He disappeared into the crowd.'

'What's wrong, Tony?' Richardson asked.

Price's cell phone trilled. Flipping it open, he identified himself; then, looking at the others, held up his finger.

'Hello, Inspector Dionetti. I'm glad you called. I have a few questions for you about the second man at the shooting . . .'

Sitting in his elegant, book-lined study, Dionetti contemplated an Etruscan bust. 'You said that you wanted to know if anyone came around asking about the Rocca brothers,' he said.

'And?'

'An old friend of mine – Peter Howell, the former SAS –'

'I know who he is,' Price interrupted. 'What did he want?'

Dionetti described his meeting with the Englishman and finished by saying: 'I regret I won't be able to get more information. But to ask too many questions . . .'

'What did you tell Howell?'

Dionetti licked his lips. 'Howell asked if we had identified the bodies. I told him they were the Rocca brothers.

I had no choice. Howell has other contacts in Venice. If I hadn't told him, they would have.'

'What else?' Price demanded.

'He saw the results of the explosion –'

'And you volunteered that it was a C-twelve.'

'What else could I do. Howell was a soldier. He knows about these things. Listen to me, Antonio. Howell is on his way to Palermo, where the Roccas came from. He is travelling alone, an easy target.'

Price thought about that. 'All right,' he said finally. 'But if Howell contacts you from Palermo I want to know about it.'

After hanging up, Price looked at the face on the screen. 'It's Peter Howell,' he announced to the others.

He encapsulated what Dionetti had told him and gave an overview of Howell's career.

'What would such a man be doing with Jon Smith?' Bauer demanded.

'Covering his back,' Richardson said grimly. 'Smith's no fool. He wasn't about to go meet Danko alone.' He turned to Price. 'That bastard Dionetti has a big mouth. Can we still trust him?'

'As long as we pay him,' Price replied. 'Without us Dionetti's one step away from bankruptcy. Five hundred years of family tradition –' He snapped his fingers. '– gone! Just like that. And he was right: Howell would have found out about the Roccas and the C-twelve, one way or another.'

'It seems that Smith is not the only loose end,' Bauer observed.

'True,' Richardson agreed. 'But Palermo is a dangerous place – even for a man like Peter Howell.'

7

Upon arriving from Houston, Jon Smith drove directly from Andrews to his Bethesda home. He showered, packed a change of clothes for a week, and called a car service to take him to Dulles Airport.

He was arming the security system when the secure phone rang.

'Klein here, Jon. Have you made the necessary arrangements?'

'I'm booked on the Delta flight to Moscow, sir. It leaves in three hours.'

'Good. I've spoken with the president. He's given Covert-One the green light to proceed as it sees fit – but fast.'

'Understood, sir.'

'Here's the information you'll need.' After Klein gave him the details, he added: 'I know there's history between you and Randi Russell, Jon. Don't let it get in the way of what you need to find out.'

Smith reined in his anger. Tact wasn't one of Klein's strong suits.

'I'll report in every twelve hours, sir.'

'Good luck then. Let's hope that whatever the problem is, the Russians have a handle on it.'

As the Delta L-1011 lumbered into the night sky, Smith settled himself in the comfortable business-class seat. He ate sparingly, then slept all the way to London. After refuelling, the aircraft continued its easterly journey, landing at Sheremetevo early in the morning. Travelling on his military ID, Smith had no problem at customs and immigration. After a forty-minute cab ride he arrived at the new Sheraton hotel near Red Square.

Smith placed a DO NOT DISTURB sign on his door, washed away the travel grit, and slept another four hours. Like most soldiers, he had long ago mastered the art of getting rest when he could.

A little after noon, he stepped out into the raw Moscow spring and walked the six blocks to a covered arcade fronting a nineteenth-century building. The shops were upscale, offering everything from furs and perfumes to precious icons and Siberian 'blue' diamonds. Smith threaded his way past prosperous-looking shoppers, wondering which belonged to Russia's new business elite and which were outright criminals. In the new Russia the distinction blurred.

He walked almost to the end of the arcade before he saw the address Klein had given him. The gold lettering – in Cyrillic and English – read: BAY DIGITAL CORPORATION.

Through the plate-glass window Smith saw a reception desk, and behind it, a series of workstations as modern as any found on Wall Street. Elegantly dressed men and women went about their business with brisk efficiency, but a particular one caught his eyes. She was in her mid-thirties, tall, with gold hair cut short. She had the same straight nose and firm chin that belonged to another woman he'd known, the same dark eyes . . . as Sophia had had.

Smith took a deep breath and entered. He was

about to introduce himself to the receptionist when the blond woman looked up. For an instant Smith couldn't breathe. It was as if his Sophia had suddenly come back to life.

'Jon?'

Randi Russell could not hide her surprise, which drew curious looks from the rest of the staff. She hurried over to the receptionist's desk.

'Why don't we talk in my office,' she said, trying to keep her tone businesslike.

Smith followed her to a small but pleasantly decorated office, filled with framed watercolours of the Santa Barbara coastline. Randi Russell closed the door and looked him up and down.

'I can't believe it,' she said, shaking her head. 'When? How . . . ?'

'It's good to see you again, Randi,' Smith said quietly. 'I'm sorry I didn't let you know I was coming. It was a last-minute trip.'

Randi's eyes narrowed. 'Nothing is last-minute with you, Jon. How did you know where to find me?'

Smith knew that in the aftermath of the Hades tragedy Randi had been stationed as a CIA field operative in Moscow. But it had taken Klein to ferret out the exact nature of her cover and where Smith could locate her.

Smith looked around the room. 'Is it safe to talk here?'

Randi pointed to what looked like a DVD player. 'The latest in bug detection. Besides, our cleaners "sweep" the place every night.'

Smith nodded. 'All right. First, I knew you were in Moscow but not where to find you. Others helped with that. Second, I need your help because a man – a good

80

man – is dead and I want to find out what happened to him.'

Randi considered his words. She could tell when people were lying, even professionals whose stock in trade was mendacity. Her instincts told her that Smith was giving her the truth – or at least as much of it as he could.

'I'm listening, Jon.'

Smith sketched out who Danko was, then described his encounter with the Russian in minute detail. He did not shy away from the grisly details of the massacre at St Mark's. Randi was no stranger to violence.

'Are you sure the hunters weren't after you as well?' she asked.

'If I'd been the primary target, I'd be dead,' Smith replied grimly. 'Their target was Danko; they made sure he was dead. Only then did they turn on me.'

Randi shook her head. 'Saved by a piano. My God! I can't believe that you chased after them unarmed. You're lucky that someone got to them first.' She took a deep breath. 'What is it you want, Jon – to avenge Danko or to get into Bioaparat?'

'Yuri sacrificed his life to bring me a secret,' he replied. 'If I uncover it, I'll find whoever killed him. But I think that whoever it is, he or they are also linked to Bioaparat.'

'What do you want from me?'

'Your best contacts in Russia, people in authority, people you would trust.'

She stared at the watercolours. 'Oleg Kirov, a major-general in the Russian Federal Security Service. He's very much like the Danko you describe: realistic, trustworthy, a patriot. His number two is Lara Telegin. Very bright, politically savvy, very good in the field.'

'I remember meeting Kirov when I was working for USAMRIID,' Smith said. 'But I don't know him well enough to call out of the blue. Can you set up a meeting?'

'Of course. But Kirov will want to know if you're acting in any official capacity – and so would I.'

'I'm not working for USAMRIID or any intelligence agency. That's the truth.'

She looked at him wryly. 'As far as it goes.' She held up her hands to ward off his protest. 'Hey, I know how these things work. So does Kirov.'

'This means a lot to me, Randi.'

She brushed away his thanks, and an uncomfortable silence descended between them.

'There are things I need to tell you,' Smith said at last. 'Personal things.'

He described his visit to Sophia's grave and told her about the closure he had managed to find. 'After the funeral, I felt there were things you and I had to say to each other, but never did. We just walked away from each other.'

Randi stared at him. 'I know what you mean. But back then, a part of me still blamed you for what had happened to Sophia. It took me a long time to work through that.'

'Do you still blame me?'

'No. There was nothing you could have done to help her. You didn't know about Tremont and his killers, or that Sophia was a threat to them.'

'I needed to hear you say that,' Smith told her.

Randi looked at the framed photo on her desk of her and Sophia in Santa Barbara before the horror. Although over a year had passed, Randi had not been able to forgive herself for not having been there when her sister had needed her most. While Sophia lay dying in that hospital bed, Randi had been thousands of miles away, working deep undercover in Iraq, helping the resistance to Saddam Hussein's regime. She had not learned how or why Sophia had been murdered until weeks later, when Jon Smith had materialized in Baghdad like some dark djinn.

Amid the rubble of her grief, Randi had managed to find unbroken vessels she could cling to. But her feelings for Smith remained ambivalent. She was grateful that he had been with Sophia in her last moments, that she had not died alone. Yet as she became more and more entangled in the web that was Hades she couldn't help but wonder if Smith could somehow have prevented her sister's murder. There too, the issue had been maddenly unclear. She knew that Smith had loved Sophia deeply and would never have knowingly put her in harm's way. Yet, when she stood at her sister's grave, she still believed that he could have done something to save her.

Randi brushed away that last thought and turned to Smith.

'It'll take a little while to set up the meeting with Kirov. Would you like to meet for a drink later?'

'Very much.'

They settled on the lounge in the Sheraton, after Randi had closed up the office.

'What exactly is Bay Digital?' Smith asked. 'And what do you do here?'

'You mean the people who sent you didn't mention that?' Randi smiled. 'Jon, I'm shocked. I happen to be the Moscow office manager of a very successful venture-capital firm looking to invest in promising Russian high-tech startups.'

'Except the funding doesn't come from private investors or hedge funds,' Smith said.

'Be that as it may, anyone with money can open all doors in Russia. I have contacts that range from the Kremlin, through the army, and even into the Russian mafia.'

'I always said you had friends in low places. And is there such a thing as high-tech in this country?'

'Better believe it. The Russians don't have our equipment, but give them the right tools and they shine.' She touched his arm. 'It really is good to see you again, Jon – whatever your reasons for being here. Is there anything you need right now?'

Smith pictured Danko's widow and child. 'Tell me what Russians bring when they call on a woman who's just lost her husband – and doesn't know it yet.'

8

At 7:36 A.M. Houston time, Dr Adam Treloar boarded
a British Airways flight for its nonstop run over the
Pole to London's Heathrow Airport. Upon arrival, he
was escorted to the transit lounge where, as a first-
class passenger, he availed himself of the services of a
masseuse. After a quick shower, Treloar picked up his
freshly pressed suit from a valet and headed for gate
sixty-eight, where he was shown into the forward cabin
of another BA flight, this one to Moscow. Twenty-eight
hours after he had started his journey, Treloar cleared
Russian customs and immigration without incident.

Treloar adhered strictly to the itinerary that he and
Reed had worked out. After a taxi dropped him off at
the new Hotel Nikko across the river from the Kremlin,
Treloar registered, then gave the porter an extravagant tip to bring the bags up to his room. Next, he
exited the hotel and hailed another taxi, which took
him to the cemetery on Mychalczuk Prospekt. The old
woman selling flowers by the entrance was astonished
to receive twenty American dollars for a bouquet of
wilted daisies and sunflowers. Treloar proceeded to a
stretch of relatively new graves laid out under a stand
of birch trees. He placed the flowers at the foot of a
distinctive Orthodox cross that commemorated the final
resting place of his mother, Helen Treloar, née Helena
Sviatoslava Bunin.

FBI background investigators had duly noted that

Treloar's mother had been born in Russia when Treloar had applied for the post of chief medical officer. But no red flags went up. Competing for medical talent against the private sector, NASA was only too happy to land an expert like Adam Treloar, who came to the agency after fifteen years with Bauer-Zermatt A.G. No one asked why Treloar had given up his seniority at such a prestigious firm or why he had accepted a 20 percent pay cut. Instead, the space agency had handed over Treloar's impeccable credentials and glowing references and told the Bureau to fast-track the background check.

With the end of the Cold War, travel to Russia had become easier than ever. Thousands of Americans went to visit relatives whom, in many cases, they had seen only in photographs. Adam Treloar went back, too, to visit his mother after her divorce and return to her native Moscow. For the next three years, he flew in every spring to spend a week with her.

Two years ago, Treloar had informed his superiors at NASA that his mother had terminal cancer. They commiserated and told him he could have as much personal leave as he needed. The dutiful son increased his visits to three a year. Then, last fall, when Helena Bunin at last succumbed, he went back for an entire month, ostensibly to settle her affairs.

Treloar was certain that the FBI was keeping track of his visits to Moscow. But he also knew that, like any bureaucracy, it was content as long as it recognized a pattern, and that pattern did not change. Over the years, Treloar had created just such a pattern, altering it only when he had a foolproof reason to do so. Since this was the six-month anniversary of his mother's death, it would have seemed out of place if he hadn't gone to visit her grave.

During the taxi ride back to his hotel, Treloar reviewed what he had done. The cabdriver from the airport, the porter at the hotel, the old woman at the cemetery, the other cabdrivers – all would remember him because of the generous tips. If anyone came checking, the pattern of his visit was clear. Now it would seem natural to rest for a few days in Moscow before heading back. Except that the NASA physician had more on his agenda than sightseeing.

Treloar retired to his room and slept for several hours. By the time he awoke, darkness had descended over the city. He showered, shaved, put on a fresh suit, and, bundled up in a warm overcoat, went out into the night.

The thoughts came unbidden as he walked. As much as they rankled him, he could never make them go away. So he surrendered, allowing them to wash over him, breathing shallowly until they were spent.

Adam Treloar believed himself to be marked as Cain had been marked. He was cursed by terrible desires that he could neither control nor escape from. They were the reason why he had bargained away his career at Bauer-Zermatt.

In another lifetime, Treloar had been the star of Bauer-Zermatt's virology division, preening in the respect of his peers and the adulation of his subordinates – one subordinate in particular, a sloe-eyed fawn so beautiful that Treloar had found the temptation irresistible. But the fawn had turned out to be a goat, tethered to one of Bauer-Zermatt's competitors. The goat was meant to snare the unwary suitor, compromise him, and force him to bend to the competitor's will.

Treloar had never seen the trap; he'd only had eyes for the fawn. But he saw plenty, later, when men arrived at his apartment and played sex tapes in which he had a starring role. They offered a cold choice: exposure or cooperation. Because of the proprietary nature of Bauer-Zermatt's research, every employee had to sign a strictly worded contract whose provisions included a morals clause. Treloar's tormenters made a point of reminding him about that as they replayed the video. They drove him to face the fact that his options were few: hand over information about the company's research, or face exposure. Of course, exposure would not be the end of it. Public branding as a deviant would follow. Then, after all the publicity, the civil – and probably criminal – charges, it would be futile for him to try to find another job anywhere in the medical research community.

Treloar was given forty-eight hours to consider his choices. He wasted the first twenty-four doing just that. Then, as he looked into a future that held nothing but ruins, he realized that his blackmailers had overreached: they had placed him in a position where he had nothing to lose by fighting back.

By virtue of his seniority at Bauer-Zermatt, Treloar was able to secure a meeting with Dr Karl Bauer himself. In the elegant surroundings of Bauer's Zurich office, he laid out his trespasses and the way in which he was being blackmailed. He offered to make amends any way he could.

To Treloar's surprise, Bauer seemed nonplussed at the turn of events that had befallen his wayward employee. He listened without comment, then instructed Treloar to come back the next morning.

To this day, Treloar had no idea what had transpired behind the scenes. The following morning, when he appeared before Bauer, he was told that he would never hear from the blackmailers again. Evidence of his peccadilloes was no longer in the public domain. There would be no repercussions – ever.

But there would be recompense. Bauer informed Treloar that in return for saving his future in the medical research community, Treloar would soon leave the company. An employment offer would arrive from NASA; he would accept it. His colleagues would be told that he was seizing the chance to do the kind of research he could never be involved in if he stayed at Bauer-Zermatt. Once he arrived at NASA, he would place himself at the disposal of Dr Dylan Reed. Reed would be his guide and mentor, and Treloar would obey him without question.

Treloar recalled the cold, precise way in which Bauer had handed down his edict. He remembered the flash of anger, then the amusement in Bauer's eyes when Treloar had timorously asked what kind of research he would be doing at NASA.

'Your work will be of secondary concern,' Bauer had told him. 'It is your connection to your mother, to Russia, that interests me. You will be seeing her on a regular basis, I think.'

Treloar shouldered his way against the wind as he turned away from the bright lights of Gorky Square and into the dark streets that led into the Sadovaya District. The bars became seedier, the homeless and the drunks more aggressive. But this was not Treloar's first visit to Sadovaya, and he was not afraid.

Half a block away, he saw the familiar flashing neon sign: KROKODIL. A moment later, he rapped on the heavy door and waited for the Judas hole to open. A pair of black, suspicious eyes examined him, then the bolt was released and the door opened. On his way in, Treloar gave the giant Mongolian bouncer a twenty-dollar bill for the cover charge.

Shrugging off his coat, Treloar felt the last of his thoughts dissolve beneath the hot lights and the screaming music. Faces turned his way, eyes impressed by his Western suit. Gyrating bodies bumped him, more by design than by accident. The manager, a thin, ferretlike creature, hurried over to greet his foreign customer. Within seconds, Treloar had a glass of vodka in his hand and was being escorted along the edge of the dance floor to a private area of velvet-covered couches and soft ottomans.

He sighed as he relaxed among the cushions. The warmth of the liquor made his fingertips tingle.

'Shall I fetch you a sample?' the ferret whispered.

Treloar nodded happily. To pass the time, he closed his eyes and let the music roar through him. He stirred when something soft grazed his cheek.

Standing in front of him were two blond-haired boys, their eyes a perfect blue, their complexions flawless. They could not have been more than ten years old.

'Twins?'

The ferret nodded. 'And better, virgins.'

Treloar groaned.

'But they are very expensive,' the ferret warned him.

'Never mind that,' Treloar said hoarsely. 'Bring us some *zakuski*. And soft drinks for my angels.'

He patted the cushions on either side of him. 'Come to me, my angels. Give me a taste of heaven . . .'

Six kilometres from the Krokodil are the three high-rises known collectively as Dzerzhinsky Square. Until the early 1990s, it had been the headquarters of the communist KGB; after democratization, the complex was taken over by the newly formed Russian Federal Security Service.

Major-General Oleg Kirov, hands behind his back, stood in front of the windows of his fifteenth-floor office, looking out at the Moscow skyline.

'The Americans are coming,' he murmured.

'What did you say, *dusha?*'

Kirov heard the tap of heels on hardwood, felt slender fingers slide across his chest, inhaled the warm, sweet perfume borne on the words. He turned and took the beautiful brunette into his arms, kissing her hungrily. His passion was returned as he felt her tongue teasing his, her hands slipping to his belt, then lower.

Kirov pulled back, gazing into the provocative dark eyes that tantalized him.

'I wish I could,' he said softly.

Lieutenant Lara Telegin, Kirov's aide-de-camp, stood with arms akimbo, surveying her lover. Even in the drab military uniform she looked like a runway model.

'You promised me dinner tonight,' she pouted.

Kirov couldn't help but smile. Lara Telegin had graduated at the top of her class at the Frunze military academy. She was an expert marksman; the same hands that caressed him could take his life in a matter of seconds. Yet she could be as shameless and provocative as she was professional.

Kirov sighed. Two women in one body. Sometimes he wasn't sure which was the real one. But he would enjoy them both for as long as he could. At thirty, Lara was just beginning her career. Inevitably she would move on to other posts, and finally a command of her own.

Kirov, twenty years her senior, would go from being her lover to her godfather – or, as the Americans liked to say, a 'rabbi' who would look after the interests of his favourite.

'You didn't tell me about the American,' Lara said, all business now. 'Which one is it? We get so many these days.'

'I didn't tell you because you were gone all day and I had no one to help me with this infernal paperwork,' Kirov grumbled. He handed her a computer printout.

'Dr Jon Smith,' she read. 'How very common.' She frowned. 'USAMRIID?'

'Our Dr Smith is anything but common,' Kirov said dryly. 'I met with him when he was stationed at Fort Detrick.'

'"Was"? I thought he still is.'

'According to Randi Russell, he still has an association with USAMRIID but is on indefinite leave. She called to ask if I would see him.'

'*Randi Russell* . . .' Lara let the name hang.

Kirov smiled. 'No need to get catty.'

'I only become catty when there's good reason,' Lara replied tartly. 'So she's paving the way for Smith . . . who, it says here, was engaged to her sister.'

Kirov nodded. 'She died in the Hades horror.'

'And would Russell – whom we both suspect operates a CIA front – vouch for him? Are the two of them running some kind of operation? What's going on, *dusha*?'

'I think that the Americans have a problem,' Kirov said heavily. 'Either we're part of it or they need our help. In any event, we will find out soon enough. You and I will be seeing Smith tonight.'

In the waning afternoon Smith stepped out of the apartment block on Ulitsa Markovo. He turned his collar against the wind and stared up at the grim concrete face of the building. Somewhere within the anonymous windows on the twentieth floor Katrina Danko would be attending to the heartbreaking task of telling her six-year-old daughter, Olga, that she would never see her father again.

To Smith, the task of calling on the relatives of the dead was a task that pained him like no other. Like all wives and mothers, Katrina had known why he was here from the minute she opened the door and laid eyes on him. But she had iron in her spine. She had refused to surrender to tears, asking Smith how Yuri Danko had died and whether he had suffered. Smith told her as much of the truth as he could, then said that arrangements had already been made to fly Danko's remains to Moscow as soon as the Venetian authorities released them.

'He talked a great deal about you, Mr Smith,' Katrina had told him. 'He said that you were a good man. I see that is true.'

'I wish I could tell you more,' Smith said sincerely.

'What good would that do?' Katrina asked. 'I knew the kind of work Yuri was involved in – the secrecy, the silences. But he did it because he loved his country. He was proud of his service. All I ask is that his death not be in vain.'

'I can promise you it won't be.'

Smith walked back to his hotel and spent the next hour lost in thought. Seeing Danko's family added a personal sense of urgency to his mission. Of course he would make sure that Katrina and her daughter were well provided for. But that wasn't enough. Now more than ever he needed to know who had killed Danko, and why. He wanted to be able to look his widow in the eye and say, no, the man you loved did *not* die in vain.

As night descended, Smith made his way to the lobby bar. Randi, wearing a navy blue power suit, was already waiting for him.

'You look pale, Jon,' she said quickly. 'Are you all right?'

'I'll be fine. Thanks for meeting me.'

They ordered pepper-flavoured vodka and a plate of *zakuski* – pickled mushrooms, herring, and other snacks. After the waitress withdrew, Randi raised her glass.

'To absent friends.'

Smith echoed her toast.

'I spoke with Kirov,' Randi said, and gave him the details on the upcoming meeting. She glanced at her watch. 'You'll have to get going. Is there anything else I can do?'

Smith counted out some rubles and left them on the table. 'Let's see how things go with Kirov tonight.'

Randi came close and slipped a business card in his hand. 'My address and phone number – just in case. You have secure communications, right?'

Smith patted his pocket. 'The latest in digitally encrypted cell phones.' He gave her the number.

'Jon, if you find out anything I should know . . .' She let the rest of her thought hang.

Smith squeezed her hand. 'I understand.'

Jon Smith had been to Moscow a number of times, but he had never had occasion to visit Dzerzhinsky

Square. Now, standing in the cavernous lobby of the Zamat 3 building, all the stories he'd heard from Cold War warriors came back to him. There was a soulless indifference about the place that no amount of fresh paint could hide. The echoes off the varnished floorboards sounded like the footsteps of the condemned – men and women who, since the birth of communism, had been dragged through there on their way to the interrogation chambers in the cellars. Smith wondered how those who worked there now dealt with the ghosts. Were they aware of them? Or was the past hurriedly dismissed for fear that, like a golem, it might come back to life?

Smith followed his junior-officer escort into the elevator. As the car rose, he mentally reviewed the details Randi had provided on Major-General Oleg Kirov's career, and that of his deputy, Lara Telegin.

Kirov seemed to be the kind of soldier who straddled the past and the future. Raised under the communist regime, he had distinguished himself in combat during Afghanistan, Russia's Vietnam. Afterward, he had thrown his lot in with the reformers. When a fragile democracy took hold, Kirov's patrons rewarded him with a post in the newly formed Federal Security Service. The reformers were eager to destroy the old KGB and purge the diehards in its ranks. The only people they trusted to carry out that cleansing were battle-tested soldiers like Kirov, whose loyalty to the new Russia was unquestioned.

If Kirov represented a bridge to the future, Lara Telegin was that future's best hope. Educated in Russia and England, Telegin was the new breed of Russian technocrat: multilingual, worldly in her outlook, a technological wizard who knew more about the Internet and

Windows than did most westerners.

But Randi had emphasized that when it came to matters of national security, the Russians were still secretive and suspicious. They could drink with you all night, regale you with their most intimate or embarrassing experiences. But if you asked the wrong question about the wrong subject, offence would be taken instantly, the trust broken.

Bioaparat is about as sensitive an issue as there is, Smith thought as he was shown into Kirov's office. *If Kirov takes what I tell him the wrong way, I could be back on the plane before morning.*

'Dr Jon Smith!'

Kirov's voice boomed across the room as he went over and shook Smith's hand. He was a tall, barrel-chested man with a full head of silver hair and a face that might have been stamped on a Roman coin.

'It's good to see you again,' he said. 'That last time was . . . Geneva, five years ago. Correct?'

'Yes, it was, General.'

'Allow me to introduce my adjutant, Lieutenant Lara Telegin.'

'A pleasure, Doctor,' Telegin said, openly appraising Smith and approving what she saw.

'The pleasure is mine,' Smith replied.

He thought that with her dark eyes and raven hair, Lara Telegin was the archetypal temptress out of a nineteenth-century Russian novel, a siren who wooed otherwise rational men to their doom.

Kirov indicated the sideboard. 'Can I offer you a refreshment, Dr Smith?'

'No, thank you.'

'Very well. In that case, as you Americans are so fond of saying: what's on your mind?'

Smith glanced at Lara Telegin. 'No disrespect intended, Lieutenant, but the subject is highly confidential.'

'None taken, Doctor,' she replied tonelessly. 'However, I am cleared for COSMIC-level material, the kind that you would take to your president. Besides, I understand that you are not here in any official capacity. Are you?'

'The lieutenant has my full confidence,' Kirov added. 'You may speak freely here, Doctor.'

'Fine,' Smith replied. 'I will assume that this conversation is not being monitored and that the premises are secure.'

'Take that as a given,' Kirov assured him.

'Bioaparat,' Smith said.

The single word elicited the reactions he'd expected: shock and concern.

'What about Bioaparat, Doctor?' Kirov asked quietly.

'General, I have good reason to believe that there's a security breach at the facility. If material has not already gone missing, there is a plan under way to steal some of the samples you hold there.'

'Preposterous!' Lara Telegin snapped. 'Bioaparat has some of the most advanced security systems in the world. We have heard these kinds of allegations before, Dr Smith. Honestly, sometimes the West thinks that we are little more than unruly schoolchildren playing with dangerous toys. It's insulting and –'

'Lara!'

Kirov's voice was soft, but the command behind it was unmistakable.

'You must forgive the lieutenant,' he said to Smith. 'She resents when the West appears to be patronizing or paternalistic – which is sometimes the case, wouldn't you agree?'

'General, I'm not here to criticize your security arrangements,' Smith replied. 'I wouldn't have come all this way if I didn't believe that you have a serious problem – or that you wouldn't at least hear me out.'

'Then please, go on about our "problem."'

Smith regrouped and took a deep breath. 'The most likely target is your store of smallpox.'

Kirov paled. 'That's insane! No one in their right mind would try to steal that!'

'"Right minds" wouldn't try to steal anything you keep at Bioaparat. But we have information that the theft is in the works.'

'Who is your source, Doctor?' Telegin demanded. 'How reliable is he? Or she?'

'Very reliable, Lieutenant.'

'Would you produce him for us so that we might satisfy ourselves?'

'The source is dead,' Smith replied, trying to keep his voice level.

'Convenient,' she observed.

Smith turned to Kirov. 'Please listen to me. I'm not saying that you or the Russian government is involved in this. The theft is being engineered by third parties who, right now, are unknown. But for them to get the sample out of Russia requires the cooperation of people inside Bioaparat.'

'You're suggesting that either the research or security personnel are involved,' Kirov said.

'It could be anyone who has access to the smallpox samples.' Smith paused. 'I'm not passing judgment on your people or your security, General. I know that most of those who work at Bioaparat are as loyal as the people who work in our facilities. But I am telling you that you have a problem – which will become *our* problem, and probably the world's – if those samples get out.'

Kirov lit a cigarette.

'You came all this way to tell me this,' he said slowly. 'But you also have a plan, don't you?'

'Shut down Bioaparat,' Smith said. 'Right now. Throw a military cordon around it. Nothing goes in – for sure, nothing and no one comes out. In the morning, you inspect the virus stocks yourself. If they're all there, fine, we're safe, and you can go after the mole.'

'And you, Dr Smith? Where would you be during all this?'

'I would ask you to grant me observer status.'

'Don't you trust us to tell you that all the stocks are intact, Doctor?' Telegin taunted.

'It's not a matter of trust, Lieutenant. If the situation were reversed, wouldn't *you* want to be on-site at our facility?'

'There's still the issue of your source,' Kirov reminded him. 'Understand, Doctor. To do what you ask requires me to go to the president himself. Certainly I can vouch for your credentials. But I need a very good reason to disturb his sleep. If I have the name of your source, if I can check his pedigree – that would validate a great deal of what you have told us.'

Smith turned away. He had known that it might come down to this, trading Yuri Danko's identity in order to secure Kirov's cooperation.

'The man has a family,' he said at last. 'I need your word that they will not be punished and that if they want to, they can leave.' He held up his hand before Kirov could reply. 'That man was not a traitor, General. He was a patriot. He came to me only because he didn't know how high up the conspiracy went. He

99

gave up everything he had here so that Russia *wouldn't* be blamed if anything happened.'

'I can understand that,' Kirov replied. 'You have my assurance that the family will not be harmed. Furthermore, the only person I will speak to is President Potrenko – unless you tell me that *he* is somehow tainted?'

'I can't believe that to be the case,' Smith replied.

'Then we are in agreement. Lara, call the duty officer at the Kremlin. Tell him that it's urgent and I'm on my way.'

He turned to Smith. 'Now, that name, please.'

'I think you are extending the American a great deal of trust,' Lara Telegin said as she and Kirov walked through the underground garage to his car. 'Maybe too much trust. If he is a liar, or worse, a provocateur, you could end up having to answer some embarrassing questions.'

Kirov returned his driver's salute and stepped aside to allow Lara to get into the car.

'Embarrassing questions,' he said once they were settled. 'Is that all?'

She glanced at the partition that separated the driver's compartment from the rest of the car, making sure that it was all the way up. Such actions were ingrained in her, a result of her military intelligence training.

'You know what I mean,' she said. 'For a soldier, you hold extremely progressive views. They have made you your share of enemies.'

'If by "progressive" you mean that I wish Russia to join the twenty-first century, then I plead guilty,' Kirov replied. 'And if I have to take the odd risk to ensure that

100

such views prevail against the Neanderthals who would send us back to a bankrupt political system, so be it.'

He gripped the door handle as the car shot out into the wide boulevard that runs by Dzerzhinsky Square.

'Listen to me, Lara,' he continued. 'Men like Jon Smith do not recklessly give their word. You can be sure that he is not on some fool's mission. Individuals high in American government believe the information important enough to send Smith over. Do you see what I mean? What Smith has been allowed to do, told to do – not his words – legitimizes what the Americans believe they have.'

'A traitor's word,' she said bitterly.

It had taken her all of twenty minutes to confirm that Yuri Danko was missing and that his whereabouts were unknown. *Except the Americans, damn them, know that he's dead!*

'On the face of it, Danko was a traitor,' Kirov agreed. 'But you can see his dilemma: what if he had gone to his superior, or even higher up the command chain, and that person had turned out to be part of this "conspiracy"? Danko would still be dead and we would know nothing.'

Kirov stared through the bulletproof window at the streetlights flashing by.

'Believe me, I hope that the Americans are wrong,' he said softly. 'I would like nothing more than to show Smith that Bioaparat is totally secure and that he has been the victim of a hoax. But until I *can* do that, I must give him the benefit of the doubt. You understand, *dusha*?'

She squeezed his hand. 'Better than you think. After all, I have been learning at the feet of the master.'

The big sedan bored through the Kremlin's Spassky

Gate, stopping only at the security checkpoint where passengers' IDs were checked. A few minutes later, Kirov and Telegin were escorted into the section of the Kremlin that houses the president's apartment and personal working quarters.

'I had better wait here,' Telegin said as they stood in the grand, domed foyer built by Peter the Great. 'There's bound to be more information coming through on Danko.'

'There will be – and Smith will give it to us,' Kirov replied. 'But right now, I think it's time you got used to presenting yourself to your civilian masters.'

Telegin could scarcely hide her surprise and trepidation as they followed the duty officer up the double staircase. They were shown into an elegantly appointed library where a figure wrapped in a thick robe sat by a crackling fire.

'Oleg Ivanovich, you had better have good reason to rob an old man of his sleep.'

Viktor Potrenko cut a patrician-looking figure as he rose to shake Kirov's hand.

'May I present my adjutant, Lieutenant Lara Telegin,' Kirov said.

'Lieutenant Telegin,' Potrenko murmured. 'I have heard good things about you. Please, sit.'

Lara thought that Potrenko lingered in holding her hand. Maybe the rumours about the seventy-five-year-old president were true – that he had a fondness for young women, particularly ballerinas.

When they were seated, Potrenko continued, 'Now what is all this business about Bioaparat?'

Swiftly, Kirov laid out the gist of his conversation with Smith. 'I think that this is something we must take seriously,' he concluded.

102

'Do you?' Potrenko mused. 'Lieutenant Telegin, what are your thoughts?'

Lara understood that her next words could very well put her career in the crosshairs. But she also knew that the two men before her were masters of nuance and inflection. They would spot a lie or an equivocation faster than a hawk sees a hare.

'I'm afraid that I must play devil's advocate, Mr President,' she said, then explained her reservations about taking Smith's words at face value.

'Well spoken,' Potrenko commended her. He turned to Kirov. 'Don't lose this one.' He paused. 'So, what are we to do? On the one hand, the Americans gain nothing by crying foul. On the other, it stings to believe that a theft of this magnitude can occur under our very noses – without us even being aware.'

Potrenko rose and stepped close to the grate, warming his hands. It seemed a very long time before he spoke.

'We have a Special Forces training facility outside Vladimir, do we not?'

'We have, Mr President.'

'Call the commander and authorize a quarantine around Bioaparat effective immediately. You, Lieutenant Telegin, and Dr Smith will fly there at first light. If a theft has occurred, you will notify me immediately. Either way, I want a comprehensive review of the security procedures.'

'Yes, Mr President.'

'Oleg?'

'Sir?'

'If even a gram of smallpox is missing, alert our virus hunters at once. Then arrest everyone on-site.'

9

After landing at the Naples airport, Peter Howell took a taxi to the docks, where he boarded the hydrofoil for the thirty-minute ride across the Straits of Messina. Through the big windows of the lounge, he watched as Sicily came into view, first the craters of Mount Etna, then Palermo itself, nestled beneath the limestone bulk of Monte Pellegrino that tapered off into a plateau at sea level.

Settled by Greeks, invaded by Romans, Arabs, Normans, and Spaniards, Sicily has been a waystop for soldiers and mercenaries for centuries. As one of the breed, Howell had been on the island both as a visitor and a warrior. After stepping off the hydrofoil, he went into the heart of the city – the Quattro Centri, or Four Corners. There he found accommodations in a small *penzione* where he had stayed before. It was well away from the tourist traffic yet within walking distance to the places Howell needed to go to.

As was his habit, Howell reconnoitred those areas of the city he intended to visit. Not unexpectedly, nothing had changed since his last trip, and the map he carried in his head served him well. Returning to the *penzione*, he slept until the early evening, then headed for the Albergheria, a warren of narrow streets in Palermo's craftsmen's district.

Sicily was famous for its knife makers and the quality of their wares and Howell had no problem buying a finely honed ten-inch blade with a sturdy leather handle. Now that he had a weapon, Howell proceeded to the docks, where the taverns and rooming houses were definitely not mentioned in the tourist guides.

Howell knew that the bar was called La Pretoria, although there was no sign on the stone walls. Inside was a large, crowded room with sawdust on the floor and timbers lining the ceiling. Fishermen and boatbuilders, mechanics and sailors sat at long communal tables drinking grappa, beer, or cold, flinty Sicilian wine. Wearing corduroy pants, an old fisherman's sweater, and a knitted cap, Howell attracted little attention. He bought two grappas at the bar and carried the drinks to the end of one of the tables.

The man sitting across from him was short and thick-set, with an unshaven face scarred by the sea and wind. Cold grey eyes regarded Howell through the haze of cigarette smoke.

'I was surprised to hear from you, Peter,' he said in a hoarse voice.

Howell raised his thimbleful of grappa. '*Salute*, Franco.'

Franco Grimaldi – one-time member of the French Foreign Legion, now a professional smuggler – put down his cigarette and lifted his glass. He had to do this because he had only his right arm, having lost the left one to a Tunisian rebel's sword.

The two men tossed back their drinks and Grimaldi jammed the cigarette back between his lips.

'So, old friend. What brings you to my parlour?'

'The Rocca brothers.'

Grimaldi's fleshy lips creased into what might have been misconstrued as a smile. 'I hear things did not go well for them in Venice.' He looked at Howell shrewdly. 'And you just came from there, didn't you?'

'The Roccas executed a contract, then someone executed them,' Howell replied, his voice hard, flat. 'I want to know who that was.'

Grimaldi shrugged. 'It's best not to inquire too closely into the Roccas' dealings – even if they are dead.'

Howell slipped a roll of American dollars across the table. 'I need to know, Franco.'

The Sicilian palmed the money like a magician.

'I heard that there was a special contract,' he said, cupping the side of his mouth as he held his cigarette.

'Specifics, please, Franco.'

'I cannot tell you. Usually the Roccas made no secret about their contracts – especially after a few drinks. But they were very quiet about this job.'

'And you knew about it because . . . ?'

Grimaldi smiled. 'Because I sleep with their sister, who kept house for her brothers. She knew everything that went on within those walls. She is also highly excitable and loves to gossip.'

'Do you think you might use your charms to get a few more details?'

Grimaldi's smile became even wider. 'It would be difficult work, but for a friend . . . Maria – that is her name – probably hasn't heard the news yet. I will break it to her, then let her weep on my shoulder. Nothing like grief to lubricate the tongue.'

Howell gave him the name of the *penzione* where he was staying.

'I will call you later this evening,' Grimaldi said. 'Meet me at the usual place.'

As Howell watched Grimaldi slip his way around the tables and out the door, he noticed a pair of men sitting at one of the smaller tables near the bar. They were dressed like locals, but their body-builder physiques and

106

close-cropped haircuts betrayed their true identities. *Soldiers.*

Howell was familiar with the big American base outside Palermo. During his days with the SAS he'd had occasion to use it as a staging ground for joint operations with U.S. Navy SEALs. For security reasons, most of the personnel stayed within the base perimeter. When they ventured out, it was usually in groups of six or more, and then only to the popular clubs and restaurants. There was no reason for these strapping specimens to be here unless . . .

C-12.

The explosives used to kill the Rocca brothers were an *American* creation. Tightly controlled. But certainly available at one of the largest U.S. bases in Southern Europe.

Had the Roccas' paymaster – possibly the individual who had hired them to kill Danko – also been the one to booby-trap the gondola?

As he rose from the table, Howell took another look at the two Americans.

Or had it been a soldier's mission from the very beginning?

Just before midnight, the *penzione's* sleepy porter knocked on Peter Howell's door to inform him that he had a phone call. He was surprised to discover that his guest was dressed as though ready to go out.

Howell spoke briefly on the phone, tipped the porter, and disappeared into the night. The moon rode high in the sky, illuminating the shuttered shops of the Vuccira market. Howell crossed the empty square to the Piazza Bellini, then drifted along the Via Vittorio Emannuele, the city's major thoroughfare. At the Corso Calatofini, he turned right, now just a hundred yards shy of his destination.

Dominating the Via Pindemonte is the Convento dei Cappuccini – the Convent of the Capuchins. While a striking example of Middle Ages architecture, the monastery's real attraction lies below ground. In the catacombs that surround the *convento* are buried over eight thousand bodies, belonging to both lay and religious persons. Preserved through various chemical processes, they are placed in the niches along the corridors, and are dressed in the clothes the interred themselves had provided prior to their death. Those bodies that aren't lined up along the cold, sweating limestone walls rest in glass coffins, stacked floor to ceiling.

Although open to the public during the day, the catacombs had been a favourite hiding place of smugglers for centuries. There were a dozen ways in and out, and Peter Howell, who had studied the catacombs carefully, knew them all.

As he approached the gates that fronted the parklike entrance to the monastery, Howell heard a low whistle. He pretended not to notice Grimaldi slip out of the shadows until the smuggler was only a few steps away. The moonlight created dancing pinpricks of light in Grimaldi's grey eyes.

'What have you found out?' Howell demanded.

'Something worth getting out of bed for,' the smuggler replied. 'The name of the man who hired the Roccas. He's frightened. He thinks that after the Roccas, he's next. He wants money to get off the island and hide on the mainland.'

Howell nodded. 'Money isn't a problem. Where is he?'

Grimaldi motioned the Englishman to follow him. They skirted the tall wrought-iron fence, moving into the shadows created by the monastery's high walls. The smuggler slowed, then crouched by a small gate cut into the fence. His fingers were busy working the lock when Howell spotted the anomaly.

The lock was already open!

Howell moved like a wraith. As soon as Grimaldi pushed open the gate, he delivered a blow meant to stun, not kill, to the side of the head. Grimaldi let out a soft sigh and dropped, unconscious.

Howell didn't pause. Slipping through the gate, he made his way along the hedgerow that formed a corridor to the entrance of the catacombs. He spotted nothing, which meant –

The trap was outside *the perimeter, not inside!*

Just as he whirled around, Howell heard the creak of the gate's hinge. Two shadows hurtled towards him. In the split-second that the moonlight caught their faces, he recognized the soldiers from the tavern.

Instantly the knife appeared in his hand. Howell held his ground until the last possible second, then, like a matador, pivoted to allow the first soldier to rush past him. He swung the blade up and across, its cutting edge drawing across the man's midsection.

Howell didn't wait to see the killer drop. Feigning right, he moved left, but that didn't fool the second soldier. He heard a soft *phut*! as a silenced automatic spat. The hot breath of the bullet almost kissed his temple. Howell dropped low, kicked out with his legs, and drove his heel into his assailant's kneecap.

Instantly Howell grabbed the pistol, but before he could train the weapon on the soldier he saw Grimaldi stagger to his feet. The bullet meant for the soldier tore through Grimaldi's throat, dropping the smuggler. As the second soldier fled, Howell tucked the gun into his waistband, ran over to Grimaldi, and dragged him inside the gate up to the entrance of the catacombs. As he expected, this door was also unlocked.

A few minutes later, Howell was deep inside the monastery's turnnels. The light from a lamp he had found revealed his catch for the night: Grimaldi lay next to a large, concrete-lined ring whose cover had already been pried off. The wounded soldier, the front of his jacket covered with blood, was propped up against the three-foot-high concrete ring as well.

'Name.'

The soldier's breathing was ragged, his face turning grey from the blood loss. Slowly he raised his head. 'Screw you!'

'I went through your clothes,' Howell said. 'No wallet, no identification, not even labels on your shirts. Only people with a great deal to hide go to those lengths. So what are *you* hiding?'

The soldier spat, but Howell was too quick. Standing, he hauled his captive up to the lip of the ring.

'Did you kill the monastery watchmen?' he demanded. 'Is that where you disposed of them?'

Grabbing the soldier by the neck, he forced him halfway over the concrete ledge.

'Is that where you were going to throw *me*?'

The soldier screamed as Howell, holding him by his jacket collar, forced him over the yawning black hole. From fifty feet below rose the stench of brackish water.

Howell looked down at the red dots that darted at the very bottom.

'Rats. There's probably enough water down there so that the fall won't kill you. But they will. Slowly.' He jerked the man back.

The soldier licked his lips. 'You wouldn't . . .'

Howell stared at him. 'You're wounded. Your partner is long gone. Give me what I need and I promise you won't suffer. Listen.'

Howell pushed him to the ground, then went over and picked up the inert form of Franco Grimaldi. He carried him to the well and without the slightest hesitation heaved him over the side. A second later there was a terrific splash followed by the high-pitched chatter of rats embracing their victim.

The soldier's eyes rolled in terror.

'Name?'

'Nichols. Travis Nichols. Master Sergeant. My partner is Patrick Drake.'

'Special Forces?'

Nichols groaned as he nodded.

'Who sent you after me?'

Nichols stared at him. 'I can't . . .'

Howell grabbed him and jerked him close. 'Listen to me. Even if you live you'd be nothing more than a loose thread that needs cutting. Especially when they discover that I'm not dead. The only chance you have is to tell me the truth. Do that and I'll do what you need.'

Nichols slumped against the concrete ring. His words stumbled out on bright red bubbles.

'Drake and I were part of a special squad. Wet work. Communications by cutouts only. One of us would get a phone call – a wrong number, only it wasn't. Then we'd go to the post office where we had a rented box. The orders would be waiting.'

'Written orders?' Howell asked dubiously.

'On flash paper. Nothing more than a name or a place. After that, we'd meet a contact and he'd fill us in.'

'In this case, the contact was Grimaldi. What were your orders?'

'To kill you and get rid of the body.'

'Why?'

Nichols looked up at Howell. 'You and I are the same. You know nobody gives reasons for things like that.'

'Who is "nobody"?'

'The orders could have come from any one of a dozen sources: the Pentagon, army intel in Frankfurt, the NSA. Take your pick. But with wet work, you know that the source had to be right up there, real high. Listen, you can throw me to the rats but that's not going to get you a name. You know how these things work.'

Howell did.

'Does the name Dionetti mean anything to you?'

Nichols shook his head. His eyes were glassy.

Howell knew that no one except Marco Dionetti – the man who had opened his home and extended him his friendship – knew that he was travelling to Palermo. Dionetti . . . with whom he would have to have a little chat.

'How were you to report that this mission was successful?' Howell asked Nichols.

'Drop off a message at another post office box – no later than noon tomorrow. Number sixty-seven. Someone will come by . . . Oh, Christ, it hurts!'

Howell brought his face very close to Nichols's lips. He needed one last thing from Nichols, and prayed that the soldier had enough strength left to give it up. He strained to hear as the soldier finally let slip his most precious secrets. Then he heard the soft gurgle of the death rattle.

Leaving the lamp where it was, Howell took a moment to compose himself. Finally he hoisted the corpse and dropped it over the side of the well. Quickly, so that he wouldn't have to listen to the rats, he pushed the heavy lid in place and locked it down.

10

At first glance, the Bioaparat complex might have been mistaken for a small college campus. The slate-roofed, red-brick buildings were accented with white-trimmed doors and windows, and were connected to one another by flagstone walks. Dew sparkled in the grass beneath old-fashioned carriage lamps. There were several quadrangles with stone benches and precut concrete tables where employees could enjoy lunch or a game of chess.

The effect was slightly less bucolic during the day, when it was easy to see the razor wire topping the twelve-foot-high concrete wall encircling the compound. Then as now, guard patrols with machine guns and Dobermans were visible. Inside some of the buildings was more elaborate, sophisticated security.

There was a reason why no expense had been spared when it came to Bioaparat's appearance: the facility was open to international bioweapons inspectors. The consulting psychologists had recommended that the facility evoke a warm, familiar environment that was nonthreatening yet that commanded a level of respect. Many designs had been studied; in the end, a campus layout had been chosen. The psychologists had argued that most of the inspectors were or once had been academics. They would feel comfortable in such sur-roundings, which spoke of pure, benevolent research. Having been put at ease, the inspectors would be more likely to allow themselves to be guided along, rather than play medical detectives.

The psychologists had been right: the multinational teams who had visited Bioaparat were impressed as much by the ambience as by the state-of-the-art facilities. The illusion was fostered by familiarity. Almost all the equipment at Bioaparat had come from the West: American microscopes, French ovens and test tubes, German reactors, and Japanese fermenters. The inspectors associated such tools with specific research, primarily into *Brucella melintensis*, a bacterium that preys on livestock, and a milk protein called casein, which stimulates high growth in various seeds. Scores of workers dressed in starched white lab coats going about their business in pristine laboratories completed the desired effect. Having been lulled by the sense of order and efficiency, the inspectors were prepared to take what they saw in Building 103 at face value.

Building 103 was a Zone Two structure, built along the lines of a matryoshka doll. If the roof were removed, one would see a box-within-a-box complex. The outermost shell was reserved for administrative and security personnel who were directly responsible for the safekeeping of the smallpox samples. The first of the two inner shells was a 'hot' area that contained animal cages, specially designed labs for work with pathogens, and giant, sixteen-ton fermenters. The second shell, the actual kernel, held not only the vaultlike refrigerator where the smallpox was stored, but rows of stainless steel centrifuges and drying and milling machines. There, experiments designed to ferret out the mystery of *Variola major* were conducted. The nature of the tests, their duration, the amount of smallpox used, and the results all were tabulated in a computer that only the international inspection teams could access. Such safeguards had been designed to prevent unauthorized use of smallpox in experiments such as gene splicing or replication.

The inspection teams had never found evidence of anything other than approved research in Building 103. Their reports praised the Russian scientists for their attempts to discover whether or not smallpox might hide the key to diseases that still plagued mankind. Finally, after reviewing the formidable security arrangements – which relied almost exclusively on electronic and video surveillance, and so kept the need for human beings to a minimum – the inspectors signed off on the integrity of Building 103. After all, not so much as a gram of variola had ever been unaccounted for.

Russian President Potrenko's call to the Special Forces training unit outside Vladimir was logged in at 1:03 A.M. Six minutes later, one of the duty officers was knocking on the door to Colonel Vassily Kravchenko's cottage. At half past the hour, Kravchenko was in his office, listening to Potrenko's detailed orders to install an undetectable quarantine that would seal Bioaparat from the outside world.

A short, stocky man, Kravchenko was a veteran of Afghanistan, Chechnya, and other places where his Special Forces had been sent. Wounded in action, he'd been relieved of active duty and sent to Vladimir to oversee the training of new recruits. After hearing what Potrenko had to say, the timing of the call gratified him: he had two hundred soldiers who had just completed their field exercises. With them, he could seal off the entire town of Vladimir, much less the Bioaparat complex.

Kravchenko answered Potrenko's questions quickly and succinctly, assuring him that within the hour, he could have his men in position. No one inside the compound or in the town would be any the wiser.

'Mr President,' he said. 'What are my exact orders if someone attempts to exit Bioaparat after the quarantine is in place?'

'Give one warning, Colonel. Only one. If he resists or attempts to escape, use of deadly force is hereby authorized. I need not remind you why.'

'No, Mr President.'

Kravchenko was all too familiar with the hellish concoctions stored in the ultrasecret holds of Bioaparat. He had also witnessed chemical warfare in Afghanistan, and its results were indelibly printed on his memory.

'I will execute your directive as ordered, Mr President.'

'And I will expect to hear from you when the cordon is in place, Colonel.'

While Kravchenko and Potrenko were finishing their call, Lieutenant Grigori Yardeni of the Bioaparat Security Detail (BSD) was in his office in Building 103. He was watching the bank of closed-circuit television monitors when the cell phone in his pocket went off.

The voice was garbled by a synthesizer and sounded like a strangled whisper. 'Do it now. And prepare to use the Option Two. Do you understand?'

Yardeni managed to get the words out, barely: 'Option Two.'

He sat there for a moment, frozen by the implications of what he'd just heard. So many nights he had imagined receiving the call that now, having come, it seemed unreal.

You've been waiting your whole life for this chance. Get on with it!

There were sixty cameras situated throughout Zones One and Two, all of them hooked up to video players. The machines themselves were in a fireproof cabinet equipped with a time lock that could be opened only at the end of a shift, and only by Yardeni's superiors. In addition, the video players were absolutely tamperproof. Yardeni had long ago realized that he had no options as to how to carry out the theft.

The lieutenant was a strapping young man, well over six feet, with curly blond hair and chiselled features. He was a favourite at the Little Boy Blue cabaret, a male strip club in Vladimir. Every Tuesday and Thursday, Yardeni and a few other BSD officers rubbed baby oil over their bulked-up frames and gyrated in front of screaming women. They made more money in those few hours than in a month working for the state.

But Yardeni had always had bigger ambitions. A fanatical devotee of action films, his favourite star was Arnold Schwarzenegger, except that he was getting a little too old. Yardeni thought there was no reason why someone with his looks and physique couldn't replace Arnold. He'd heard that Hollywood was a mecca for tough, good-looking hustlers with attitude.

For the past three years, Yardeni had been scheming to get to the West. A problem he had in common with thousands of other Russians was money: not only for the prohibitive exit taxes and air tickets, but enough to live on afterwards. Yardeni had seen pictures of Bel Air; he had no intention of arriving in Los Angeles penniless, forced to live in the Russian-immigrant ghetto.

The lieutenant checked the clock above his desk and rose, his military-style tunic straining across his chest. It was after one o'clock, that time of night when the body is in its deepest slumber, when it is most vulnerable to death. Except for the human and animal patrols outside and the security inside, Bioaparat, too, slept.

Yardeni reviewed the procedures he already knew by heart, then steadied himself and opened the door. As he made his way through Zone One, he thought about the man who'd approached him almost a year ago. Contact had been made at the Little Boy Blue, and at first he had thought that the man, one of the very few in the audience, was a homosexual. That impression lasted only until the man revealed just how much he knew about Yardeni's life. He described his parents and sister, detailed his high school and army careers, how Yardeni had been his division's boxing champion only to be cashiered when in a fit of rage, he had almost killed a fellow soldier with his bare fists. The man had commented that for all intents and purposes, Yardeni's career would flatline here in Bioaparat, where he would sit daydreaming about what might have been while baby-sitting those who actually got to go to the shining cities.

Of course, one could always change one's destiny . . .

Trying not to think about the cameras, Yardeni proceeded to Zone Two through a corridor that was referred to as a 'sanitary passageway.' It was really a progression of small, sterile rooms linked by connecting doors equipped with coded locks. The locks did not hinder Yardeni; he had a key card and the master codes.

Entering the first cubicle, a changing room, he stripped and hit the red button on the wall. A fine decontamination mist enveloped him.

The next three cubicles held separate items of the antiplague suit: blue socks and long underwear; a hood and cotton smock; the respirator, goggles, booties, and safety glasses. Before leaving the last changing room, Yardeni reached for something that he had put in a locker at the beginning of his shift: a brushed aluminium Thermostype container, the size of a flask.

He lifted the container in his gloved hand. It was a marvel of engineering. From the outside, it appeared to be nothing more than an expensive Western toy, functional but overly extravagant. Even if one unscrewed the top and looked inside, nothing would seem amiss. Only when the base was twisted counterclockwise would the container reveal its secret.

Carefully, Yardeni inched the base around until he heard the click. Inside the double walls, tiny canisters released their contents of nitrogen. Immediately, the container became cold to the touch, like a glass filled with shaved ice.

Slipping it into the pocket of his antiplague suit, Yardeni opened the door to the Zone Two lab. Inside, he made his way past stainless-steel worktables to what the researchers jokingly referred to as the Coke machine. It was actually a walk-in refrigerator with a door of specially constructed, hermetically sealed Plexiglas. It always reminded Yardeni of the bulletproof barriers at the cashiers' booths in the American Express office.

He slipped the coded key card into the slot, punched in the combination, and listened to the long, slow hiss as the door swung back. Three seconds later, it closed behind him.

Pulling open one of the drawers, Yardeni gazed down at row after row of vials made of tempered glass. Working quickly, he unscrewed the container at its midsection and placed the top half to one side. Set in the base were six slots, much like the chambers of a revolver.

He placed one ampoule into each of the slots, then replaced the top section, making sure that it was tightly in place.

Using his key card, he exited the Coke machine and made his way out of the lab. The procedure in the changing rooms was reversed as he deposited parts of the suit into burn bags. After a second decontamination mist, he was ready to get dressed, except that this time he changed into casual clothes – jeans, sweatshirt, and a baggy parka.

A few minutes later, Yardeni was outside, breathing deeply in the night air. A cigarette steadied him. Option Two, the voice had said. That meant something had gone wrong. Instead of Yardeni choosing his moment to purloin the variola, he had had to take it now. And quickly, too, because for some reason Moscow had become suspicious.

Yardeni knew all about the Special Forces command outside Vladimir. He'd befriended some of the trainees in town bars; they were tough and capable, not the kind of men that even he would ever want to tangle with. But the rounds of vodka had bought him valuable information. He knew exactly what kind of exercises the Special Forces went through and how long it took to execute them.

Yardeni crushed his cigarette under his boot and began walking away from Building 103, headed for one of the guard posts on the perimeter. Tonight, as every night for the past month, comrades from his old army unit would staff it. Yardeni would tell them he was going off-shift; they would joke that he could still do the last show at the Little Boy Blue. And if someone bothered to check the computerized roster, let him.

◇◇◇

For the past fifty minutes, Kravchenko had been working swiftly and silently. No lights had gone on in the training ground, no alarms had sounded. His soldiers were rousted and assembled under the cover of darkness. As soon as the troops had been mustered, the first armoured personnel carriers rumbled through the gates. Kravchenko couldn't do anything about the engine noise and didn't pay it any mind. Both the citizens of Vladimir and the Bioaparat employees who worked the evening shifts were used to nighttime military exercises.

Riding in the command APC, Kravchenko guided his column down the two-lane highway that led out of his compound. His orders had been clear; if a traitor was on-site, he would be surrounded. The one thing Kravchenko, an eminently practical man, could guarantee was that no one could break the quarantine.

'Grigori?'

'It's me, Oleg.' Yardeni strolled up to the brick post. Standing outside finishing a cigarette was a fellow BSD guard.

'Is your shift over?'

Yardeni feigned boredom. 'Yeah. Arkadi clocked in early. He owes me time from last month. Now I can go home and get some sleep.'

Arkadi was Yardeni's relief, who at this time was, Yardeni assumed, asleep next to his fat wife, not due to come in for another four hours. But Yardeni had coaxed the computer to tell a different story.

'One moment, please.'

Yardeni turned in the direction of the voice coming through the open window of the post. Inside was a guard he had never seen before. He glanced at his friend.

'You didn't tell me that Alex was out tonight.'

'The flu. This is Marko. He usually works days.'

'Fine. But would you tell him to let me out of this dump? I'm getting cold.'

When Oleg opened the door of the post, Yardeni realized it was already too late: the other guard was already checking the computer.

'I have your relief clocked in, Lieutenant, but there's no shift change on the roster,' he said. 'Technically, you're leaving your post unattended.'

The guard's accusatory tone decided Yardeni's next action. His friend Oleg had his back to him. He never saw Yardeni's arm come around his neck, and felt only a sharp tug before his neck snapped.

The second guard was fumbling for his holstered gun when Yardeni drove the knuckles of his right hand into his windpipe. After the guard sank to his knees, struggling to breathe, it was easy enough to kill him by breaking his neck, too.

Yardeni staggered out of the booth and slammed the door. Instinct and training took over. He began walking, the old infantry refrain repeating itself over and over in his mind: *One foot in front of the other, and in front of the other, and in front . . .*

Outside the perimeter wall, Yardeni saw the lights of Vladimir. He heard the lonely whistle of a still-distant train. The whistle snapped him back to reality, reminded him what he had left to do. Leaving the road, he headed into the woods that surrounded Bioaparat. He had spent many hours there, and finding the right paths on a moonlit night was easy enough. He set a brisk pace and moved off.

Yardeni called up specific images as he ran. A contact would be waiting. He would have the passport that identified Yardeni as a visiting Canadian businessman. There would be a plane ticket for an Air Canada flight and a thick wad of American currency to tide him over until he reached Toronto and the bank where his money and new ID papers had been deposited.

Forget Oleg! Forget that other one! You're almost free!

Yardeni was deep into the woods when he slowed and finally stopped. His hand dropped to his zippered parka pocket, his fingers curling around the cold aluminium container. The marker to his new life was secure.

Then he heard it – the faint roar of heavy vehicles approaching. They were moving west, towards the compound. Yardeni had no problem identifying them by sound alone: APCs, filled with Special Forces. But he did not panic. He was familiar with the procedures they would follow. As long as he was outside the perimeter they would establish, he was safe. He started to run again.

A half mile out of town, Kravchenko saw the security lamps that bathed the perimeter of Bioaparat in white, hot light. Ordering his column off the highway, he guided the vehicles along secondary roads and cart paths until the APCs created an unbreakable steel ring around the facility. Roadblocks were set up at all the arteries leading into and out of the complex. Observation units were posted thirty metres from the brick wall, at fifty-metre intervals. Snipers using thermal scopes were hidden in those spaces. At 2:45 A.M., using a satellite relay, Kravchenko informed his president that the noose was in place.

'Sir?'

Kravchenko turned to his second-in-command. 'Yes, number two?'

'Sir, some of the men have been . . . wondering. Is something wrong inside? Has there been an accident?'

Kravchenko drew out cigarettes. 'I know that some of the men have families in town. Tell them not to worry. That is *all* you may tell them – for now.'

'Thank you, sir.'

Kravchenko exhaled the smoke with a soft hiss. He was a good commander who understood the need for honesty when leading men. Nothing else worked for very long. But in this case he did not feel it prudent to add that even as he spoke, an Ilyushin military transport plane belonging to the army's biohazard containment unit was being readied in Moscow. The time to worry would come if or when that plane left the ground.

The passenger train that pulled into Vladimir at exactly 3:00 A.M. had begun its journey twelve hundred miles to the west, in Kolima in the Ural Mountains. Vladimir was its last stop – a brief one – before the final three-hour run to Moscow.

The engineer had been looking out the window of his locomotive as he'd pulled into the station. He grunted at the sight of the solitary passenger standing on the platform. The only reason Vladimir was a scheduled stop was to pick up soldiers headed for Moscow on leave. Tonight he decided that he could shave a few minutes off his schedule.

The tall figure, wrapped in a greatcoat, did not move

as the train rolled past him. Standing a few feet from the edge of the platform, he continued to scan the darkness beyond the weak station lights.

Ivan Beria, born in Macedonia thirty-eight years ago, was a patient man. Raised in the cauldron of ethnic hatred and bloodletting that was the Balkans, he had learned firsthand how patience worked: your grandfather recounts how ethnic Albanians killed off most of your family. The story is retold so many times that it seems the events took place only yesterday. So when the opportunity for revenge eventually presents itself, you seize it with both hands – preferably around your enemy's neck.

Beria was twelve when he had killed his first man. He kept on killing until all the family blood debts were settled. By the age of twenty, his reputation as an assassin was made. Other families, whose sons or husbands were dead or maimed, turned to him, offering the gold on their hands or around their necks as payment for services to be rendered.

Beria graduated swiftly from settling family feuds to becoming a freelance operator whose services were available to the highest bidder, usually the KGB. As twilight descended over communism, the security apparatus turned more and more to freelancers in order to maintain deniability. At the same time, as Western investment began to permeate Russia, the same capitalists who arrived to do business were also interested in more exotic investments. They were seeking a special kind of man who, because of the worldwide computer links between police and intelligence agencies, was becoming more and more difficult to come by in the West. Through his KGB contacts, Beria discovered that the pockets of American and European entrepreneurs were very deep, especially when it was necessary to cripple or eliminate a competitor.

Over a five-year period, Beria kidnapped over a dozen executives. Seven of them were killed when the ransom demands were not met. One of his targets was a senior official with a Swiss firm called Bauer-Zermatt. Beria was astonished to discover that when the ransom was paid, there was *twice* the amount of money that he'd stipulated. Included was a request that Beria not only free the executive but that he severely inhibit Bauer-Zermatt's competitor's desire to move into the region. Beria was more than happy to oblige, and that marked the beginning of his long and very profitable relationship with Dr Karl Bauer.

'You! Are you getting on? I have a schedule to keep.'

Beria looked at the fat, florid-faced conductor, his baggy uniform crumpled from having been slept in. Even in the fresh air, he smelled the sour stench of liquor coming off the man.

'You don't leave for another three minutes.'

'This train leaves when I say it does, and to hell with you!'

The conductor was about to step off the platform when, without warning, he found himself slammed up against the train car's steel flank. The voice in his ear was as soft as a serpent's tongue.

'The schedule has changed!'

The conductor felt something being jammed into his hand. When he dared to glance down, he discovered a roll of American dollars in his fist.

'Go give the engineer whatever he needs,' Beria whispered. 'I'll tell you when we leave.'

He pushed the conductor away, watched him half run, half stumble towards the locomotive. He checked his watch. The man from Bioaparat was late; even the bribe would not delay the train for very long.

Beria had arrived in Vladimir earlier in the week. His principal had told him to expect a man coming out of Bioaparat. Beria was to guarantee safe passage of both the man and what he was carrying to Moscow.

Beria had waited patiently, staying mostly in a cold little room in the town's better hotel. The call he'd been expecting had come only a few hours ago. His principal spoke of a change in plans, a need to improvise. Beria had listened and assured the principal that he could accommodate these unforeseen developments.

He checked his watch. The train should have left five minutes ago. There was the fat conductor, waddling back from the locomotive. He, too, was looking at a watch.

Beria recalled the armoured column he had heard and glimpsed earlier that evening. Thanks to his principal, he knew everything he needed to about the Special Forces, where they were headed, and why. If the man from Bioaparat hadn't made it out of the compound –

He heard the pounding of heavy boots on the platform. His hand dipped into his coat pocket, his fingers curling around the butt of his Taurus 9mm. He relaxed his grip as the figure ran under a pool of light. He recognized the features that had been described to him.

'Yardeni?'

The lieutenant's chest was heaving with exertion. 'Yes! And you are –'

'The one you were told would meet you. Otherwise, how would I know your name? Now get in. We're late.'

Beria pushed the young guard up the train car's platform. When the conductor came up, wheezing, he held more money under his nose.

'This is only for you. I want privacy. And if there are any delays on the way to Moscow, you will tell me at once. Understand?'

The conductor snatched the money.

The train was moving even as Beria steered Yardeni down the narrow corridor of the car and into a first-class compartment. The seats had been converted to sleeperettes, complete with small soiled pillows and threadbare blankets.

'You have something for me,' Beria said, locking the door and pulling down the shade.

Yardeni took his first good look at his contact. Yes, the sepulchral voice on the phone could have belonged to someone like this. Suddenly he was very glad that he was younger, bigger, and stronger than the monklike figure wrapped in black.

'I was told that you would have something for *me*,' he replied.

Beria pulled out a sealed envelope, watching as Yardeni opened it and examined the contents: a Canadian passport, an Air Canada ticket, cash, several credit cards.

'Is everything in order?' he asked.

Yardeni nodded, then reached into his jacket pocket and pulled out the aluminium canister.

'Be careful. It's very cold.'

Beria did not touch the cylinder until he'd put on gloves. He held it for a moment, like a money trader hefting a pouch of gold dust, then set it aside. He brought out an identical container and handed it to Yardeni.

'What's this?' the young guard demanded.

'Hold on to it. That's all you need to know for now.' He paused. 'Tell me what happened at Bioaparat.'

'Nothing happened. I went in, got the material, and came out.'

'You were on-camera the whole time?'

'There was nothing I could do about that. I told your people –'

'When are tapes reviewed?'

'At the beginning of the new shift, about four hours from now. What does it matter? It's not like I'll be going back.'

'There was no problem at the gate?'

Yardeni was a very smooth liar; he just didn't know the kind of man he was up against.

'None.'

'I see. And you managed to get out before the Special Forces arrived.'

Yardeni couldn't hide his surprise. 'I'm here, aren't I?' he barked. 'Listen, I'm tired. You have anything to drink?'

Silently, Beria withdrew a pint of brandy and handed it to Yardeni, who examined the label.

'French,' he remarked as he tore off the foil seal.

Yardeni raised the bottle, took a generous swallow, then sighed. After unlacing his boots, he removed his parka and folded it into a pillow. As he stretched out, Beria stood up.

'Where are you going?' Yardeni asked.

'To the bathroom. Don't worry. I won't wake you when I return.'

Beria stepped into the corridor, locked the door behind him, and walked to the end of the car. He lowered the top half of a window just enough so that the antenna on his cell phone would protrude through the crack. Seconds later, the connection to Moscow was established, the voice on the other end as clear as if the party was standing next to him.

11

The pounding on the door wrenched Smith out of a light sleep. He fumbled for the bedside lamp as two militiamen burst in, followed by Lara Telegin.

'What the hell's going on?' he demanded.

'Please come with me, Doctor,' Telegin replied. Stepping closer, she lowered her voice. 'There have been developments. The general needs to see you in his office immediately. We'll be waiting outside.'

Smith dressed quickly and followed Telegin to a waiting elevator. 'What happened?'

'The general will brief you,' Telegin said.

They walked through an empty lobby to a sedan idling at the kerb outside. The ride to Dzerzhinsky Square took less than ten minutes. Smith detected no unusual activity in the building until they reached the fifteenth floor. The halls were filled with uniformed personnel rushing from office to office, dispatches in hand. In the cubicles, young men and women were hunched over computer keyboards, talking quietly into headsets. A keen urgency crackled in the air.

'Dr Smith. I would say good morning except it is anything but that. Lara, close the door, would you?'

Smith took stock of Kirov, thinking that he too must have been rousted from his bed not long ago.

'What do you have?'

Kirov passed him a glass of tea set in a filigree metal holder. 'Earlier this morning, President Potrenko ordered the Special Forces contingent outside Vladimir to surround the Bioaparat complex and establish a *cordon sanitaire*. This was done without incident.

'For the next several hours, everything was quiet. However, thirty minutes ago, a roving patrol reported that two guards had been found dead – murdered – at their post.'

Smith felt a cold sensation deep in his stomach. 'Did the Special Forces intercept anyone coming out?'

Kirov shook his head. 'No. Nor did anyone try to get in.'

'What about the security inside the complex – specifically Building 103?'

Kirov turned to Telegin. 'Play the tape.'

She aimed the remote at a wall-mounted monitor. 'This is the video from the security cameras inside 103. Please note the time stamp in the lower-right corner.'

Smith watched the black-and-white images on the screen. A big, uniformed guard walked down a corridor and disappeared into Zone Two. Another set of cameras picked him up in the changing rooms in the decontamination areas.

'Freeze that!' Smith pointed to the canister that the guard, now in full biohazard gear, was holding in his left hand. 'What's that?'

'You'll see for yourself in a minute. Lara?'

The tape rolled on. With growing incredulity, Smith watched the guard enter the refrigerated walk-in safe and begin removing ampoules.

'Tell me that's not smallpox.'

'I wish I could,' Kirov replied.

The suited-up thief completed his work and returned to the first of the decontamination chambers.

'Where are the backup security measures?' Smith

demanded. 'How the hell could he just walk in like that?'

'The same way your security personnel at USAMRIID can walk into your vaults,' Lara Telegin snapped. 'Our system is almost a duplicate of yours, Doctor. We rely just as heavily on coded locks and electronic counter-measures as you do in order to reduce the risk of the human factor. But in the end, it always comes down to one man.' She paused. 'Bioaparat guards are subjected to an intensive screening procedure. Still, you cannot see into a man's soul, can you?'

Smith's eyes were riveted on the screen, which showed a close-up of Grigori Yardeni's face.

'He doesn't care if the camera captures him. It's as though he knows there's nothing he can do about it.'

'Precisely,' Kirov said, and quickly explained why the guards on duty could not tamper with the tapes made during their watch.

'If we hadn't installed this feature, it would have taken far longer to identify the thief. As it is –'

'As it is, he knew he was never coming back. How the hell could he have gotten through the quarantine?'

'Please note the time,' Kirov said, pointing to the corner of the screen. 'The theft occurs *before* the Special Forces are in position. This one had the devil's own luck: he managed to get out only minutes before Colonel Kravchenko began deploying his troops.'

'Is that why he killed the guards at the post – because he was in a hurry?'

'I'm not sure.' Kirov looked at him carefully. 'What are you getting at, Doctor?'

'This guy had to have had a solid plan,' Smith said. 'Okay, he knew he was going to get caught on camera. He didn't care; he must have made some provisions for

132

that. But I don't believe he intended to kill the guards. It makes no sense. Why take the chance that the bodies might be discovered before he completes his escape? I think he had to act *sooner* than he'd anticipated, that he *knew* the Special Forces were on their way – and why.'

'Are you suggesting he had an informer, an accomplice, on the outside?' Telegin demanded.

'How does it look to *you*, Lieutenant?' Smith retorted.

'We will consider that possibility later,' Kirov said. 'Right now, we must track down this Grigori Yardeni. The amount of smallpox he took . . .'

Smith closed his eyes. A hundredth of that amount could, if properly dispersed, infect a population of a million or more.

'What countermeasures have you initiated?'

Kirov pressed a button on his desk and a wall panel slid back to reveal a giant screen. The action it depicted was in real time.

He indicated a moving red dot. 'An Ilyushin transport from the Medical Intelligence Division – our virus hunters – is en route to Vladimir. They will be the ones to enter Bioaparat – no one else.'

He pointed to a blue circle. 'This is the quarantine established by the Special Forces team. Here' – he gestured to three yellow dots – 'we have the reinforcements from Sibiyarsk, already in the air. They consist of a battle-ready battalion that will cordon off Vladimir.'

He shook his head. 'Those poor people will wake up to discover they're prisoners.'

Smith turned to the monitor, which still showed the hulking figure in the antiplague suit. 'What about him?'

Telegin's fingers danced across the keyboard and a military record appeared on the screen. As she ran the translation software, Smith got an even clearer look at Yardeni. Then the Cyrillic alphabet morphed into English.

'Not exactly the kind of guy you'd expect to pull something like this,' he murmured. 'Except this.' He pointed to the paragraph dealing with Yardeni's history of violence.

'True,' Kirov agreed. 'But aside from his bad temper, there was nothing to indicate that Yardeni would contemplate this sort of treason. Consider: he has no relatives or friends living abroad. He accepted the Bioaparat assignment as a way to do penance and reinstate himself in the armed forces.'

He looked at Smith. 'You are familiar with Bioaparat, especially its security. Unlike our other facilities, it is on par with anything in the West, including the CDC. International inspectors – Americans among them – were more than satisfied with our systems.'

Smith understood what Kirov was trying to do: make him an advocate. The Russians had *not* been negligent. Their security was good. This was internal sabotage, impossible to predict or to prevent.

'We all suffer the same nightmares, General,' Smith said. 'You just happened to wake up to one.'

He forced himself to sip some tea. 'How long has Yardeni been on the loose?'

Telegin punched up the medical report. 'According to the Special Forces battle surgeon, the guards were murdered around 2:30 A.M.'

'Just over three hours ago . . . He could have gone a long way in that time.'

She threw up another image on the big screen, displaying concentric circles – green, orange, and black.

'Bioaparat is in the centre. The smallest circle – black

– represents the distance that a reasonably fit man could cover, like a soldier on a training run. The orange circle extends the range if Yardeni has a car or a motorcycle.'

'What are those triangles?' Smith asked.

'Checkpoints established by the local militia. We've faxed them his photo and particulars.'

'What are their orders?'

'Shoot on sight, but not to kill.' She noted Smith's startled expression. 'Our directive describes him as a multiple killer. Also, that he is HIV-positive. Believe me, Doctor, no militiaman will touch Yardeni after he's down.'

'I was thinking more about what he's carrying. If a bullet shatters the container –'

'I understand your concern about the container, but if Yardeni is spotted, we cannot let him walk away.'

'What's the last circle?'

'The worst possibility of all: Yardeni had a conspirator with a plane waiting at the Vladimir airfield.'

'Have there been any takeoffs?'

'None recorded, but that doesn't mean anything. The new Russia has a surplus of experienced pilots, most of them former air force. They can land on a highway or in a field, pick up their load, and be gone in minutes.'

'President Potrenko has ordered interceptors into the area,' Kirov added. 'Any light aircraft will be challenged. If it does not comply with instructions, it will be brought down immediately.'

The wall monitor fascinated Smith. It seemed a living organism, constantly mutating as the symbols winked and moved. But he felt that in spite of the impressive array marshalled against the renegade officer, something was missing.

Moving over to the screen, he traced his finger along

a white line that began east from Vladimir and ran west to Moscow.

'What's this?'

'The rail line between Kolima in the Urals and Moscow,' Kirov replied. He looked at Telegin. 'Was there a train scheduled through Vladimir last night?'

Telegin went to work on the keyboard.

'There was,' she announced. 'It pulled into Vladimir at three o'clock.'

'Too soon for Yardeni to have caught it.'

Telegin frowned. 'Not necessarily. According to the schedule, it should only have been there a few minutes. But it didn't depart on time. It stayed an extra twelve minutes.'

'Why?' Kirov demanded.

'No reason given. In fact, it stops only when there are soldiers headed to Moscow on leave –'

'But there were no soldiers, were there?' Smith said.

'Good guess, Doctor,' Telegin said. 'No one was scheduled to go on leave.'

'So why did the engineer hang around?'

Kirov stepped over to the computer console. The time of the murder of the two guards was juxtaposed against the time when the train left Vladimir. Then that window was measured against the amount of time it would take a man to get from Bioaparat to the train station.

'He could have done it!' Kirov whispered. 'He could have made the train because it didn't leave on time.'

'It was late because somebody held it up!' Smith said savagely. 'Yardeni took the most obvious route. That son of a bitch knew the roads would be blocked sooner than later. He didn't have a plane. He had an accomplice, someone who, if necessary, could hold up the train long enough for him to get to it.'

He turned to Telegin. 'Then all he had to do was ride it into Moscow.'

She was punching the keyboard furiously, then looked up. 'Sixteen minutes,' she said hoarsely. 'It gets into Moscow's central station in sixteen minutes!'

Ivan Beria shifted with the sway of the train; beyond that, he did not move.

Nor had he taken his eyes off Grigori Yardeni. The stress of the theft and the subsequent flight, coupled with the effects of the brandy, had done its work. The Bioparat guard had fallen asleep within minutes of the train's leaving Vladimir.

Beria leaned towards Yardeni. He lay so still as to appear dead. Beria cocked his ear and caught the rattle of shallow breathing. Yardeni was in a very deep sleep. It wouldn't take much to make it deeper still.

He slapped him on the cheeks, twice. 'We're almost there. Time to get up.'

Beria looked out the window as the train threaded its way through the giant railyard. In the reflection, he watched Yardeni yawn and stretch, roll his head to work out the kinks in his neck. His voice was thick with sleep.

'Where do we go from here?'

'Our separate ways,' Beria replied. 'I will get you through the station and into a taxi. After that, you're on your own.'

Yardeni grunted and made a move towards the door.

'Where are you going?' Beria demanded.

'To the toilet – with your permission.'

'Sit down. Everybody in the car has the same idea. You'll end up in line. No point in giving anyone that good a look at you, is there?'

Yardeni considered, then sat down again. He ran his hand over one of the parka pockets to reassure himself that the documentation and money were where they should be. Satisfied, he thought he could hold his water until they reached the station.

When the train entered the tunnel between the yard and the station, the overhead lights flickered, went out briefly, then flickered back on.

'Let's go,' Beria said.

The corridor was filling up with people. Because of his height, Yardeni had no problem keeping Beria in sight, even in the sputtering light. Oblivious to the muttered curses, he elbowed his way to the exit.

The train eased into its siding and shuddered to a stop. The conductor lifted the platform that covered the steps. Beria and Yardeni were the first ones off, walking swiftly to the front of the train and towards the doors leading to the station proper.

The big van boomed along Moscow's still-empty boulevards. Inside, Smith, Kirov, and Telegin sat in captain's chairs bolted to the floor. Telegin was in front of a monitor displaying the city's traffic patterns; every few seconds she spoke to the driver on her headset.

Kirov, too, wore a headset. Ever since leaving Dzerzhinsky Square, he had been in constant communication with an elite unit of the Federal Security Service.

He swivelled his chair around to face Smith. 'The train is in – right on schedule, wouldn't you know.'

'How far away are we?'

'Thirty seconds, maybe less.'

'Reinforcements?'

'On the way.' Kirov paused. 'Are you familiar with

our flying squads?' When Smith shook his head, he continued. 'Unlike your FBI SWAT, we prefer to send ours in undercover. They dress like tradesmen, green-grocers, street workers – you wouldn't recognize them until it was too late.'

'Let's hope it isn't.'

Through the one-way window, Smith saw the station, a massive, nineteenth-century structure. He braced himself as the driver veered into a sharp turn and braked hard in front of the main building. He was on his feet even before the van stopped rocking.

Kirov grabbed his arm. 'The flying squad has Yardeni's picture. They'll take him alive, if possible.'

'Do they have mine – so they don't shoot me by mistake?'

'As a matter of fact, yes. But stay close to me anyway.'

The three ducked under the ornate portico and ran into the station. The interior reminded Smith of a museum, all polished granite, bas relief, and three massive glass domes. There were few travellers, but the sound of their footsteps was like the rumble of a distant herd. In the centre was a large area with rows of benches; along the sides were souvenir shops, refreshment stands, and news kiosks, most of them still shuttered. Smith glanced at the large black arrivals/departures board suspended from the ceiling.

'How many others are due in?'

'We're in luck,' Lara Telegin replied. 'This is the first one. But in twenty minutes, the commuter trains arrive. The crowds will be unmanageable.'

'Which track?'

She pointed to the right. 'Over there. Number seventeen.'

As they ran for the doors leading to the sidings, Smith

turned to Kirov and said, 'I don't see any of your people around.'

Kirov tapped the plastic receiver in his ear. 'Believe me, they're here.'

The air on the platforms was heavy with diesel fumes. Smith and the others ran past orange and grey electric locomotives, resting in their sidings, until they came up against a stream of people going the other way. Moving to the side, they began scanning faces.

'I'm going to find a conductor,' Telegin said. 'Maybe if I show him Yardeni's picture, he'll remember the face.'

Smith continued to study the passersby who trudged along, their faces puffy from sleep, their shoulders bowed under the weight of suitcases and packages bound with string and rope.

He turned to Kirov. 'There aren't enough passengers. These must be coming from the last cars. Whoever was riding up front is already in the station!'

Ivan Beria was standing in front of a newsstand that had just opened for business. He threw down a few kopeks and picked up a newspaper. Leaning against a pillar, he positioned himself so as to have an unobstructed view of the entrance to the men's washroom.

Given Yardeni's size and the dose of slow-acting poison that had been in the brandy, Beria estimated that the big guard would not make it out of the washroom alive.

Any second, he expected someone to run out screaming that a man inside was having a seizure.

But no, there was Yardeni, strolling out of the washroom, looking considerably happier, checking – like a peasant – to make sure that his zipper was done up.

Beria slipped his hand into his coat pocket, to his

Taurus 9mm, when his eyes registered the anomaly: a man wearing overalls, like a sanitation worker, was in the process of emptying a bin into his push cart. The only problem was that as soon as he saw Yardeni, he forgot all about the garbage.

Where there's one, there are more.

Beria slipped around the pillar so that Yardeni wouldn't spot him and quickly surveyed the station. Within seconds he picked out two more men who were out of place: a deliveryman hauling bread, and one who tried to pass himself off as an electrician.

Beria knew a great deal about the Federal Security Service. He was aware that the interest was both reciprocal and intense. But he could not believe they were there for him. Clearly the object of their attention was Yardeni.

Recalling what Yardeni had told him about his clean getaway from Bioaparat, Beria cursed. The guard would pay dearly for his lies.

Beria watched him stroll among the benches toward the kiosks. The three plainclothes agents trailed, forming a rough triangle behind him. One was speaking into a wrist mike.

Then Beria noticed a tall, rangy man come through the doors to the platforms. This was no Russian, though the one following him certainly was. The face of Major-General Kirov was indelibly printed in Beria's memory.

Beria noted that the foot traffic in the station had picked up. Good. He would need as much cover as possible. Beria stepped out from behind the pillar just long enough for Yardeni to catch a glimpse of him. He didn't think that Yardeni's shadows could have discerned exactly what Yardeni had seen to make him move in that direction, but they would surely follow.

Beria counted off the seconds, then slipped out from behind the pillar again. Yardeni was less than fifteen feet away. Beria had his hand on his gun, ready to draw it, when, without warning, Yardeni stumbled, teetered, then crashed to the floor. Immediately, the shadows closed in.

'Help me . . .'

Yardeni had no idea what was happening to him. First his chest had felt like it was on fire; now it seemed to be caught in the jaws of a giant vice that was mercilessly squeezing the life out of him.

As he thrashed on the cold marble floor, his vision began to blur. But he could still make out the features of the man who had brought him this far. Instinctively, he reached out to him.

'Help me . . .'

Beria didn't hesitate. Putting on a concerned expression, he moved directly to the stricken man and the under-cover agents.

'Who are you?' one of them demanded. 'Do you know this man?'

'We met on the train,' Beria replied. 'Maybe he remembers me. God, look at him. He's delirious!'

The poison was causing Yardeni to foam at the mouth, cutting off his speech. Beria was very close now, kneeling.

'You'll have to come with –' one of the agents began.

He got no further. Beria's first shot tore away his throat. His second caught another agent in the temple. The third found the remaining man's heart.

'Shoot him!'

The booming words startled Beria. He rose to discover travellers lying on the floor, hiding as best they could under the benches. But at the doors was Kirov, pointing at him, shouting to a young woman who had come up on Beria's blind side.

'Lara, shoot him!'

Beria whipped around to face Lara Telegin, who had her gun levelled at him. His peripheral vision caught three more figures racing towards them.

'*Go!*' she called out softly.

Beria didn't hesitate. He ducked behind the woman and raced for the exits.

After making sure that Beria was safely away, Telegin braced herself in the shooter's classic stance. As calmly as if she were on the practice range, she shot the remaining members of the undercover team. Then, without pause, she wheeled around to face a disbelieving Kirov.

It took Smith only a split second to realize that Telegin's treachery had frozen the general in her crosshairs. Without thinking, he launched himself at the Russian an instant before he heard the shot. Kirov cried out once as he and Smith went down.

Smith scrambled to his feet and squeezed off two quick shots. Telegin screamed as the bullets tore into her, slamming her body against a pillar. For an instant, she hung like that, her head lolling to one side. Then her gun clattered to the floor, her knees gave way, and she slid down, lifeless as a broken marionette.

Smith turned to Kirov, who had propped himself up against a door. He ripped open his jacket, pulled down the sleeve, and saw the bloodied flesh where Telegin's bullet had struck his upper arm.

Kirov clenched his teeth. 'It's a through-and-through. I'll live. Get over to Yardeni.'

'Telegin –'

'To hell with her! I just hope that you aren't a good shot. I have a lot of questions for her.'

Smith zigzagged through the cowering crowd, making his way around the bodies of Kirov's fallen men. When he reached Telegin, one look told him that she would never be answering any more questions. Quickly, he turned to Yardeni and realized that the same was true for him.

Militiamen and police were flooding the station. Kirov was on his feet, unsteady and in pain, but strong enough to bark out orders. Within minutes, travellers were being herded out of the area.

Brushing aside a medic, Kirov went over to Smith and knelt down by the two bodies.

'The foam around his mouth . . . ?'

'Poison.'

Kirov stared at Lara Telegin's glassy eyes, then reached out and closed the lids. 'Why? Why was she working with him?'

Smith shook his head. 'With Yardeni?'

'Him, too, probably. But I meant Ivan Beria.'

Then Smith remembered the man in the black overcoat, nowhere to be seen now. 'Who is he?'

Kirov winced as the medic firmly sat him down and went to work on his wound.

'Ivan Beria. A Serb freelance operator. He has a long and bloody history in the Balkans.' He hesitated. 'He was also a KGB favourite. Most recently he's been contracting out his skills to the *mafiya* and certain Western interests.'

Smith caught something in Kirov's tone. 'It's personal, isn't it?'

'Two of my best undercover agents in the *mafiya* were murdered in a particularly brutal fashion,' Kirov replied flatly. 'Beria's fingerprints were all over that job. I'm going to put an alert –'

'No, don't touch him!' Smith yelled as the medic was reaching for Yardeni's body. Stepping over to the corpse, he felt gently along the inside folds of the parka.

'Travel documents,' he said, producing Yardeni's passport and air tickets.

His fingers continued to work inside the parka. Suddenly, something very cold brushed his fingertips.

'Get me some gloves!' he called to the medic.

Seconds later, Smith eased out the shiny metal container and carefully laid it on the floor.

'I need ice!'

Kirov moved in for a better look. 'It's intact, thank God!'

'Do you recognize the container design?'

'It's standard issue for the transport of ampoules from the Bioaparat safe to the laboratories.' He spoke briefly into his mike, then looked at Smith. 'The biohazard unit will be here in a few minutes.'

While Kirov issued orders for the station to be cleared, Smith placed the container into a bucket of ice that the medic had managed to find. The nitrogen in the thermal layer kept the container at just above freezing, rendering the virus inactive. But Smith had no idea how long the charge would last. Keeping the canister on ice would provide some measure of safety until the biohazard team arrived.

Suddenly Smith realized how quiet the station had become. Looking around, he discovered that all the militia had pulled back, taking the last of the travellers and station workers with them. Only he and Kirov were left, surrounded by bodies.

'Have you been in combat, Dr Smith?' Kirov asked.

'Call me Jon. And yes, I have.'

'Then you're familiar with this silence . . . after the

145

gunfire and screaming are over. It's only the survivors who get to see what they've wrought.' He paused. 'It's the survivor who can thank the man who saved his life.'

Smith nodded. 'I know you would have done the same. Tell me more about Beria. How does he fit in?'

'Beria is not only an executioner, he is a facilitator. If you want something delivered or spirited out of the country, he's the man who'll guarantee it gets done.'

'You don't think that he and Yardeni – with Telegin's help – planned and executed the theft themselves, do you?'

'Executed, yes. Planned, no. Beria's forte is not in strategy. He is – how would you put it? – a hands-on operator. His job would have been to shepherd Yardeni after he got out of Bioaparat.'

'Shepherd him where?'

Kirov held up the Canadian passport. 'The American-Canadian border is porous. Yardeni wouldn't have had any problem smuggling the smallpox into your country.'

The idea made Smith's flesh crawl. 'You're saying that Yardeni was a thief *and* a courier?'

'A man like Yardeni does not have the wherewithal to provide himself with a new passport, much less pay for the services of Beria. But someone did. Someone wanted to get his hands on a smallpox sample and was willing to pay mightily for the privilege.'

'I'm sorry I have to ask: where does Telegin fit in?'

Kirov looked away, feeling torn by her betrayal.

'You don't strike me as a man who believes in coincidence, Jon. Consider this: Yardeni has been in place for some time. But his masters choose this particular moment to activate him. Why should it have coincided with your arrival in Moscow? Did they know you were coming? If so, they would have deduced that they had one last chance to steal from Bioaparat. And why was Yardeni told to proceed with the theft? Because someone tipped him off that the Special Forces were on their way.'

'*Telegin* warned Yardeni?'

'Who else could it have been?'

'But she wasn't acting on her own . . .'

'I think Lara was the eyes and ears of whoever planned this. As soon as she knew you were in Moscow she contacted her principals, who told her to go ahead and have Yardeni execute the theft. They could not afford to risk the access that Yardeni provided them.'

He paused and glanced at the body of his lover. 'Think about it, Jon. Why would Lara have risked everything – her career, future . . . love – if the rewards were not overwhelming? She would never have found such bounty in Russia.'

Kirov looked up as the station doors opened and the biohazard team, dressed in full antiplague suits, came through. Within minutes, the container that Telegin and Yardeni had died for was being sealed in a stainless-steel box and wheeled to a vaultlike truck, ready to be removed to Moscow's premier research facility, the Serbsky Institute.

'I'm going to initiate the search for Beria,' Kirov said as he and Smith walked out of the station.

Smith watched the virus hunters' truck pull away from the station, escorted by motorcycle outriders.

'Something you said, General. About Beria being a facilitator. What if Yardeni *wasn't* his primary responsibility?'

'What do you mean?'

'Yardeni was important – pivotal – in that he was the inside man. He was the one who actually had to go in and get the sample. But how valuable was he to anyone *after* that? A liability is more like it. Yardeni didn't die from a gunshot wound. Beria poisoned him.'

'What are you getting at?'

'That Beria's directive was to protect the smallpox, not Yardeni.'

'But Yardeni was carrying the samples. You saw the container.'

'Did I, General? All I saw was *a* container. Don't you want to know what's inside?'

The shuttle bus from the train station rolled through the thickening Moscow traffic. Because of the hour, Ivan Beria was one of only six passengers on board. Sitting by the rear exit doors, he watched a stream of militia cars wail down the boulevard to the station and listened as the other passengers speculated about what was happening.

If they only knew . . .

Beria was not concerned that the bus might be stopped. Not even Major-General Kirov, the man who had placed a hundred-thousand-ruble reward on his head, could organize so thorough a search in so short a time. Kirov's first act would be to check with the taxi dispatchers. Police at the train station would be shown a photograph and asked if anyone answering that description had gotten into a private car. Kirov might eventually think about the bus, but not soon enough to do him any good.

The bus clattered across streetcar tracks, then struggled up a ramp onto the circular highway that rings the city. He checked to make sure that the container he'd taken from Yardeni was secure in his pocket. Confusion and misdirection were his allies: they would buy him the time he needed. As soon as Kirov checked Yardeni's corpse, he would discover the container Beria had given the Bioaparat guard. Kirov would believe that it held the smallpox samples stolen from Building 103. His first thought would be to get them to a secure location, but he would have no reason to check them. By the time that was done, the smallpox would be safely in the West.

Beria smiled and turned to the windows as the sprawling complex of Sheremetevo Airport came into view.

The outriders peeled away as the truck carrying Yardeni's container turned into the underground garage of the Serbsky Institute. The sedan with Kirov and Smith pulled up close enough to the truck for the two men to observe the unloading of the stainless-steel biohazard safe.

'It'll be taken to the Level Four labs two stories below,' Kirov told Smith.

'How long before we know what we have?'

'Thirty minutes.' Kirov paused. 'I wish it could be faster, but procedures must be followed.'

Smith had no quarrel with that.

Accompanied by a squad of newly arrived Federal Security Service agents, they took an elevator to the second floor. The institute's director, a thin, birdlike man, blinked rapidly when Kirov informed him that his office was now a central command post.

'Let me know the instant the test results are available,' Kirov told him.

The director snatched his lab smock off the coat rack and beat a hasty retreat.

Kirov turned to Smith. 'Jon. Under the circumstances it's time you told me exactly why you came here and who you're working for.'

Smith considered the general's words. Given the possibility that the Russians had not been able to contain the smallpox theft within their borders, he had no choice but to contact Klein immediately.

'Can you set me up with communications?'

Kirov gestured at the telephone console on the desk. 'All the lines are secured satellite links. I'll wait out –'

'No,' Smith interrupted. 'You need to hear this.'

He dialled the number that magically always connected him to Klein. The voice on the other end was crisp and clear.

'Klein here.'

'Sir, it's me. I'm in the director's office at the Serbsky Institute. Major-General Kirov is with me. I need to bring you up to speed, sir.'

'Go ahead, Jon.'

It took Smith ten minutes to give a complete account of events. 'Sir, we expect to have test results in' – he checked his watch – 'fifteen minutes.'

'Put me on the speaker, please, Jon.'

A moment later, Klein's voice flooded the room. 'General Kirov?'

'Yes?'

'My name is Nathaniel Klein. I do the same work that Valeri Antonov does for your government. In fact, I know Valeri quite well.'

Smith watched the colour drain from Kirov's face.

'General?'

'Yes, I'm here. I . . . I understand what you're telling me, Mr Klein.'

Kirov understood all too well. Valeri Antonov was

more a shadow than a man. Rumoured to be Potrenko's most trusted adviser, he was never seen at council meetings. In fact, few people had *ever* seen him. Yet his influence was undeniable. That Klein knew of Antonov's existence – that he knew him *quite well* – spoke volumes.

'General,' Klein said. 'I recommend that until we have more information, you do not alert any of your state security organizations. Mention plague and you'll have a panic on your hands that Beria will use to his advantage.'

'I agree, Mr Klein.'

'Then please take what I'm about to say in the spirit it's offered: is there anything that I or any U.S. agency can do to help you?'

'I appreciate the offer – sincerely,' Kirov replied. 'But right now, this is an internal Russian matter.'

'Are there any standby measures you'd suggest we take?'

Kirov looked at Smith, who shook his head. 'No, sir. Not at this time.'

A second line on the console buzzed. 'Mr Klein, please excuse me for a moment.'

Kirov picked up the other call and listened intently. After speaking a few words in Russian, he turned to Smith.

'The test results on the contents of the first ampoule are complete,' he said tonelessly. 'It is tea, not smallpox.'

Klein's breath whistled across the ether. 'How many ampoules are there?'

'Five. There is no reason to think that the other results will be any different.'

'Beria made a switch!' Smith said. 'He took Yardeni's container and gave him a dummy to carry.' He paused.

'That's why Yardeni was poisoned. Beria *wanted* us to find what he was carrying, to think that we'd caught the thief in time.'

'That makes sense,' Kirov said. 'If Beria's original plan had stood, we would have discovered the theft later. By then, Yardeni would have died, but identifying the body would have taken time. The pieces of the puzzle would have been scattered all over Moscow. Beria would have had ample time to finish his mission.'

'What exactly is his mission?' Klein spoke up.

'To spirit the smallpox out of the country,' Smith said slowly.

Kirov looked at Smith. 'The airport! Beria's carrying the smallpox, headed straight for Sheremetevo!'

The implications of Kirov's conclusion stilled the conversation. *Smallpox on a commercial airliner bound for God knows where . . . It was insane!*

'Why Sheremetevo, General?' Smith asked.

'It's the only logical place to go. How else could he hope to get the virus out of the country?'

'I'm afraid he's right, Jon. General, is there any way you can get to Beria *before* he gets to Sheremetevo?'

'Given his head start, no chance. The best I can do is call President Potrenko and have him shut it down.'

'I suggest you do that immediately. If a plane with Beria onboard gets off the ground, we have the makings of a holocaust!'

Ivan Beria got off the bus after it had pulled into the departures area of the international terminal. Because of the time difference between Moscow and Western capitals, most flights left early in the morning. Those having business in Zurich, Paris, London, or even New

York would arrive just as the wheels of commerce in those cities started to churn.

Beria scrutinized the uniformed patrols loitering by the check-in counters. Detecting no unusual activity or heightened security, he walked down the concourse towards the duty-free and gift shops. On the way, he slowed his stride a fraction to glance at the monitor that listed the morning's departures. The flight he'd been told to look for had just commenced boarding.

Beria walked up to the plate-glass window of the duty-free shop and pretended to study the perfume and cigar displays. As he moved closer to the entrance, he watched for the man whom he was supposed to meet.

A minute crawled by as passengers entered and left the shop. Beria began to wonder if his contact was inside. There was no way to check, since he couldn't enter the duty-free area without a boarding pass.

Then he saw what he was looking for: a shiny, bald pate sticking out of the crowd. As he moved closer, he noted the second distinguishing feature: the distinct egg-shaped eyes that gave Adam Treloar his perplexed, slightly startled expression.

'David,' he called out softly.

Treloar, who had been milling around the entrance to the shop, almost fainted when he heard the code name. He looked around, trying to find the speaker, then felt a touch at his elbow.

'David, I thought I had missed you.'

Treloar stared at the cold, dark eyes of the man standing in front of him. The thin smile, meant to reassure, reminded him of a razor slash.

'You're late!' Treloar whispered. 'I've been waiting –'

He heard Beria's chuckle, then gasped as an incredibly tight grip seized his arm. He offered no resistance as

153

Beria steered him to a refreshment stand and sat him down at the end of the counter.

'Oranges and lemons . . .' Beria said in a singsong tone.

For an instant, Treloar's mind went blank. Desperately, he tried to remember the words that would complete the phrase.

'Say . . . Say the bells of Saint Clemens!'

Beria smiled. 'Give me your carry-on.'

Treloar reached for the small leather bag at his feet and placed it on the counter.

'The liquor.'

Treloar dug out a small bottle of plum brandy that he'd bought at the hotel gift shop.

Unscrewing the cap, Beria raised the bottle to his lips and pretended to drink. He passed it to Treloar, who mimicked him. At the same time, Beria slipped the container from his pocket onto the counter.

'Smile,' he said conversationally. 'We are two friends sharing a drink before one of us has to leave.' Treloar's eyes bulged as Beria unscrewed the container. 'And because we can't finish the bottle, I give you the rest to enjoy during your flight.'

Carefully, he poured a few ounces of brandy into the container. 'Now, if the inspectors wish to check, you open it and let them smell what's inside.'

Pushing back his stool, Beria gripped Treloar's shoulder. 'Have a safe flight.' He winked. 'And forget that you ever saw me.'

The all-points bulletin on Ivan Beria reached Sheremetevo security just as Adam Treloar was going through the metal detector. The guard manning the scanner noted a cylindrical object in the carry-on and asked the American to step aside. Another guard opened the bag, removed the container, and unscrewed it. Smelling a distinctive plum odor, he smiled and closed the top.

Handing it back to Treloar, he offered some advice: 'Your brandy is too cold. It tastes much better when it's warm.'

By the time a squad of militia flooded the international terminal, Treloar was safely ensconced in his first-class seat. The American Airlines 767 was pulled back from the gate just as airport security began reviewing their surveillance tapes, searching for anyone who resembled Ivan Beria.

American flight 1710, nonstop to London with continuing service to Washington's Dulles Airport, was number two for takeoff behind a Paris-bound Air France Airbus. The call from the minister of defence reached the flight director in the control tower as 1710 was given the go signal by traffic control.

'Shut it down!' the director screamed over the loudspeaker.

Twenty-two faces turned and stared at him as if he were quite insane.

'Shut *what* down?' one of the controllers asked.

'The airport, you imbecile!'

'All of it?'

'Yes! Nothing leaves the ground.'

All activity in the tower was focused on relaying a FULL-STOP message to aircraft taxiing into position on the active runways and waiting on the aprons. No one had time to think about the planes that had taken off. By the time they did, American 1710 had banked over Moscow and was climbing smoothly to its designated cruising altitude of thirty-six thousand feet.

12

Because of the time difference between Moscow and the eastern seaboard of the United States, it was still the middle of the night when Anthony Price pulled up to the northern guard house at Fort Belvoir, Virginia.

After the computer had scanned his credentials, he drove up the crushed-shell driveway to General Richardson's quarters, a stately Victorian surrounded by a manicured lawn. Lights were burning on the third floor, as Price had expected.

The deputy director of the National Security Agency found Richardson in his study, the gleaming bookshelves filled with leather volumes, mementos, and framed military citations. The general rose behind his desk and gestured at the coffee tray.

'Sorry to have dragged you out of bed, Tony, but I wanted you to see this for yourself.'

Price, who seldom slept more than four hours a night, helped himself to coffee, then came around so that he could see the computer screen.

'The latest message from Telegin,' Richardson said, indicating the descrambled text.

Price read the first few sentences, then looked up. 'So everything at Bioaparat went according to plan. What's the problem?'

'Read the rest.'

Price's eyes narrowed. 'Jon Smith? What the hell is he doing in Moscow?'

'According to Telegin, poking around in our business. Seems that he almost tipped Kirov off in time.'

'But both Beria and Treloar escaped ... Haven't they?'

Richardson rubbed his tired eyes. 'That's the reason I called you: I don't know. Telegin was supposed to report once both men were safely away. She hasn't. Check this out.'

Richardson hit several keys and the latest CNN updates filled the screen.

'A problem at the Moscow train station,' he said. 'Someone decided to have an O-K-corral shootout. The Russians clamped down hard and fast, so the details are sketchy. But you have to wonder: what happened to Telegin?'

'If you haven't heard from her, she's dead,' Price said flatly.

'Or taken. If Kirov has her –'

'He doesn't! Telegin was a pro. She never would have let herself be taken alive.' He pointed to the screen. 'Says here there are at least five dead – all security personnel. I know Beria is good, but to take out that many he had to have had help. I think Telegin stepped in.'

After a moment's silence, Richardson said, 'Assuming that Beria got away clean, we still have a problem. Kirov and Smith will be all over Telegin – her movements, contacts, the works. She may have left footprints.'

Price paced along Richardson's museum-quality Oriental rug. 'I'll head for Fort Meade. A shooting in a Moscow train station? Hell, that's a terrorist act, NSA territory. Nobody will raise an eyebrow when I get people working on this.'

'What about Smith?' Richardson asked.

'He's army, so *you* start checking. He's got to be

working for someone, and as far as I'm concerned, he's making way too many connections. First Yuri Danko, now showing up in Russia . . .'

'Randi Russell is CIA undercover in Moscow.'

'I don't think that Smith flew seven thousand miles for a piece of ass, Frank. We need to know who's issuing him his marching orders – then we cut him off at the knees!'

The first thing Randi Russell noticed when she deactivated the alarm and opened the door to Bay Digital was that she was not alone. Although the security system indicated no intrusion, she caught the faint odour of clove tobacco smoke.

'Carrot Top, is that you?' she called out.

'I'm in here, Randi.'

Sighing, Randi locked the door behind her. She'd come in early, hoping to use the peace and quiet to catch up on some reports.

'Where in here?'

'The file room.'

'Damn!'

Gritting her teeth, Randi marched to the very back of the office. The file room was really a large, walk-in vault where the latest computer equipment was kept. Theoretically, she was the only one with the combination.

Randi stepped into the temperature-controlled chamber where she found the intruder busy downloading the latest video game from the confidential files of a Japanese electronics company.

'Carrot Top, I warned you about that,' she said, trying to sound severe.

Sasha Rublev – nicknamed Carrot Top for his mass

of wiry, reddish-orange hair – beamed at her. Tall and lanky, with liquid green eyes that Randi knew drove girls crazy, he was all of seventeen years old – and undoubtedly Russia's premier computer genius.

'Sasha, one of these days you'll trip an alarm and you'll be calling me from the local militia precinct.'

Sasha feigned hurt. 'Randi, how could you possibly think that? Your security is very good, but . . .'

A cakewalk for someone like you.

Randi had discovered Sasha Rublev at a computer seminar Bay Digital hosted for Moscow University students. The gangly teenager had caught her attention not only because he was the youngest person in the room but because he was quietly working at a laptop, hacking his way into the Russian Central Bank's mainframe to check on the level of gold reserves.

Randi knew at once that Rublev was an undiscovered prodigy. Over cheeseburgers and Cokes, she was amazed to learn that this son of a Moscow subway conductor possessed an IQ that was off the charts but, because of the bureaucracy, remained mired in the antiquated high school system. Eventually she got permission from Sasha's family for him to work for Bay Digital a few hours a week and on weekends. As the bond between mentor and mentee grew, Randi gave him access to some of the most advanced equipment in the office, in return for Sasha's solemn promise not to misuse it. But like a playful puppy, Sasha insisted on bringing her gifts – information whose sources she didn't want to know about.

'Okay,' she said. 'What's so important that it couldn't wait until I got in?'

'The shooting at the railroad station.'

'I was listening to the news on the way in. What about it?'

Sasha's fine-boned fingers danced over the keyboard. 'They're saying it was the work of Chechen rebels.'

'And?'

'So why shut down the Moscow airport?'

Randi stared over his shoulder at the screen. Sasha had hacked his way into the Federal Security Service's mainframe and was reading the latest traffic about the imminent shutdown of Sheremetevo Airport.

'The Chechens are targeting the airport?' he asked skeptically. 'I think not. Something big is happening, Randi. And the FSS doesn't want anyone to know.'

Randi thought for a moment. 'Close the link,' she said quietly.

'Why? I'm using five cutouts. Even if they pick up on the intrusion, they'll think that it's coming from Bombay.'

'Sasha . . .'

Mindful of her tone, he quickly closed the laptop.

'Randi, you look worried. Don't be. The cutouts are –'

'It's not the cutouts, Sasha. It's what you said: why close the airport?'

The logistics of shutting down a major airport are the stuff of nightmares. Smith and Kirov arrived to find hundreds of bewildered travellers milling around in the concourse, besieging the check-in counters, seeking explanations from harried airline employees who had none to offer. Armed militia were stationed at every entrance and exit, making the travellers virtual prisoners. Three-man patrols swarmed through the concourse shops, lavatories, and stockrooms, checking the baggage and cargo areas, the employees' lounges and changing areas, even the chapel and the day-care centre. Rumours flew and anger mounted. As the two combined, the level of fear among those trapped in the international terminal grew exponentially.

'Someone in the surveillance room thinks he spotted Beria on the tape,' Kirov told Smith as they threaded their way through the concourse.

'I sure as hell hope so,' Smith replied as the two men headed for the airport's security command post.

Smith and Kirov burst into the security command room, which resembled a large television studio. In front of a twenty-foot console sat six technicians monitoring the ninety cameras strategically placed throughout the complex. The cameras were on timers and were operated by remote control. With a few taps of the keyboard, technicians could focus or shift them to cover a particular area.

Above the console were wall-mounted screens that offered the security director a real-time, bird's-eye view of the terminal. Hidden away in a temperature-controlled area were the video machines, faithfully recording everything that the cameras picked up.

'What do you have?' Kirov demanded.

The security director pointed to one of the monitors. The black-and-white picture showed two men sitting at a refreshment counter.

'The image is poor,' he conceded. 'But that appears to be your man.'

Kirov moved in for a closer look. 'That's him all right.' He turned to Smith. 'What do you think? You saw him at close distance.'

Smith studied the image. 'It's him. Do you think he's talking to the man beside him?'

Kirov turned to the director. 'Can you enhance the image?'

The director shook his head. 'I've done as much as possible with the equipment I have.'

'Do you have any other shots of them together?' Smith asked.

'That's the only one. The cameras are on timers. They captured only that one shot of Beria before moving to another sector.'

Smith took Kirov aside. 'General, I realize that Beria is our principal target, but we need to know who that guy is. What if your service were to scan the tape?'

Kirov pointed to the blurred faces on the screen. 'Look at how the light falls. And that column there – there's nothing we can do to improve the photograph. We don't have the software.'

Smith tried another tack: 'You know Beria better than anyone else. Has he ever worked with a partner?'

'Never. Beria has always been a solo operator. That is one of the reasons he has eluded capture: he leaves no one we can connect him to. I think he's using the other man for cover.'

Something about the picture refused to let Smith go. 'General, I may be able to get the tape enhanced.'

'At your embassy?' Kirov asked.

Smith shrugged. 'What do you say?'

Kirov considered. 'Very well.'

'Telegin – did she have a laptop or a cell phone?'

'Both.'

'I can check them too.'

Kirov nodded. 'I'll have a security officer escort you to my building. Both items are in the kitchen.'

'Which brings me to my last question,' Smith said. 'What if Beria *isn't* in the terminal?'

Kirov's eyes widened as he grasped the implications of Smith's words. 'I need the designations and destinations of the last three flights that left before shutdown,' he told the director.

Smith looked at the time imprinted on the videotape, then at the screen where the security director was pulling up the departures schedule.

'Swissair 101, Air France 612, American 1710. Beria could have made it onboard any one of them.'

'Get me the tapes of the cameras that cover the jetways to those flights,' Kirov snapped. 'And the passenger manifests.'

As the director hurried away, Kirov turned to Smith. 'It's *possible* Beria made those flights, Jon, but unlikely. The odds are that he got out of the airport but is still in the city.'

Smith knew what Kirov was intimating. There were three airliners, with a combined load of over a thousand people, headed into Western Europe. Was Smith prepared to create a series of international incidents on the possibility that Beria was onboard one of those planes?

'And if the situation were reversed, General?' Smith asked. 'If the destination wasn't Zurich, Paris, or London, but Moscow? Wouldn't *you* want to know? Or would you be okay with the "odds"?'

Kirov stared at him, nodded, then reached for the phone.

Kirov was closer to the truth than he realized: Beria had gotten out of the airport, and he was still in Moscow. But not for much longer.

Beria had left the airport the way he'd arrived – by

163

shuttle bus. Except this one took him directly to Moscow's central bus depot.

Entering the chilly, dilapidated building, Beria went directly to the counter and purchased a one-way ticket to St Petersburg. With twenty minutes to spare, he went into a washroom that smelled of urine and industrial cleaner and splashed water on his face. When he came out, he bought several greasy pastries from a woman behind a stall and wolfed them down with a glass of tea. Fortified, he joined the line of passengers waiting at the departure bay.

Beria scanned the faces around him. They belonged mainly to older people, some of whom, he guessed, were travelling with all their worldly possessions packed into cardboard suitcases or taped-up packages. Beaten down by circumstances, invisible to the new moneyed class, they were less than anonymous. No militia would ever bother checking their papers; no cameras would record their departure. Best of all, everyone would keep to themselves, not wanting to borrow from their neighbour's hardship.

Beria slipped to the back of the bus, to the long seat that ran the width of the vehicle. He huddled in the corner and listened to the grinding of the transmission as the driver backed out. Soon afterwards, the roar of the engine diminished, the traffic beyond the window stilled, and at last, he slept.

It took Smith and Kirov thirty minutes to review the jetway tapes of the passengers who'd boarded the three flights to Europe.

'Four possibles,' Smith said. 'That's what I come up with.'

Kirov nodded. 'No distinct resemblance to Beria, just faces we couldn't quite define.'

Smith checked the clock in the security command post. 'The first plane, Swissair 101, will reach Zurich in two hours.'

'Let's make the calls,' Kirov said heavily.

Ever since the golden age of terrorism in the early 1980s, plans have been in place to deal not only with aerial hijackers carrying explosives but with those armed with chemical-biological weapons. Kirov got on the line to his counterparts in Swiss Internal Security, the French Deuxième, and England's M15. When representatives of the three agencies were ready, he motioned to Smith, who was talking to Nathaniel Klein on a separate line. He then patched Klein into the conference call without informing the others that the American was listening in.

'Gentlemen,' he opened. 'We have a developing problem.'

Kirov did not dwell on the background of the crisis; he told his listeners what they needed to know at that moment. Every minute that passed meant that much less time to prepare.

'You say that it's possible, but by no means certain, that this Beria character is onboard our flight,' the Frenchman said. 'Is there any way you can confirm this?'

'I wish that were possible,' Kirov replied. 'But unless I find Beria in the next two hours, we must work on the assumption that he made it onboard one of those aircraft.'

'What about his file?' the deputy director of M15 asked. 'I'm told that we, for one, have precious little on this creature.'

'Everything we have is being shipped via secure E-mail,' Kirov responded.

'Does Beria know you followed him to the airport?' the Swiss asked. 'Is it possible that he already suspects that he might be apprehended? I ask because it is imperative we know what we're dealing with: does Beria have any reason to unleash this bioweapon in midair?'

'Beria is acting as a courier, not as a terrorist,' Kirov told him. 'It is in his financial interest to deliver what was stolen from Bioaparat. He is not an ideologue or a martyr.'

The three Europeans on the line began to discuss how best to react to the crisis hurtling towards them. Their options were few, the choice predictable.

'Since the first flight lands on our soil, it begins with us,' the Swiss said. 'We will treat this as a potential terrorist threat and take appropriate measures. If Beria is on that plane, he will be rendered harmless by all available means. We will have personnel and equipment ready to secure the smallpox.' He paused. 'Or to deal with it as best we can should contamination occur. If, on the other hand, we find that Beria is *not* onboard, we will let everyone know immediately.'

'Even sooner than that, *mon vieux*,' the Frenchman said. 'Air France arrives in Paris seventy-five minutes after the Zurich flight.'

'I recommend that an open line be established to monitor events as they develop,' the Englishman interjected. 'That way, we can follow the process of elimination – if there is one.'

'I'd like to remind you of one thing, London,' Kirov spoke up. 'The flight is headed for your capital, but it's an American crew and plane. I have an obligation to inform the ambassador.'

'As long as that doesn't result in a jurisdictional squabble here,' London replied.

'I'm sure it won't,' Kirov said. 'Now, if there are no further comments or suggestions, I recommend that we terminate this call to allow you to deploy your resources.'

There were none. One by one, the parties hung up until only Klein remained on the line.

'Are you coming home, Jon?' he asked.

'A suggestion, sir?'

'Go ahead.'

'I think it'd be better for me to remain in the arena, sir. If General Kirov can provide me with transportation, I can be in European airspace before the Swissair flight touches down. I can monitor the situation in-flight, then direct the pilot to whichever city the target plane lands in. I'll be at ground zero, giving both of you real-time reports.'

'What do you think, General?' Klein asked.

'I like the idea of having our own bioweapons expert on-site,' the Russian replied. 'I'll arrange for transportation immediately.'

'That would have been my recommendation, too. Good luck, Jon. Keep us posted.'

Twenty minutes later, Jon Smith was being escorted into Kirov's apartment. Under the watchful eyes of the security man, he went into the kitchen, where he found the laptop and the cell phone that had belonged to Lara Telegin.

The escort drove Smith to the embassy, watching as he

cleared the marine guard post and disappeared behind the gates. Driving off, what he didn't see was Smith doubling back.

Smith walked fast to the arcade, only a mile away from the embassy. He was relieved to see Randi as soon as he stepped through the front door.

'Why is it I expected to see you today?' she asked quietly.

'We need to talk, Randi.'

Smith's arrival drew amused smiles from the staff, in particular a redheaded boy whose look made Randi blush.

'They think you're my lover,' she told Smith after they were in her office.

'Oh . . .'

She laughed at having caught him off-guard. 'It's not the worst thing people could think of you, Jon.'

'Actually, I'm flattered.'

'Now that we've gotten that out of the way, what can I do for you?'

Smith brought out the videotape, laptop, and cell phone.

'As you probably heard, there's a situation at the airport.'

'A "situation" as in the Russians are shutting it down.'

'Randi, all I can tell you is that they're looking for someone. Believe me, it's important to us that they find him.'

He explained the problem with the videotape. 'It's a question of enhancement. The Russians just don't have the software and expertise to do it fast.'

Randi pointed to the laptop and phone. 'What about those?'

'The massacre at the railroad station and the situation

at Sheremetevo are direct results of communications between two conspirators,' Smith replied. 'I don't expect the phone to give up much. But the laptop . . . Maybe E-mails were exchanged. I don't know.'

'If your conspirators were professionals – and I assume they were – they'd be using encryption and firewalls. It could take a while to crack them.'

'I'd appreciate your taking a shot.'

'Which brings us to the next problem. You don't think that I can just waltz this stuff into the embassy, do you? I'm here on nonofficial cover. My contact with the CIA station chief is nonexistent. I'd have to contact Langley and have them alert the SC. The minute I do that, headquarters will want to know why I'm hitting the panic button.'

She paused. 'Going that route means you have to tell me a whole lot more than I think you want to – or can.'

Smith shook his head in frustration. 'Okay, I understand. I thought that maybe –'

'I didn't say there wasn't an alternative.' Quickly, Randi went on to tell him about Sasha Rublev.

'I don't know . . .' Smith said.

'Jon, I know what you're thinking. But consider this: the FBI hires teenage hackers to help track down cyber terrorists. And I'd be looking over Sasha's shoulder every minute.'

'You trust the kid that much?'

'Sasha is part of the new Russia, Jon, a Russia that looks out to the world, not one that keeps it at bay. As for politics, to Sasha it's the most boring thing in the world. Besides, I'm guessing that you didn't just trip over this laptop. The Russians must have sanctioned the hunt.'

Smith nodded. 'They have. All right. I have to leave

Moscow in about an hour. You have my number. Call me the minute your boy genius comes up with anything.'

He smiled at her. 'And thanks, Randi. Very much.'

'I'm happy to help, Jon. But there is a quid pro quo. If there's anything I need to know –'

'You'll hear it from me, not CNN. Promise.'

13

The Swiss have one of the most highly organized terrorist-response teams in the world. Superbly trained, expertly equipped, the twenty-man unit known as the Special Operations Group was on its way to Zurich International Airport within minutes of receiving the go signal from the minister of defence.

By the time Swissair 101 was twenty minutes out, the commandos were in position. Half of them wore the uniform of the Swiss border patrol, whose ubiquitous presence at airports and railroad stations went unnoticed by travellers accustomed to visible security. The other half were dressed as mechanics, fuellers, baggage handlers, and caterers – the kind of people anyone would expect to see around parked aircraft.

The plainclothes contingent, heavily armed with MP-5 submachine guns and smoke and stun grenades, would be the first-wave assault troops if the situation degenerated into a hostage crisis. The uniformed patrols were the second perimeter, ready to move if Beria somehow managed to slip past the invisible cordon that would be established around the aircraft.

Finally, there was a third ring, made up of Swiss Army sharpshooters who had positioned themselves on the roofs of the international terminal and the maintenance hangars. They would have an unobstructed view of the plane as it taxied to the last gate. There, an attempt would be made to collar the jetway to the fuselage.

The attempt would fail. The captain would announce a malfunction and advise his passengers that a ramp would be wheeled up to the forward hatch.

Once the passengers started moving down the ramp, the snipers would try to pick out Beria and lock on to him. If successful, there would be no fewer than three rifles covering the target at any given moment. According to plan, the plainclothes commandos would execute the takedown, wrestle Beria to the ground, and neutralize him. But if for any reason there was a problem, the snipers were cleared for centre-mass/head-shot fire.

Wearing a caterer's baggy white overalls, the SOG commander quietly radioed the control tower and received the latest word: flight 101 was on final approach. Word was passed along; the safeties of weapons were thumbed off.

The bus rattled into the St Petersburg station just as Swissair 101 touched down in Zurich. Following the crowds, Ivan Beria drifted into the terminal, headed for the lockers. Removing a key, he opened a locker and pulled out a cheap suitcase.

The washroom was abominable, but a tip to the attendant got Beria a private stall that was reasonably clean. He took off his coat, jacket, and pants, and from the suitcase pulled out a new navy blue blazer, grey slacks, a sports shirt, and comfortable loafers. Also in the suitcase were a fleece-lined jacket, several plastic bags filled with souvenirs from the Hermitage Museum, and a billfold containing an airline ticket, passport, credit cards, and American currency. Beria flipped open the passport and scrutinized his picture, in which he wore the clothes he'd just put on. He thought he looked like a John Strelnikov, a naturalized American citizen who worked as a civil engineer for a Baltimore-based construction company.

Beria packed up his old clothes in the suitcase and left the bathroom. In the station, he stopped at a refreshment stand, put down the suitcase, bought himself a Coke, and moved on. Given the homeless population that meandered through the station, the suitcase would disappear before he reached the front doors.

Outside, he got into a cab and offered the driver ten American dollars over the negotiated rate if he got him to the airport in thirty minutes. The driver made it with two minutes to spare.

Beria knew that by now his photograph and particulars had been wired to every major transportation facility in the country. It didn't matter. He had no intention of coming into contact with the authorities.

Walking through the newly refurbished terminal, he reached the area reserved for tour groups and slipped into a gaggle of sixty-odd travellers clustered in front of the Finnair counter.

'Where's your badge? You need your badge.'

Beria smiled pleasantly at the harried young woman whose badge read OMNITOURS: TREASURES OF THE CZARS.

Handing over his passport and ticket, he mumbled, 'Lost it.'

The woman sighed, grabbed his paperwork, and steered him to a counter where she brought out a paper badge.

'John Strel . . .'

'Strelnikov.'

'Right. We'll just put down 'John,' okay?'

Using a felt pen, she wrote the name on the badge, peeled away the backing to expose the adhesive, and pressed it firmly onto Beria's lapel.

'Don't lose it!' she scolded. 'Otherwise you'll have problems at customs. Do you want to do any duty-free shopping?'

Beria said that might be nice.

'You'll get your passport and tickets back after immigration,' the woman said, already moving to quell another crisis elsewhere in the group.

Beria was counting on that. Much better to have some exhausted American tour guide deal with the exit visas and airline tickets.

After purchasing some cologne that he placed in his Hermitage souvenir bag, Beria joined the line shuffling through immigration. He watched as in the booth, two bored officials stamped the passports that the tour guide had brought them. Hearing his name, he stepped forward, retrieved his passport, and proceeded through customs into the departure lounge.

Beria took a seat beside a middle-aged couple who turned out to be from San Francisco. Since he pretended that his English was only passable, his new friends did most of the talking. Beria learned that the Finnair flight to Washington's Dulles Airport would take about ten hours and that the dinner service would likely be decent but certainly not memorable.

The Ilyushin C-22 executive jet had just crossed into German airspace when Smith received word that Beria was not onboard Swiss-air 101.

'That's a positive confirmation?'

'Absolutely,' Klein replied over the satellite phone.

'They eye-balled every single passenger. He wasn't there.'

'The Paris flight comes down in nineteen minutes. Are they ready?'

'The people I talk to say yes. Privately, they're telling me that the government is passing peach pits. If something happens and later word gets out that they allowed the plane to land . . . well, you can imagine the fallout.'

'Do you think the government will spring a leak?'

'It's a real possibility. The French have an election coming up in two weeks. The opposition is looking for any kind of ammunition it can get its hands on.'

Smith returned to an idea that had occurred to him back in Moscow, but which he hadn't voiced.

'Sir, what if we were to give the French a hand?'

'How?'

'Their Airbuses aren't equipped with the SecFax system. American 1710 can receive secure satellite facsimile transmissions. You could talk directly to the captain, bring him up to speed, then ship him a photofax of Beria.'

Smith waited out the silence. What he proposed was, at the very least, dangerous. If his suggestion was carried out and something went terribly wrong on the American flight, the consequences would be nothing short of disastrous.

'Let me check something,' Klein said finally. 'I'll get back to you.'

A few minutes later, he was back. 'I spoke with American's director of security in Dallas–Fort Worth. He says 1710 is carrying a sky marshal.'

'Even better. Get him –'

'Her, Jon.'

'Forgive my presumption. The pilot must have a way

to communicate with her. Once he does, she can cover the plane.'

'We have to allow for the possibility that Beria is travelling incognito.'

'Kirov never mentioned that Beria was a master of disguise. Possibly that's because he's never operated outside familiar borders before. A trained agent would be able to see through makeup and prosthetics.'

'Do you propose we inform Kirov – or anyone else?'

'It's our plane, sir. If the agent spots him, we can give the French the all-clear and warn the British that he's on the way. Any lead time we could give them would be invaluable.'

Another moment of silence followed.

'All right, Jon. I'll get things going on this end. The flight's ninety minutes out of Heathrow. Stay airborne until I call back.'

Catching a whiff of exotic perfume, Adam Treloar stirred in his spacious first-class seat. He heard the faint rustle of silk against flesh, then caught a pair of shapely buttocks swaying past his line of sight. As though she sensed she was being watched, the woman, a long-legged redhead, turned. Treloar blushed as her eyes settled on him; his embarrassment deepened as she smiled and raised her eyebrows as though to say, *you naughty boy!* Then she was gone, disappearing behind the partition into the area where the drinks and food were prepared.

Treloar sighed, not because he coveted the girl; females of any age did not interest him sexually. But he appreciated beauty in all its forms. In certain parts of the Caribbean, on private yachts, he had watched, rapt, as loveliness like that was subjugated in order to stimulate the appetites of the audience.

An announcement from the pilot interrupted his reverie:

'Ladies and gentlemen, we'd like to inform you that the latest weather in London calls for light drizzle, with a temperature of sixty-two degrees. We are on schedule, with an estimated time of arrival of one hour and five minutes from now.'

Boring, Treloar thought.

He was still musing about the inanity of such announcements when the woman reappeared. She seemed to be walking more slowly, as though taking time to stretch her legs. Once again, Treloar felt himself brushed by her cool gaze; his blush returned.

The woman's name was Ellen Diforio. She was twenty-eight years old, a certified martial arts expert, and championship shooter. She was in her fifth year in the federal marshal service, her second in the sky marshal division.

Wouldn't you know it? My last gig, and this *has to happen.*

Fifteen minutes earlier, Diforio had been thinking about a date she had that night with her Washington lawyer boyfriend. Her daydreams had been interrupted by a seemingly innocuous announcement that the in-flight duty-free shop had a special offer on Jean Patou 1000 perfume. The code words had snapped Diforio back to reality. She had counted off ten seconds, picked up her bag, and left her business-class seat, heading in the direction of the washrooms. She had kept on going into first class, around the panel into the service area, and then, surreptitiously, into the cockpit.

Diforio read the security director's message and studied the photofax intently. Her orders were clear: determine whether or not this individual was on board. If she spotted him, she was not to make any contact or attempt to restrain him. Instead, she was to report back to the cockpit immediately.

'What about a weapon?' Diforio had asked the pilot. 'It doesn't say anything about a gun or a bomb. There's no bio, either. Who is this guy?'

The pilot shrugged. 'All I know is that the British have scrambled the SAS guys. It's that serious. If he's onboard and we make it down, they take him out on the ground.' He looked pointedly at her handbag. 'Do me a favour: no Annie Oakley stuff back there.'

Making her way through the first-class cabin, Diforio noted the embarrassment of the man with the funny, egg-shaped eyes.

Not this clown.

She was very much aware of the effect she had on men and planned to put it to good use. Seventeen or seventy, they all took notice; some were a little subtler than others. But if she wanted to, she could get them to look at her directly. A hint of a smile, a twinkle in her eyes was all it would take.

The first-class and business cabins were a wash. Not that she had expected to find the target there. Guys like this Beria character liked to hide themselves in a mob. Diforio pulled back the curtain and stepped into the economy section.

The cabin was configured for 3–3–3 sitting, the seats separated by two aisles. While pretending to check the magazine rack, Diforio scanned the first six rows along the left-hand aisle: retirees, kids on a college break, young families travelling on a budget. She began walking to the back of the plane.

A few minutes later, Diforio was at the lavatories at the end of the bulkhead. She'd gotten a good look at all the passengers in the perimeter, plus two who had exited the washrooms. The rest of the seats were filled; none of the occupants resembled the target.

Now the tricky part.

Diforio went back the way she'd come, stepped into the business section, came around the partition, then went back into economy. Arching her back, she made it look like she was trying to work out cramped muscles. Curious male faces turned sympathetic – and appreciative – when her breasts pushed against the shell beneath her jacket. She encouraged the ogling with a slight smile as she moved down the right-hand aisle, her gaze flitting over but never alighting on individual faces. Again, her luck held. All the seats were occupied; the male passengers either asleep, reading, or working on business papers. She was grateful that the movie had ended and most of the window shades were up, allowing the sunlight to pour in.

Once again, Diforio found herself at the back of the plane. She walked past the lavatories, then up the left-hand aisle, double-checking to make sure that she hadn't overlooked any seats. A moment later, she was in the flight deck.

'Negative on the target,' she reported to the pilot.

'You're sure?'

'First and business are clean. No one even remotely resembles this guy. You have a full house in economy – two hundred thirty-eight people. One hundred seventeen are women – and believe me, they *are* women. Twenty-two are children under the age of fifteen; forty-three are kids in their twenties. Out of sixty-three possible males, twenty-eight are over sixty-five and look it. Another sixteen are over fifty. That leaves nineteen possibles – and no match.'

The pilot nodded with his chin at the copilot. 'Danny'll set up a link with Dallas. Tell 'em what you found – or didn't.' He paused. 'Does this mean I can start breathing again?'

The communications gear on the C-22 allowed Smith to eavesdrop on the French security operations channel. He listened as agents of the Deuxième Bureau reported on the disembarkation of Air France flight 612. Three-quarters of the passengers were off and still there was no sign of Beria. Smith was turning his attention to the American flight, less than twenty minutes from touchdown, when the satellite phone chirped.

'It's Klein. Jon, I just got a report from Dallas. The marshal on 1710 reports that there's no one onboard who resembles Beria.'

'That's impossible! The French have just about off-loaded. Nothing there. He *has* to be on American.'

'Not according to the air marshal. She's almost positive that Beria isn't there.'

'*Almost* isn't good enough.'

'I realize that. I've relayed her findings to the Brits. They're grateful, but they're not going to ease up. The SAS is in position and will stay there.'

'Sir, I think we have to consider the possibility that Beria took some other flight or that he's using another way to get into the States.'

Klein's breath whistled over the line. 'Do you think he'd be so brazen as to try that? He must know that we've pulled out all the stops to bring him down.'

'Beria started a job, sir. He's killed in the course of carrying it out. Yes, I think he's determined enough to try to reach us.' He paused. 'Moscow is the main point for flights to the West, but it's not the *only* way out.'

'St Petersburg?'

'It handles a lot of flights to and from Scandinavia and northern Europe. Aeroflot, Scandinavian Airlines, Finnair, Royal Dutch – they all have steady traffic in and out of there.'

'Kirov will have an embolism when I suggest that Beria might have gotten as far as St Petersburg.'

'He's gotten awfully far as it is, sir. This guy isn't running; he's following a well-thought-out plan. That's what's keeping him one step ahead of us.'

Smith heard something on the French channel. He excused himself, listened briefly, then got back to Klein. 'Paris confirms that their flight's clean.'

'What's your next step, Jon?'

Smith thought for a moment. 'London, sir. That's where I get off.'

14

With puffs of blue tyre smoke and the stink of super-heated brakes, American 1710 touched down at London's Heathrow Airport. Per instructions from the Special Air Service commander, the pilot informed his passengers that a mechanical problem had developed with the jetway assigned to their gate. The control tower was rerouting them to another part of the field where ramps could be rolled up against the hatches.

The flight attendants passed through the first- and business-class cabins, reassuring passengers that they would make their connecting flights.

'What about the continuation to Dulles?' Treloar asked.

'Our time on the ground will be as brief as possible,' the steward replied.

Treloar prayed that he was right. The nitrogen charges inside the canister were good for another twelve hours. The stop at Heathrow was usually ninety minutes; the flying time to Dulles, six hours fifteen minutes. After customs and immigration, he would have a three-hour window to get the smallpox into a refrigerated facility. There was little room for the unforeseen.

Stepping out onto the ramp, Treloar discovered that the aircraft was parked next to a giant maintenance hangar. As he descended the steps, he saw baggage carts being loaded and two airport buses idling near the hangar doors. At the bottom of the steps, a pleasant young customs officer invited him to step into the hangar, which was set up as a temporary processing and in-transit facility.

As Treloar and his fellow travellers shuffled along, they had no idea that hard eyes tucked against sniper-scopes were scrutinizing their every move. They could not have guessed that the young men in customs and immigration uniforms, along with the baggage handlers, bus drivers, and maintenance people, were all heavily armed undercover SAS operatives.

Just before Treloar disappeared through the door leading into the hangar, he heard a high-pitched shriek. Turning, he saw a trim, executive jet land gracefully on the runway two hundred yards away. He imagined that it belonged to an obscenely wealthy entrepreneur, or to some sheik, never suspecting that inside the Ilyushin C-22 a man was, at that moment, receiving a detailed description of him from a sniper who happened to have Treloar's forehead in his crosshairs.

'The Brits say that 1710 is clean, sir.'

Klein's voice whistled through the secure link. 'I got the same report. You should have heard Kirov when I gave him the news. All hell's breaking loose in Moscow.'

Sitting in the parked Ilyushin, Smith continued to watch the activity around the American 767. 'What about St Petersburg?'

'Kirov's compiling a list of all flights that have left up to now. He's scrambling to get the terminal's departure tapes, as well as putting men on the ground to start interviewing employees.'

Smith bit his lip. 'It's all taking too long, sir. With every hour, Beria gets further and further away.'

'I know. But we can't hunt until we have a target.' Klein paused. 'What's your next move?'

'There's nothing I can do in London. I asked American to get me on 1710 and they obliged. It's scheduled to leave in about seventy-five minutes. That'll put me in Washington sooner than if I were to wait for military transport.'

'I don't like the idea of your being without a secure link.'

'The flight deck crew will know that I'm onboard, sir. If there's any word from Moscow, you can radio the plane.'

'Under the circumstances, that'll have to do. In the meantime, try to get some rest on the flight. This thing is just getting started.'

Anthony Price was in his expansive office on the sixth floor of the NSA headquarters at Fort Meade, Maryland. As deputy director, Price was responsible for the agency's day-to-day operations. Right now, that meant keeping his staff on top of the situation in Moscow. So far, the Russians were sticking with the story that Chechen rebels were responsible for the massacre – which suited Price just fine. It gave him a legitimate reason to cover the incident. And the longer the Russians chased the phantom terrorists, the easier it would be for Beria and Treloar to slip through the net.

Price looked up when he heard the knock on his door. 'Come in.'

Price's senior analyst, a stout young woman with a librarian's fussy air about her, entered.

'The latest update from our resources on the ground in Moscow, sir,' she said. 'Seems that General Kirov is very concerned about some surveillance video out of Sheremetevo in Moscow.'

Price felt a constriction in his chest but managed to keep his voice level. 'Really? Why? Who's on the tape?'

'No one knows. But for some reason the Russians red-flagged it. Apparently the video is very poor.'

Price's mind was racing. 'That's it?'

'For now, sir.'

'I want you to stay on top of that video. Anyone hears word one about it, I want to know.'

'Yes, sir.'

After the analyst left, Price turned to his computer and called up the flights coming into Dulles. There was only one reason that the Russians would be so interested in the video surveillance tapes: Beria had been seen *with* somebody. And that person could only be Adam Treloar.

American 1710 was scheduled to arrive in a little over six hours. Russian photo analysis and enhancement was hardly state of the art. It would take their machines hours to float up images. By that time, 1710 should be on the ground and Adam Treloar would be safe.

Price sat back in his executive leather chair, removed his glasses, and tapped a stem against his front teeth. The situation in Moscow had degenerated into a near-fiasco. That Beria had escaped the carnage at the train station was nothing short of miraculous. Equally amazing was the fact that he'd gotten to Sheremetevo in time to hand off the smallpox to Adam Treloar.

But the surveillance cameras had caught a connection between the two men. Kirov had the connection. As soon as he'd reconstructed Treloar's picture, he would run it against the customs and immigration databanks. He would discover exactly when Treloar had entered and left Russia. He would alert the CIA and FBI liaisons at the embassy.

Then we'd start running Treloar to ground, if for no other reason than he was seen with Beria . . . But does Kirov suspect that Treloar is the actual courier?

Price didn't think so. So far, everything indicated that the hunt was centred on Beria. And the Russians were getting close. The bulletins coming in from NSA assets in St Petersburg indicated intense counterintelligence activity in there.

Price pulled up another set of arrivals. There it was, the Finnair flight, five hours out of Dulles. Could the Russians pull together their information and confirm that Beria had flown out of St Petersburg? If they sounded the alarms, how long would it take FBI to throw a net over Dulles?

Not long.

'That's all the time you have, friend,' Price said to the screen.

Reaching for the phone, he punched in Richardson's secure number. The master plan had called Beria's presence in the United States a contingency. But with the exposure of Treloar inevitable, that status was about to change.

Major-General Kirov had been on his feet for the better part of twenty-four hours. Painkillers, Lara Telegin's unspeakable betrayal, and an insatiable desire to find Ivan Beria kept him going.

Staring out his office window at the gathering twilight, Kirov reviewed the situation. In spite of what he had told Klein, the search for Beria was still concentrated in Moscow. He had listened to what the American had had to say, and had been openly sceptical about his theory that the killer had run to St Petersburg in order to get out of Russia. Kirov believed that the fiasco at the train station had completely shattered Beria's intricate plan. Obviously a contact, perhaps ready to take the smallpox, had been waiting close by. Equally true was that the shooting would have frightened him off. Certainly there would have been a fallback rendezvous point. But between the police, the militia, and the security forces, Kirov had more than eight thousand men scouring the city, all searching for a single face. The monster from the Balkans could move around only at great peril to himself – and to his contact. Knowing Beria as well as he did, Kirov believed that he had gone to ground somewhere in the city. That being the case, it was just a matter of time before he was flushed and the stolen smallpox retrieved.

But for all his certainty, Kirov knew better than to place all his bets on a single roll of the dice. Honouring his promise to Klein, he had called the head of the Federal Security Service in St Petersburg. The FSS and the police already had Beria's description and particulars; the call from Moscow put some starch into their search. Kirov had instructed the FSS commander to concentrate his resources on the train and bus stations – places where Beria would most likely have entered the city – and on the airport. At the same time, passenger manifests and airport security videos were to be thoroughly checked. If there was the slightest possibility that Beria had been or still was in St Petersburg, Kirov was to be notified immediately.

◇◇◇

Two hours after American 1710 had departed London, Adam Treloar finished his dinner wine and stowed his meal tray into the arm-rest of his seat. Ambling to the lavatory, he washed his hands and brushed his teeth using the supplies provided in the amenities kit. On the way back to his seat, he decided to stretch his legs.

Pulling back the curtain, he stepped into business class and walked down the left-hand aisle of the darkened compartment. Some of the passengers were watching a movie on their personal video screens; others were either working, reading, or sleeping.

Treloar continued all the way to the back of the economy section, made the turn at the lavatories, and returned up the right-hand aisle. Back in the business section, he stopped abruptly as a calculator fell at his feet. He leaned down to pick it up and was handing it to the passenger in the aisle seat when he chanced to look across at the man by the window, asleep.

'Are you all right?' the passenger whispered.

Treloar nodded and took two quick steps forward, slipping behind the curtain into first class.

Impossible! It can't be him.

His breath came in deep gasps as he tried desperately to calm himself. The sleeping man in the window seat had had his face to him: Jon Smith.

'Can I get you something, sir?'

Treloar stared at the flight attendant who'd come up to him. 'No . . . thank you.'

He hurried back to his seat, settled in, and pulled a blanket over himself.

Treloar remembered meeting Smith in Houston. He had made the mistake of revealing that he had over-heard Reed talking about Venice and Smith. Reed had warned him that Smith was not his business. He had assured Treloar that there was no reason why the doctor should ever again cross Treloar's path.

Then what's he doing here? Is he following me?

The questions pounded at Treloar as he glanced down at his carry-on, tucked beside the bulkhead. In his mind's eye, he saw the shiny canister, and inside, the ampoules with their deadly golden-yellow liquid. Too paralyzed to move, he tried to rein in his panic.

Think logically! If Smith knew about the smallpox, would he have allowed you to get onboard in London? Of course not! You'd be in chains right now. So he doesn't know. His being here is a coincidence. It must be!

His reasoning calmed him a little, but as soon as one set of questions was answered, another popped up: Maybe Smith *was* aware that he was carrying the virus, but there hadn't been time to safely arrest him in London. Maybe the British had refused to go along. Maybe Smith was allowing him to get back home because he needed the time to establish a controlled situation at Dulles. They would fall on him as soon as he disembarked . . .

Treloar pulled the blanket up closer under his chin. Back in the sunshine and safety of Houston, Reed's plan had sounded so easy, so perfect. Yes, there was an element of danger, but it was infinitesimally small compared to the rewards he stood to reap. And before the danger, there had been the delights of Moscow.

Treloar shook his head. He had memorized what it was he was supposed to do upon arrival at Dulles. Now, Smith's unexplained presence had turned a careful plan to ashes. Guidance, explanations, reassuring words were needed.

Reaching out from under the blanket, Treloar pulled out the inflight phone. At this point in the operation, communications were strictly forbidden. But with Smith only a few feet away that rule no longer applied. Treloar fumbled with his credit card and scanned it in the slot cut into the hand unit. Seconds later, the transaction was approved and he was on-line.

The room next to Randi's office had been set up as a small conference centre, complete with the latest audio-visual equipment, flat-screen monitors, and a professional video/DVD-editing unit that rivalled anything found in Disney's animation department. On most Friday afternoons, the staff would get together, eat junk food, and watch the latest movies on DVD courtesy of Amazon.com.

Sitting next to Sasha Rublev, Randi watched as the gangly teenager used the editing and enhancement software to massage the blurred image of the face on the tape. Sasha hadn't moved from the computer for hours. Every now and again he stopped just long enough to chug down a Coke; then, fortified, he'd return to his task.

All the while Randi had been nothing more than a silent observer. She was fascinated how Sasha coaxed pixel after pixel out of what appeared to be nothing more than a smudge. Little by little the image of a man's face came into focus.

Sasha made one final pass at the keyboard, then rolled his head to work out the kinks in his neck.

'That's it, Randi,' he said. 'I can't get it any better.'

Randi squeezed his shoulder. 'You did great.'

She stared at the picture of a fleshy face punctuated by puffy cheeks and thick lips. The eyes were the most startling features: large and egg-shaped, they seemed to bulge from their sockets.

'He's an ugly man.'

Randi started at the sound of Sasha's voice. 'What do you mean?'

'He looks like a troll. There's something evil about him.' He paused. 'The train station . . . ?'

'I don't know,' Randi replied truthfully. She gave Sasha a quick hug. 'Thank you. You've been a great help. I need a couple minutes to finish up in here and then we'll go get us some Egg McMuffins. Okay?'

Sasha pointed to the laptop and the cell phone on the conference table. 'What about those?'

Randi smiled. 'Maybe later.'

As soon as she was alone, Randi established a secure E-link with the embassy's senior foreign service officer who was, in fact, the CIA station chief. As soon as he acknowledged her, she fired off an urgent request for any and all information about the man whose photo would follow.

Randi fed a printout of the image into the fax machine and, checking her watch, thought that she should get a reply in about thirty minutes. As she reached for her purse, she thought of Jon Smith and wondered why this 'ugly' man was so important to him.

'Stay calm, Adam. Just stay calm.'

Adam Treloar sat jammed into the corner of his spacious window seat. He was grateful for the privacy afforded in the first-class cabin and the drone of the engines. Nonetheless he spoke in whispers.

'What am I supposed to do, Price?' he demanded. 'Smith is onboard this plane. I *saw* him!'

Anthony Price swivelled his chair to face the windows fitted with bulletproof, one-way glass. He chose a random point in the sky and fixed his gaze on it. Then he emptied his mind of everything except the issue at hand.

'But he hasn't seen *you*, has he?' he said, trying to sound as reassuring as possible. 'And he won't. Not as long as you're careful.'

'But what's he doing here in the first place?'

Price would have dearly loved to know that.

'I'm not sure,' he said carefully. 'As soon as we're through I'll start checking. But remember: *Smith is not your concern*. And there is absolutely no reason for him to be interested in you.'

'Don't lie to me!' Treloar hissed. 'You think I don't know about Smith's role in the Hades horror?'

'Smith is no longer with USAMRIID,' Price replied. 'And here's something you may not know: his fiancée was killed during Hades. Her sister works in Moscow for a venture capital firm.'

'Are you saying Smith was there for personal reasons?'

'Could well be.'

'I don't know . . .' Treloar muttered. 'I don't like coincidence.'

'But sometimes that's all it is,' Price said soothingly. 'Adam, listen to me. I have you flagged at Dulles. You'll breeze through customs and immigration. One of our people will be waiting for you with a car. You're home free. So just relax.'

'Just make sure nothing goes wrong. If they find –'

'Adam!' Price said sharply. 'We don't need to get into that.'

'Sorry . . .'

'Call me as soon as you're in the car. And don't worry.'

Price broke the connection. Treloar had always been the weak link in the chain. But also indispensable. He was the only member of the Compact who had established a reason for going to Russia on a regular basis. He was also a scientist who knew how to handle smallpox. But that didn't stop Price, who hated the weak, from despising him.

'Just make it home, Adam,' he whispered to the sky. 'Make it home and you will certainly get your just rewards.'

15

After leaving the Washington city limits, Nathaniel Klein drove along U.S. 15 until he reached Thurmont, Maryland. There he took Route 77, slipped past Hagerstown, and followed Hunting Creek until he reached the Catoctin Mountain Park Visitors Center. Skirting the forest ranger's station, he headed up two-lane blacktops until he came to a sign that read NO STOPPING, SLOWING, TURNING OR STANDING HERE. To reinforce the message, an army Humvee rattled off the shoulder and into the middle of the road.

Klein pulled over his nondescript Buick sedan, lowered his window, and held out his ID. The officer, who had been alerted to expect Klein, scanned the card. Satisfied, he instructed Klein to proceed. As soon as he was under way, the car phone sounded.

'Klein here.'

'Kirov in Moscow. How are you, sir?'

By the sounds of it, better than you. But all he said was, 'Fine, General.'

'I have information.' There was a slight hesitation, as if the Russian was trying to find the right words. Finally, they came out in a rush: 'Beria made it to St Petersburg, just as you suspected. Frankly, I am at a loss to understand how this is possible.'

'You're sure?' Klein demanded.

'Positive. A bus driver was stopped at a checkpoint on the Moscow–St Petersburg highway. He was shown a photograph and identified Beria.'

'How far outside St Petersburg was this checkpoint?'

'A little bit of luck here: only an hour. I immediately concentrated my resources in the city, particularly the airport. No American carriers had left up to that point.'

Klein breathed a little easier. Wherever Beria was going, it wasn't here.

'But there was a Finnair flight that left almost ten hours ago,' Kirov said. 'It's carrying an American tour group.'

Klein closed his eyes. 'And?'

'The immigration officer remembers the tour leader giving him a stack of passports. He took his time going through them. One of the names caught his attention because it was a Russian name on an American passport. Ivan Beria now calls himself John Strelnikov. If the Finnair flight is on schedule, it will land at Dulles in fifteen minutes.'

Klein stared through the windshield at the lodges coming into view.

'General, I'll have to call you back.'

'I understand. Godspeed to you, sir.'

Klein drove past the rustic dwellings until he saw the largest one, fronting a small pond. He pulled in, got out, and hurried to the front door. Nathaniel Klein had arrived at Aspen, the presidential lodge at Camp David.

Developed in 1938 as a retreat for Franklin Delano Roosevelt, the area known as Camp David had been called the Catoctin Recreational Demonstration Area (RDA), used by federal employees and their families. Its security fence surrounded one hundred and twenty-five acres sheltered by a thick growth of oak, hickory, aspen, poplar, and ash. The guest lodges – used by foreign dignitaries, the friends and family of the president, and other visitors – were set in private surroundings and connected to Aspen by a series of footpaths.

Through the trees Klein caught a glimpse of Marine One, the presidential helicopter. Under the circumstances, he was glad that the flying time to Washington was only thirty minutes.

The Secret Service agent opened the door for him and Klein stepped into a small, pine-panelled foyer. A second agent escorted him through the homey living room to the large, comfortable room that served as the presidential office.

Samuel Adams Castilla, the chief executive, sat behind a stressed-pine desk, going through paperwork. Wearing a cardigan over a denim shirt, the former New Mexico governor rose and offered Klein his large, weathered hand. Behind titanium-rimmed glasses, cool, slate-grey eyes appraised the visitor.

'Usually I'd say it's good to see you, Nate,' the president said. 'But since you mentioned it was urgent . . .'

'I'm sorry to intrude on your privacy, Mr President, but this can't wait.'

Castilla ran a palm across his five o'clock shadow. 'Does it relate to what we talked about in Houston?'

'I'm afraid it does.'

The president gestured at one of the couches. 'Bring me up to speed,' he said crisply.

Five minutes later, Castilla knew more than he had ever wished to know.

'What's your recommendation, Nate?' he asked quietly.

'Commence FIREWALL,' Klein said tightly. 'We don't want a single one of those passengers walking out of the terminal.'

Developed in collaboration with the FAA, the FBI, and the Pentagon, FIREWALL was a dedicated response to any terrorist incursion into the United States. If the warning came early enough, every port of entry would be flooded by security officials waiting for a target whose description and particulars were already in hand. Klein knew that it was too late to do this at Dulles. The best he could do was to alert every available uniformed and undercover officer in the complex and initiate a hunt. Even as agents were scrambling, the FAA would be faxing a passenger manifest to the central command post.

The president stared at him, nodded, and reached for the phone. In seconds he had Jerry Matthews, the head of the FBI, on the line, and was explaining what had to be done.

'I don't have time to give you all the details right now, Jerry. Just get FIREWALL going. I'm faxing you a description of the suspect as we speak.'

The president took the sketch Klein held out and fed it into the machine.

'His real name is Ivan Beria, Jerry. He's a Serb national. But he's calling himself John Strelnikov and is travelling on a fake U.S. passport. He is not, I repeat *not*, an American citizen. And Jerry? This is a level-five situation.'

Five was the highest designation, meaning that the individual in question was to be considered not only armed and dangerous but a clear and immediate danger to national security.

The president hung up and turned to Klein. 'He'll get back to me as soon as the ball's rolling.' He shook his head. 'He asked – respectfully, mind you – what my sources were.'

'I appreciate your position, sir,' Klein replied.

'It's one of my making.'

After the nightmare of Hades and the subsequent election, Samuel Castilla had sworn that the United States would never again be caught off-guard. While he respected the work of the traditional agencies, he saw a dire need for a new group – small, elite, run by a single individual beholden to no one, reporting only to the chief executive.

After a great deal of thought, Castilla had chosen Nathaniel Klein to head what would become known as Covert-One. Using funds carefully siphoned off from various government departments, employing only the most talented and trustworthy men and women, Covert-One had grown from an idea into a presidential iron fist. *This time*, Castilla thought, *we have the chance to stop the monster instead of wading through the horror it'll spawn*.

The ringing phone intruded on his reverie. 'Yes, Jerry.'

Castilla listened, put his hand over the mouthpiece, and turned to Klein.

'They have a hit on Strelnikov. Immigration clocked him in eight minutes *before* FIREWALL went into effect.' He paused. 'Do you want to maintain the alert, Nate?'

Suddenly, Klein felt very old. Beria had fooled them again. Eight minutes was an eternity to someone like him.

'It's a whole different ballgame now, sir. We have to go to a backup plan.' Quickly he outlined what he had in mind.

The president got back on the line. 'Jerry, listen carefully . . .'

Even as Castilla spoke, the director of the FBI scrambled the Bureau's elite antiterrorist teams stationed at Buzzard's Point. A description of Beria was being sent to the computer screens of their cars. Within thirty minutes, the first squads would be interviewing taxi dispatchers, skycaps, limousine drivers, anyone who might have seen or come into contact with the suspect.

'Let me know the minute you have something,' Castilla said and ended the call. He turned to Klein. 'Exactly how much smallpox was stolen?'

'Enough to start a wildfire of an epidemic across the eastern seaboard.'

'What about our vaccine supplies – besides the amount stock-piled by USAMRIID for military use?'

'Barely enough to inoculate half a million people. I'm anticipating your next question, Mr President: how long to manufacture enough? Too long. Weeks.'

'Nonetheless, we have to try. What about Britain, Canada, Japan – can we buy from them?'

'They have less than we do, sir. And they would need that to protect their own populations.'

For a moment, there was silence.

'Is there any reason to believe that Beria came here *with the express intent* of unleashing the virus?' the president asked.

'No, sir. Ironically, that's our one ray of hope. Beria has never been anything other than a killer for hire, a facilitator. His politics revolve around the price paid for services rendered.'

'Facilitator? Are you suggesting that he's *delivering* the smallpox to someone over here?'

'I appreciate that it's a difficult concept to entertain, Mr President. After all, if a terrorist wanted to stage a biochem attack against us, it would be much safer to assemble the weapon *outside* the country, rather than here.'

'But the smallpox is already a weapon, isn't it, Nate?'

'Yes, sir. Even in its raw form, it is extremely potent.

Deposit it in New York City's water supply and you create a crisis of massive proportions. But, Mr President, if you take the same amount and reconfigure it so that it can be used in an aerosol dispersal system, you can crop dust, if you will, a much greater area.'

The president grunted. 'You're saying, why waste the potential when you can maximize it.'

'Exactly.'

'Assuming, for a moment, that Beria is a courier, how far can he get?'

'Hopefully we can contain him to the D.C. area. Beria has a couple of problems: he doesn't speak English well, and he's never been in this country, much less in this specific area. One way or another, he will draw attention to himself.'

'In theory, Nate. But he won't be signing up for tours of the White House. He'll deliver the virus and get the hell out of Dodge. Or try to.'

'Beria has to have help on this end,' Klein conceded. 'But again, the geographic area is limited. We should also remember that the people using Beria do not want the virus released until it suits them to do so. That means they have to store it – safely. And that requires a very good laboratory. We're not looking in tenements or abandoned warehouses, Mr President. Somewhere in the surrounding counties is a state-of-the-art lab that was created just for this purpose.'

'All right,' he said finally. 'The hunt for Beria is under way. We'll also start searching for this lab. Right now, we keep a lid on what's happening. Total media blackout. Is that about right?'

'Yes, sir. About the media: Kirov has done a yeoman's job of keeping the situation in Russia under wraps. But if there's a leak, that's where it will spring. I suggest that when you call President Potrenko, you ask him what steps he's taking to hold the blackout in place on his end.'

'Noted. Now what about this second man you mentioned, the one Beria may or may not have met in Moscow?'

'He's the wild card, sir,' Klein said softly. 'If we can finger him, we can use him to get to Beria.'

As soon as he heard the double *ping* indicating that the aircraft was at the gate, Adam Treloar was out of his seat and moving to the forward hatch. The rest of the first-class passengers fell in behind him, creating a buffer between him and the man who could not be allowed to catch a glimpse of him.

Treloar drummed his fingers on his carry-on, impatient for the hatch to roll up. His instructions had been precise. He repeated them over and over again until he knew the litany by heart. The only question was, would he be able to carry them out without interference?

The hatch disappeared into the bulkhead, the flight attendant stepped back, and Treloar charged past her. He set a fast pace, moving through the jetway and into a harshly lit corridor that dead-ended at an escalator. He walked down it and found himself at the immigration booths. Beyond them were the baggage carousels and the customs checkpoints.

Treloar had expected and would have preferred crowds. But Dulles was not as busy as Kennedy or Los Angeles, and no international flights had come at the same time or just a little ahead of American 1710. He went up to an empty counter and offered his paperwork to an officer who scanned the passport and asked inane questions about where he'd been. Treloar gave him the truth about his mother, how he had gone to Russia to visit her grave and tend to it. The officer nodded solemnly, scribbled something on the customs form, and waved him along.

Treloar had baggage, but he wasn't about to waste time waiting for it to come down the chute. The instructions had been very specific on that point: he was to get out of the terminal as quickly as possible. Walking past the carousels, Treloar dared to glance over his shoulder. At the other end, Jon Smith was at an immigration counter reserved for diplomats and aircrews. Why would he . . . ? Of course! Smith was Pentagon. He would be travelling on a military ID, not on a civilian passport.

Holding his card, Treloar approached the customs agent.

'Traveling light, sir,' the agent commented.

Remembering his instructions, Treloar explained that he had had his bags sent on ahead, using a bonded courier service that catered to well-heeled travellers who were not inclined to wrestle with their own suitcases. Familiar with the arrangements, the agent waved him through.

Out of the corner of his eye, Treloar caught Smith walking up to the same agent. He veered right, so as not to walk across Smith's line of sight.

'No, sir,' the agent called out. 'You go left.'

Treloar turned abruptly and almost ran into the tunnel that connected to the terminal.

'Dr Smith?'

He turned to the customs agent walking up to him. 'Yes?'

'There's a call for you, sir. You can take it in there.'

The agent opened the door to an interview room where detained travellers were questioned. Pointing to a phone on the desk, he said, 'Line one.'

'This is Smith.'

'Jon, it's Randi.'

'Randi!'

'Listen. There isn't much time. I just got a positive ID on that guy in the picture. He's Adam Treloar.'

Smith clenched the receiver. 'You're sure?'

'Positive. We cleaned up the video enough to get a good print, which I shipped over to the embassy. Don't worry. Whatever the cat is, it's still in the bag. I made Treloar a prospective investor and asked for a standard background check.'

'What did you find out?'

'His mother was Russian, Jon. She died a while ago. Treloar comes over frequently, to pay his respects, I guess. Oh, and he was on the same flight as you – American 1710.'

Smith was stunned. 'Randi, I can't thank you enough. But I have to run.'

'What do you want me to do with the laptop and the cell phone you brought in?'

'Can you get your boy genius to work on it?'

'I figured as much. I'll call you as soon as I have something.'

Smith left the office, quickly walked back to the customs counter and found the agent who had alerted him to the call.

'I need your help,' he said urgently, displaying his military ID. 'There was a passenger onboard 1710. Can you find out if he's cleared customs yet? The name is Adam Treloar.'

The agent turned to his terminal. 'Got him right here. Treloar. Went through about two minutes ago. Do you want –?'

Smith was already on the move, heading out of the restricted area towards the concourse, dialling Klein's number as he ran.

'Klein here.'

'Sir, it's Smith. The guy with Beria is American. Dr Adam Treloar. He's a NASA scientist and he was on the London-to-Washington flight.'

'Can you find him?' Klein demanded urgently.

'He has a two-minute start on me, sir. I might be able to run him down before he leaves the terminal.'

'Jon, I'm at Camp David with the president. Hold on, please.'

Smith kept threading his way through the traffic in the concourse as he waited for Klein to come back on the line.

'Jon, listen to me. A FIREWALL alert was issued earlier, for Beria. But he slipped through it. Now that we know who he was seen with it's imperative that you find Treloar. We have FBI agents in the area –'

'No good, sir. It'll take too long to bring them up to speed. I think I have the best shot.'

'Then take it.'

Smith raced down the tunnel. He knew the layout of Dulles intimately. After clearing customs and immigration, passengers walked through the arrivals area to other gates, or, if D.C. was their final destination, to the area where the specially built transit buses waited.

These vehicles could raise their platforms to reach the boarding area. Once the passengers were on, the chassis was lowered and the buses would go across the airport to the main terminal. There, the docking process would be repeated, and the passengers would disembark and head for the exits.

Smith ran past the shops and newsstands, darting among travellers, straining to catch a glimpse of Treloar. Reaching the end of the concourse, he found himself in a large holding area. Along one wall were elevator-style glass doors that passengers went through to get on the buses. Only one bus was parked at the dock. Smith shouldered his way through the crowd of twenty-odd travellers who were in the process of boarding.

Ignoring the shouts of protest, Smith elbowed his way onto the bus, his eyes flitting from face to face. He checked every passenger. Treloar wasn't there.

Smith rapped hard on the partition separating the cabin from the driver's compartment. A startled, black face looked back at him and the ID he jammed against the glass.

'Did another bus just leave here?' he shouted.

The driver nodded and gestured at a bus that was better than halfway between the arrivals area and the main terminal.

Smith turned and cut his way through the growing crowd in the bus. He spotted an emergency exit and dashed towards it. Alarms sounded as he threw open the door with the large red warning sign stencilled across its face.

Flying down the ramp that led to gate aprons, Smith spotted an airport supervisor's sedan idling next to a string of baggage carts. He flung open the door and jumped behind the wheel. He jammed his foot on the accelerator and the sedan shot onto the taxiways, narrowly missing an oncoming fueller.

The drive across the parking aprons took less than thirty seconds. Abandoning the vehicle, Smith raced up to the bus. Because the chassis was eight feet off the ground, he could make out only the heads of the passengers as they disembarked.

Swinging through another emergency door, Smith found himself in an identical holding area filled with passengers waiting to board. Turning, he saw the backs of those who had just come off the bus. He scanned the sea of faces around him. Treloar *couldn't* have slipped out. Not that fast.

Then he saw him, only a glimpse at first. But it was unmistakably Treloar, beyond the sliding glass doors that opened to the sidewalk outside where cabs, limousines, and private vehicles waited.

Barging ahead, Smith jammed through the doors in time to see his quarry about to step into a black Lincoln sedan with heavily tinted windows.

'Treloar!'

Charging down on him, Smith saw terror in those odd eyes, noted the way Treloar was clutching his carry-on tightly against his chest.

Treloar jumped into the car and slammed the door. Smith reached the vehicle just in time to get his fingers around the door handle. Then, without warning, the big car screeched away from the kerb, throwing him heavily to the sidewalk. Smith tucked his shoulder, letting it absorb the impact, and rolled with the momentum. By the time he was back on his feet, the Lincoln was well into traffic.

Two airport policemen ran up and grabbed him by the arms. Thirty precious seconds were wasted as Smith struggled to identify himself. Finally he was able to get Klein on the line.

'Did you get the plate number?' Klein demanded after Smith told him about the car.

'No. But I saw the last three digits. And there was an orange sticker in the lower left corner. Sir, the Lincoln is registered to a U.S. government agency.'

16

'Where are we going?'

The heavily tinted glass between the front and rear compartments prevented Adam Treloar from seeing the driver. His voice, coming through hidden speakers, had a raspy quality.

'There is no need for concern, Dr Treloar. Arrangements have been made. Please sit back and enjoy the ride. There will be no further communication until we've reached our destination.'

Treloar's eyes darted to the door locks. He pushed the button to raise them, but to no avail.

What's happening here?

No matter how hard he tried to calm himself, Treloar could not erase the image of Smith: on the plane, in the customs area, spotting him, the recognition dawning across his face. Treloar considered it a miracle that the transfer bus had pulled away from its bay before Smith managed to get onboard. But that hadn't stopped him. Smith was like some savage hound, refusing to give up the chase. Treloar had caught a glimpse of him in the main terminal, just seconds before he'd raced through the exit doors. But even then Smith had almost caught up to him. Treloar recoiled when he flashed on the hand curling over the door handle, trying to force it open.

I'm safe now, he thought, trying to reassure himself. *The car was waiting as they promised. Smith won't be able to touch me where I'm going.*

The rationale provided some comfort, but it could not still other questions: *Why* was Smith after him? Did he *suspect* that Treloar was carrying the smallpox? Did he *know?*

Impossible!

Treloar was well versed in the protocols regarding a bioweapons alert. If Smith had had the slightest suspicion that he was the courier, Treloar never would have made it off the jetway without being arrested.

Then why? What had prompted Smith to focus on him?

Treloar sat back in the soft leather seat, gazing out at what appeared to be nightscape. The car was moving swiftly along the highway that led from the industrial parks around Dulles into the city proper. The driver didn't seem to be worried about being stopped for speeding.

Just as well, as far as Treloar was concerned. The sooner they reached their destination, the sooner he would have his answers.

The news of Adam Treloar's escape did not sit well with Nathaniel Klein.

'I know you did your best, Jon,' he said, speaking over a secure line. 'But now we have Beria *and* Treloar to deal with.'

Smith was huddled next to a pillar outside the main terminal.

'I understand, sir. But with Treloar, we have a break. The tags on the car that picked him up were government.'

'I'm running them even as we speak,' Klein replied. 'What I don't understand is why he bolted.'

209

'Because he's guilty, sir,' Smith said coldly. 'There was no reason for Treloar to evade me. It was clear that he remembered me from Houston. So why run? What was he so afraid of?' Smith paused. 'And where was he going in such a hurry? He didn't even pick up his luggage.'

'But according to you, he had a carry-on.'

'That he was holding on to as if the crown jewels were inside.'

'Hold for a moment,' Klein said. 'Something's coming through on those tags.'

Smith heard the sound of a printer, then Klein was back on the line.

'The car that was waiting for Treloar is registered to NASA.'

Smith was stunned. 'Okay. Treloar has enough seniority to have a driver meet him. But that still begs the question: why run?'

'If he is running, Jon, would he have arranged for such obvious transport?'

'Sure – because he never expected to see me or to be the object of any attention.' Smith paused. 'Let's find the car and ask him, sir.'

'Let's do one better. I'll have a federal BOLO alert put out on Treloar.'

The implications of what Klein suggested were far reaching. A BOLO alert meant that every law enforcement officer within a hundred miles of the capital would have Treloar's description and orders to pick him up on sight.

'In the meantime,' Klein concluded, 'I want you here at Camp David. The president is expecting a briefing on Beria. I want him to hear your report firsthand.'

◇◇◇

The Lincoln wound its way up Wisconsin Avenue and crept down a quiet, leafy street. An alumnus of Georgetown University Medical School, Treloar recognized the area as Volta Place – a neighbourhood on the fringe of campus, slowly being gentrified block by block.

The locks popped up and the driver held the door open. Treloar hesitated, then, picking up his carry-on, slowly stepped out of the car. He took his first good look at the driver – built like a linebacker, with a square, expressionless face – and at his destination, a pleasant, recently renovated townhouse with painted white brick and black trim on the door and shutters.

The driver opened the gate in the wrought-iron fence that bordered the tiny lawn. 'You're expected, sir.'

Treloar walked up the flagstone path and was reaching for the lion's-head knocker when the door swung open. He stepped into a postage-stamp-size foyer of polished hardwood and Oriental carpet.

'Adam, it's good to see you.'

Treloar almost fainted at the sound of Dylan Reed's voice behind the door.

'Don't be so shocked,' Reed said, closing and locking the door. 'Didn't I tell you that I'd be here? Everything's all right now.'

'It *isn't* all right!' Treloar exploded. 'You don't know what happened at the airport. Smith –'

'I know *exactly* what happened at Dulles,' Reed cut him off. 'And I know about Smith.' He eyed the carry-on. 'Is that it?'

'Yes.'

Treloar handed him the carry-on and followed Reed into a small kitchen that looked out on a patio.

211

'Excellent job, Adam,' Reed was saying. 'Truly excellent.'

Picking up a towel, he removed the canister from the carry-on and deposited it in the freezer.

'The nitrogen charge –' Treloar began to say.

Reed checked his watch. 'I know. It's good for another couple of hours. Don't worry. We'll have it safely stored by then.' He gestured at a round table in the breakfast nook. 'Why don't you sit down. I'll get you a drink and you can tell me everything.'

Treloar heard the rattle of ice cubes and the clink of glass. When Reed returned, he was carrying two tall glasses filled with ice and a bottle of good scotch.

After pouring generous measures, he raised his glass: 'Well done, Adam.'

Gulping his drink, Treloar shook his head violently. Reed's equanimity was driving him crazy.

'I'm telling you, everything's *not* all right!'

Fuelled by the whiskey, the words rushed out of him. He held back nothing, not even his exploits at the Krokodil, not caring because Reed had made it clear long ago that he knew all about those proclivities. Every minute of his trip was accounted for so that Reed could follow his reasoning.

'Don't you see?' he asked plaintively. 'It *couldn't* have been a coincidence that Smith was on the same flight as me. Something must have happened in Moscow. The contact, whoever he was, must have been followed. They saw us together, Dylan. They can link him to me!

'And then that scene at the airport – Smith trying to catch me. *Why?* Unless he knew –'

'Smith doesn't know anything.' Reed poured Treloar more scotch. 'Don't you think that if you were a suspect, half the FBI would have been waiting for you?'

212

'Yes, I thought of that! I'm not an idiot. But the coincidence –'

'There – you just said it: coincidence.' Reed leaned forward, his expression earnest. 'I think that a lot of this has been my fault. When you called me from the plane, I gave you instructions that, I realize, you followed to the letter. But I was wrong. I should have told you *not* to run if Smith approached you. It would have been curiosity on his part, remembering you from Houston. Nothing more.'

Believe me, it was more,' Treloar replied sullenly. 'You weren't there.'

True. But you were never far from my mind . . .

'Listen to me, Adam,' Reed said. 'You're safe. You did what was necessary and you made it back home. Think: what can anyone say? You went to visit your mother's grave. That's all documented. You saw a little bit of Moscow. No harm there. Then you came home. The airport? You were in a rush. You didn't have time to pick up your bag. And Smith? You never actually got a good look at him, did you?'

'But why was he after me in the first place?' Treloar demanded.

Here, Reed realized, only a piece of the truth would work.

'Because your contact at Sheremetevo was caught on tape – and you along with him.'

Treloar groaned.

'Listen to me, Adam! They have a tape of two men sitting side by side at an airport counter. That's *all* they have. No voice, nothing to connect the two of you. But because they know what the courier was carrying, they're looking at everyone.'

'They know about the smallpox,' Treloar said dully.

'They know it's *missing*. And that the courier had it. But *he's* the one they're after, not you. No one suspects you of anything. You just happened to be sitting next to this guy.'

Treloar washed his face with his hands. 'I don't know if I could stand it, Dylan . . . To be questioned.'

'You'll be fine because you haven't done anything,' Reed repeated. 'Even if you were polygraphed, what could you say? Did you know the identity of the man sitting next to you? *No*. Were you supposed to meet him? *No*. Because the contact could just as easily have been a woman.'

Treloar swallowed more scotch. Looking at the situation that way, he felt a little better. There was so much he could say no to.

'I'm exhausted,' he said. 'I need to get some sleep, somewhere where no one will disturb me.'

'Already arranged. The driver will take you to the Four Seasons. There's a suite waiting for you. Take as much time as you need. Call me later.'

Throwing his arm over Treloar's shoulder, Reed walked him to the door. 'The car's outside. Adam, thank you. All of us thank you. Your contribution has been invaluable.'

Treloar had his hand on the doorknob. 'The money?' he asked under his breath.

'There's an envelope at the hotel. Inside, you'll find two numbers. One is for the account, the other is the bank director's private number in Zurich.'

Treloar stepped out into the gloaming. The wind had picked up and he shivered. He looked back once and saw only the black door, closed.

The car was not waiting in front of the townhouse. Treloar looked up and down the street, then spotted it halfway down the block. He thought he understood why: there were no parking spaces.

Walking down the street, the scotch warming his belly, he replayed Reed's reassuring words. He was right: everything that had happened in Russia was behind him. No one had any evidence against him. Besides, he knew so much about Reed, Bauer, and the others that they would always have to protect him.

The idea of holding such power lulled Treloar. Looking up, he expected to see the Lincoln on his left. Instead, it was further down the block, a stone's throw from Wisconsin Avenue. He shook his head. He was more tired than he realized and must have miscalculated the distance. Then he heard the soft slap of leather on concrete, footsteps approaching.

Treloar saw the shoes first, then the pant legs with razor-sharp creases. When he looked up, the figure was less than two feet away.

'*You!*'

Treloar's eyes rolled wildly as he stared at Ivan Beria.

Beria took a quick step towards him. Treloar could smell his breath, heard the soft whistle that escaped Beria's nostrils.

'I missed you,' Beria said softly.

Treloar cried out weakly as a sharp pain shot through his chest. For an instant he thought he was having a heart attack.

'When you were a little boy, did you prick balloons with a needle? That's all it is, really. Just a balloon.'

Absurdly, Treloar clung to the image even as the tip of Beria's stiletto wriggled into his heart. He sighed once and felt all the air rush out of his lungs. Lying there on the sidewalk, he could see the people walking along Wisconsin and Beria stepping off the sidewalk. He must have tried to call out, because Beria turned and looked at him. Then, as his eyes closed, so did the door of the black Lincoln.

Dr Dylan Reed had put Adam Treloar out of his mind as soon as the door had closed behind him. Having made the arrangements himself, he knew what was in store for the hapless scientist. By the time he returned to the kitchen, Dr Karl Bauer and General Richardson – the latter dressed in mufti – were waiting.

Richardson held up a cell phone. 'I just heard from Beria. It's done.'

'Then we have to get moving,' Reed replied.

He glanced at Bauer, who had already removed the canister from the freezer and was opening it on the counter. At his feet was a lightweight titanium chest the size of a picnic cooler.

'Are you sure you want to do that here, Karl?'

Bauer finished opening the canister before replying. 'Open the chest, please, Dylan.'

Kneeling, Reed pulled the handles. There was a faint hiss as the seals came apart.

The interior was surprisingly small, but Reed knew this was because the chest was merely a larger version of the canister that had been carried from Russia. Its thick walls were studded with liquid nitrogen capsules, which, when fully activated, would keep the interior at a steady temperature of minus two hundred degrees centigrade. Developed by Bauer-Zermatt A.G., the chest was standard issue when it came to the transport of toxic cultures.

Using thick, specially lined gloves, Bauer removed the inner chamber in which the ampoules rested. Looking at them, he thought they resembled miniature missiles, lined up ready to fire. Except that by the time the protocols were altered, they would be vastly more potent than any nuclear weapon in the American arsenal.

Although Bauer had been handling viruses for more than forty years, he never forgot what he was dealing with. He made sure that his hands were absolutely steady and that there was no moisture on the counter or anywhere near his feet before he slowly lowered it into a special cradle in the chest. Closing the lid, he entered an alphanumeric combination into the security lock pad and set the temperature.

Looking up, he said, 'Gentlemen, the clock is running.'

The row houses of Volta Place shared a common characteristic: each had a small garage behind the backyard that opened up on an alley. Reed and Richardson carried the chest into the garage and stowed it in the cargo compartment of a Volvo station wagon. Bauer stayed behind a moment to make sure that nothing that could link the three men to this location had been left behind. He was not concerned about fingerprints or fibres or any other forensic minutiae; in a few minutes, a special NSA cleaning crew would arrive to wash and vacuum the interior. The NSA maintained several such safe houses in the Washington area. For the cleaners, this was just another stop in a busy schedule.

As Bauer walked to the garage, he heard the wail of sirens coming from the direction of Wisconsin Avenue.

'It would appear that Adam Treloar is about to play his final role,' he murmured as the three got into the station wagon.

'Too bad he isn't around to read the reviews,' Reed said, and edged the car into the alley.

17

Peter Howell stood on the top tier of the wide steps leading into the Galleria Regionale on the Via Alloro. Sicily's most prestigious gallery boasted paintings by Antonello da Messina as well as the magnificent fifteenth-century fresco *Triumph of Death* by Laurana, which particularly appealed to Howell.

Staying well away from the tourists hiking up and down the steps, alert for anyone who might be taking an undue interest in him, Howell pulled out his secure phone and dialled the number Jon Smith had given him.

'Jon? Peter here. We need to talk.'

Forty-five hundred miles away, Smith pulled over onto the soft shoulder of Route 77.

'Go ahead, Peter.'

Continuing to scan the foot traffic around the gallery, Howell described his meeting with the smuggler, Franco Grimaldi, the subsequent attempt on his life, and his encounter with Master Sergeant Travis Nichols and his partner, Patrick Drake.

'Are you sure they were U.S. military?' Smith asked.

'Absolutely,' Howell replied. 'I set up watch at the post office, Jon. An officer came to the box, just like Nichols said he would. But there was no chance to take him – and no way I can get on your base outside Palermo.' Howell paused. 'What are your soldier boys up to, Jon?'

'Believe me, I'd love to know.'

The sudden appearance of American military personnel – soldiers as assassins – added a new dimension to an already complex equation, one that demanded to be addressed immediately.

'If Nichols and his partner were sanctioned killers, someone had to be paying them,' Smith concluded.

'My thoughts exactly,' Howell replied.

'Any ideas as to how to ferret out the money man?'

'Actually, yes,' Howell replied, then proceeded to explain.

Ten minutes later, Smith pulled back on Route 77. Reaching the entrance to Camp David, he was given a military escort to Rosebud, the guest cabin closest to Aspen. He found Klein sitting in front of a fieldstone fireplace, talking on the phone.

Klein waved Smith to sit, finished his monosyllabic conversation, and turned to Smith.

'That was Kirov. His people are questioning everyone in the Bioaparat complex, trying to walk back the cat to Yardeni's contacts. So far, no luck. Yardeni seems to have been one closemouthed SOB. He didn't go around spending money he shouldn't have had, or bragging about how soon he'd be living the high life in the West. No one remembers seeing him with any foreigners. Kirov's checking his phone calls and mail, but I'm not holding my breath.'

'So whoever reached out to Yardeni did so very carefully,' Smith observed. 'They made sure he was the right man for the job – no family, corrupt, someone who could keep his mouth shut.'

'That's my guess.'

'What else does Kirov have?'

'Nothing. And he knows it.' Klein snorted. 'He tried hard not to sound too relieved that it's now our problem. Can't blame him, though.'

'It's still *Russian* smallpox that's at the root of all this, sir. If word gets out –'

'It won't.' Klein checked his watch. 'The president is expecting my call in fifteen minutes. What do you have?'

Smith spoke quickly and succinctly, describing everything that had happened in Russia as well as his confrontation with Treloar at Dulles. Klein's eyebrows shot up in surprise when Smith detailed how U.S. soldiers were now involved. Then he presented his suggestions for the next course of action.

Klein took a moment to consider. 'I like most of it,' he said finally. 'But a couple of points might be a hard sell.'

'I don't see where we have options, sir.'

Klein's reply was interrupted by a call his secretary put through. Smith noticed a gleam in his eyes as he listened.

Placing a hand over the mouthpiece, he whispered, 'The BOLO nailed Treloar!'

Even as Smith leaned forward in his chair, Klein's expression slackened.

'You're sure?' he demanded. After a pause: 'No witnesses? No one saw *anything*?'

Klein listened some more, then said, 'I want the detectives' reports and the crime-scene photos faxed to my desk immediately. And yes, cancel the BOLO.'

The receiver rattled in its cradle.

'Treloar,' Klein said, grinding his back teeth. 'D.C. cops found him in Volta Place, near Wisconsin, stabbed to death.'

Smith closed his eyes, picturing the frightened bald man with the funny eyes.

'They're positive?'

'A passport and other ID were found on the body. It's him. Someone got very close and stuck what the cops think was a stiletto into his heart. They're saying it was a mugging.'

'A mugging . . . Did they find anything around the body, a carry-on?'

'Nothing.'

'Had he been robbed?'

'Money and credit cards were gone.'

'But not the wallet or the passport. Those would be left behind to help with the ID.' Smith shook his head. 'Beria. Whoever was using Treloar knew he was the link. A weak link. They used Beria to get rid of him.'

'"They" being . . . ?'

'I don't know, sir. But the handoff's been made. "They" have the smallpox. Treloar was expendable.'

'Beria . . .'

'That's why Beria went to St Petersburg, why he was on that Finnair flight. He wasn't running. He came over to eliminate the weak link.'

'Anyone could have done that.'

'The execution? Yes. But wouldn't it be better to use a man who is – or was – unknown to us? We have a description, but no fingerprints, no real understanding of movement or methodology. Beria is perfect because he's as anonymous as an assassin can be.'

'So there *was* an exchange at Sheremetevo.'

Smith nodded. 'Treloar had the smallpox all along.' He paused. 'And I was sitting thirty feet away from him.'

Never taking his eyes off Smith, Klein picked up the phone. 'Let's not keep the president waiting.'

Smith was surprised to see the chief executive in casual attire and informal surroundings. After Klein had made the introduction, Castilla said, 'Your reputation precedes you, Colonel Smith.'

'Thank you, Mr President.'

'So, what are the latest developments?'

Klein launched into the murder of Adam Treloar and how it factored into the overall situation.

'Treloar,' the president said. 'Is there any way you can use him to trace the rest of the conspirators?'

'Believe me, sir, we're going to put his life under a microscope,' Klein replied. 'But I'm not holding out much hope. The people we're dealing with have been very careful in choosing their allies. The one in Russia – Yardeni – yielded no clues as to who his paymasters might be. The same may be true with Treloar.'

'Let's get back to those "people" you're talking about. Do you believe that they might be foreign nationals? Someone like Osama Bin Laden?'

'I don't see Bin Laden's fingerprints on this, Mr President.' Klein glanced at Smith. 'The fact that the conspirators' reach is so great – from Russia all the way to NASA in Houston – indicates a certain level of sophistication. Someone who's very familiar with how we and the Russians operate, where we keep our jewels, and how we guard them.'

'Are you suggesting that someone in this country could have orchestrated the theft in Russia?'

'The smallpox is in this country, Mr President. The man who stole it, the man who carried it are both dead at the hands of an assassin who, until recently, was a relative unknown in the West. There is no Arab connection here. Add to that, the material we're dealing with is not only lethal, but requires a sophisticated facility to turn it into a bioweapon. Finally there's the involvement of U.S. military personnel, at least on the periphery.'

'*Military personnel?*' the president asked.

Klein turned to Smith, who gave the chief executive a *précis* of the events that took place in Palermo.

'I'm going to start digging into the backgrounds of these two soldiers, Mr President,' Klein said, then paused. 'So the answer to your question is yes – it's very likely that someone here is running the show.'

The president took a moment to digest this.

'Monstrous,' he whispered. 'Unbelievably monstrous. Mr Klein, if we knew *why* they want the smallpox, wouldn't that tell us *what* they intend to do, maybe even *who* they are?'

Klein's tone betrayed his frustration. 'It would, Mr President. But the "why" is just another puzzle.'

'Let me get this straight. There's a potential plague source that may be somewhere in the D.C. area. You also have a killer loose –'

'Mr President,' Smith interrupted, 'the killer may actually be our best bet.'

'Would you care to elaborate, Mr Smith?'

'The conspirators have eliminated the two men whom we might have gotten to. They brought over their own assassin for precisely that reason. I think they're holding him in reserve in case there's more wet work to be done.'

'Your point being?'

'Beria is our last link to the conspirators, Mr President. If we find him and manage to take him alive, he might give up enough to point us in the right direction.'

223

'Does an all-out hunt for this killer run the risk of too much publicity? Maybe it'll frighten him off.'

'It would have, sir,' Klein broke in. 'Except for one thing: Beria murdered a man in cold blood on a Washington street. He's no longer a terrorist but a common murderer. If we link him to the killing, every law-enforcement agency in five states will be after him.'

'Again: wouldn't this only drive him deeper underground?'

'Not really, sir. Beria and the men who control him would think they know exactly the kind of forces that are being marshalled against them. They would circumvent them. And they would feel safe because they'd think they knew exactly what law enforcement's next step would be.

'Plus, if we hunt Beria without publicity, and the conspirators have no idea what it is we're doing, they might believe that the threat of his capture outweighs his usefulness,' Smith added. 'In which case, he'd end up like Yardeni and Treloar.'

'Point taken, Mr Smith,' the president agreed. 'I presume you have a plan for Beria?'

'Yes, I do, sir,' Smith replied quietly, and began to describe it.

Inspector Marco Dionetti of the Venice Questura stepped nimbly from the police launch to the dock in front of his palazzo. He returned the constable's salute and watched the boat as it disappeared into the passing canal traffic, the vessels lit up from bow to stern.

At the front door, Dionetti deactivated the security system before entering. His cook and servant were both old women who had been in his household for decades. Neither was any match for a burglar, and since the palazzo had enough treasures to fill a small museum, precautions were necessary.

Dionetti picked up the mail waiting for him in the foyer. Proceeding to the drawing room, he settled into a club chair and slit open the letter from the Offenbach Bank in Zurich. He sipped his aperitif and nibbled on black Kalamata olives while scrutinizing the balance in his account. The Americans might be many things – none of them good – but they never missed a payment.

Marco Dionetti did not concern himself with the big picture. He did not care why the Rocca brothers had to kill or why they had to die. True, his conscience had been pricked when he'd sold Peter Howell. But Howell had travelled to Sicily and would never be heard from again. In the meantime, the Dionetti legacy, courtesy of American dollars, would continue to flourish.

After a refreshing shower, Dionetti took his solitary meal at the great table that could seat thirty. When coffee and dessert had been served he dismissed the servants, who retired to their quarters on the fourth floor. Lost in thought, Dionetti nibbled on strawberries drenched in Cointreau and daydreamed of where he might vacation, courtesy of American largesse.

'Good evening, Marco.'

Dionetti choked on the fruit in his mouth. He stared in disbelief as Peter Howell entered the room as calmly as if he were an invited guest and took a seat at the other end of the long table.

From inside his smoking jacket Dionetti whipped out a Beretta, levelling it across twenty feet of ancient cherrywood.

'What are you doing here?' he demanded hoarsely.

'Why, Marco? Was I supposed to be dead? Is that what they told you?'

Dionetti's mouth worked like that of a landed fish. 'I don't know what you're talking about!'

'Then why hold a gun on me?'

Very carefully Howell opened his palm and placed a small vial on the table.

'Did you enjoy your dinner, Marco? The *risotto di mare* smelled excellent. And the strawberries – are you enjoying them?'

Dionetti stared at the vial, then at the few berries at the bottom of his bowl. He tried to push away the dark thoughts crowding his mind.

'Are you guessing that I somehow managed to poison the fruit, Marco? After all, I got past your security. Your servants never suspected there was anyone in the house. Would it have been so difficult to drop a little atropine into the dessert?'

The gun barrel began to waver as Dionetti absorbed what Howell was saying. Atropine was an organic poison found in the belladonna family. Tasteless, odourless, it killed by attacking the central nervous system. Frantically Dionetti tried to remember how fast the poison worked.

'On someone of your height and weight, I should think about four, five minutes – given the amount I used,' Howell informed him. He tapped the vial on the table. 'But here is the antidote.'

'Pietro, you have to understand –'

'I understand that you betrayed me, Marco,' Howell replied harshly. 'That is *all* I need to understand. And if you didn't have something I need you'd be dead by now.'

'But I can kill you right now!' Dionetti hissed.

Howell shook his head in reproof. 'You took a shower, remember? You left your gun in its holster on the bathroom counter. I took the bullets, Marco. If you don't believe me, shoot.'

Dionetti squeezed the trigger. All he heard were clicks, like nails being driven into his coffin.

'Pietro, I swear –'

Howell held up his hand. 'Time is crucial to you, Marco. I know that American soldiers killed the Roccas. Did you help them?'

Dionetti licked his lips. 'I told them how the Roccas intended to make their escape.'

'And you knew this how?'

'I received my instructions over the telephone. The voice was electronically altered. I was told to first help the Roccas, then the soldiers who would follow.'

'And me.'

Dionetti's head bobbed furiously. 'And you,' he whispered.

His mouth was dry. His voice sounded like it was coming from very far away. He felt his heart hammering against his ribs.

'Pietro, please! The antidote . . .'

'Who pays you, Marco?' Howell asked softly.

It would be a waste of time to ask Dionetti about the Americans. They never would have revealed themselves to him. Following the blood money would be the best bet.

Howell rapped the table with the vial. 'Marco . . .'

'Herr Weizsel . . . the Offenbach Bank in Zurich. For God's sakes, Pietro, give me the antidote!'

Howell slid his cell phone the length of the table. 'Call him. I'm sure that a client of your stature has his home number. Make sure I can hear the access codes.'

Dionetti fumbled the phone and jabbed at the keypad. As he waited for the connection he could not take his eyes off the vial.

'Pietro, *please*!'

'All in good time, Marco. All in good time.'

18

The LearJet touched down at Kona Airport on the Big Island shortly before twilight, Hawaii time. Under Bauer's supervision, three technicians off-loaded the virus container and placed it in a waiting Humvee. The ride to the Bauer-Zermatt compound took forty-five minutes.

Because the complex had once been an army medical research facility, certain construction requirements had been met. Both to prevent intruders from getting in and highly lethal bugs from escaping into the island population, the area between the sea cliff and the lava fields had been cored out. The giant pit had been lined with thousands of cubic yards of concrete, creating an enormous, multi-storey cradle. This was then divided into three levels, or zones, the deepest one reserved for the laboratories that would house the most dangerous viruses. When Bauer had taken over the facility, virtually everything he needed was already in place. After one year and a hundred million dollars, the required updating had been completed and the operation went on-stream.

Once the Humvee was safely inside the massive garage, the container was off-loaded onto a mechanized trolley, which took it to a waiting elevator. Three floors below, Bauer was greeted by Klaus Jaunich, the head of his handpicked research staff. Jaunich and his team of six had been brought over from the company's Zurich headquarters for the express purpose of working on the smallpox. All of them had been with Bauer for years; all had profited beyond their wildest dreams from their association with him.

And all understand that I am privy to secrets that could break them in an instant, Bauer thought, smiling at Jaunich.

'It's good to see you, Klaus.'

'The pleasure is mine, *Herr Direktor*.'

Jaunich was a study in contrasts. A big, bearlike man in his late fifties, he had an uncommonly soft voice. His bearded moon face bespoke a lumberjack, yet the image was dispelled as soon as he smiled, revealing tiny baby teeth.

Jaunich motioned to his two waiting associates, their orange containment suits making them look like astronauts. They lifted the container off the trolley and, carrying it between them, proceeded to enter the first of four decontamination chambers, waystations to the laboratory itself.

'Does the *Direktor* wish to view the procedure?' Jaunich inquired.

'Naturally.'

Jaunich led the way to a glass-enclosed mezzanine that overlooked both the decontamination chambers and the lab. From this vantage point, Bauer watched as the delivery team moved from one chamber to the next. Because the decontamination procedure was necessary only when leaving the lab, going in took only a few minutes.

Inside the lab, the team opened the chest. Bauer leaned forward and spoke into the microphone.

'Be very careful with the transfer,' he cautioned the two men.

'*Ja, Herr Direktor,*' came the tinny response over the loudspeakers.

Bauer tensed as the pair dipped their hands into the cloud of nitrogen and slowly withdrew the revolverlike chamber that housed the ampoules. In the background, the door to the refrigerated vault, not much different from the Coke machine at Bioaparat, opened.

'We haven't much time,' Bauer murmured. 'Is the rest of the team ready?'

'More than ready,' Jaunich assured him. 'The entire process will be completed in less than eight hours.'

'You will start the procedure without me,' Bauer said. 'I will retire, then join you for the final steps in the recombination process.'

Jaunich nodded. Obviously Bauer would want to be present at the beginning of what would eventually be viewed as a milestone in biochemical engineering. But the circumstances that had brought the smallpox here – whatever they were – had clearly taken their toll on the old scientist. Before venturing into the tense laboratory atmosphere, he needed to rest.

'Be assured that every step of the procedure will be videotaped, *Herr Direktor.*'

'As it should be,' Bauer insisted. 'What we will accomplish here today has never been attempted before. The Russians couldn't do it at Bioaparat. The Americans are too frightened to even try. Think, Klaus: the first steps in the genetic alteration of one of mankind's greatest scourges, the beginning of a transformation that will render all past and present vaccines impotent! The result? The perfect battlefield weapon.'

'For which there is only one cure,' Jaunich finished. 'Strict quarantine.'

Bauer's eyes gleamed with anticipation. 'Exactly!

Since there is no known antidote, whichever country is infected must immediately shut down its borders. Take Iraq, for example. Baghdad pays no heed to our warnings to desist from a certain course of action. The decision is made to engage in a preemptive strike. Our little princess is introduced into the water or food supply. People contract the disease; the death toll mounts swiftly and exponentially. The population is desperate to flee, but the borders are sealed. The word has spread: any Iraqi must be considered infected. Even those trying to escape through the mountains would be hunted down and slaughtered.'

Bauer opened his hands like a magician releasing his dove. 'Poof! In one fell swoop the enemy is no more. He cannot fight because there's no longer an army. He cannot resist because his infrastructure has collapsed. He cannot remain in power because what is left of his people will turn on him. The only option is unconditional surrender.'

'Or pleas for a vaccine,' Jaunich observed.

'A plea that will fall on deaf ears, since there is no vaccine.' Bauer savoured the moment. 'Or so the victim will be told.' He smiled. 'But first things first: the samples must be readied for the recombination. If all goes well, we can see about the antidote.'

He clamped his hand on Jaunich's shoulder. 'I leave the undertaking in your more than capable hands and will see you in a few hours.'

Several time zones to the east, in Houston, Megan Olson pulled her cherry-red Mustang into the NASA parking area reserved for members of the space shuttle. She locked the car and walked quickly into the administration building. Dylan Reed's message had interrupted her dinner with a pleasant but boring aerospace engineer. The last word to scroll across her beeper had been URGENT.

Megan went through the security checkpoints and stepped into an elevator that whisked her to the sixth floor. Although the area was brightly lighted, there was an eerie silence in the corridors. The door to Reed's office was ajar, the light slanting into the hall. Megan knocked and entered.

The office was divided into a working space and a much larger conference area dominated by a long, oval table. Megan blinked. Seated at the table were the shuttle mission pilot, Frank Stone, and the commander, Bill Karol. Next to them sat the mission director, Harry Landon, and the deputy director of NASA, Lorne Allenby. The latter two appeared tired, their clothes rumpled as if they'd just gotten off a long flight. Megan thought that might actually be the case. With the launch date less than forty-eight hours away, Landon and Allenby should have been at the Cape.

'Megan,' Dylan Reed said. 'Thanks for coming on such short notice. I think you know everyone here.'

Megan exchanged murmured greetings as she slipped into a chair beside the mission pilot, Frank Stone.

Reed massaged the back of his neck, then braced himself on the table with both arms, his attention focused on her.

'Have you heard?'

Megan shook her head. 'Heard what?'

'Adam Treloar was killed this afternoon in Washington.' He paused. 'A mugging gone bad.'

'Oh my God! How? What happened?'

'The D.C. police don't have a lot to give us – or to go

on,' Reed replied. 'Adam had just returned from Russia – his mother is buried there. He had a reservation at a hotel so I assume he was going to stay overnight before flying down to the Cape. He was walking near Wisconsin Avenue – not a bad area, I'm told – when the son of a bitch accosted him.' Reed ran his fingers through his hair. 'What happened next is anyone's guess. No one saw or heard anything. Adam was dead by the time a passerby finally happened upon him and called the police.' He shook his head. 'Such an incredible waste!'

'Dylan, we're all pretty shook up over what happened,' Lorne Allenby, the NASA executive said. 'But we have to move things along.'

Reed waved his hand to acknowledge as much. When he turned to her, Megan felt her heart pounding.

'You're Treloar's backup. Because of the situation, you're being moved up to active duty as one of the mission specialists. Are you ready, Megan?'

Her mouth went dry, but she thought her words sounded strong and confident. 'Absolutely. It's not the way I wanted to get the slot, but yes, I'm ready.'

'You don't know how glad all of us are to hear that,' Reed said. He looked around the table. 'Questions?'

Frank Stone, the mission pilot, spoke up. 'No questions, just a vote of confidence. I've trained with Megan. I know she's ready.'

'Second that,' added Bill Karol, the commander.

'Landon?' Reed asked.

The mission director shifted in his seat. 'I've read the training reports. I know that Megan can handle the experiments Adam and you set up.' He offered a thumbs-up.

'Glad to hear it,' Allenby said. 'The bean counters in Congress are watching this mission like vultures. Having played up what we expect to glean from these experiments, I have to pony up results.' He turned to Megan. 'Bring back something that makes all of us look good.'

Megan managed a weak smile. 'I'll do my best.' She looked around the table. 'And thank you all for your vote of confidence.'

'Okay, then,' Reed said. 'I'll call the rest of the team tomorrow. I know that some of you are jet-lagged, so why don't we call it a night and meet again tomorrow morning before flying out?'

Everyone nodded gratefully and the room emptied quickly, leaving only Reed and Megan.

'You're the chief of the biomedical research programme, Dylan,' she said quietly. 'You and Treloar were pretty close. How do *you* feel about my being onboard?'

'At the end of the day, I can't say that I knew Adam all that well. You know how he was – taciturn, kept to himself mostly. Not the kind of guy who went for a few beers after work or played Saturday softball. But he was part of the team – a vital part – and I will miss him.' He paused. 'As far as you're concerned, I couldn't ask for a better backup up there.'

Megan tried to harness her conflicting emotions. A part of her was already racing ahead to all the details that had to be looked after: preparation at the Cape, integrating herself into the team and the launch procedure. She knew that normally the crew was quarantined for seven days prior to launch, although recently the period had been shortened. Still, she would have to undergo an extensive physical to make sure she wasn't harbouring any bugs.

Another part of her couldn't get the image of the odd-looking Treloar out of her mind. Reed was right: Treloar had been something of a loner. Not having known him personally made it easier to accept the fact of his death. Still, the way he had died made her shudder.

'You okay?' Reed asked.

'Fine. Just trying to take it all in.'

'Come on. I'll walk you to your car. Try to get a good night's sleep. Tomorrow, you hit the ground running.'

Megan had a small unit in an apartment complex that catered to short-term NASA personnel. After a restless, toss-filled sleep, she woke up and hit the pool before anyone else was there. Returning to her apartment, she discovered a note taped to her door.

Getting over her initial shock, Megan dressed quickly and made her way downstairs. Setting a fast pace, she reached the coffee shop on the next block a few minutes later. Given the hour, the place was almost empty. She had no problem spotting him.

'Jon!'

He rose from a booth in the corner. 'Hello, Megan.'

'My God, what are you doing here?' she asked, slipping into the seat across from him.

'I'll tell you in a minute.' He paused. 'I heard about your being assigned to the mission. You deserve the shot, no matter the circumstances.'

'Thank you. Obviously I'd rather it didn't happen this way, but –'

The waitress came by and they ordered breakfast.

'I wish you'd called,' she said. 'I leave for the Cape in a few hours.'

'I know.'

She studied him carefully. 'You didn't come all this way just to congratulate me – although I'd like to think so.'

'I'm here because of what happened to Treloar,' Smith said.

'Why? According to the media, D.C. homicide is handling the case.'

'They are. But Treloar was the chief medical officer, an important member of the NASA team. I was sent down here to find out if something in Treloar's background and activities might give us a lead as to why he was killed.'

Megan's eyes narrowed. 'I don't understand.'

'Megan, listen to me. You're taking his place on the flight. You must have worked with him. Anything you can tell me about him would help.'

They lapsed into silence as the waitress returned with their orders. The idea of food suddenly made Megan nauseated. She steadied herself and organized her thoughts.

'First of all, almost all my training was supervised by Dylan Reed. In a way, the title of chief medical officer is misleading. It's not like you go up there to hand out aspirins or Band-Aids. The duties are pure research. As head of the biomedical research programme, Dylan worked closely with his chief medical officer, Treloar. And he duplicated those experiments with me, in case I had to take Treloar's place. So I never really worked closely with Treloar at all.'

'What about personally? Was he close to anyone? Was there any gossip about him?'

'He was a loner, Jon. I never heard that he dated, much less had anyone steady. I *can* tell you that working with him wasn't much fun. A brilliant mind, but no personality, no humour, nothing. It was as if a part of him – the medical genius – flourished, while the rest of him never grew up at all.'

She paused. 'Your investigation isn't going to impact the launch, is it?'

Smith shook his head. 'No reason it should.'

'Look, the best I can do is give you the names of the people who worked directly with Treloar. Maybe they'll have something for you.'

Smith was certain that he already had those names – and more. He'd spent half the night going over Adam Treloar's files, forwarded from the FBI, the NSA, and NASA. Still, he listened carefully as Megan ran down her list.

'That's really all I know,' she concluded.

'Plenty for me to work with. Thank you.'

Megan managed a smile. 'Given what you're doing, I don't suppose there's any chance of your getting down to the launch? I could get you great seats.'

'I wish I could,' he replied, and meant it. 'But maybe I'll see you at Edwards when you touch down.' Edwards Air Force base in California was the shuttle's primary landing station.

They were silent for a moment, then Megan said, 'I've got to get going.'

He reached across the table and, covering her hand, held it tightly. 'Come home safe.'

Lost in thought, Megan walked back to her apartment. Adam Treloar was dead – murdered – and Jon Smith had suddenly materialized in Houston. He had neatly sidestepped the issue of who had sent him. He had questioned her skilfully but had given nothing in return. What was Smith *really* doing here? Who was he after and why? There was only one way to find out.

Back in her apartment, Megan took out her digitally

encrypted phone and dialled the number she had memorized long ago.

'Klein here.'

'It's Megan Olson.'

'Megan . . . I thought you'd be on your way to the
shuttle launch by now.'

'I'm leaving in a little while, sir. There have been
developments I felt you should know about.'

Quickly she outlined her conversation with Jon Smith.
'That he was being evasive is putting it mildly,' she said.
'Is there anything you want to do for him?'

'Negative,' Klein replied briskly. 'Smith is involved
because of his USAMRIID expertise.'

'I don't understand, sir. How does that come into
play?'

Klein paused. 'Listen carefully, Megan. There's been
a leak in Russia, at Bioaparat.' He paused as Megan
caught her breath. 'A sample was stolen. Adam Treloar
was in Moscow at the time. The Russians have him on
tape with the courier who was carrying the material.
A handoff was made. We're certain that Treloar carried
the stuff into this country. Then, when his usefulness
had run out, he was murdered.'

'What happened to what he was carrying?'

'Gone.'

Megan closed her eyes. 'What did he bring in?'

'Smallpox.'

'Dear God!'

'Listen to me, Megan. You're at ground zero. We
thought that Treloar might be dirty. Now we're sure
that he was. The question is, did he have accomplices
in the shuttle programme?'

'I don't know,' Megan replied. 'It seems impossible.
These are all dedicated individuals. As far as I can

tell, there's nothing suspicious going on.' She shook her head. 'But then again, I missed Treloar, didn't I?'

'*Everybody* missed him,' Klein replied. 'Don't beat yourself up over that. The key is to find the smallpox. Covert-One is working on the assumption that it's somewhere in the D.C. area. Whoever has it would not want to transport it any more than is absolutely necessary. And from London, Treloar could have taken a nonstop flight anywhere – Chicago, Miami, Los Angeles. He *chose* D.C. for a reason. We think that's where the storage facility has been set up.'

'Do you still want me to go ahead and fly on the shuttle?'

'Absolutely. But until that bird is off the pad, don't draw attention to yourself. If you spot anything suspicious, call me immediately.' He paused. 'And Megan, if we don't have a chance to talk again, good luck and come home safely.'

Klein broke the connection and Megan found herself staring at a dead phone. She had been very tempted to ask Klein if Jon Smith also worked for Covert-One, if *that* had been the reason for his evasiveness. Like her, Jon was someone with no commitments, few attachments, and was a crisis-proven specialist. Megan recalled the day when, during one of her brief visits stateside, Klein had materialized in her life, quietly offering to make her part of something special, unique, giving her a greater sense of purpose and direction. She also remembered him telling her how she would probably never meet another member of Covert-One, that part of her usefulness lay in the worldwide contact network she had built up, men and women she could turn to for information, favours, sanctuary.

Klein would never tell me . . . And neither would Jon if he were involved.

As she double-checked her packing, Megan thought of what Klein and Jon had said to her, to come home safely. But if Klein didn't find the smallpox, would there be anything to come home to?

The NASA security office occupied the northeast corner of the administration building's second floor. Smith handed over his Pentagon ID and waited as the duty officer scanned it into the computer.

'Where's your commanding officer?' Smith asked.

'Sir, I'm sorry. We're in the middle of a shift change. Colonel Brewster has left the building; Colonel Reeves is running late due to . . . ah, personal matters.'

'I can't wait around for the colonel. Clear me through.'

'But, sir –'

'Lieutenant, what is my clearance?'

'COSMIC, sir.'

'Which means that I can examine anything in this facility, right down to your last fitness report. Correct?'

'Yes, sir!'

'Now that we're clear on that, here's what we'll do: you will follow the appropriate procedures to log me in. You will not mention my arrival to anyone except Colonel Reeves, with whom you will talk to face to face. If the colonel wishes to speak with me, inform him that I will be in the Records Room.'

'Yes, sir. Is there anything the Records Room can get for you?'

'Just tell the staff to ignore me. Now let's get moving, Lieutenant.'

As he was buzzed through the bulletproof doors,

Smith thought that his bad-guy act had achieved the desired effect: the subordinate was cowed; his peer, Colonel Reeves, would be annoyed and curious, but also wary. There was good reason why Reeves would not likely go around asking about Smith.

Technically, NASA is a civilian programme. But in the early 1970s, when the agency finally decided on the kind of shuttle it needed and how to launch it, it discovered that it had no alternative but to turn to the air force. A devil's bargain was struck: in return for the Pentagon's deeming the shuttle 'an essential military requirement,' NASA would not only get to use the air force's Atlas and Titan booster rockets for its launches, it would also be the beneficiary of a steady revenue stream. The other side of the coin was that the agency was at the mercy of the Pentagon's whims and interference. Colonel Reeves held senior rank with the NASA hierarchy, but those who carried the Pentagon's coveted COSMIC pass represented the true masters.

Smith followed the lieutenant through a maze of corridors that dead-ended at a fireproof door. After punching in the codes, the officer pulled back the door and stepped to the side to allow Smith to enter. The room was at least ten degrees cooler than the rest of the floor. There was no sound save for the hum of machines, ten of the fastest computers ever built, linked to data-storage towers and PC units nestled in individual workstations.

Smith felt the eyes of the Records Room staff flicker over him, but their curiosity was short-lived. He followed the officer to a workstation well away from the others.

'This is Colonel Reeves's unit,' the duty officer explained. 'I'm sure he won't mind if you use it.'

'Thank you, Lieutenant. I don't expect to be too long – assuming I'm not interrupted.'

'Understood, sir.' He handed Smith a cell phone. 'Just dial three-zero-nine when you're through, sir. I'll come and get you.'

Smith settled himself in front of the monitor, activated the computer, and fed in the floppy he'd brought with him. Within seconds, he had overridden all the security blocks and had the entire Houston NASA network at his fingertips.

The information on Adam Treloar that Smith had received from the other federal agencies was merely a starting point. Smith had travelled to Houston to begin tracking Treloar where he had lived and worked. He needed the internal and external phone logs, inter-office E-mail, anything that resembled a trail – electronic or otherwise. There he would learn how Treloar had lived, whom he'd spoken with and met, how often, where, for how long. He would peel back the traitor's life like a stalk of celery, searching for that one anomaly, coincidence, or pattern that would be the first link in the chain leading to Treloar's coconspirators.

Smith tapped a few keys and began at what seemed like a logical point: who knew that Treloar had been to Russia? Hidden in these wafer-thin chips and fibre optics might be instructions – and names to go with them.

When Dylan Reed arrived at his office, he had no way of knowing that Smith had already begun his search. So intent was he on the morning's crowded agenda that he almost ignored the *ping* from his computer, signalling an alert. Absently, he punched in a sequence of numbers, his mind still on the first meeting of the day. The name that popped up on the screen got his immediate attention: Adam Treloar.

Someone's snooping!

Reed's hand flew to the phone. Seconds later, he was listening as the security duty officer explained Smith's presence in the Records Room.

Reed strained to remain calm. 'No, it's fine,' he told the officer. 'Please tell Colonel Reeves that our visitor is not to be disturbed.'

Our visitor! An intruder!

Reed took a moment to steady himself. What the hell was Smith doing here? Word out of Washington was that the police were treating Treloar's death as just another mugging, albeit with unintended consequences. Even the newscasts found the story mundane, a development that had pleased Reed, Bauer, and Richardson.

Reed slammed his palm against the leather blotter on his desk. Damn Smith! He recalled how frightened, almost terrified, Treloar had been of Smith. Now, the same iciclelike fingers that had danced up and down Treloar's spine had turned themselves on him.

Reed took a deep breath. Bauer had been right to suggest that Reed flag all files relating to Treloar, in case someone came looking.

And someone has . . .

The more Reed thought about it, the less surprised he was that Smith was the intruder. Smith had a reputation for tenacity that made an already dangerous man potentially lethal. Reed made sure that his nerves were settled before he dialled General Richardson at the Pentagon.

'This is Reed. That potential problem we talked about? It's real.' He paused. 'Hear me out, but I think you'll agree: we have to activate the solution.'

19

A Secret Service sedan was waiting for Jon Smith when he stepped out of Ronald Reagan National Airport. Halfway to Camp David, the call he had been expecting came through.

'Peter, how are you?'

'Still in Venice. I have some interesting news for you.'

Without going into the details of his interrogation of Dionetti, Peter Howell told Smith about the Swiss connection – Herr Weizsel at the Offenbach Bank in Zurich.

'Would you like me to have a chat with the Swiss gnome, Jon?'

'Better hold off on that until I get back to you. What about Dionetti? We don't want him sounding any alarms.'

'He won't be doing that,' Howell assured him. 'He has a severe case of food poisoning and is expected to be in the hospital for at least a week. Plus he knows that I have all his financial records and can ruin him with one phone call.'

Howell didn't think it necessary to delve into details.

'I'll stay put until I hear from you,' Howell said. 'If necessary, I can be in Zurich in two hours.'

'I'll keep you posted.'

The driver dropped Smith off at Rosebud, where Klein was waiting for him.

'Good to have you back, Jon.'

'Yes, sir. Thank you. Any word on the smallpox?'

Klein shook his head. 'But have a look at this.' He passed Smith a rolled-up sheet of paper.

The ink sketch contained some of Beria's features but wasn't precise enough to clearly define the assassin. Beria's appearance was nondescript to begin with – a major advantage for a hired killer. The composite reflected a man who could have been just about anyone. It would be sheer, blind luck if law enforcement stumbled across him – which was precisely what Klein wanted Beria's handlers to believe. With a few cosmetic changes to his appearance, Beria was perfectly safe: his controllers would continue to believe that his usefulness outweighed his potential liability.

Rolling up the sheet, Smith tapped it against his palm. He thought that Klein was taking an enormous risk: by denying law enforcement access to the true likeness of Beria, he was effectively limiting the hunt. But on the other end of the scale was a collateral benefit: when the composite hit the street and Beria's controllers saw it, they would not be spooked. Investigation of Treloar's death would be expected. That an eyewitness had provided police with a general description would not be seen as suspicious. Smith did not think that the controllers would become careless, but they would remain relaxed, presuming no immediate threat to their long-range plans.

'How'd it go in Houston?' Klein asked.

'Treloar was damn careful,' Smith said. 'Whatever contacts he made, he was meticulous in covering up his tracks.'

'Nonetheless you accomplished your primary mission.'

'I've chummed the waters, sir. Whoever was running Treloar knows I'm snooping.' He paused. 'Is the president going along with your recommendation about the vaccine, sir?'

'He's been talking to the drug companies,' Klein replied. 'They're coming onboard.'

Given the circumstances, it was vital that the major pharmaceutical companies realign their production facilities in order to produce as much smallpox vaccine as possible in as short a time as possible. Even if the stolen smallpox was genetically altered, the current vaccine might prove at least partially effective. But to manufacture the necessary amount would mean stopping the flow of other products. The losses incurred would be staggering, as would those related to manufacturing the vaccine. That the president had already agreed to underwrite the companies' losses was only half the battle. The companies would want to know why the vaccine was needed so urgently, and where such a large outbreak had occurred. Since it was impossible to hold back such information – it would inevitably find its way to the media – the location of the alleged epidemic had to be remote, yet fairly populated.

'We decided to use the Indonesian archipelago,' Klein said. 'The internal chaos in that region has pretty much closed off all incoming and outgoing traffic. There are no tourists left, and Jakarta has banned foreign media from the country. Our play is that there have been sporadic outbreaks of smallpox, leading to the possibility that the virus can multiply and spread if left unconfined. Thus the need for such a large amount on such short notice.'

Smith considered. 'I like it,' he said finally. 'The current Indonesian regime is a pariah in the eyes of most governments. But there will be panic when word leaks.'

'Can't be helped,' Klein replied. 'Whoever has the smallpox will put it to use very soon – a matter of weeks, if not days. As soon as we identify and take down the conspirators – and recover the virus – we can spin the story to indicate that the initial diagnoses and reports were wrong. It wasn't smallpox after all.'

'God willing that will be the case.'

Smith turned as Major-General Kirov, dressed in mufti, entered the room. He was startled by the Russian's appearance.

The fit, middle-aged Kirov had morphed into a slightly seedy-looking individual in a well-worn, off-the-rack suit. His tie and shirt-front were dotted with food and coffee stains; his thin-soled shoes were as badly scuffed as his cheap briefcase. His hair – now a wig – was long and unruly; a touch of makeup – expertly and judiciously applied – added an alcoholic's redness to his eyes and deepened the dark crescents under them. Kirov had re-created himself in the image of a man who was uncomfortable for the eye to dwell on. He reflected failure, dissolution, and hopelessness – the attributes of a failing salesman that the smart set, living and working in the chic area around Dupont Circle, wouldn't care to acknowledge.

'My compliments on your makeover, General,' Smith said. 'Even I had to look twice.'

'Let's hope the same is true for Beria,' Kirov replied sombrely.

Smith was glad to have the burly Russian by his side. After the debacle at Bioaparat and Moscow, Kirov had convinced the Russian president to send him to the United States to help with the hunt for Ivan Beria.

Klein had thought that Kirov, who had spent a year in Washington and knew the ethnic districts well, would be invaluable. He had argued as much to the president, who had concurred with Potrenko and allowed Kirov to come over.

But in Kirov's hard, bright eyes Smith saw the real reason why the general was here. Kirov had been betrayed by a woman he'd loved and trusted, who had been corrupted by unknown forces linked to a killer he'd let slip away. Kirov badly needed to make amends, to regain his honour as a soldier.

'How do you want to proceed, Jon?' Kirov asked.

'I need to stop at home,' Smith replied. 'After you get settled in, we can go to Dupont Circle.'

Since no one at the Russian embassy was aware of Kirov's presence in the city, Smith had suggested that the general stay with him and use the Bethesda house as the base for their hunt for Beria.

'Are you sure you don't want long-range cover?' Klein asked.

As much as Klein trusted Kirov's abilities and instincts, he was still reluctant to put both men out in the field without cover. True, Smith had gone to Houston to find a trail that Treloar might have left behind. But his real intention had been to touch the tendrils of the web that still linked Treloar to the conspirators, his controllers. By letting them know that he was ready to investigate the very heart of where Treloar had lived and worked, Smith hoped to provoke a response that would force the controllers to come after him . . . Which meant bringing Beria out of his hole.

'We can't take the chance that Beria would spot the cover, sir,' Smith replied.

'Mr Klein,' Kirov said, 'I understand – and share – your

concern. But I promise you I will not let anything happen to Jon. I have a distinct advantage over any cover you might provide. I *know* Beria. If he's wearing a disguise, I'll see through it. There are characteristics and mannerisms that he won't be able to hide.' He turned to Smith. 'You have my word. If Beria is out there, if he comes for you, he is ours.'

Ninety minutes later, Smith and Kirov arrived at Smith's ranch-style home in Bethesda. As Smith walked him through the house, Kirov noted the paintings, wall hangings, and *objects* from cultures around the world. The American was indeed a well-travelled man.

While Smith showered and changed, Kirov made himself comfortable in the guest bedroom. They met in the kitchen where, over coffee, they pored over a large-scale map of Washington, focusing on the multiethnic neighbourhood around Dupont Circle. Since Kirov was already familiar with the area, a plan came together quickly.

'I know we didn't talk about this with Klein,' Smith said as they got ready to leave. 'But . . .' He held out a SIG-Sauer pistol.

Kirov looked at it then shook his head. He went into the bedroom and came back with what looked like an ordinary black umbrella. He held it at a forty-five degree angle, moved his thumb along the handle, and suddenly, a one-inch blade popped out of the tip.

'Something I brought along from Moscow,' Kirov said conversationally. 'The blade has a fast-acting animal tranquillizer – Acepromazine. It can bring down a hundred-kilo boar in seconds. Besides, if for some reason your police were to stop me, I could explain away an umbrella. A gun would be much harder.'

Smith nodded. He might be the bait, but Kirov would be the one doing the close-in work. He was glad that the Russian wasn't going to face Beria unarmed.

Smith slipped the SIG-Sauer into his shoulder holster. 'All right, then. I'll give you forty minutes lead time, then follow you in.'

Moving along the streets like a wraith, Kirov studied the human traffic swirling around him. Like other areas close to Washington's core, Dupont Circle had undergone a revival. But tucked in between trendy cafés and designer boutiques were the Macedonian bakeries, Turkish carpet shops, Serbian emporiums filled with beaten brass and copper planters, Greek restaurants, and Yugoslav coffeehouses. Kirov knew how strong the pull of the familiar would be to a man operating in an unfamiliar environment, even if that man was a vicious killer. This ethnic mix was just the kind of environment that Ivan Beria would gravitate to. There he could find familiar food, listen to music he had grown up with, overhear accents he recognized. Kirov, who could eavesdrop in many Slavic languages, was also perfectly at home there.

Turning into an open-air quadrangle bordered by shops and stalls, Kirov took a seat in the shade of an umbrella-topped table. A Croat woman who spoke only halting English took his order for coffee. The Russian held back a smile as he overheard her running invective at the proprietor.

Sipping the thick, sweet coffee, Kirov surveyed the foot traffic, noting the women's colourful blouses and skirts and the men's baggy pants and leather jackets. If

Beria came here, he would wear the rough, practical clothing of a Yugoslav working man – maybe a cap, too, to cast a shadow over his features. But Kirov had no doubt that he would recognize him. In his experience, the one aspect of his appearance an assassin could never disguise was the eyes.

Kirov understood there was a good chance that given the opportunity Beria would recognize him as well. But Beria had no reason to think that Kirov was in the United States. His primary concern would be to avoid the police, as sparse as the patrols were in the area. He wouldn't expect a face from the past, so far from home. By the same token, Kirov did not expect to see Beria strolling up to the nearest pastry shop to buy a snack. He might know where the assassin was *likely* to venture out, but he had no idea where he was at that moment.

With hooded eyes, Kirov surveyed the changing scene around him. He also scanned the entrances and exits to the quadrangle, where people appeared from and disappeared to. He noted the signs posted in the shop windows indicating the business hours, and made a mental note to check the alleys and the delivery bays.

If Beria had to come out to perform his wet work, this was an area he would feel comfortable in. This might cause him to feel that he had the upper hand, and a confident man could sometimes be a blind one.

Three-quarters of a mile from where Kirov was contemplating the possible takedown zone, Ivan Beria opened the door to his two-bedroom apartment on the top floor of a building that specialized in short-term leases to the city's white-collar transients.

Facing him was the driver of the Lincoln, a big, silent

man with a nose that had been broken at least several times and a deformed left ear that resembled a tiny cauliflower. Beria had met such men before. Comfortable with violence and unerringly discreet, they were the perfect messengers for the principals who hired him.

Motioning the driver inside, Beria locked the door and accepted the proffered envelope. He tore it open and quickly read the contents, written in Serb. Stepping away, he smiled to himself. The principals always underestimated the number of people who had to be eliminated. In this case, Beria had already been paid for the Russian guard and the American scientist. Now he was being asked to remove one more.

Turning to the driver, he said, 'Picture.'

Silently, the driver took back the letter and handed over a picture of Jon Smith, taken by a security camera. The subject was facing the lens, his face free of shadows. The resolution was very good.

Beria smiled thoughtfully. 'When?'

The driver held out his hand for the picture. 'As soon as possible. You must be ready to go the minute you're called.'

The driver raised his eyebrows, silently asking if there was anything else. Beria shook his head.

After the driver left, Beria went into the bedroom and removed a digitally encrypted satellite phone from his pack. A moment later, he was speaking to a Herr Weizsel at the Offenbach Bank in Zurich. The account in question had just been fattened by two hundred thousand American dollars.

Beria thanked the banker and hung up. *The Americans are in a hurry.*

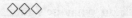

Naked, Dr Karl Bauer stepped out of the final decontamination room. On the bench of the changing room were underclothes, socks, and a shirt. A freshly pressed suit hung on the door hook.

A few minutes later, Bauer was dressed and on his way to the glass-enclosed mezzanine where his chief of staff, Klaus Jaunich, waited.

Jaunich gave a slight bow and held out his hand. 'Magnificent work, *Herr Direktor*. I have never seen anything like it.'

Bauer shook his hand and acknowledged the compliment. 'Nor are we likely to witness something like that ever again.'

After resting, Bauer had returned to the laboratory. Even though he had worked through most of the night, he felt elated and full of energy. He knew from experience that this was only the adrenaline flowing through his system and that fatigue would inevitably catch up to him. Nonetheless, Jaunich was right: it *had* been magnificent work. Using his laserlike concentration, he had applied a lifetime of knowledge and experience into taking the first steps that would transform an already deadly virus into an unstoppable, microscopic firestorm. Now he felt almost cheated because he would be unable to take those last few steps toward completion.

'We knew from the beginning, didn't we, Klaus,' he said, voicing his thought. 'That we would never be able to see this creation through to the end. The physics of this earth deny me my ultimate triumph. To complete it, I must give it away.' He paused. 'Now it will be up to Reed to go where we cannot.'

'So much trust in one man,' Jaunich murmured.

'He will do what he's told,' Bauer replied sharply.

'And when he returns, we will have what, until now, we've only dreamed of.'

He patted the big man on the shoulder. 'It will be all right, Klaus. You'll see. Now, the transport?'

'The sample is ready for shipment, *Herr Direktor*. The aircraft is standing by.'

Bauer clapped his hands. 'Good! Then you and I must have a celebratory drink before I leave.'

20

Beneath the blaze of lights, she looked like a sculpture heralding in the new millennium. From her vantage point three miles away, Megan Olson stared in awe at the space shuttle, mated to the giant external tank and the two slightly smaller solid rocket boosters.

It was two o'clock in the morning on a windless, moonlit night at Cape Canaveral. Megan's nose tingled from the briny air and her nerves trilled with anticipation. Usually, the crew was up and about by three o'clock, but Megan had been unable to sleep much past midnight. The thought that in fewer than eight hours she would be onboard the shuttle, boring into space, left her breathless.

Megan turned and walked the length of the path that ran by the ground floor of the building where the crew was quartered. A hundred yards away, razor wire glittered atop the Cyclone fence surrounding the compound. She heard the distant cough of a security Jeep as it ground its way around the perimeter. The security at the Cape was both impressive and unobtrusive. The uniformed air police were the most visible, always a magnet for the television cameras. But beyond them were the plainclothes detachments that roved the entire facility twenty-four hours a day, making sure that no one and nothing interfered with the launch.

Megan was about to head back to her room when she heard footsteps nearby. Turning, she saw a figure move from the shadows of the building into the light.

Dylan Reed?

It was a standing joke that not only did Reed not hear his alarm clock, but that he could sleep through liftoff if allowed to do so. So what was he doing up and about an hour before roll call?

Raising her arm, Megan was about to call out to him when a bright headlight appeared around the corner. Instinctively, she drew back as a sedan with the NASA logo on the door slipped close to where Reed was standing. Staying in the shadows, Megan watched an older man get out of the car and approach Reed.

Someone he was expecting. Who? And why break the quarantine?

Quarantine was a vital part of the launch process, although this time its duration had been reduced, of necessity, from the usual seven days. Allowing an outsider to come into direct contact with a crew member at this late stage was unheard of.

As the visitor and Reed moved away from her and into a pool of light, Megan saw something around the man's neck: a health stabilization card, indicating that whoever he was, the visitor had been given a clean bill of health by NASA doctors.

Satisfied that Reed's guest was cleared to be in a restricted area, Megan started to move away. But something in the back of her mind resisted. She'd always relied on her intuition and instinct; listening to both had saved her life more than once. They whispered to her now that she should not do the polite thing and walk away, giving Reed his privacy.

Megan hung back. Because the two men stood facing each other, she couldn't hear what they were saying. But there was no mistaking that something passed from

257

the visitor to Reed: a shiny, metallic cylinder about four inches long. Megan saw it only for a split second before it disappeared into the pocket of Reed's overalls.

Megan watched the visitor grip Reed's shoulder, then get back into his car and drive away. Reed seemed to gaze after the taillights until they were reduced to two pinpricks, then he turned and began walking towards his quarters.

He has preflight jitters, just like the rest of us. Someone close to him came out to see him off.

But the explanation rang hollow. Reed was a veteran of six shuttle missions, almost nonchalant about the process. Nor could it have been a relative. Once the quarantine was in effect, family members had no contact with the crew. They were relegated to a special viewing area three miles from the launch.

Someone in the programme. Someone I never met.

Before heading for the mess hall where the crew would have their last real meal until they returned, Megan stopped off at her room. She considered her options, one of which was to casually broach the subject with Reed. After all, he had been her supporter ever since she had arrived at NASA; over time, she'd come to think of him as a friend. Then she remembered Adam Treloar, the missing smallpox, and the desperate search that was secretly under way. Klein's directive had been unequivocal: she was to report *anything* suspicious. Although Megan was certain that there was a perfectly innocent explanation for Reed's behaviour, she nonetheless reached for the phone.

At six-thirty, the crew entered the clean room to suit up. Since Megan was the only woman on the mission, she had a cubicle to herself. Closing the door, she cast a critical eye over her launch/entry suit or LES. Made to measure and weighing a hefty ninety pounds, it was comprised of more than fifteen individual pieces, including a flotation device, gravity pants, and a diaper. Megan had questioned the need for the latter until Reed had explained to her exactly how much pressure was exerted on the body during the entry into orbit. It was virtually impossible for the bladder not to void.

'Looking very stylish, Megan,' Frank Stone, the mission pilot, commented when she stepped into the men's changing area.

'I like the patches best,' Megan replied.

'Tell my wife that,' Bill Karol, the commander piped up. 'She designed them.'

Each mission had a unique patch, designed either by the crew-members or their relatives. This one depicted the shuttle racing into space. Inside the round borders were stitched the names of the crew.

The crew paired off to check each other's suits, making sure that every piece was snug and secure. Then one of the mission specialists, David Carter, led the group in a brief prayer. The moment helped lift the pall created by Adam Treloar's untimely death.

With a little over three hours to liftoff, they trooped out of their quarters and into a blaze of camera lights. The walkout was the last chance for outside observers, all carefully screened and wearing special passes, to see the astronauts. Passing through the gauntlet, Megan waved briefly for the media. When she smiled, a reporter called out, 'One more! Just like that.'

The ride to the gantry in the UPS-style van took only a few minutes. Once there, the crew boarded an elevator that took them up 195 feet to the white room, the final staging area where they put on their parachutes, harnesses, communications hats, helmets, and gloves.

'How are you holding up?'

Megan turned to see Reed beside her, dressed and ready.

'Okay, I guess.'

'Preflight butterflies?'

'Is that what's going on inside my stomach?'

He leaned closer. 'Don't go spreading this, but I get them too.'

'Not *you*!'

'Especially me.'

Maybe it was the way she was looking at him that brought out his next words: 'Is anything wrong? You look like you want to ask me something.'

Megan brushed the air with her hand. 'It's the moment, I guess. You dream and train and work for it, and then one day, it's there.'

Reed patted her shoulder. 'You'll do fine. Just remember what Allenby said: we're all counting on those experiments you have scheduled.'

'Ladies and gentlemen, it's that time,' one of the prep crew called out.

Megan breathed a sigh of relief as Reed turned away. During her telephone conversation with Klein, the head of Covert-One said that he would immediately check on Reed's mysterious visitor, try to establish a solid ID, and get back to her. Since she hadn't heard from him, Megan assumed that Klein was either still checking or that he had come up with a perfectly satisfactory answer that he hadn't been able to relay to her.

'Showtime,' Reed announced. He gestured at Megan. 'After you, ma'am.'

Megan took a deep breath, crouched, and ducked through the flight-deck hatch. Making her way to the ladder, she descended to the mid-deck where, in addition to the sleep stations, food and storage lockers, and the bathroom, were three special liftoff chairs for her, Randall Wallace, another mission specialist, and David Carter, the payload specialist.

Settling herself in the take-down chair, which would be folded and stored after liftoff, Megan found herself on her back, her knees pointed at the ceiling.

'Third mission and I still can't get used to these seats,' Carter grumbled as he slipped into the chair beside hers.

'That's because you keep putting on the pounds, my man,' Wallace needled him. 'All that home cooking.'

'At least I have a home to come back to,' Carter shot back.

Tapping an imaginary cigar, Wallace did his imitation of Groucho Marx. 'Must be love.'

The banter died as the prep crew came in and strapped the astronauts into the seats.

'Mikes?'

Megan tested hers and nodded as much as she could, given the tight leeway. As her mates were strapped in, she listened to the orbiter crew going through the liftoff checklist with mission control.

Their work finished, the prep crew stepped back. Although Megan couldn't see them, she imagined how solemn their expressions were.

'Ladies and gentlemen, Godspeed. Come home safely.'

'Amen to that,' Carter muttered.

'I should have brought a good book to read,' Wallace mused. 'Megan, how are you doing there?'

'Just peachy, thank you. Now if you boys don't mind, I have my own checklist to review.'

Several hundred miles to the northeast, Jon Smith finished his second cup of coffee and checked his watch. By now, Kirov would have had enough time to settle into position in Dupont Circle. On his way out, Smith took one last look at the monitors connected to the exterior security cameras. Located on a corner lot, his house was bordered by tall trees that effectively hid it from its neighbours. The backyard was all lawn, with no bushes or shrubs where an intruder could hide. Motion sensors embedded in the stone walls of the house continually scanned the area.

If someone managed to get past the sensors, he would discover a sophisticated alarm system built into the dual-pane windows and the door locks. If these were somehow breached, pressure pads throughout the house would activate, triggering both an alarm and an incapacitating gas through the sprinkler system. Tested in federal prisons, the gas took down its targets in less than ten seconds, which was why Smith kept a gas mask in his night-table cabinet.

Although Smith believed that Beria would not attempt to kill him with a long-range shot, he thought it prudent to double-check the perimeter. Satisfied that it was secure, Smith went back through the kitchen that connected directly to the garage. He was reaching to shut off the small television perched on the counter when he saw an image that made him stop. He hesitated briefly, then smiled and reached for the phone.

◇◇◇

At twenty-one minutes to liftoff, the voice of the flight director, Harry Landon, came over the crew's headsets.

'Folks,' he said in his Oklahoma twang, 'seems we got ourselves an unexpected development.'

Even though they were aware that three hundred people at mission control were listening to every sound they made, the crew could not contain a collective groan.

'Don't tell me we're going to have to do this all over again,' Carter groused.

'What's the problem, mission control?' the pilot asked crisply.

'Did I say a problem? No. I said a *development*.' There was a brief pause. 'Olson, are you all done with your flight check?'

'Yes, sir,' Megan replied, her heart racing.

Don't tell me I screwed up. Anything but that.

'In that case, do you want to take this call?'

Involuntarily, Megan tried to sit up but got nowhere. Who could be calling her? *Oh, Jesus!*

'Harry,' she said in panicky voice. 'I don't know if that's such a good idea.'

'Now don't you fret. I'll patch it through only to you.'

The last thing she heard before the static was Carter's 'Rats!'

'Megan?'

Her pulse quickened. 'Jon? Is that you?'

'I couldn't let you leave without saying good luck.'

'Jon, how did you . . . ? I mean, how *could* you –'

'No time to explain. Are you okay? Are you ready?'

'Ready, yes. Okay? Well, I'm still getting used to sitting on a ton of liquid fuel.'

263

'I wanted to wish you well . . . Make sure you come home safe and sound.'

Megan smiled. 'I will.'

'Sorry, folks,' Landon broke in. 'Time's up.'

'Thanks, Harry,' Megan said.

'I'm going to put you back in the loop. Ready?'

'Go ahead.'

Megan steeled herself for some gentle ribbing, which never materialized. In the fifteen minutes to countdown, the rest of the crew were busy exchanging instructions and details. Closing her eyes, she whispered a few words from the Twenty-fourth Psalm. She had barely finished when the shuttle shifted a little. An instant later, the ignition procedure for the solid boosters kicked in and a loud, low rumble enveloped the craft.

Through the chatter of ground control double-checking liftoff, Megan heard: 'Houston, we have *Discovery* lift-off!'

As the external tank fed the shuttle's main engines, Megan felt as though she were strapped to a bone-jarring roller coaster – except that there was no stopping this ride. Two minutes and six seconds after liftoff, the solid boosters separated from the orbiter, falling away to the ocean, where they would be retrieved. Powered by the fuel from the external tank that fed her main engines, *Discovery* struggled to break free of gravity. The higher and faster she ascended, the closer the crew got to the maximum 3-G pressure. Megan had been warned that it would be like having a gorilla strapped to your chest.

Wrong. More like an elephant.

Six minutes later, at an altitude of 184 miles, the main engines stopped firing. Its job done, the external fuel tank separated and fell away. Megan was amazed by the sudden silence and by how smooth the ride had suddenly become. Turning her head, she understood why: beyond the sliver of a window in her line of sight were the stars. She and *Discovery* were in orbit.

21

The preceding evening, Ivan Beria had rendezvoused with the driver of the Lincoln outside the Metro stop at Q Street and Connecticut Avenue. The driver had further information and instructions for Beria, who studied them as the car wended its way out of the city towards Bethesda.

The driver was necessary because Beria could not afford to be seen on the streets – and because he had only the most rudimentary driving skills. A killer who could carve a man up in seconds, he was lost in and confused by the traffic streaming in and out of the city. In an emergency, he could not be sure of executing an escape. There was one other advantage to the car besides transport: it was perfect for surveillance. Washington was filled with executive sedans. This one would not look out of place in a neighbourhood such as Bethesda.

Approaching Smith's house, the driver slowed as though searching for a particular number. Beria got a good look at the rambling ranch-style house, set well back from the street. He noted the trees that ran along the property line and that, he surmised, continued around the back. There were lights in the windows but no shadows indicating movement.

'Come around again,' Beria told the driver.

Next time, Beria looked closely at the other houses on the block. Most had toys and bicycles on the front lawn, a basketball hoop over the garage door, a small powerboat perched on a trailer chocked in the driveway. By contrast, Smith's house looked vacant, brooding. It was, Beria thought, the house of a man who lives alone and prefers it that way, whose work demands solitude and secrecy. Such a house would have a far more sophisticated – and deadly – warning system than anything advertised by the security company patches on the doors of the other homes.

'I have seen enough,' he told the driver. 'We will come back tomorrow morning.'

Now, a few minutes after nine o'clock in the next morning, Beria was in the backseat of the Lincoln as it idled at the far corner of Smith's street. The driver was standing outside, smoking. To passing joggers and dog walkers, he appeared to be waiting for a client.

In the cool stillness of the interior, Beria reviewed all the information on Smith. His principal wanted the American doctor out of the way quickly. But there were obstacles. Smith did not go to an office. His home appeared to have good security. Therefore, the execution would have to be done out in the open, wherever an opportunity presented itself. Another problem was the unpredictability of Smith's movements once he was outside his home. He had no set schedule, so the principal could not say where he would be at any given time. This meant that Beria had to follow Smith as closely as possible and look for an opening. Working in his favour was the fact that the American did not have an escort, did not – as far as the principal knew – carry a weapon. Most important, he had no inkling that he was in any kind of danger. Beria checked his watch; forty-five minutes had elapsed since he'd arrived.

The Lincoln listed as the driver got back behind the wheel. 'Smith's coming out.'

267

Beria looked through the windshield down the street where a navy blue sedan was backing out of a garage. According to the principal, this was Smith's vehicle.

'And we begin,' Beria said softly.

As Smith drove into the city, he constantly checked his mirrors. After a few miles he tagged the black Lincoln that changed lanes whenever he did. He called Kirov on the cell.

'It's the Lincoln from the airport. On my tail. I think Beria's nibbling.'

'I'm ready,' Kirov assured him.

Breaking for a light, Smith checked his rearview. The Lincoln was still three cars back.

Once in the city, Smith drove as fast as traffic permitted, changing lanes, leaning on his horn. He hoped Beria would buy the image of a man late for an important appointment, a man preoccupied, his guard down, easy prey. He wanted the assassin to focus on him to the exclusion of everything and everyone else. That way, he would never see Kirov coming.

He's in a hurry, Beria thought. *Why?*

'He's headed for Dupont Circle,' the driver said, keeping his eyes on the traffic.

Beria frowned. His apartment was in that area. Could Smith have already discovered it? Was that his destination?

The sedan picked up speed on Connecticut Avenue, turned left on R Street, and then right on Twenty-first Street.

Where's he going?

The sedan slowed as Smith approached the top of the triangle at S Street. Beria watched him park the car in a lot, then cross Twenty-first Street. This area, with its Eastern European restaurants and shops, was familiar to him. Since arriving in Washington, it was the only place he had ventured into where he felt comfortable.

He's here to try to pick up the scent. Or maybe someone saw my picture.

Beria had seen the police composite on the news. He thought it a poor rendering, nothing like him at all. But maybe someone had seen him in the area, even though Beria rarely left his apartment until after dark.

No. If he suspects I'm here, he would not have come alone. He's not sure. He's guessing.

'Stay where I can find you,' Beria told the driver.

The driver pointed to a restaurant called Dunn's River Falls. 'I'll be in the lot.'

Stepping out of the car, Beria trotted across the street in time to see Smith duck under an archway bordered by a bar and a poster shop. Now he knew exactly where his quarry was headed: the small quadrangle between Twenty-first Street and Florida Avenue. He thought it quite clever of Smith to hunt him in a place that Beria might naturally gravitate to. But it was also a location Beria knew he could control.

Beria disappeared under the arch, then stepped under the awning of a Macedonian coffee shop. At one of the tables, a group of old men were playing dominoes; the soft crooning of a native folk song crackled over indoor-outdoor speakers. There was Smith, walking towards the fountain in the centre of the quadrangle. Not so quick now, looking around as though expecting someone. Beria thought he could smell Smith's discomfort, the unease of someone who realizes that he's out of place. His hand dipped into his jacket pocket, fingers curling around the cork handle of his spring-loaded stiletto.

269

Thirty paces ahead, Smith felt his pager vibrate against his kidney. Kirov was signalling that Beria was in the zone, within fifty feet of Smith. Slowing his pace even more, Smith drifted across the front of a stall with rugs draped over clotheslines. Stopping, he checked his watch, then looked around as though searching for someone in particular. Given the hour, there were customers about – mostly people on their way to work or to open their shops, stopping to get a coffee and pastry. Smith thought Beria would accept that this was a logical time to meet an informer who might be passing through.

The pager vibrated again – twice. Beria was within twenty-five feet and closing. Smith felt a cold tingle dance along his spine as he moved past the carpet display. Still looking around, he saw neither Beria nor Kirov. Then he heard soft footfalls behind him.

From his vantage point in the doorway of a closed dry goods store, Kirov had picked up Beria the instant he'd stepped through the arch. Now he approached him on the diagonal, his specially designed sneakers making his footsteps soundless.

Don't look around, Jon. Don't bolt. Trust me.

Beria was now less than a dozen feet behind Smith, closing fast. As his hand came out of his pocket, Kirov caught a glimpse of the cork handle and a flash of stainless steel as Beria depressed the mechanism that causes the blade to spring into place.

Kirov carried his ordinary-looking black umbrella. It swung lightly in his grip as he closed the distance to Beria. At the precise moment when the assassin took another step, his back leg lifted slightly, calf raised, Kirov brought the umbrella down. The razor-sharp tip sheared the fabric of Beria's pant leg, caught flesh, and cut down a quarter inch. Beria whirled around, stiletto glinting in the pale sunlight. But Kirov was already two steps away. Beria caught sight of him and his eyes widened in shock. The face from Moscow! The Russian general from the train station!

Beria took a step towards Kirov but never reached him. His right leg faltered and gave way. The stiletto fell from his grip as he pitched forward. The drug that had coated the umbrella tip was singing through his veins, blurring his vision, turning his muscles to putty.

Glassy-eyed, Beria was faintly aware of being propped up by a pair of strong arms. Kirov was holding him, smiling, talking in Serb, telling him what a bad boy he'd been and how he'd been looking for him everywhere. Beria opened his mouth but could only gurgle. Now Kirov was drawing him close, whispering something. He felt Kirov's lips brush his cheek, then a shout, in Serb, from someone insulting his manhood.

'Come on, lover,' Kirov said softly. 'Let's get you out of here before this turns nasty.'

Beria twisted around and saw the old men making rude gestures at him. Now Smith was beside him, propping him up by his other shoulder. Beria tried to move his feet but found that he could only drag them. His head lolled and he saw the underbelly of the arch. Outside the quadrangle, the roar of traffic was like that of a giant waterfall. Kirov was sliding open the door to a blue van, bringing out a collapsible wheelchair. Hands on his shoulders forced him to sit. Leather straps snaked around his wrists and ankles. He heard the whine of an electric motor and realized that the wheelchair had been rolled onto a ramp that was being raised. Then Kirov was pushing the chair into the van, locking the wheels. Suddenly everything disappeared except for the Russian's cold, blue eyes.

'You don't know how lucky you are, you murdering bastard!'

After that, he heard nothing at all.

The back porch of Peter Howell's hideaway on the Chesapeake shore looked out on a still pond fed by a meandering stream. It was early evening, almost eight hours since Beria had been taken. The low sun warming his face, Smith sat back and watched a pair of hawks circling for prey. Behind him, he heard Kirov's heels fall on the tongue-and-groove boards.

Smith had no idea who really owned this rustic retreat, but as Peter Howell had told him in Venice, it was both very private and well equipped. Clean and comfortable, the cabin had a larder stocked with dry goods. Under the floorboards in the main room, in a small oubliette, was a cache of arms, medicines, and other essentials, indicating that the owner was undoubtedly in Howell's line of work. Out back, in what looked like a large toolshed, was something else.

'It's time, General.'

'He should be left a little while longer, Jon. We don't want to do this again.'

'I read the same medical literature you do. Most men break after six hours.'

'Beria isn't most men.'

Smith walked across the porch and leaned on the railing. From the moment he and Kirov had conceived the operation, they had known that, when taken, Beria would not talk. Not without inducements. It wouldn't be anything so primitive as electroshock or rubber truncheons. There were sophisticated chemicals that, in certain combinations, were very effective and reliable.

272

But they had drawbacks. One could never be sure if the recipient might have an unexpected reaction, go into shock, or worse. Such a risk could not be taken with Beria. He had to be broken cleanly, completely, and above all, safely.

Smith did not deceive himself. Whether it was electricity, chemicals, or anything else, it all amounted to torture. The idea that he had to sanction its use sickened him, both as a human being and as a physician. He'd told himself over and over again that in this case, such tactics were justified. What Beria was a party to could expose millions to a horrible death. It was vital to get at the information in his head.

'Let's go,' said Smith.

Ivan Beria was surrounded by white. Even if he kept his eyes closed, which was most of the time, he saw white.

When he had regained consciousness, he discovered that he was standing in a deep, cylindrical tube, a kind of silo. About fifteen feet high, its walls were perfectly smooth, coated with plaster that had been painted and then finished with something to make it shine. High beyond his reach were two big flood lamps that burned continuously. There was a total absence of darkness, not even a hint of shadows.

At first, Beria thought that it was some makeshift holding cell. The thought had reassured him. He'd had brief experiences with jail cells. But then he discovered that the diameter of the silo was barely large enough to accommodate his shoulders. He could lean a few inches in any direction, but he could not sit down.

After a while, he thought he heard a faint hum, like

a distant radio signal. As the hours passed, the signal seemed to get stronger and the walls whiter. Then they started to close in on him. That was the first time Beria had closed his eyes, briefly. When he opened them, the whiteness was even starker, if such a thing were possible. Now he dared not open his eyes at all. The hum had crescendoed into a roar and beyond it, Beria heard something else, something that might have been a human voice. He had no idea that he was screaming.

Without warning, he staggered back, falling through a concealed door that Kirov had opened. Grabbing Beria's arm, he yanked the assassin out of the silo and immediately slipped a black hood over his head.

'Everything's going to be all right,' Kirov whispered in Serb. 'I'm going to take away the pain, all of it. You'll have some water, then you can talk to me.'

Suddenly, violently, Beria threw his arms around Kirov, holding him as a drowning man would a piece of driftwood. All the while Kirov continued to talk to him and still him, until Beria took his first halting steps.

Smith was shocked by Beria's appearance – not because he was scared or hurt, just the opposite: he looked exactly as he had the last time Smith had seen him.

But there were differences. Beria's eyes were glassy and washed out, like those of day-old fish on ice. His voice was a monotone, with no timbre or texture to it. When he spoke, it was as though he'd been hypnotized.

The three of them sat on the porch around a little table with a small running tape recorder. Beria sipped water from a plastic cup. Next to him, Kirov watched his every move. In his lap, covered by a cloth, was a gun, the barrel pointed at Beria's shoulder.

'Who hired you to kill the Russian guard?' Smith asked softly.

'A man from Zurich.'

'You went to Zurich?'

'No. We spoke on the telephone. Only the telephone.'

'Did he tell you his name?'

'He called himself Gerd.'

'How did Gerd pay you?'

'Money was deposited into an account at the Offenbach Bank. It was handled by Herr Weizsel.'

Weizsel! The name Peter Howell had gotten out of the corrupt Italian policeman, Dionetti . . .

'Herr Weizsel . . . Did you meet him?' Smith asked softly.

'Yes. Several times.'

'And Gerd?'

'Never.'

Smith glanced at Kirov, who nodded, indicating that he believed Beria was telling the truth. Smith agreed. He had expected that Beria would have worked through cutouts. Swiss bankers were some of the best frontmen in the business.

'Do you know what it was you took from the Russian guard?' Smith continued.

'Germs.'

Smith closed his eyes. *Germs . . .*

'Do you know the name of the man you passed the germs to at the Moscow airport?'

'I think it was David. It wasn't his real name.'

'Did you know that you would have to kill him?'

'Yes.'

'Did Gerd tell you to do this?'

'Yes.'

'Did Gerd ever mention any Americans? Were you ever contacted directly by any Americans?'

'Only my driver. But I don't know his name.'

'Did he ever talk to you about Gerd or anyone else?'

'No.'

Smith paused, trying to keep his frustration in check. Whoever was running this operation had constructed seemingly impenetrable firewalls between themselves and the assassin.

'Ivan, I don't want you to listen to this.'

'All right.' Beria looked away, his expression vacant.

'Jon, he's got nothing left to give up,' Kirov said. 'We might be able to get a few more details, for what they're worth.' Kirov spread out his hands. 'What about the Lincoln?'

'It's a NASA fleet vehicle. Dozens of drivers use it. Klein's still running down the particulars.' He paused. 'We should have snatched the driver. By now, he's reported that Beria's missing. The controllers will assume the obvious. They'll be much more careful from here on in.'

'We talked about that,' Kirov reminded him. 'It would have been impossible for just the two of us to take down Beria and the driver. We would have needed reinforcements.'

'Beria gave us two names: the Offenbach Bank and this Herr Weizsel,' Smith said, and told Kirov about the Venice connection.

The Russian looked up. 'Weizsel would have had to deal with Gerd. He would have talked to him, maybe even met him . . .'

Smith completed the thought: 'So he would know Gerd's real name, wouldn't he?'

22

When Ivan Beria failed to appear within the allotted time, the driver of the Lincoln walked away from the car. In that neighbourhood, chances were good that it would be stolen within the next few hours. After that, it would either be professionally stripped in a chop shop or dismembered by petty thieves. Either way, it would disappear.

Even if the authorities somehow got to it first, the car would yield few clues. The driver always wore gloves; there would be few if any forensics to link him to the car. Nor did his name appear on any NASA paperwork. The car had been checked out in the name of a driver currently working in Pasadena, California.

At the Metro stop on Connecticut Avenue and Q Street, the driver called his principal. Quietly, he explained what had happened and suggested that the assassin had been taken. The party on the other end instructed the driver to go immediately to Dulles Airport. In a designated locker he would find two overnight bags, one with money and identity papers, the other with a change of clothes. There would also be a ticket for Cancún, Mexico, where he was to stay until further notice.

As soon as he hung up with the driver, Anthony Price called Dr Karl Bauer, who had returned to Hawaii after delivering the altered smallpox sample to Dylan Reed at Cape Canaveral.

'The problem you sent your boy to fix?' he said

abruptly. 'Now it's worse than before.' After giving Bauer the scant details, he added: 'If Beria's been taken, then you can bet it's Smith who has him. In the end, Beria will talk – if he hasn't already.'

'If he does, what of it?' Bauer demanded. 'He never saw any of us. He doesn't know our names. Treloar is dead. The trail stops with him.'

'The trail has to stop with Beria!' Price snapped. 'He needs to be dealt with.'

'While he's in Smith's custody?' Bauer replied sarcastically. 'Pray tell me how you propose getting to him.'

Price hesitated. Smith wouldn't keep Beria in a federal prison or holding cell. He'd squirrel him away where no one could find him.

'Then we have to move up the schedule,' he said. 'Create a diversion.'

'Doing so would endanger Reed and the entire project.'

'*Not* doing it endangers us! Listen to me, Karl. Reed was going to run the experiment the day after tomorrow. There's no reason why he can't run it now.'

'All the experiments are on a fixed schedule,' Bauer replied. 'It might look suspicious if Reed changes the sequence.'

'Given the consequences, a change in sequence will be the last thing anyone thinks about. The key is to get the mutation down as quickly as possible – and cover our butts.'

There was silence on the other end of the line. Price held his breath, wondering if the old scientist would play along.

'Very well,' Bauer said at last. 'I will contact Reed and tell him to move up the schedule.'

'Tell him to work as fast as possible.'

'As fast as is *prudent*.'

Price was at the end of his tether. 'Don't split hairs on me, Karl. Just tell him to get on with it.'

Karl Bauer stared at the now-silent phone. He thought that Anthony Price was one of those bureaucrats who become infected with a Napoleon complex, intoxicated with their seemingly limitless power.

Leaving his office, Bauer took the elevator to the sub-basement. This was the heart of his communications centre, a room the size of an air traffic control centre where technicians, using three private satellites, kept their fingertips on the electronic pulse of the Bauer-Zermatt empire. There was also a fourth satellite, which, until now, had remained inactive. Crossing the room, Bauer entered his private chamber and locked himself in. He seated himself at the console, activated the high-definition screen, and began typing on the keyboard. The satellite, built by the Chinese in Xianpao, launched by the French out of New Guyana, sprang to life. As hardware went, it was a relatively unsophisticated piece of equipment, but then again, it had only one purpose and a very short life span. When its job was done, an explosive charge would destroy any evidence that it had ever existed.

Bauer piggybacked on the NASA frequency, prepared his message for the microburst transmission, and opened the circuits. In nano-seconds, the message was beamed to the satellite, which in turn relayed it to the shuttle. Its mission accomplished, the satellite immediately went dormant. Even if the burst was inadvertently noticed, it would be almost impossible to fix not only its origin but also the relay point. With the satellite silent, it would appear that the burst had come from a black hole in space.

Sitting back in his chair, Bauer steepled his fingers.

Of course there would be no direct reply from the shuttle. The only way Bauer would be sure that his transmission was received would be to tap into the shuttle-NASA transmissions. When he heard Reed's voice, he would know.

Traveling at 17,500 miles per hour at an altitude of 202 miles, *Discovery* was on its fourth orbit around the earth. Stowing away her temporary seat, Megan Olson worked her way out of her launch/entry suit and into comfortable overalls studded with Velcro-lined pockets. She noted that her face and upper body were puffy. Virtually every wrinkle had disappeared and her waistline had shrunk a good two inches. This occurred because there was little gravity to pull down blood and bodily fluids. After four to six hours, the excess fluids would be removed through the kidneys.

With the help of her teammates, Carter and Wallace, Megan activated the shuttle's power, air conditioning, lights, and communications. The payload bay doors were opened to release the heat built up by the firing of the solid rocket booster and main engines during liftoff. They would stay open for the duration of the mission and help regulate the temperature inside the orbiter.

As she worked, Megan listened to the chatter among the commander, Bill Karol, the pilot, Frank Stone, and mission control. It was all routine give-and-take about the shuttle's status, speed, and position – until she heard Karol's puzzled voice.

'Dylan, are you copying this?'

'Roger that. What's up?'

'Something just came in over the circuits for you. But there was no mission-control input.'

Megan heard Reed chuckle. 'Probably one of my lab guys slipped on a headset. What's the message?'

'Apparently there's been a change in the order of your experiments. Megan's been bumped to number four. You take the opening slot.'

'Hey, that's not fair,' Megan spoke up.

'Been listening in, have you?' Reed said. 'Don't worry about it, Megan. You'll make your bones.'

'I know. But why the change?'

'I'm checking the schedule right now.'

'I'm on my way up.'

Drifting in microgravity, Megan manoeuvred her way up the ladder to the flight deck. Reed was suspended like a diver in neutral buoyancy behind the pilot and the commander, checking his log.

Glancing up, he remarked, 'You look ten years younger.'

'Please, five years. And I feel bloated. What's up?'

Reed passed her the log. 'It's a last-minute schedule change I forgot to mention. I'm going to run the critter tests first and get them out of the way. Then you can have the place all to yourself and your Legionnaires' disease microbes.'

'I was really hoping to get into it first thing,' Megan replied.

'Yeah, I know. First trip. All the excitement. But if I were you, I'd grab some sack time while I slave over a hot petri dish.'

'Would you like a hand with the tests?'

'Appreciate the thought, but no thanks.' Reed took back the log. 'Well, I'd better go open up the Factory.'

The Factory was the crew's nickname for the Spacelab.

On the monitor, Megan watched Reed manoeuvre his way to the mid-deck, then float into the tunnel that connected to the Spacelab. It never failed to amaze her that only the curved walls of the tunnel and its outer skin separated Reed from the frozen waste of space.

Megan turned to Bill Karol. 'Who sent that transmission?'

Karol checked his screen. 'There's no name attached, just a number.'

Steadying herself, Megan read over his shoulder. The six-digit number was familiar but she couldn't grasp why.

'Someone was in a hurry,' Stone, the pilot, said laconically. 'Probably a last-minute snafu in the ground lab.'

'But you said this didn't come through mission control,' Megan said.

'What I meant was that there wasn't any of the usual chatter. But hell, Megan, who else could have sent it?'

As the two men returned to their duties, Megan backed away. Something was not right. A moment ago she'd remembered where she'd seen that number before. It was Dylan Reed's NASA ID. How could he possibly have sent a message to himself?

As soon as Dylan Reed entered the Spacelab, he overrode the circuits that controlled the cameras' recording activity at the Biorack. Pulling back the Velcro strap on one of his pants pockets, he removed the stubby, titanium cylinder that Bauer had given him less than twenty-four hours ago. Although the tube had been carefully sealed, Reed understood that he was dealing with a 'hot' product that had been left unrefrigerated for too long. He opened the freezer and slipped the tube next to the maize cells and nematode worm specimens, then reset the cameras.

Relieved that the variola was secure, Reed began to

prepare the Biorack for the procedures he would carry out. At the same time, he tried to fathom what had happened back on earth to cause Bauer to move up the schedule so dramatically. The last he'd heard, Beria had been set in motion to remove Smith. Since Bauer had been able to transmit his message, and there had been no emergency relays from ground control indicating any unusual developments, the logical conclusion was that Beria had run into a problem – serious enough for Bauer to act.

Reed knew that Bauer would not contact him again unless it was absolutely necessary. The pilot and the flight commander would not be suspicious about one message lacking the usual NASA double-speak; a second would be challenged and investigated. Since at the moment Reed had no way of contacting Bauer, he had to rely on blind faith and finish the work the old Swiss had begun.

Reed would have preferred to be rested for his task. As it was, he would have to ignore the liftoff fatigue and pace himself for the gruelling session ahead. As he slipped his feet into the restraints embedded in the floor in front of the Biorack, he estimated the amount of time the job would take. If his calculations were right, the rest of the crew would be having their dinner just as he was finishing up. They would all be in one place, just as he wanted.

Nathaniel Klein's eyes were as hard and flat as river rock. Sitting in Rosebud's living room, he listened without comment as Smith presented his account of how Beria had been taken and the details of the subsequent interrogation.

'A known killer is connected to a Swiss bank and one of its principal officers,' he murmured.

Smith indicated the cassette on the coffee table. 'Beria gave up a lot more than that. Some of the top people in Russia and Eastern Europe have had him on their payrolls. Events that seemed to make no sense to us can all be traced back to assassinations and blackmail that Beria was a party to.'

Klein grunted. 'Fine. We have a lot of dirt and one day it might be useful. But there won't be a "one day" unless we find the smallpox! Where are Beria and Kirov right now?'

'At a secure location. Beria's heavily sedated. Kirov's watching him. The general forwarded a request: he'd like to bring Beria back to Moscow – quietly – as soon as possible.'

'We can certainly arrange that – as long as you're sure he has nothing left to tell us.'

'I'm sure, sir.'

'In that case, I'll arrange transport at Andrews.'

Klein rose and paced in front of the picture window. 'Unfortunately, taking Beria didn't solve *our* problem. You know how notorious the Swiss are about keeping their financial dealings secret. The president might be able to get them to open up the Offenbach Bank without disclosing why we need their cooperation, but it's a long shot.'

'This can't be a government-to-government operation, sir,' Smith said quietly. 'We don't have the time, and like you, I suspect that the Swiss would stonewall us.' He paused. 'But Herr Weizsel might be more forthcoming. I have Peter Howell standing by in Venice.'

Klein glanced at Smith and understood what it was he was really talking about. He took a moment to weigh the risks.

'All right,' he said at last. 'But make sure that he

understands there can't be any exposure or comebacks.'

Smith went into the small room that had become Klein's nerve centre at Camp David and made the call.

'Peter, Zurich is a go.'

'I thought it might be,' the Englishman replied. 'I'm booked on the early evening flight.'

'Peter, I got to Beria. He gave up Weizsel but that's it. I need to know the name of the paymaster.'

'If Weizsel knows, so will you. I'll talk to you from Zurich, Jon.'

'Good. Now, do you happen to have a tape recorder handy? I have something that might be useful . . .'

Smith walked back into the living room and told Klein that Peter Howell was on his way to Switzerland. 'Has there been any word on the Lincoln, sir?'

Klein shook his head. 'As soon as you called to say that you had Beria, I reached out to a contact in the D.C. metropolitan police force. He put the car on the hot sheets, making it look like it had been involved in a legitimate hit-and-run. Nothing so far. And nothing on the driver either.' He paused. 'At first I thought that there was a logical explanation for the NASA sticker on the car. Now . . .'

'Treloar was NASA,' Smith said. 'Why wouldn't he have had a car waiting to pick him up at Dulles? He wasn't expecting to be followed or chased.'

'But then that same vehicle trailed *you*, didn't it?' He looked at Smith carefully. 'And something else that's connected to NASA. Dr Dylan Reed had a late-night visit from an individual we haven't been able to identify.'

Smith glanced at Klein sharply. He knew that Klein lived in a world where secrets were shared only when absolutely necessary. Now the head of Covert-One was admitting that he had a source right in the heart of NASA.

'Megan Olson,' Smith said. 'At this point, with the launch so close, it can't be anyone else. You should have told me, sir.'

'There was no need for you to know about Megan,' Klein replied. 'By the same token, she doesn't know about you.'

'Why tell me now?'

'Because we still don't have any lead on the smallpox. You'll recall that I believed it was in the D.C. area because that's where Treloar flew in.'

'Right. From London, he could have gone anywhere.'

'Now I'm thinking that perhaps there's a connection between Treloar and Reed.'

'Is that why Megan is down there, to watch Reed?' Smith demanded.

'Why don't you tell me if there's anything *you* know about Reed that might indicate he could be involved in something like this.'

Smith shook his head. 'I don't know Reed all that well. But his reputation at USAMRIID was sterling. Do you want me to go back and see what I can find?'

'No time,' Klein replied. 'I need you for something else. If we don't solve this mystery, there'll be plenty of time to investigate Reed when the shuttle comes home.'

Klein picked up two dossiers. 'These are the files on the two soldiers Howell encountered at Palermo.'

'They look pretty thin, sir,' Smith observed.

'Don't they? The records have been sanitized. Dates, locations, assignments, chain of command – a lot unaccounted for. And the phone number Nichols gave up doesn't exist.'

'Sir?'

'Not officially. Jon, I haven't done more because I don't know what we're dealing with here. But we must find out where this military thread leads. I want you to do exactly what you did in Houston: touch the web and see what kind of spider crawls out.'

Three hours after leaving Venice, Peter Howell checked into Zurich's Dolder Grand Hotel.

'Do you have any messages for me?' he asked the front desk clerk.

Howell was handed a thick vellum envelope. Opening it, he found a single sheet of scented notepaper with an address written on it. Although the message was unsigned, Howell knew its author – an octogenarian grande dame who had been involved in espionage ever since World War II.

How on earth can Weizsel afford to dine at Swan's Way on a banker's salary? Howell wondered, and thought it might be a good idea to find out.

After changing into a business suit, Howell took a taxi into the heart of the city's financial district. By now it was eight o'clock and the area was deserted except for several brightly lighted storefronts. One of them had a golden swan perched over the doorway.

The interior was pretty much what Howell had expected: upscale rathskeller with beamed ceilings, stucco, and heavy furniture. The waiters were in black tie, the silver was heavy and gleaming, and the maître d' seemed puzzled why this tourist thought he could dine at his establishment without a reservation.

'I'm Herr Weizsel's guest,' Howell told him.

'Ah, Herr Weizsel . . . you are early, sir. Herr Weizsel's

table is prepared for nine o'clock. Please have a seat in the lounge, or the bar, if you prefer. I will direct him to you.'

Howell drifted off into the lounge where, a few minutes later, he was involved in an animated conversation with a young woman whose bosoms threatened to overflow the confines of her evening dress. Nonetheless, he still managed to spot the maître d' talking to a young man, pointing him out.

'Should I know you?'

Howell glanced over his shoulder at a tall, thin man with swept-back hair and eyes so dark they appeared black. He guessed that Herr Weizsel was in his late thirties, spent a small fortune on his clothes and stylist, and looked down at most of the world with undisguised contempt.

'Peter Howell,' he said.

'An Englishman . . . Do you have business with the Offenbach Bank?'

'I have business with you.'

Weizsel blinked rapidly. 'There must be some mistake. I have never heard of you.'

'But you've heard of Ivan Beria, haven't you, old son?'

Howell had his hand on Weizsel's arm, just above the elbow. Weizsel's mouth worked furiously as Howell pressed down on a nerve.

'There's a nice, quiet table in the corner. Why don't we have a drink?'

Howell steered the banker into the corner of a banquette and slipped in beside him, effectively trapping Weizsel.

'You can't do this!' Weizsel gasped, rubbing his elbow. 'We have laws –'

'I'm not here about your laws,' Howell cut him off. 'We're interested in one of your clients.'

'I can't discuss confidential matters!'

'But the name Beria rang a bell, didn't it? You service his account. I don't want the money. All we need to know is who sends it in.'

Weizsel glanced around, looking at the growing crowd at the bar. He strained to catch the maître d's eye.

'Don't bother,' Howell told him. 'I gave him money not to disturb us.'

'You are a criminal!' Weizsel declared. 'You are holding me against my will. Even if I give you what you want, you will never leave –'

Howell placed a small recorder on the table. Plugging in an earpiece, he handed it to Weizsel. 'Listen.'

The banker did as he was told. After a moment, his eyes widened in disbelief. Yanking out the earpiece, he flung it across the table. Peter Howell thought that it had been farsighted of Jon Smith to provide that particular portion of the interrogation where Beria mentioned Weizsel.

'So my name is spoken. What of it? Who is this man?'

'You recognized his voice, didn't you?' Howell said softly.

Weizsel fidgeted. 'Perhaps.'

'And perhaps you remember it belonging to someone called Ivan Beria.'

'What if I do?'

Howell leaned in close. 'Beria is an assassin. He works for the Russians. How much Russian money do you handle, Herr Weizsel?'

The banker's silence was telling.

'I thought so,' Howell continued. 'So let me tell you

what will happen if you *don't* cooperate. I will make sure the Russians learn that you were quite forthcoming when it came to their money – where it comes from, how and when it's moved, all those little details they thought were safe because, after all, they paid you handsomely for your discretion.'

Howell paused to let the import of his words sink in. 'Now,' he picked up, 'once the Russians know this, they will be upset – understandably so. Explanations will be demanded. Excuses will not be tolerated. And once trust has been broken, my dear Weizsel, you are finished. You've dealt with enough Russians to know that they never forget, never forgive. They'll want revenge, and your precious Swiss laws and police won't stand in their way. Am I making myself clear?'

Weizsel felt his stomach sour. The Englishman was right: the Russians were barbarians, swaggering about Zurich, flaunting their newfound wealth. And every banker wanted a piece of their booty. No questions were asked. Demands made became demands satisfied. The Russians groused about the fees, but in the end they paid. They also made it very clear to brokers like Weizsel that they could not run, could never hide, if they broke trust. The Englishman was the kind of man who could make it seem that Weizsel had betrayed his clients. And nothing the banker could say or do would change the Russians' minds once they were convinced of his treachery.

'What was the name again?' Weizsel asked almost inaudibly.

'Ivan Beria,' Howell replied. 'Who feeds him his money?'

23

Five hours had elapsed since Dylan Reed had sequestered himself in the Spacelab. During this time, he had monitored the crew's movements and conversations via his headset. Twice, Megan Olson had asked if he needed some help; another time she wanted to know how much longer he would be. She was eager to start her own experiments.

She wouldn't be so anxious if she knew what was going on in here, Reed thought grimly.

Politely but firmly he told Megan that she and the others would have to wait until he was finished.

Because Reed had to monitor the crew, the work was taking much longer than he had hoped it would. Another distraction was the almost nonstop conversation between the crew and mission control. Nonetheless, Reed worked as quickly as he could, pausing only to rest his hands, which, encased in the long rubber gloves attached to the box, tended to cramp.

The enormity of what he was doing almost overwhelmed him. Staring through the microscope, he gazed upon a world of smallpox that had never been seen before – except by its creator, Karl Bauer. In his Hawaii laboratory, the Swiss scientist had managed to take the variola virus and reengineer it so that it tripled in size. He was then able to open it up so that it would be receptive to even further growth. But Bauer had been constrained by earth's gravity; Reed was not.

The genesis of Bauer's work could be traced back to one of the first shuttle missions. Astronauts had discovered a two-day-old bag of sandwiches that they had forgotten to eat. The food was stored in a sealed plastic bag that was floating like a beach ball. Opening the bag, the crew thought the sandwiches would be fine – until one member pointed out that the only way the bag could float was because the bacteria in the food had produced enough gas to make the bag puff up.

This impromptu observation gave scientists incontrovertible proof that bacteria grow faster and bigger in a microgravity environment.

When Karl Bauer read the NASA report on the phenomenon, he immediately concluded that what was true for bacteria might also apply to viruses. The initial research proved heady, but hampered by gravity, Bauer was unable to reach a definitive conclusion. Years would pass until he found Reed and a way to conduct the final experiments in space.

Now what Reed observed was a variola ten times as large and potent as anything on earth. Its protein bubbles, which on earth would burst at a certain size, retained their integrity and lethal capacity. As a battlefield weapon, this strain would have no equal. Reed shuddered when he imagined how quickly entire populations would be decimated if this variant was released through an air-burst bomb. The variola would speed its way from the respiratory tract to the lumph nodes, then spread to the spleen, bone marrow, and other lymphatic organs. Eventually it would make its way to the small blood vessels in the skin. With a normal strain of smallpox, such a process would take five to ten days. Reed estimated that the incubation and infection period would now be measured in minutes.

The body would simply have no chance to rally any defence.

Reed withdrew his hands from the Glovebox, wiped them, and took a moment to compose himself. Then he activated his throat mike.

'Hey, folks. I'm just about done here. Is it dinnertime yet?'

'We were just about to call you,' Stone replied. 'Everyone's ordered steak and eggs.'

Reed managed to laugh. 'Wait until you see what it looks like.' He paused. 'I'd like everybody in the mess so I can go over the schedule.'

'Roger that. We'll save you some of that steak. See you in a little while.'

Reed closed his eyes and willed himself to stay calm. He switched off his mike but not his earpiece. He did not want to hear the next sounds the crew would make. They would be nothing human. But to gauge how fast the variola acted, he had no choice but to listen.

Returning to the Biorack, he once again donned the rubber gloves and carefully filled the small tube with the altered variola. Securing the tube, he removed it from the Glovebox through a small air lock and placed it in the freezer.

Using the footholds, he moved to the back of the lab and opened a locker. Inside was a fully contained extravehicular mobility unit, or EMU, the suit used on space walks. After slipping inside it, Reed was reaching for his helmet when he caught his reflection in the visor. He hesitated as the faces of his fellow crew members floated in the coated Plexiglas, people he had worked and trained with for months, even years, people whom he genuinely liked. But not enough to show them compassion or mercy.

In that reflection, Reed also saw the faces of his two brothers, killed during a terrorist attack on the U.S. embassy in Nairobi, and that of his sister, a Peace Corps volunteer, abducted, tortured and finally murdered in the Sudan. What Reed was doing was not for the greater glory of science, and certainly not for public recognition or acclaim. This new strain would never see the light of day – unless circumstances dictated that it be unleashed. General Richardson and Anthony Price were the kind of men who did not tolerate the kind of losses Reed had suffered. To them, payback wasn't just a few cruise missiles lobbed into some tents or bunkers, but a swift and total devastation by an invisible, unstoppable army. By helping build this army, Reed believed he was laying a marker at the graves of his kin, keeping a promise made long ago that their sacrifices would never be forgotten.

Securing his helmet, Reed made his way back to the Biorack. He plugged his air-supply hose into an independent feed that crew members used during space walks. Calmly and deliberately he broke the seal on the Glovebox. Within seconds, the dried variola particles in the dish began forming spores as tiny as dust particles. Inexorably they found their way to the rent on the Glovebox seals and outside. Reed stared in fascination as spores seemed to hang there. For an instant, he was seized by the irrational thought that they might attack him. Instead, the circulation stream caught them and they swirled like a minuscule comet into the connecting tube linking the Spacelab to the main body of the orbiter.

'Are you coming, Megan?' Carter asked as the two of them completed their report to mission control.

Maneuvering past the sleep stations, Megan called over her shoulder, 'Yup. I'm starving.'

At that moment, both crew members heard a squawk over their headsets. '*Discovery*, this is mission control. We understand you're looking to break for dinner?'

'That's affirmative, mission control,' Carter replied.

'*Discovery*, our instruments show a possible pressure leak in the air lock on the lower deck. Be much obliged if someone could check it out.'

Stone's voice came over the sets: 'Megan, Carter, you're the closest.'

Carter looked at Megan with puppy-dog eyes. 'I'm *really* hungry!'

Reaching into one of the sleep stations, Megan pulled out a deck of cards from under a strapped-down pillow. She tore away the cellophane, shuffled carefully so that no cards would slip out, and held the deck out to Carter.

'Cut. High card wins.'

Carter rolled his eyes, reached for the deck and turned over a ten. Megan came up with a seven.

Carter laughed and propelled himself towards the food station. 'I'll save you some Oreos!' he called back.

'Sure, thanks.'

'You okay to do it, Megan?' Stone asked.

She sighed. 'I'm fine. Just make sure that Carter doesn't hog the veal cutlets or whatever.'

'Roger that. See you in a bit.'

Megan knew that 'a bit' meant at least an hour. Checking out an air lock meant getting into an EMU.

Gripping the handles, she descended the ladder to the lower deck. Tucked behind the cargo and the equipment that the shuttle carried was the air lock. The red light over its door was blinking, indicating a possible malfunction.

'Damn wire is all it is,' Megan muttered and pushed off.

'Watch this.'

Carter tore open a packet of orange juice, held it up, and squeezed out some of the liquid. Forming a rough sphere, the juice floated in front of Carter, who pierced it with a straw and began to sip. In seconds, the solid that was a liquid had disappeared.

'Very nice,' Stone said. 'You can come do magic tricks at my kid's next birthday.'

'Uh-oh, the sauce is loose,' Randall Wallace called out.

Stone turned to find that while he had been talking to Carter, the shrimp-cocktail sauce had lost contact with his spoon. He picked up a tortilla and made a swiping motion to catch it.

'Wonder what's keeping Dylan,' Carter said through a mouthful of chicken with gravy, which he was eating out of a plastic baggie.

'Dylan, do you copy?' Stone said into his mike.

There was no reply.

'Probably in the can,' Carter said. 'He has this thing for barbecue beans. Maybe he smuggled some on board.'

Beans, along with broccoli and mushrooms, were never on the shuttle menus. Excess gas was much more painful in space, and flight physicians still weren't sure how gases behaved in microgravity.

Carter coughed.

'You're eating too fast,' Stone chided him.

Carter's reply was drowned out by a fit of hacking.

'Hey, maybe he's choking on something,' Wallace said.

As Stone moved towards him, Carter suddenly grabbed the pilot by the shoulders. Another paroxysm swept through him and he vomited blood up into the air in front of him.

'What the hell!' Stone cried.

His words were cut off as he clutched his chest and began to claw at his jumpsuit. His body felt like it was burning up. When he wiped his face, the back of his hand came away all bloody.

Karol and Wallace watched in horror as their shuttle mates rolled over, their arms and legs kicking out as though in seizure.

'Get up to the flight deck and seal yourself in!' Karol roared.

'But –'

'Do it!' As he shoved Wallace towards the ladder, a voice from mission control came over his headset.

'*Discovery*, do you have a problem?'

'Damn right we do!' Karol shouted. 'Something's tearing Carter and Stone apart –'

Karol's body spasmed. 'Oh, Jesus!' As he doubled over, a trail of blood swirled away from his eyes and nostrils. Somewhere far away he heard the urgent voice from mission control.

'*Discovery*, do you copy?'

A reply formed in his mind, but before he could get the words out, a red haze descended across his eyes.

Working inside the air lock on the lower deck, Megan heard the cries and groans over her headset. She jabbed the transmit button on her EMU.

'Frank? Carter? *Wallace?*'

All she heard now was static. Her communications unit was malfunctioning.

Ignoring the wiring she'd been checking, Megan reached for the lever to open the air lock. To her horror, it refused to budge.

In the Spacelab, Dylan Reed clutched a stopwatch in his gloved hand. The mutated variola was working with frightening speed. He knew that he should measure exactly how fast it was infecting and destroying the crew. Bauer had been adamant that human test subjects were the only way to gauge the lethal capacity of the new small-pox. It was also a way to get rid of any potential witnesses. But to do that would have meant looking at the stopwatch. Dylan Reed would have had to open his eyes, something he didn't dare do because then he'd surely see the faces behind the screams.

A world away, mission director Harry Landon was in a cubicle down the hall from mission control, catching up on some much-needed sleep. A twenty-year NASA veteran, ten of those years spent in the pressure cooker of the Cape, Landon had learned to rest whenever the opportunity presented itself. He was also able to wake up instantly, alert and ready.

Landon sensed the hand even before he felt it on his shoulder. Rolling over, he found himself gazing into the face of a young technician.

'What is it?' he demanded.

'There's a problem onboard *Discovery*,' the tech replied nervously.

Landon swung off the cot, grabbed his glasses off a

filing cabinet, and moved for the door. 'Mechanical? Flight? What?'

'Human.'

Landon didn't break stride as he called back over his shoulder. 'What do you mean, "human"?'

'It's the crew,' the tech stammered. 'Something's wrong.'

Something *was* wrong – terribly so. Landon sensed it as soon as he entered mission control. All the techs were huddled over their consoles, talking urgently to *Discovery*. From the snatches he heard as he passed by, Landon realized that no one onboard the orbiter was responding.

Moving to his command post, he barked, 'Get me visual!'

'We can't, sir,' someone called back. 'The video feed must be down on their end.'

'Then get me audio!'

Landon slipped on a headset and tried to keep his voice level. '*Discovery*, this is the mission director. Come in, please.' Static crackled against his eardrum. '*Discovery*, I say again, this is the mission director –'

'Mission control, this is *Discovery*.'

The strangled voice made Landon's blood run cold. 'Wallace, is that you?'

'Yes, sir.'

'What's going on up there, son?'

Landon had to wait out more static. When Wallace was back, he sounded as if he was choking.

'Wallace, what's wrong?'

'Control . . . Control, do you read?'

'Wallace, just tell us –'

'We're all dying . . .'

24

During the shuttle's pioneer years, in the early 1980s, procedures were set in place to deal with the inevitable mishap, malfunction, or tragedy. Enumerated in the so-called Black Book, they were first implemented in January 1986, after the disaster that took *Challenger* 51-L.

Harry Landon had been present in mission control that day. He still remembered the mission director's expression of horror when the shuttle exploded seventy-three seconds after liftoff. Then he watched as the director, tears streaming down his face, reached for the Book and began making the necessary calls.

Landon's fingers trembled as he fumbled for the key to unlock the drawer he'd prayed he would never have to open. The Book was a slender three-ring binder. Landon opened it to the first page, reached for the phone, then hesitated.

Getting to his feet, he plugged his headset into the intercom system that connected him to all the headsets used by the staff.

'Ladies and gentlemen,' he said sombrely. 'If I can have your attention . . . Thank you. You all heard the last communication from *Discovery*. If it's accurate – and we don't know that it is – then we are in the middle of a true catastrophe. The best thing we can do for our people up there is to follow procedures and be ready to respond to any request for assistance. Continue to monitor all aspects of the flight and of the shuttle's condition. If there's deviation or anything unusual – no matter how insignificant – I want to know about it. I want the data team to review all the tapes, every conversation, every transmission. Whatever happened up there happened quickly. But there had to be a trigger. I want to know what it was.'

Landon paused. 'I know what you must be thinking, and going through. I know what I'm asking you to do is difficult. But we cannot lose hope that there may be survivors. That's whom we're working for. Whoever's left, we want to bring them down safely. Nothing else matters.'

He looked around. 'Thank you all.'

The silence that had settled over the room began to break up. Landon was relieved that the grim expressions were replaced by ones of resolve and determination. He had always believed that the people he worked with were the best; now they were proving him right.

Landon's first call went to Rich Warfield, the president's science adviser. A physicist by training, Warfield was familiar with the shuttle programme. He immediately grasped the magnitude of the mishap.

'What can I tell the president, Harry?' he asked. 'He'll want the bottom line, no bullshit.'

'Okay,' Landon replied. 'First, there has been no communication with *Discovery* since Wallace's last transmission. In it, he indicated that the crew was dying or dead. I'll have someone play you the actual tape in case the president wants to hear for himself.

'As for the shuttle, it appears stable. There's been no change in flight path, speed, or trajectory. All onboard systems are green.'

'Give me your educated guess, Harry,' Warfield prompted.

'All air-supply readings are normal,' Landon replied. 'That means no toxic contaminants. No smoke, no fire, no gases.'

'What about food poisoning?' Warfield suggested. 'Could it be something as mundane as that?'

'The crew would have been having their first meal. But even if all the food were contaminated, I doubt that the poison could have spread so quickly – or virulently.'

'What about the payload?'

'This wasn't a classified flight. The Spacelab had the usual menagerie of frogs, insects, and mice to be used for experiments . . .'

'But what, Harry?'

Landon double-checked the experiments' schedule. 'Megan Olson was slated to begin work on Legionnaires' disease. That's the only bug in the programme. She never got started on it.'

'Could the bug have filtered out somehow?'

'Chances are ten thousand to one that it did. We have all sorts of sensors to detect a leak in the Biorack. But let's say it did. Legionnaires' doesn't work that fast. Whatever killed the crew did so in a matter of minutes.'

For a moment there was silence.

'I know it's not my area of expertise,' Warfield said finally. 'But if you carve away the other possibilities, it still sounds to me like a bug got loose.'

'Off the record, I'm tempted to agree with you,' Landon replied. 'But I wouldn't go planting that idea in the president's mind. Right now, we just don't know.'

'The president will have questions,' Warfield said heavily. 'I think you know what the first one will be.'

Landon closed his eyes. 'This is the procedure, Rich.

During launch, the range safety officer tracks the flight. His finger is never far from the destruct button. If anything goes wrong, well . . . You remember *Challenger*? After the external tank blew and the shuttle exploded, the solid rocket boosters kept going. The RSO brought them down.

'The shuttle has a destruct sequence that can be activated by us when it's on its way down. At that point, it's still far enough out that if we had to, we could blow it up without any danger to the population below.'

Landon paused. 'Rich, when you tell him this, remind him that he's the one who has to give that order.'

'All right, Harry. Let me pass along what we have so far. Don't be surprised if he calls you direct.'

'The minute I know more, I'll let you know,' Landon said.

'Harry, last thing: *can* we bring the shuttle down on autopilot?'

'Hell, we can bring a seven-forty-seven down that way. The question is, will we want to?'

Landon's next call went to the range safety officer, who had already been apprised of the emergency. Landon explained as much as he could, then added that the original duration of this mission had been eight days.

'Clearly that's not the case anymore,' he said. 'It's not a question of *if* but *when* we bring her down.'

'And once she's in range?' the RSO asked quietly.

'Then we'll see.'

Landon continued down the list, which included calls to General Richardson and Anthony Price. In addition to being the air force chief of staff, Richardson was also codirector of the Space Security Division, which was

303

responsible for identifying and monitoring everything that was either approaching earth or in orbit around it. As head of the National Security Agency, Price was on the list because the shuttle sometimes flew classified missions sponsored by the NSA.

Every time he finished a call, Landon looked around, hoping that one of his people would have some news for him. He recognized this as the gesture of a desperate man; under the circumstances, any conversation he might have been having would have been interrupted if contact with the shuttle had been reestablished.

For the next two hours, Landon continued to work the phones. He was grateful that at least for now, he didn't have to deal with the media. Many in NASA resented the fact that shuttle flights were now considered so mundane that coverage was not warranted. During the ill-fated *Challenger* launch, CNN had been the sole network providing live feed. Today, only NASA cameras had recorded *Discovery*'s liftoff.

'Landon, circuit four!'

Landon didn't even bother to see who was speaking. He found the channel and heard a faint voice through the crackle of static.

'Mission control, this is *Discovery*. Do you copy?'

Dylan Reed was still in the Spacelab, in his protective EMU, his boots in the floor restraints that kept him positioned in front of the auxiliary communications panel. The several hours of deliberate incommunicado seemed like an eternity to him. He'd turned off the radio so that he wouldn't have to listen to the desperate voices floating from mission control. Now, to proceed with the next phase of the operation, he had reestablished contact.

'Mission control, this is *Discovery*. Do you read?'

'*Discovery*, this is the mission director. What is your status?'

'Harry, is that you?'

'Dylan?'

'It's me. Thank God, Harry! I didn't think I'd ever hear another human voice.'

'Dylan, what happened up there?'

'I don't know. I'm in the lab. One of the EMUs was showing default. I climbed in to check it out. Then I heard . . . Jesus, Harry, it sounded like they were being strangled. And the commo gear was down –'

'Dylan, hang on, okay? Try to stay calm. Is there anyone else in the lab?'

'No.'

'And you've had no communication with the rest of the crew?'

'No. Harry, listen. What –?'

'We don't know, Dylan. That's the long and the short of it. We got a garbled message out of Wallace but he couldn't tell us what happened. It had to be something fast and extremely lethal. We're thinking a bug got loose. Do you have anything like that on board?'

Actually what I have is a shuttle that's one big hot zone.

But what he said was: 'Christ, Harry! What are you talking about? Look at the manifest. The worst we're carrying is Legionnaires' and that's still in the biofreezer.'

'Dylan, you have to do this,' Landon said in a measured tone. 'You have to go back into the orbiter and see . . . and tell us what you see.'

'Harry!'

'Dylan, we have to know.'

'What if they're all dead, Harry? What am I supposed to do for them?'

'Nothing, son. There's nothing you can do. But we're going to bring you home. No one leaves their post until you're back on the ground, safe and sound.'

Landon was about to add 'I promise,' but the words couldn't make it past his lips.

'All right, Harry. I'll go check out the orbiter. I want to keep the commo link open.'

'We need you to check the video feed. We have no picture.'

That's because I fixed the cameras.

'Roger that. Leaving the lab now.'

The bulky space suit made his movements awkward, but slowly Reed floated through the connecting tunnel, taking care not to snag any part of his suit. Even the slightest tear would be fatal.

The sight in the mid-deck made him gag. Stone, Karol, and Carter had been reduced to bloated corpses covered in sores, floating freely or snagged to pieces of equipment by an arm or a leg. Trying not to look, Reed manoeuvred his way around them to the ladder. Up in the flight deck, he found Wallace strapped to the commander's chair.

'Mission control, this is *Discovery*.'

Landon responded instantly. 'Go ahead, Dylan.'

'I found everyone except Megan. Jesus, I can't tell you . . .'

'We need to know what they look like, Dylan.'

'The bodies are bloated, sores, blood . . . I've never seen anything like it.'

'Are there any signs of the contaminant?'

'Negative. But I'm not taking off the EMU.'

'Of course not. Can you tell what they were eating?'

'I'm on the flight deck, with Wallace. Let me go downstairs.'

After a few minutes, Reed was back on the link. In reality, he hadn't moved. 'Looks like whatever was brought onboard. Chicken, peanut butter, shrimp . . .'

'Okay, we're checking the source of the food right now. If it was contaminated, the agent might have mutated in microgravity.' Landon paused. 'You need to find Megan.'

'I know. I'll check mid-deck again, the john . . . If she's not there, she'll be on the lower deck.'

'Contact me as soon as you find her. Mission director out.'

Thank God!

Although her transmit button was still malfunctioning, Megan had heard every word between Reed and Landon. She slumped forward, her helmet clicking against the air-lock door. Hundreds of questions raced through her mind: How could the rest of the crew be dead? What could have overtaken them? Was it something they had brought onboard? It'd been less than an hour since she'd last seen Carter and the others. Now they were *dead*?

Megan forced herself to calm down. She glanced at the nest of wires in the open panel above the door. Clearly there was a mix-up in the wiring. Following the instructions printed on the panel door, she had tried to reverse a number of connections but so far hadn't found the faulty one.

Relax, she told herself. *Dylan will be down here in a few minutes. When he doesn't find me out there, he'll realize I'm in here. He'll open the door from his end.*

Megan took as much comfort in the thought as she

could. She wasn't prone to claustrophobia, but she could feel the air lock – no bigger than a pair of broom closets set side by side – closing in on her.

If only the damn mike worked! To be heard by another human would be the sweetest thing.

Then fix the mike, she told herself.

Dylan's voice came over her headset: 'Mission director, I'm in the lower deck. No sign of Megan yet. I'll check the storage holds.'

Even though she knew that sound was baffled in space, Megan raised both hands and began pounding on the door. Maybe somehow Dylan would hear her.

'Mission director, I've checked most of the hold. Still nothing.'

Landon's voice floated through Megan's headset: 'Suggest you try the air lock. Maybe she got in there.'

Yes, try the air lock!

'Roger that, mission director. I'll cut commo until I reach the air lock.'

As soon as Reed approached the door, he saw Megan's face behind the porthole. The joy and relief in her eyes speared him. He switched on the intercom mode on his communications set.

'Megan, can you hear me?'

He saw her nod.

'I'm not receiving. Is your transmitter down?'

Megan nodded, then floated up and pointed to the commo unit built into the chest of her EMU. She gave the universal thumbs-down signal and worked her way back to the porthole.

Reed looked at her. 'Okay. I understand. Not that it makes any difference.'

Megan wasn't sure she'd heard him correctly and mimed a shrug.

'You don't understand,' Reed said. 'Of course you don't. How could you? Megan . . .' He hesitated. 'I can't help you get out.'

Her eyes widened in terror and disbelief.

'Let me tell you what's out here, Megan. A virus. The kind the world has never seen before because it's not *of* this world. It was born on earth, but it was given life here, in the Spacelab. That's what I was working on.'

She was shaking her head, her lips moving frantically in soundless words.

'You should try to stay calm,' Reed continued. 'You heard me talking to mission control. They know everyone's dead. They have no clue what happened up here. And they never will.'

Reed wet his lips. '*Discovery* has become a kind of *Marie Celeste*, a doomed ghost ship. Of course, there are differences. *I'm* still alive and so are you – for the time being. NASA can and will bring the orbiter down on autopilot. As long as I'm alive, they're not going to push the autodestruct button.'

Reed let a beat go by. 'They won't have to.'

Megan felt hot tears spill over her cheeks. She was faintly aware that she was screaming but that had no impact on Reed. His expression remained as cold and remote as arctic ice.

'I wish it were someone other than you, Megan,' he was saying. 'Really I do. But Treloar had to be eliminated and you were his backup. Now, I don't expect you to understand. But since I was the one who brought you into the programme and gave you this chance, I feel I owe you an explanation. You see, we need to keep our bioweapons' arsenal strong. All those treaties we signed – do you think places like Iraq, Libya, or North Korea give a damn about them? Of course not. They're too

309

busy developing their own weapons. Well, now we'll have something that will trump whatever they come up with. And we'll be the *only* ones to have it.

'The sample I made? A thimbleful is enough to eradicate any country we choose. I realize that's not a very scientific measurement, but you get my drift. If you don't believe me, look at what happened here, how quickly the smallpox went to work, the consequences . . .'

Never in her life had Megan felt so powerless. Reed's voice droned in her ears like something from a nightmare. She could not believe such words coming from a man she had thought she knew, a colleague, a mentor, someone she'd trusted implicitly.

He's insane. That's all I need to know. And what I need to do is get out of here!

When Reed spoke again, it was as though he'd read her mind.

'You've done most of my job for me, Megan, locking yourself in like that. The fire will do the rest. I didn't mention that? Well, there's going to be an awful lot of confusion when this thing lands. The only thing on mission control's mind will be to get me out of here safely. After that, if something explodes, well . . .' He shrugged. 'You've been a part of history, Megan. I'll never forget you – or the others.'

His eyes never left hers as he touched a panel on his commo unit. 'Mission director, this is Reed. Do you copy?'

She heard Landon's voice: 'Copy, Dylan.'

'I have an update. I . . . I found Megan. She's dead . . . like the others.'

There was a moment's silence on the other end. 'I copy, Dylan. I'm so sorry. Listen, we're working to bring you home. Can you get to the flight deck?'

'Affirmative.'

'We won't need any help, but if something goes wrong . . .'

'Understood. Harry?'

'Yes?'

'You've opened the Black Book, right?'

'Yes, Dylan.'

'There's a name that's not in there. Dr Karl Bauer. He knows more about bugs than anyone alive. I think you might want to consult with him about the quarantine.'

'Roger that. We'll get Bauer to the landing site. We're running emergency descent models right now. As soon as we have a firm trajectory, we'll let you know.'

Reed smiled faintly and, looking directly at Megan, said, 'Roger, mission director. *Discovery*, signing off.'

25

The helicopter ferrying Jon Smith from Camp David landed in the cargo transport area of Andrews Air Force Base. Smith hopped out and trotted across the tarmac to the white panel truck parked next to a sleek executive jet.

'Hello, Jon,' Major-General Kirov said, watching the corpsmen pull a stretcher out of the truck.

'Did everything go as planned?' Smith asked.

'It did,' Kirov replied. 'These men' – he indicated the corpsmen – 'arrived at your house exactly on schedule. They were very quick, very efficient.'

Smith glanced at Ivan Beria, a blanket tucked up to his chin, as he was wheeled by.

'Is he all right?'

'The tranquilizers worked perfectly,' Kirov replied.

Smith nodded.

As the stretcher disappeared into the jet, Kirov turned to Smith. 'I am grateful to you – and to Mr Klein – for allowing me to help. I only wish I could do more.'

Smith shook the Russian's hand. 'I'll stay in touch, General. I think we got everything we could out of Beria, but if he says anything interesting . . .'

'You'll be the first to know,' Kirov assured him. 'Good-bye, Jon Smith. I hope that we will meet again, under more pleasant circumstances.'

Smith waited until Kirov was onboard and the hatch was closed. By the time the jet was racing down the runway he was in his car, being waved through perimeter security. As he headed for the highway, his thoughts drifted from what had been accomplished to what was still left to do.

In Moscow it was the middle of the night, but the lights were still burning in the offices of the Bay Digital Corporation.

In the conference room, Randi Russell was working on her fourth cup of coffee, watching Sasha Rublev as he worked to ferret out the secrets of the laptop Jon Smith had delivered. Surrounded by hardware wired into the laptop, Sasha had been at his keyboard for over seven hours, downing the occasional Coke to maintain his energy level. Three times Randi had suggested they quit for the night, but each time Sasha simply waved her words away.

'I'm close,' he would mumble. 'Just a few more minutes.'

By now Randi had decided that Sasha did not measure time like mere mortals.

She drained her coffee, stared at the dregs, and then said: 'Okay, that's it. And this time I mean it.'

Sasha held up one hand, kept typing with the other. 'Wait for it . . .'

He jabbed a key triumphantly and slumped in his chair. 'Look,' he said proudly.

Randi couldn't believe her eyes. The big monitor, which had been filled with nothing but a series of unintelligible symbols all evening, suddenly morphed into a string of deciphered E-mails.

'Sasha, how –?' Randi shook her head. 'Never mind. I'd never understand.'

Sasha beamed at her. 'The person this computer belongs to used CARNIVORE, your FBI's latest encryption program.' He looked at her shrewdly. 'I thought no one outside America had this.'

'Me too,' Randi murmured.

Using the mouse, she scanned the E-mails, unable to believe what she was reading.

What the hell is the Cassandra Compact?

Returning to Bethesda, Jon Smith fixed himself a quick snack and took it into his study. The faint odour of drugs and a broken man's fear hung in the house. Smith opened a window and sat down with the files Nathaniel Klein had given him.

Travis Nichols and Patrick Drake . . . both U.S. Army sergeants. Both from the same small town in central Texas where young men went either into the oil fields or the military. Seasoned combat veterans, they had seen action in Somalia, the Gulf, and most recently, Nigeria.

Smith's interest was piqued when he read their fitness reports from the Advanced Warfare School at Fort Benning, Georgia. Nichols and Drake had graduated one and two in their class, cold, hard men whose keen edge had been further honed by instructors in the blackest combat arts.

Then they disappear . . .

Now Smith knew what Klein had meant about the lapses. In each of the last five years there were months where the soldiers' whereabouts could not be accounted for. No notations had been made by commanding officers; no ship-out or transport orders were available.

Experienced in the ways of the military, Smith could

guess where Nichols and Drake had disappeared. Scattered throughout the army were special units. The most public of these were the Rangers. But there were others, whose members were culled from the most experienced and battle-hardened troops. In Vietnam, they had been known as LRRPs – Long Range Reconnaissance Patrols; in other parts of the world, they had no designation whatsoever.

Smith was aware of three such outfits but suspected there were more. He knew no one in any of them, and didn't have the time or the resources to start a hunt from scratch. There was only one way to go: with the phone number that Peter Howell had coaxed from the dying Travis Nichols's lips.

For the next hour, Smith considered one plan of action after another. From each one he took away a detail or two that, when strung together, formed a coherent whole. Then he went over it again and again, probing for weaknesses, eliminating questions, trying to give himself the best possible advantage. He knew that the minute he made the call to that as yet unknown person at the other end of a number that didn't exist, his life would hang on his every word and action.

Outside, the insects and birds began their nocturnal litany. As Smith rose to close the window, his phone rang.

'Jon, it's Randi.'

'Randi! What time is it over there?'

'I don't know. I've lost track. Listen, Sasha broke through the laptop's firewalls. All the E-mails – and everything else – are in the clear.'

By her tone, Smith knew that Randi wanted an explanation.

'I need what you have, Randi,' he said quietly. 'No questions asked. Not now.'

'Jon, you asked me to do you a favour. I did. From the little I've read, this stuff's explosive. There are references to Bioaparat and to something called the Cassandra Compact –'

'But I haven't seen any of that,' Smith said urgently. 'That's why I need it – to try to find out what's going on.'

'You have to tell me one thing,' Randi replied. 'This "situation," whatever it is, is it localized in Russia? Or has something gotten out?'

Smith had come up against Randi's single-mindedness before. He knew she wasn't vying for glory; she was an intelligence agent trying to do her job. Somehow he had to convince her that his interests and hers were the same.

'Something has gotten out,' he said.

She stared at him. 'Not like Hades, Jon. Not again!'

'It isn't like that at all,' Smith assured her. 'We have a situation here at home. Believe me, all stops have been pulled out on this. The orders come from the highest level. Do you understand? The *highest* level.' He allowed his words to sink in. 'What you've done will help me enormously,' he continued. 'Please believe me: there's nothing more you can do on your end. At least not right now.'

'So I take it you don't want me to signal Langley.'

'It's the *last* thing I want you to do. I'm asking you to trust me, Randi. Please.'

After a moment's hesitation, she replied, 'It's not a matter of trust, Jon. I just don't want . . . I couldn't bear to stand by and let another situation like Hades develop.'

'No one does. And it won't happen.'

'Will you at least keep me posted?'

'As much as I can,' Smith replied truthfully. 'Things are moving fast here.'

'All right. But remember your promise.'

'You won't hear it on CNN.'

'I'll ship you the contents now. What do you want me to do with the laptop?'

Smith considered his options. By all rights he should have the computer returned to Kirov. But what if Lara Telegin wasn't the only traitor? He couldn't run the risk that somehow vital secrets would fall into the wrong hands.

'I'm sure that you have a secure safe,' he said. 'Preferably something tamperproof.'

'I have one of the new flash vaults. Anyone trying to get in is in for a nasty surprise.'

'Good. One last thing: the cell phone.'

'It had a bunch of numbers in its memory – all on the Russian military exchange. I'll send you copies.'

Hearing a *ping*!, Smith turned to his monitor as an incoming message scrolled across the screen.

'I'm receiving your feed,' he said.

'I hope it's what you need.' Randi hesitated, then added, 'Good luck, Jon. I'll be thinking of you.'

Smith turned his attention to the screen and scanned the E-mails one by one. The sender was code-named Sphinx; the receiver, Mephisto.

As he continued to read, the enormity of what was referred to as the Cassandra Compact grew before his eyes. Lara Telegin – Sphinx – had been in contact with Mephisto for over two years, feeding him top-secret information on Bioaparat, its personnel and security. The most recent notes mentioned Yuri Danko and Ivan Beria by name.

Who were you feeding? Who is Mephisto?

Smith worked his way deeper into the E-mails. Suddenly he spotted something and scrolled back. It was a congratulatory note. Mephisto had been awarded a citation. There was a reference to a ceremony on a certain date.

Veterans Day . . .

Using his USAMRIID access code, Smith got into the Pentagon site and punched in the date. Instantly the specifics of the ceremony appeared, including pictures. There was a shot of President Castilla holding the citation. And the soldier who was about to receive it.

'Are you absolutely sure?' Klein asked.

Smith thought Klein sounded tired, but maybe it was just the connection.

'Yes, sir,' he replied. 'The E-mail refers to a specific date. There was only that one ceremony. Only one such citation was awarded. There's no mistake.'

'I see . . . Given this new development, have you come up with a way to proceed?'

'Yes, sir.'

It had taken Smith two hours to revise the plan he'd come up with prior to Randi Russell's call. Quickly he gave Klein the details.

'It sounds awfully dangerous, Jon,' Klein said softly. 'I'd feel a whole lot better if you weren't going in alone.'

'Believe me, I'd like to have Peter Howell around but there's no time to get him here. Besides, I need him in Europe.'

'And you're sure you want to proceed immediately?'

'As long as you can get those items I mentioned, I'll be ready.'

'Consider it done. And Jon, you will be wearing a transmitter, won't you?'

Smith held up a tiny fibreoptic patch that looked identical to a small round Band-Aid, the kind that might be used on a shaving cut.

'If something goes wrong, sir, you'll at least know how far I got.'

'Don't even think that.'

After hanging up, Smith took a moment to compose himself. He thought of everything that had happened up to this point, all the lives that had been sacrificed on the altar of the Cassandra Compact. Then he saw Yuri Danko coming towards him across St Mark's Square . . . and Katrina, his widow.

Without hesitation, he reached for the phone, made sure the scrambler was activated, and dialled the number Peter Howell had passed along. If anyone tried to trace the call, they'd find themselves zipping from one cutout to another all over the country.

On the other end, the phone was ringing. The receiver was picked up and an unearthly voice, electronically distorted, answered: 'Yes?'

'This is Nichols. I'm home. Hurt. I need to come in.'

26

General Frank Richardson inadvertently knocked the cigar burning in the cut-glass ashtray.

'Say again,' he spoke into the phone.

A patchy, mangled voice came back at him. '. . . is Nichols . . . Hurt . . . coming in.'

Richardson clenched the receiver. 'Go to safe point Alpha. Repeat: safe point Alpha. Copy?'

'Copy.'

The connection was broken.

Richardson stared at the telephone as though he expected it to ring again. But the silence in his office was broken only by soft ticks of the grandfather clock and the distant drones of Humvees as security details went about their patrols around Fort Belvoir.

Nichols . . . Hurt . . . Impossible!

Richardson took a draw on his cigar to steady himself. A seasoned commander, he quickly reviewed his options and made his decision. The first call went out to the noncom barracks on the base. A crisp, alert voice answered.

Richardson's second call was to NSA deputy-director Anthony Price. He too was awake, and luckily not that far away in his town-house in Alexandria.

While Richardson waited for the two men to arrive, he listened to the tape of the conversation. Even though his secure phone was hooked up to the latest recording equipment, the quality of the speaker's voice was scratchy. Richardson couldn't tell if the call was local or long distance. He didn't think that 'Nichols' was all that far away, not if he was ready to rendezvous at safe point Alpha.

But Nichols is dead!

Richardson's thoughts were interrupted by a knock on the office door. His visitor was a big, strapping man in his midthirties with straw-coloured hair cut close to the scalp and bright blue eyes. Normally baggy fatigues were stretched taut over a linebacker's powerful muscles.

'Good evening, General,' Sergeant Patrick Drake said, saluting crisply.

'At ease,' Richardson replied. He gestured at the wet bar in the corner. 'Help yourself to a drink, Sergeant. Believe me, you'll need it.'

Fifteen minutes later, Anthony Price was escorted into the room by the general's aide-de-camp.

'Good evening, Tony.'

Price looked at Drake and raised his eyebrows. 'What's going on, Frank?'

'What's going on is *this*,' Richardson replied and jabbed the play button on the tape recorder.

He watched the expressions of the two men as they listened to the brief exchange. He detected nothing except genuine surprise – and in the case of Price, alarm.

'How the hell could Nichols have made that call?' Price demanded. He turned to Drake. 'I thought you said that he was dead, soldier!'

'With all due respect, sir, Nichols *is* dead,' Drake replied tonelessly. He looked at Richardson. 'General, I saw Nichols take a knife in the gut. You know that there's no way a man can survive that unless he gets immediate medical attention – which wasn't forthcoming.'

'You should have made sure he was dead,' Price snapped.

'Tony, that's enough!' Richardson cut in. 'I remember your afteraction report, Sergeant. But you might want to explain the details to Mr Price here.'

'Yes, sir.' Drake turned to Price. 'Sir, our contact, Franco Grimaldi, was careless. He allowed Peter Howell to spot the trap. Howell took him down first, then came after Nichols and myself as we were closing in. Howell managed to get Nichols's gun and shoot Grimaldi. At that point, I had no choice but to retreat. My orders were to conduct this operation in a clandestine fashion. If something went wrong, I was to fall back and wait for a better opportunity.'

'Which never came,' Price said sarcastically.

'The fortunes of war, sir,' Drake replied tonelessly.

'Enough backbiting!' Richardson snapped. 'Drake followed orders, Tony. That the operation went to hell in a handbasket was not his fault. The question is, who is passing himself off as Nichols?'

'Peter Howell, obviously,' Price replied. 'Clearly Nichols lasted long enough to give him the contact number.'

Richardson glanced at Drake. 'Sergeant?'

'I agree that Nichols gave up the number, sir. And the rendezvous point, too. Otherwise your caller would have asked you to identify safe point Alpha. But I don't think it was Howell.'

'Why?'

'Howell lives in this country, sir. Although he's retired, we've long suspected that he's still available for certain operations, and it came out that he and Smith worked together during Hades. I think Howell would go active if Smith asked him to, but he would do so only *outside* the country. That's why he, not

Smith, was in Palermo. I think Smith made that call, General.'

Richardson nodded. 'So do I.'

'Smith . . .' Price muttered. 'It all comes back to him. First he's in Moscow, then Beria disappears. Now he's here. Frank, you've got to take care of him once and for all.'

'Yes,' Richardson agreed. 'Which is why I instructed him to go to safe point Alpha.' He looked at Drake. 'Where you'll be waiting.'

Wearing hightops, black pants and a turtleneck, and a dark nylon jacket, Jon Smith slipped out of his house and into his car. Driving out of Bethesda, he continually checked his mirrors. No vehicle fell in behind him on the quiet suburban streets. No tail picked him up on the beltway.

Smith crossed the Potomac and entered Fairfax County, Virginia. At this time of night traffic was light, and he drove quickly through the horse country around Vienna, Fairfax, and Falls Church. South of Alexandria he found the river again and followed it almost to the border of Prince William County. Here the affluent landscape gave way to stretches of waterfront bordered by thick forest. As he approached the county line, Smith saw safe point Alpha.

The Virginia Water and Power pumping station had been built in the 1930s, when coal was cheap and health issues nonexistent. The advent of newer, cleaner units, coupled with the outcries from environmentalists, were enough to close the plant in the early 1990s. Since then, all attempts to modernize the station had floundered on the rocks of budgetary considerations. So it continued to stand on the Potomac, a dark, hulking structure looking like some abandoned factory.

Smith turned off the two-lane blacktop and, cutting his headlights, cruised up the access road. He parked under a copse of trees a quarter mile away and, setting his backpack on his shoulders, jogged the rest of the way.

The first thing he noticed as he got close was the Cyclone fence – still shiny, topped with glistening razor wire. A fat padlock, showing no rust, secured the heavy chain around the front gates. The perimeter was well lighted, the halogen lamps giving a winterlike glow to the deserted parking lot in front of the plant.

Being used but not in use . . .

Smith had come across buildings like this before. The army preferred the neglected, the abandoned, and the derelict, where it could give its special squads the kind of training impossible to duplicate on military reservations. The Virginia Water and Power plant had that peculiar feel about it . . . used but not in use.

Perfect for safe point Alpha.

Smith circled almost the entire perimeter before he found a suitable entry point, where the fence met the river's edge. Climbing over slippery rocks, he made his way around the fence, then sprinted across a section of the deserted parking lot to the nearest wall. After pausing to get his bearings he scanned the perimeter. He saw nothing, heard nothing except for the faint calls of night creatures near the water. Yet his intuition warned him that he was not alone. His call had sent a shiver along the web. He just couldn't see the spider . . . Yet.

Hugging the side of the building, Smith moved along the face of the wall, searching for an entry point.

Three stories above Smith, in the shadows of a broken window, Sergeant Patrick Drake watched Smith through night-vision binoculars. He'd picked him up as soon as Smith had climbed around the fence, the logical entry point. According to the contents of the dossier Drake had read, Smith was nothing if not logical. It was an admirable quality in a soldier, but one that made him predictable. And in this case, fatally vulnerable.

Drake had been flown to the plant by helicopter. Later on, a car would be waiting for him when he finished his work. Getting here so quickly had allowed him to familiarize himself with the plant's layout, choose the killing ground, and find a vantage point from which to observe Smith's entry.

There he was, at the door Drake had hoped he would find, testing it . . . opening it.

Drake turned away from the window and crossed the barren room that had once housed pumping machinery. His crepe-soled shoes moved soundlessly along the dusty concrete floor.

Slipping into the stairwell, he drew out his silenced Colt Woodsman. The .22 was an assassin's weapon, meant for close-range work. Drake wanted to see Smith's face before he shot him. Maybe the terror in his expression would help ease some of the pain Drake carried on account of the loss of his partner.

Or maybe I'll gut-shoot him first, so that he can feel what Travis went through.

Two floors down, Drake paused in a landing and carefully pulled back a door that opened on a second pump room. The moonlight coming through the tall windows bathed the pitted concrete floor in what could have been a layer of ice. Moving swiftly from pillar to pillar, Drake positioned himself so that he had a clear view of another door, still closed. Given where Smith had entered, this was the only entry point into the room. Like any good soldier, Smith would check every space he encountered, making sure that it was secure, that no one would surprise him when his back was turned. But in this case, not even the *logical* precautions would save him.

Somewhere outside the pump room Drake heard a footfall. Slipping off the safety on the Woodsman, he trained the barrel on the door and waited.

Smith stared at the door, its metal sheath streaked with old red paint stains. *Safe point Alpha*. Where Travis Nichols would have gone to report in. Where the owner of the horribly mangled voice would be waiting.

He wouldn't have come alone, Smith thought. He'd have brought backup. But how many?

Smith shrugged the backpack off his shoulders. Digging inside, he brought out a small, round object the size of an India rubber ball. Then he drew out his SIG-Sauer and pushed open the door with the tip of his hightop.

The blanket of moonlight destroyed his night vision, making him blink. At the same time he took one step across the threshold. Suddenly something very hard slammed into his chest. The backpack fell from his grip as he staggered back. A second blow sent him spinning against the wall.

Smith felt as though his chest were on fire. Gasping, he tried to remain standing but his knees buckled. As he slid down the wall, he saw a shadow emerge from behind a pillar.

His thumb flicked the pin on the stun grenade in his

hand. With a weak toss he threw it across the room and quickly covered his eyes and ears.

Drake advanced on Smith with the confidence of a hunter who knows he's scored a direct hit – two, in fact. Both the bullets had hit Smith centre mass. If the colonel wasn't already dead, he soon would be.

Drake was relishing that thought when he saw a black sphere arc towards him. His instincts and reactions were superb, but he couldn't cover his eyes in time. The stun grenade exploded like a supernova, blinding him. The shock wave hammered him to the ground.

Drake was young and very fit. During live fire training and on actual missions he had taken his share of explosions. As soon as he hit the ground he covered his head in case of shrapnel. He did not panic when, opening his eyes, he saw nothing but white. The flash would wear off in a few seconds. He still had his gun in his hand. He knew that he'd hit Smith and that he was down. All he had to do was wait for his sight to return.

Then Drake heard the distant wail of sirens. Cursing, he staggered to his feet. Although the room was still a blur he made it to the windows. His vision cleared enough for him to make out two red dots flickering between the trees bordering the access road.

'Goddamnit!' he roared as he heard the sirens. Smith had brought his own backup! Who were they? How many?

His vision almost normal, Drake rushed to where he'd seen Smith fall.

But he wasn't there!

The sirens were getting louder. Cursing, Drake snatched up the backpack and headed into the stairwell. He made it outside just in time to see two sedans pull up in front of the gates.

Let 'em come, he thought. *All they're going to find is a body!*

Staring at the loose wires dangling from the panel, Megan Olson struggled to fend off her despair. She had lost track of all the combinations she had tried, running different wires to different terminals. So far, nothing had worked. The shuttle's air-lock door remained firmly sealed.

Her only consolation was that she thought she'd fixed her mike. But she didn't want to test it just yet.

Calm down, she told herself. *There's a way out of here. All you have to do is find it.*

It was maddening that less than a foot away, on the other side of the door, was the emergency-release lever. All Dylan Reed had had to do was pull it.

Instead he's going to let you die. Like all the others . . .

No matter how hard she tried, Megan could not distance herself from the horror of Reed's actions. For the last several hours she had listened in on his terse, intermittent conversations with Harry Landon at mission control. In one of them, he had given a graphic description of the bodies.

But how did he get a sample?

From Treloar! Klein had told her about the theft from Bioaparat and how Treloar had helped smuggle the Russian smallpox sample into the country. But how had Treloar gotten the virus to the launch site? He was killed soon after landing in Washington.

That's when she remembered the morning of the liftoff, being unable to sleep, taking a walk in the darkness, seeing the launch pad in the distance, seeing Reed . . . Then the anonymous visitor, approaching him, handing him something, and leaving. Could it have been a last-minute transfer? It had to be.

If what Reed had received was in fact smallpox, Megan thought, then it would have remained stable until the shuttle was in orbit and Reed could store it in the biofreezer.

The Spacelab! Suddenly she remembered the message that had come in to the flight deck. Minutes later, Reed had changed the experiments' schedule, bumping her and taking the first slot for himself. He had explained it away so smoothly that no one, not even she, had questioned him.

Not even when you had seen the NASA log number for that message. Reed's number. And you asked yourself how he could possibly have sent that message to himself . . .

Megan shook her head. The questions had been there, but she had ignored them. Instead, she had accepted the events as coincidence, had chosen to believe in the integrity of the man who had brought her to the stars.

The question of why Reed would be party to such a barbaric act plagued her. Even after she'd gone over everything she knew about him, no answer was forthcoming. There was something in him, about him, that she hadn't seen. No one had.

Earlier, Megan had clung to the frail hope that Reed would return. A part of her could not believe that he would kill her in cold blood. But as the hours passed and she listened to his communication with mission control, she came to accept that as far as he was concerned, she was already dead.

Megan stared hard at the wiring panel. Because she

was able to eavesdrop on the conversations with mission control, she knew how Harry Landon intended to bring down the shuttle and, more important, how long that would take. She still had time to figure out how to escape. Once she did, she would head straight for the auxiliary communications unit in the lower bay.

But if the wiring continued to foil her and time began to run out, she had one final option. Choosing to exercise it meant that the door would open – no doubt about that. But there was no guarantee that she would survive the aftermath.

Smith staggered to his feet, ripped off his jacket, and tore at the Velcro straps of his Kevlar Second Chance bulletproof vest. It was rated to stop anything up to a 9mm slug. But even though it had absorbed Drake's .22s easily, Smith still felt as though he'd been kicked in the chest by a mule.

Getting into his car, he activated the global positioning system built into the dash. Instantly a glowing blue dot appeared on the small screen that showed a map of Fairfax County.

Smith reached for the phone.

'Klein here.'

'It's me, sir.' Smith said.

'Jon! Are you all right? I received reports of an explosion.'

'That was my doing.'

'Where are you?'

'Just outside the plant. The target's moving – by the looks of it, on foot. Whoever you sent, sir, did the job. They got here just in time to spook Drake.'

'What about Drake? Did he take the bait?'

Smith glanced at the pulsing blue dot. 'Yes, sir. He's on the move.'

It took Sergeant Patrick Drake five minutes to cover the one-mile hiking path through the woods between the power plant and the deserted recreational area where he'd parked his vehicle.

Alert for any sign of a tail, Drake drove to the outskirts of Alexandria. Pulling into the lot of a Howard Johnson motor lodge, he parked in front of the last unit in the row. Drake opened the door to find General Richardson and Anthony Price inside.

'Mission report, Sergeant?' Richardson asked.

'The target was neutralized, sir,' Drake replied smartly. 'Two hits, centre mass.'

'You're sure?' Price demanded.

'What do you want, Tony?' Richardson snapped. 'Smith's head on a platter?' He turned to Drake. 'At ease, Sergeant. You did well.'

'Thank you, sir.'

Price gestured at the backpack that Drake had brought with him. 'What's that?'

Drake dropped the pack on one of the beds. 'Something Smith left behind.'

Undoing the straps, he laid out the contents: two spare ammunition clips, a road map, a cell phone, a microcassette recorder, and a small, round object that got Price's attention.

'What's that?'

'A flash grenade, sir,' Drake said, pretending not to notice Price's shocked expression. 'It's okay, sir. The pin is secure.'

'Give us some privacy, soldier,' Price said.

As Drake went into the bathroom, Price grabbed Richardson's arm. 'Enough of this soldier-boy shit, Frank. Neither one of us needed to be here. Drake could have called in the results.'

Richardson jerked his arm away. 'That's not the way I work, Tony. I lost a soldier boy, as you call him, over in Palermo. He had a name. Travis Nichols. And in case you've forgotten, Smith got close enough to us to call me at Fort Belvoir – on a line you guaranteed was secure!'

'The number was secure!' Price shot back. 'Your man gave it up.'

Richardson shook his head. 'For someone who's done the things you have, you sure don't like getting your hands dirty, do you? You prefer to give orders and let others die while you watch the results on television, like this is all a big game.' Richardson leaned in close. 'I'm not playing a game, Tony. I'm doing this because I believe it is *necessary*. I'm doing this for my country. What do *you* believe in?'

'The same,' Price replied.

Richardson snorted. 'But you've feathered your bed with Bauer-Zermatt, haven't you? As soon as we give the world a small taste of what our bug can do, everyone will be clamouring for an antidote. Coincidentally Bauer-Zermatt will leak that it has the inside track on the research and its stock will skyrocket. I'm curious, Tony. Just how many shares did Bauer give you?'

'A million,' Price replied calmly. 'And he didn't *give* them to me, Frank. I earned them. Don't forget that I was the one who found Beria, who watched your back, making sure that no one even got a whiff of what was happening in Hawaii. So don't try to rub my nose in this hero horseshit!'

He glanced at the items Drake had removed from the

backpack. 'Now let's wrap this thing up . . .'

His words trailed off.

'What's wrong?' Richardson asked.

Price picked up the microcassette recorder, examined the casing, and popped open the cover. 'Say it ain't so,' he muttered.

'What?' Richardson demanded. 'Smith brought it along so that he could tape a confession.'

'Maybe . . .'

Price removed the cassette and pulled one of the two pins that held it in place. The assembly came away in one piece.

'And maybe not!' His face was mottled with rage. 'I *knew* I recognized this thing! Take a look, Frank.'

In the cavity Richardson saw a state-of-the-art transmitter.

'The latest in surveillance technology!' Price hissed. 'Your boy's been had! Smith knew that if something went wrong, his killer was sure to take the backpack. Somebody's heard every word we said!'

'Sergeant!' Richardson roared.

Drake bolted out of the bathroom, gun in hand. Richardson marched up to him and showed him the gutted recorder. 'Tell me again, is Smith dead?'

Drake recognized the transmitter instantly. 'Sir, I didn't know . . .'

'*Is he dead?*'

'Yes, sir!'

'All that means is that he can't tell us where the receiver is,' Price said. He looked at Richardson. 'Are you a religious man, Frank? Because prayer might be the only thing we have left!'

333

The front door to the unit opened and Richardson, Price, and Drake stepped out fast, heading for their cars.

Fifty feet away, in the shadows, Jon Smith watched them through the windshield of his vehicle.

'It's Richardson, Price, and Drake,' he said into the phone.

'I know,' Klein replied. 'I recognized their voices – except for Drake's. So did the president.'

Smith glanced at the transmitting unit, set in the passenger-seat well, that had relayed the conspirators' words to Camp David.

'I'm going to move in, sir.'

'No, Jon. Look around you.'

Smith saw two black sedans moving into position to block the front entrance of the motor court. Another pair was closing off the rear exit.

'Who are they, sir?'

'Doesn't matter. They'll deal with Richardson and Price. Just stay low until it's all over, then get the hell away. I'll expect you at the White House at first light.'

'Sir –'

The windshield exploded as a bullet shattered the safety glass. Smith threw himself across the seat as two more shots whistled into the sedan.

'You said he was dead!' Price screamed.

'He will be,' Richardson said grimly. 'Get in the car. Sergeant, you make sure this time!'

Drake didn't bother to look back. He had spotted the blacked-out sedan the instant he'd stepped out of the unit. Smith's vehicle was parked in the shadows of some

Dumpsters, a good call. But Smith had forgotten about the moon. Cold and bright, it washed the car's interior, illuminating him perfectly. Drake had taken his first shot before Smith had realized he'd been made. Now Drake was moving to make sure of his kill.

He was fifteen feet from the car when suddenly the headlights snapped on, blinding him. Drake heard the roar of the engine and realized what was happening. But even he wasn't fast enough to get out of the way in time. As Drake launched himself into the air two tons of cold metal smashed into him, catapulting him over the car.

Behind the wheel, Smith straightened up and kept his foot on the accelerator. His peripheral vision registered dark shapes spilling out of the sedans forming the blockade, but that didn't stop him. He saw Richardson and Price jump into a car and back up fast. Turning the wheel, he tried to cut them off. For a split-second, he saw Richardson's expression through the window, then felt a tremendous jolt as the two cars mashed together in a tangle of metal.

Smith hung on to the steering wheel, trying to push Richardson's car off to the side. Then he looked up and saw the two sedans at the exit. Spinning the wheel, he hit the brakes and went into a controlled skid.

Frank Richardson felt his car rock as Smith's vehicle spun away. Then he too saw the blockade.

'Frank!' Price screamed.

Richardson slammed on the brakes, but too late. Just as he threw his hands over his face the car smashed into the front ends of the angled sedans. Seconds later, a piece of jagged metal tore through his throat as he was hurled through the windshield.

Smith leaped out of his car, running hard. He got

335

close enough to see Richardson's body sprawled across the hood before a pair of strong arms caught him.

'It's too late, sir!' a voice called out.

Smith struggled but was dragged back. A moment later, a huge explosion slammed him to the ground.

Gasping and coughing, Smith struggled to breathe. Lifting his head off the asphalt, he saw a giant fireball engulf the three vehicles. Slowly he rolled away, oblivious to the shadows darting around him, the urgent voices calling to one another. A pair of hands hauled him to his feet and he found himself looking at a young, hatchet-faced man.

'You don't belong here, sir.'

'Who . . . are you?'

The man pressed a set of keys into Smith's palm. 'There's a green Chevy around the corner. Take it and go. And, sir? Mr Klein said to remind you about your meeting at the White House.'

27

Numb and exhausted, Smith somehow managed to drive himself to Bethesda. Walking into the house, he dropped his clothes on the way to the bathroom, turned on the shower, and stood under the hot, stinging spray.

The pounding water drowned out the screams and explosions of the night. But no matter how hard he tried, Smith couldn't erase the image of Richardson's car slamming into the blockade, the fireball erupting, the sight of Richardson and Price, human torches.

Smith stumbled into the bedroom and lay down naked on the covers. Closing his eyes, he set his soldier's mental clock and let himself be swept away into a long, dark tunnel. He felt himself floating end over end, like an astronaut who'd lost his tether and was doomed to tumble endlessly through the cosmos. Then he felt something bump him and with a start woke up to discover that he was clawing for the gun on the night table.

Smith showered again and dressed quickly. He was heading for the door when he remembered that he hadn't checked his phone messages off the secure cell. Quickly he scanned the list and discovered a note from Peter Howell. Something was waiting for him on his computer.

Smith fired up his machine, ran the encryption program, and downloaded the file Howell had left. Reading it, he was stunned. After making a copy, he saved the text in a secure file and typed in a quick E-mail Howell would get on his mobile phone: *Job well done – and better. Come home. Drinks are on me. J. S.*

As dawn broke, Smith left the house and drove through the empty streets to the west gate of the White House. The guard checked his ID against the computerized list and waved him through. At the portico, a marine corporal escorted him through the silent corridors of the West Wing and into a small, cluttered office where Nathaniel Klein rose to greet him.

Smith was startled by Klein's appearance. The head of Covert-One hadn't shaved and his clothes looked as if they had been slept in. Wearily, he indicated that they should sit.

'You did a tremendous job, Jon,' he said quietly. 'People owe you a debt of gratitude. I'm assuming you came through unscathed.'

'Bumped and bruised but otherwise intact, sir.'

Klein's wan smile faded. 'You haven't heard a thing, have you?'

'Heard what, sir?'

Klein nodded. 'Good . . . That's good. That means the blackout is holding.' He took a deep breath. 'Eight hours ago, Harry Landon, mission director at the Cape, was told that there was an emergency onboard *Discovery*. When he managed to reestablish voice communication, he learned that . . . that the crew was all dead except for one member.'

He looked at Smith sadly and the tremor in his voice betrayed his loss. 'Megan's gone, Jon.'

Smith felt his body stiffen. He tried to speak but couldn't find the words. The voice he heard didn't seem to belong to him.

338

'What was it, sir? A fire?'

Klein shook his head. 'No. The orbiter is functioning perfectly. But something ripped through the craft and killed the crew.'

'Who's the survivor?'

'Dylan Reed.'

Smith raised his head. 'The *only* survivor? We're sure?'

'Reed's gone through the entire craft. Everyone is accounted for. I'm sorry.'

Smith had lost people before to sudden, violent death. He knew that his reaction was typical of a survivor: his mind flashed on the last time he'd seen Megan in that coffee shop near the NASA compound in Houston.

Now she was gone. Just like that.

'Landon and the rest of NASA have been tearing out their collective hair,' Klein was saying. 'They still can't figure out what went wrong.'

'How did Reed survive?'

'He was in one of those suits they use on space walks. Apparently he was preparing some experiment.'

'And the rest of the crew were in their normal work outfits, the overalls,' Smith said. 'No protection gear.' He paused. 'You said there was no fire, that something ripped through them.'

'Jon —'

'Megan told you that she saw someone with Reed just before the launch,' Smith cut him off. 'You already suspected a link between Treloar and Reed . . .' He thought for a moment. 'What did the bodies look like?'

'Landon said that Reed described them as bloated, covered with sores, bleeding from the orifices.'

Smith felt a tingle as the connections snapped together in his mind.

'I had a message from Peter Howell,' he told Klein. 'He had a long chat with Herr Weizsel. He was so cooperative that he insisted on taking Peter back to his apartment, where he accessed the Offenbach Bank's computers through his laptop. It seems that Ivan Beria had a long and profitable relationship with the bank, especially when one client employed him exclusively: Bauer-Zermatt A.G.'

Klein was stunned. 'The pharmaceutical giant?'

Smith nodded. 'Over the last three years, Bauer-Zermatt made a total of ten deposits into Beria's account, two of the last three just before the Russian guard and Treloar were eliminated.'

'What about the third one?' Klein demanded.

'That was for the contract on me.'

After a moment's silence, Klein said, 'Do you have proof?'

As though he were moving a piece in for checkmate, Smith pulled out a floppy disk. 'Proof positive.'

Klein shook his head. 'All right. Bauer-Zermatt is – was – paying Beria for assassinations. These included the Russian guard and Treloar. That links Bauer-Zermatt to the stolen smallpox. But there are two questions: *why* would Bauer-Zermatt want the smallpox? And *who* at the company authorized the hits and the payments?' He pointed to the disk. 'Is there a name?'

'No name,' Smith replied. 'But it's not hard to guess, is it? Only one man could have authorized the use of someone like Beria: Karl Bauer himself.'

Klein's breath whistled through his nostrils. 'Okay . . . But finding Bauer's fingerprints on the authorization to use Beria, or on the payments themselves, that's another matter.'

'They won't exist,' Smith said flatly. 'Bauer's much

too careful to leave such an obvious trail.' He paused. 'But why would he want the smallpox to begin with? To make a vaccine? No. We can already do that. To play with it? Tweak it genetically? Maybe. But why? Smallpox has been studied for years. It can't be used as a battlefield weapon. The incubation period is too long. The effects are not a hundred percent predictable. So why would Bauer *still* want a sample? Want it so badly that he would murder for it?'

He looked at Klein. 'Do you know how people die from smallpox? The first symptoms are a rash on the roof of the mouth, which then spreads to the face and forearms, then to the rest of the body. The pustules erupt, scabs form, erupt again. Eventually, there's bleeding from the orifices . . .'

Klein stared at him. 'Just like the shuttle crew!' he whispered. 'They died the way smallpox victims do! Are you saying *Bauer* got the stolen smallpox onboard *Discovery*?'

Smith rose and tried to dispel the image of Megan, how she had died, her last, terrible moments. 'Yes. That's what I'm saying.'

'But –?'

'In space – in microgravity – you can reengineer cells, bacteria, virtually anything in a way that can't be done on earth.' He paused. 'We wiped smallpox off the planet but we kept two sets of samples – one here, one in Russia. Ostensibly, we did this because we could not bring ourselves to eradicate a species into extinction. The truth is darker than that: we never knew when we might need it. Maybe years from now we *would* find a way to convert it into a weapon. Or if someone else did, we'd have enough material with which to produce a vaccine – hopefully.

'Bauer didn't want to wait years. Somehow he discovered a process he *thought* would work. Maybe he was fifty or sixty percent of the way there, but he couldn't finish. He couldn't be *certain*. The only way to prove that he was right was to arrange for an experiment in a unique environment where bacteria grow like lightning. He needed to do it onboard the shuttle.' Smith paused. 'And he did.'

'If you're right, Jon,' Klein said tightly, 'that means Dylan Reed is his handmaiden.'

'He's the only survivor, isn't he? The director of NASA's biomedical research programme. The guy who was conveniently suited up when all hell broke loose.'

'Are you suggesting that Reed murdered his own crew?' Klein demanded.

'That's exactly what I'm saying.'

'Why, for God's sake?'

'Two reasons: To get rid of any possible witnesses, and . . .' Smith's voice broke. 'And to run a controlled experiment on human test subjects to see how fast the virus would kill.'

Klein slumped in his chair. 'It's insane.'

'Only because whoever devised it *is* insane,' Smith said. 'Not raving, not foaming at the mouth. But insidiously, malignly insane. Yes.'

Klein stared at him. 'Bauer . . .'

'And Richardson, Price, Treloar, Lara Telegin . . .'

'To nail Bauer, we need hard evidence, Jon. We can try to trace his communications –'

Smith shook his head. 'There's no time. Here's the way I see it: we assume there's a bioweapon onboard the shuttle and that Reed is in control of it. Bauer and his accomplices will want to destroy all the evidence of what happened up there. Also, I'm sure that we'll find no evidence of any dealings with either Richardson or Price.

342

But Bauer still has to make sure that the shuttle comes down safely. He has to get Reed and the sample out of there. When is NASA bringing down the orbiter?'

'In about eight hours. They have to wait for an atmospheric window to open in order to land it at Edwards Air Force Base in California.'

Smith leaned forward. 'Can you get me in to see the president – right now?'

Two hours later, after speaking with the president, Smith and Klein found themselves in the small conference room next to the Oval Office. While they waited for the president to finish his meeting, Klein received a call from the Cape.

'Mr Klein? It's Harry Landon at mission control. I have that information you were asking for.'

Klein listened in silence and thanked Landon. Before hanging up, he asked: 'What is the status of the descent?'

'We're bringing her down as gently as we can,' Landon replied. 'I have to tell you, we've never done anything like this – outside of simulations, that is. But we'll get our people down. You have my word on that.'

'Thank you, Mr Landon. I'll stay in touch.'

He turned to Smith. 'Landon called everyone in the Black Book – and someone who Reed personally asked for.'

'Let me guess. Karl Bauer.'

'On the money.'

'Makes sense,' Smith said. 'He'd want to be on-site when Reed comes down with his baby.'

Klein nodded and pointed to the closed-circuit monitor that suddenly showed a picture. 'Showtime.'

◇◇◇

Despite the nest of worry lines and crow's-feet, the president, seated behind his desk, projected an image of authority and control. As he waited for the last member of the working group to arrive, he surveyed the individuals around him.

The Central Intelligence Agency was represented by Bill Dodge, cool, austere, his expression betraying nothing as he leafed through the latest update from NASA.

Martha Nesbitt, the national security adviser, sat next to Dodge. A veteran of the State Department, Marti, as she was called, was famous for the speed with which she assessed a situation, formulated a decision, and got the ball rolling.

Opposite her was the secretary of state, Gerald Simon, picking nonexistent lint off his hand-tailored suit, a ritual indicating that he was racked by indecision.

'I hope you've had time to gather your thoughts,' the president said. 'Because under the circumstances, we have to make the right decision the first time around.'

He looked around the group. 'As of now *Discovery* will reach its "window" to reenter the earth's atmosphere in approximately one hour. At that point, it will be another four hours before it begins its descent procedure. Seventy-five minutes later, it will land at Edwards. The question before us is simple: do we allow the craft to land?'

'I have a question, sir,' Martha Nesbitt spoke up. 'At what point do we lose the ability to destroy the orbiter?'

'There's really no such cutoff point,' the president replied. 'The fact that the shuttle carries an autodestruct package of high explosives has, for obvious reasons,

344

never been publicized. However, using satellite relays, we can activate the mechanism at any point between the orbiter's present position and touchdown.'

'But the package, Mr President, was really designed to blow the orbiter in space,' Bill Dodge said. 'The whole point being not to introduce any contaminants into our atmosphere.'

'That's true,' Castilla agreed.

'What's *also* true is that we have no idea what really happened onboard *Discovery*,' Gerald Simon weighed in. He glanced around the room. 'Five dedicated people are dead. We don't know how or why. But one is still alive. On the battlefield, we always bring out our dead. And if there's a survivor out there, we damn well go out and get him.'

'I agree,' Marti Nesbitt said. 'First of all, according to the latest information, the orbiter is sound, mechanically speaking. Second, NASA is still checking into what could have taken down the crew. Rightly, they're focusing on the food and fluids supplies. We know that bacteria grow very rapidly in microgravity. It's entirely possible that something that is harmless on earth mutated in a grotesque way and overpowered its victims before they could respond.'

'But isn't that exactly why we can't risk bringing down the shuttle?' Gerald Simon asked. 'I have to look at this from the state department's perspective. We know we have something lethal on that ship, but we're going to bring it down anyway? What kind of danger are we exposing ourselves – and the rest of the world – to?'

'Maybe no danger at all,' Bill Dodge responded. 'This isn't an Andromeda-strain scenario, Gerry. Or some X-file about an extraterrestrial plague that somehow invaded the shuttle. Whatever killed those people came from earth. But here, it obviously didn't have the lethal capacity. Take away the microgravity environment and the damn thing dies.'

'You're willing to bet the country on that theory?' Simon retorted. 'Or the planet?'

'I think you're overreacting, Gerry.'

'And I think your attitude is a little too cavalier!'

'Ladies and gentlemen!' The president's words silenced the room. 'Debate, questions, comments, fine. But no arguing or backbiting. We don't have the time.'

'Does NASA have any reasonable expectation of determining what happened up there?' the national security adviser asked.

The president shook his head. 'I asked Harry Landon that same question. The answer is no. Although the survivor, Dylan Reed, is a medical doctor, he doesn't have the time, facilities, or help to conduct any kind of meaningful investigation. We have a general description of the bodies' condition, but certainly not enough to determine the cause of death.'

He looked around the room. 'There is one thing I can say for sure: Harry Landon does not believe that there's even a *consideration* of destroying the shuttle. Therefore, neither he nor anyone from NASA can be permitted into our discussions. Having said that, and since you've all had a chance to examine the facts as we know them, we need to take a preliminary vote. Bill, we'll start with you: salvage or abort?'

'Salvage.'

'Marti?'

'Abort.'

'Gerry?'

'Abort.'

As the president steepled his fingers, Bill Dodge spoke up.

'Sir, I can understand why my colleagues voted the way they did. But we can't lose sight of the fact that we have a survivor up there.'

'No one's losing sight of that, Bill,' Marti Nesbitt started to say.

'Let me finish, Marti. I believe I have a solution.' Dodge turned to the group. 'As you're all aware, I wear a couple of hats, one of them being the codirector of the Space Security Division. Prior to his tragic accident, Frank Richardson shared that responsibility. Now we've anticipated that at some point in time, a biological incident – *if* that's what occurred – might take place onboard a manned or unmanned flight. We looked specifically at the shuttle and engineered a special facility for just such a contingency.'

'And where would this facility be?' Gerald Simon asked.

'At our flight-testing range at Groome Lake, sixty miles northeast of Las Vegas.'

'What are we talking about exactly?' the president asked.

Dodge produced a videocassette from his briefcase. 'It's best you all see for yourselves.'

He inserted the tape into the VCR below the high-definition television monitor and pressed the play button. After a flurry of snow, an image of the desert came into sharp focus.

'Doesn't look like much of anything,' the national security adviser commented.

'Intentionally so,' Dodge replied. 'We borrowed the idea from the Israelis. Given its terrain, Israel has few places to hide its strike aircraft. So they built a series

347

of underground bunkers, with runways that don't look like runways – and have a unique feature.'

On the screen, what appeared to be desert floor began to tilt down at a gradually increasing angle. Dodge froze the frame.

'This is where the runway appears to end. But underneath is a system of hydraulic jacks. The runway actually extends for another six hundred yards as it slopes into an underground bunker.'

The camera followed the dip in the runway. On either side, a string of lights came on. As the camera descended the ramp, a huge, concrete-lined bunker appeared out of the gloom.

'This is the containment chamber,' Dodge explained. 'The walls are reinforced concrete, six feet thick. The air circulation is HEPA filtered, just like at the CDC hot zone labs.

'Once the shuttle is inside, the facility is sealed. A special team would be waiting for Dr Reed when he comes out and would take him into a decontamination chamber. Another team takes samples from inside the craft to determine what, if anything, is in there.'

'And if they find something?' the secretary of state asked. 'Something we may not want to keep around?'

'Then after the team has been extracted, this happens.'

On the screen, the image burst into flames.

'What we create is the equivalent to not one but three air-burst fuel bombs. The fire and the heat incinerate everything – and I do mean *everything*.'

His presentation complete, Dodge removed the video.

'Questions, observations?' the president asked.

'Has this facility been tested, Bill?' Marti Nesbitt asked.

'We've never destroyed a shuttle, if that's what you

mean. But the army has burned tanks to a crisp. The air force, entire Titan booster rockets. I can assure you, nothing survives in there.'

'I, for one, like the idea,' Gerald Simon spoke up. 'Equally important as getting Dr Reed back is finding out what went wrong up there. If we have a chance of getting that information *and* we can destroy the craft if need be, then I'm prepared to change my vote.'

There were nods and murmurs of assent around the room.

'I need a few minutes to consider this,' the president said, getting to his feet. 'I'm going to ask all of you to remain here. I won't be long.'

In the next room, the president faced Smith and Klein. Pointing at the closed-circuit monitor, he said, 'You saw and heard it all. What's your take?'

'Isn't it an interesting coincidence that there's a facility out at Groome Lake that's not only tailor-made for the current situation, but that no one's ever heard about, sir?' Klein said.

The president shook his head. 'I never suspected that such a place existed. Dodge must have found some money in the "black" budget, where he doesn't have to worry about congressional oversight – or anyone else's.'

'This place was built and designed for one purpose, Mr President: to house the shuttle, remove the sample, and destroy the orbiter,' Smith said.

'I agree,' Klein added. 'Bauer's operation has been moving ahead for years, Mr President. Richardson would have needed at least that much time to create this facility. And Bauer wouldn't have gone into this project unless he had an accomplice he could trust absolutely. General Richardson's position on the chemical-biological treaty that you signed is a matter of public record. He fought you every step of the way.'

'And ultimately crossed the line between patriotism and treason,' Castilla said. He looked at the two men. 'I've heard your plan. But I have to ask you again: do you recommend we let this thing land?'

Three faces looked up expectantly as the president returned to the Oval Office.

'Ladies and gentlemen, thank you for your patience,' the president opened. 'After careful consideration I've decided that the shuttle should be allowed to land at Groome Lake.'

There were assenting nods all around.

'Bill, I will expect to see complete details on this facility and the plans to deal with the orbiter and its contents.'

'You'll have them within the hour, sir,' the CIA director replied smartly. 'I'd also like to remind everyone that Dr Reed has specifically requested that Dr Karl Bauer be present at the landing facility. I believe that to be a sound suggestion. Dr Bauer is a world authority on chemical-biological incidents. In the past, he has worked closely with the Pentagon – including the Groome Lake project – and maintains a top-secret clearance. He would be invaluable as an observer and adviser.'

There were murmurs of agreement around the table.

'Then we're adjourned,' the president said. 'Air Force One leaves for Nevada in two hours.'

28

After sending Dylan Reed orders to change the schedule, Dr Karl Bauer had immediately boarded his jet and winged east to his company's sprawling complex near the Jet Propulsion Laboratory in Pasadena, California.

Knowing that the shuttle could land only at the Groome Lake flight-test facility, Bauer had been careful to make his presence in California seem like a coincidence. The flight plan from Hawaii had been filed three days earlier; the staff in Pasadena had been told to expect him.

It was in his office, the windows overlooking the distant San Gabriel Mountains, that Bauer received his first call from Harry Landon. He professed total shock, then deep concern, when the mission director explained the nature of the emergency that had overtaken *Discovery*. He couldn't help but smile when Landon told him that Reed had specifically asked for him to be present at Groome Lake. Bauer replied that, of course, he would make himself available. He suggested that Landon contact General Richardson to confirm authorization for his presence.

Then the flight director, his voice breaking, told Bauer that Richardson and Price had been killed when the car they were in spun out of control. Bauer's shock was genuine. Thanking Landon, he immediately got on cnn.com and devoured the details. From all counts, Richardson and Price's deaths were just that – an accident.

Which means that there are two less witnesses. Good.

As far as Bauer was concerned, both men had served their purpose. They had been especially helpful in removing that meddlesome Smith. What remained to be done Bauer could accomplish by himself.

Although he was far away from his principal facility in Hawaii, Bauer still had the resources to listen in on the NASA-*Discovery* transmissions. Built into his desk was a small but powerful communications console that was hooked up to his laptop computer. The screen displayed the shuttle's current range and trajectory; over the headset, Bauer heard real-time exchanges between *Discovery* and mission control. NASA was following the exact game plan he'd predicted. Checking the time, he thought that, barring complications, the orbiter would reenter the earth's atmosphere in a little over four hours from now.

Bauer slipped off the headset, closed the laptop, and shut down the console. In a few hours, he would be in possession of a brand-new life form, an entity he had created and which, if ever released, would be the most fearful scourge ever to stalk the earth. The thought left him giddy. That no one – at least for a very long time – would associate him with the new virus was a matter of indifference. Bauer's mindset was that of an art collector who bought a masterpiece only to hide it away from the world. The joy, the thrill, the intoxication flowed not from the work's monetary value but from the fact that it was unique and that it was *his*. Like the collector, Bauer would be the only one who would gaze upon the new variola, test it, probe its secrets. And he already had a home for it in a special containment section of the laboratory on the Big Island.

Six hundred miles west of the Mississippi, Air Force One continued to wing its way west.

The president and the working group from the Oval Office were in the upper-deck conference room going over the latest reports from mission control. As of the hour, *Discovery* was approaching the window through which it would reenter the earth's atmosphere. According to Harry Landon, all systems onboard the orbiter were green. Although Dylan Reed remained in the pilot's chair on the flight deck, the computers at mission control had taken command of *Discovery*.

Floating through the invisible speakers, Landon's voice filled the room. 'Mr President?'

'We're all here, Dr Landon,' Castilla said into the speakerphone.

'We're ready to move through the window, sir. At this point I need to inform the range safety officer whether or not to open up the channel to the autodestruct package or to stand down.'

The president glanced around the room. 'What are the implications if you open the channel?'

'That would allow for possible . . . malfunctions, Mr President. But if the channel remains closed, there is no chance that the package can be activated.'

'I'll see to it right now, Mr Landon. You'll have the necessary authorization in a moment.'

Castilla left the conference room, passed through the Secret Service cabin, and entered the true heart of Air Force One – its communications chamber. In an area the size of a galley kitchen, eight specialists monitored consoles and tended equipment that was light-years ahead of anything the public could imagine. Shielded from electromagnetic pulses, the machines could send and receive digitally encrypted messages to and from any U.S. facility, military or civilian, anywhere in the world.

One of the three techs on duty looked up. 'Mr President?'

'I need to send a message,' Castilla said quietly.

Edwards Air Force Base lay seventy-five miles northeast of Los Angeles, on the fringe of the Mojave Desert. In addition to housing first-strike bombers and fighter aircraft, and serving as the usual landing zone for the shuttle, the base had another, much less public function: it was one of the nation's six staging areas for RAID teams that would be activated in the event of a chemical-biological incident.

Virtually unknown to the public, the Rapid Attack and Incursion Detail was similar to NEST, the body of specialists who hunted lost or stolen nuclear weapons. The contingent was housed in a squat, bunkerlike building in the western section of the airfield. In a nearby hanger were a C-130 and three Commanche helicopters that would ferry the team to the emergency site.

The Ready Room was a cinderblock-lined area the size of a basketball court. Along one wall were twelve cubicles, separated by curtains. In each was a Level Four biohazard suit, complete with a rebreather, a weapon, and ammunition. The eleven men who made up this incursion team were quietly checking their armaments. Like SWAT teams, they carried an array of weapons, ranging from assault rifles to shotguns to various sidearms. The only difference between them and SWAT was the lack of snipers. RAID's business was close-in work; responsibility for securing the perimeter with the long guns belonged either to the army or to a federal SWAT unit.

The twelfth man, Commander Jack Riley, was in his makeshift office at one end of the room. He looked over the shoulder of his commo officer, seated in front of a portable communications unit, then back at Smith.

'The shuttle's almost down, Jon,' he said. 'We're starting to cut it kind of close.'

Smith nodded at the tall, rangy man with whom he had trained at USAMRIID and later served with in Desert Storm. 'I know.'

Smith had been watching the clock too. He and Klein had left Washington for Groome Lake two hours before the president and the others had boarded Air Force One. Klien would go directly to the test site while Smith would hook up with RAID. En route to Edwards, the chief executive had spoken with Riley, apprising him of an emergency situation onboard the shuttle, but leaving out the details. He also told him that Jon Smith was on his way and that Riley and his team would take their orders from him.

'What about the Commanches?' Smith asked.

'The pilots are sitting in the cockpits,' Riley replied. 'All they need are two minutes' notice.'

'Sir, we have incoming from Air Force One,' the commo officer said.

Riley picked up the phone, identified himself, and listened closely. 'Understood, sir. Yes, he's right here.' He passed the phone to Smith.

'Yes?' Smith said.

'Jon, this is the president. We're about sixty minutes out from Groome Lake. What's the situation on your end?'

'Prepped and ready, sir. All we need are the plans for the chamber.'

'They're coming through right now. Call me when you and Riley have gone over them.'

By the time Smith hung up, the commo officer had the incoming faxes laid out on a worktable.

'Looks like an industrial incinerator,' Riley murmured.

Smith agreed. The blueprints showed a rectangular area one hundred forty feet long, forty feet wide, and sixty feet high. All four walls were constructed of specially reinforced concrete. A part of the ceiling was actually a ramp that would close and seal when the shuttle was inside. At first glance, it might have looked like a parking or storage area. But on closer examination, Smith saw what Riley had alluded to – the walls were studded with pipes that, according to the blueprints, were connected to gas lines. Smith could only imagine the kind of inferno they would create when lighted.

'We're taking it as an article of faith that the shuttle is clean on the outside, right?' Riley said. 'Nothing could have gotten out?'

Smith shook his head. 'Even if it could, the heat from reentry would scour the orbiter's skin clean. No, it's the interior that's the hot zone.'

'Our kind of playground,' Riley said.

'Yeah, except this time we might have to take it away from somebody else,' Smith said.

Riley pulled him aside. 'Jon, this operation hasn't been going exactly by the numbers. First the president calls and tells me to break out the team. All he says is that we're going to some place in Nevada. That turns out to be some spook base at Groome Lake where the shuttle's going to make an emergency landing because it encountered a biochem hazard. Now it looks like you intend to incinerate the damn thing.'

Smith walked Riley out of earshot of the rest of the team. A moment later, one of the RAID members nudged his buddy.

'Look at Riley. He looks like he's about to toss his cookies.'

In fact, Jack Riley was wishing that he'd never asked Smith what was onboard the orbiter.

Megan Olson accepted the fact that she had run out of options. The nest of wires had defeated her. None of the combinations she'd tried worked. The air-lock door remained frozen.

Standing back from the door, Megan listened to the chatter between Reed and mission control. The shuttle was only minutes from entering the atmospheric window through which it would return to earth. She had exactly that long to decide.

Megan forced herself to look at the explosive bolts set in each corner of the door. During her training, her instructors had pointed them out to her, saying that they were really a redundancy. The shuttle crew was never meant to use them. They were there in case a NASA ground team had to enter the shuttle during an emergency evacuation after the orbiter had landed.

After it lands, the instructors had emphasized. And only if entry through the main hatches was, for one reason or another, impossible. They had cautioned her that the bolts were on a timer that would give the ground team enough time to take cover.

'These things create a controlled explosion,' she recalled

the instructors saying. 'You don't want to be within fifty feet when they blow.'

Megan estimated that at best she was fourteen, maybe fifteen feet from the air-lock door.

If you're going to do it, do it now!

From her training and her rides onboard the Vomit Comet, Megan knew that the descent through the earth's atmosphere would be even more jarring than the liftoff. She recalled Carter saying that it was like riding a Brahman bull at a rodeo. Everything and everyone had to be strapped down securely. If she remained in the air lock, she would be hurled against the walls until she was unconscious – or worse. Her EMU would undoubtedly tear, so even if she survived reentry, what Reed had loosed in the ship would eat her up. But there were alternatives. She had to give herself a chance to get to the Spacelab, find Reed's monstrosity, and destroy it before the shuttle was too close to the earth.

Megan felt a calm descend over her, even though her heart was pounding like a jackhammer. She fixed her attention on the hexagonal bolts, painted red with a yellow dot in the centre. Pushing off the wall, she floated across the floor. When she reached the bottom right bolt, she pressed the yellow dot. A tiny control panel slid forward. The LCD blinked at her: ARM/DISARM. Carefully, because the EMU suit glove made her fingers clumsy, she pressed ARM.

Shit!

The timer immediately set itself for sixty seconds, a shorter time span than Megan had anticipated. She slithered to the next bolt and quickly set it. Pushing off the floor, she anchored herself and activated the top two bolts. When she was finished, she had twenty seconds left.

She took two steps, and then floated as far away from the door as was possible. Even though she had pulled down her visor, she could still see the four pulsing lights in the centre of the bolts. She knew she should have her back to the air lock, or at least stand sideways, so that the explosions wouldn't catch her in the face. But as the seconds counted down, all she could do was stare at the winking lights.

Two levels above, on the flight deck, Dylan Reed was getting the final signals from Harry Landon at mission control.

'You're right on target,' Landon said. 'Reentry looks good.'

'I can't see the counter,' Reed said. 'How much time to commo blackout?'

'Fifteen seconds.'

A communications blackout was a natural occurrence during reentry. The interruption lasted about three minutes and was still, even after all the manned flights, the most nerve-racking interval of the entire mission.

'Are you strapped in, Dylan?' Landon asked.

'As much as I can be. This suit's a little bulky.'

'Just hang on and we'll try to make the ride as smooth and fast as possible.' Landon paused. 'Ten seconds . . . Good luck, Dylan. Talk to you on the other side. Seven, six, five . . .'

Reed settled back and closed his eyes. He thought that immediately after reentry and reestablishing contact with Landon, he'd have to go back to the Spacelab and –

The shuttle bucked, the force almost tearing Reed out of his restraints.

'What the hell! Harry!'
'Dylan, what's wrong?'
'Harry, there's been –'

Reed's voice was cut off abruptly. Nothing except faint static filled the speakers at mission control. Landon whirled around to the tech next to him. 'Play back the tape!'

'What the hell! Harry!'
'Dylan, what's wrong?'
'Harry, there's been –'

'An explosion!' Landon whispered.

The working group was still in Air Force One's conference room with the president when the commo officer rushed in. Scanning the message, Castilla's face turned white.

'You're sure?' he demanded, staring at the officer.

'Landon's positive, sir.'

'Patch me through to him. Now!'

He looked around the table. 'Something blew on the shuttle.'

The bolts rocketed in Megan's direction, slamming and digging into the walls of the air lock. But because the shuttle had bucked on reentry, the door, which would have sailed right into her, was thrown violently to the left. It caromed off the wall, careened within inches of her, then slammed against another wall.

Without stopping to think, Megan pushed off and sailed for the door, grabbing it and pinning it with both arms. She held it for a moment, then released her grip and let it float away.

Moving through the cavity into the lower deck, she climbed the staircase to the mid-deck and headed for the hatch that opened on the tunnel to the Spacelab.

She blew the bolts! The bitch blew the bolts!

Reed knew it as soon as he felt the tremors course through the craft. Confirmation came in the form of winking lights on the console, indicating a door malfunction in the air lock.

Working his way out of the restraining straps, Reed manoeuvred his way to the ladder and, like a diver plunging into water, started down headfirst. He guessed that he had about two minutes to find Megan. After that, the shuttle ride would become too rough to continue pursuit. The craft would also come out of its blackout screen. Reed had no doubt that even if mission control hadn't heard the explosion, its instruments would have registered it. Harry Landon would be peppering him with questions, demanding explanations and updates.

As Reed snaked his way down the ladder, he found himself amazed by Megan's actions. It had taken guts – more than he'd thought she had – to blow the air-lock door. But odds were that she was dead. He had seen the effects of an explosion in a place as confined as an air lock.

Reed reached mid-deck and was about to keep going when he caught movement out the corner of his eye.

My God, she's alive!

Reed watched as Megan, her back to him, worked the submarinetype wheel on the tunnel door. Moving to a

361

tool case, he opened a drawer and pulled out a specially designed saw.

Seated in the lead Commanche, Jon Smith looked at the other grim-faced RAID agents. Right now, they all wore flight overalls. That would change as soon as they arrived at Groome Lake, where they would don their Level Four protective gear before entering the bunker.

Turning to Jack Riley, he spoke into his flight-helmet microphone. 'How far out are we?'

Riley held up a finger and communicated with the pilot. 'Forty minutes,' he replied. 'You can bet that Groome Lake already has us on radar. Another few miles and they'll scramble their own chopper, or even a couple of F-16s, for a look-see.'

He raised his eyebrows. 'What's the president waiting for? Air Force One has been on the ground for almost a half hour.'

As though on cue, a new voice came over Smith's headset.

'This is Bluebird calling RAID One.'

Smith responded instantly. 'This is RAID One. Go ahead, Blue-bird.' Bluebird was the designation for Nathaniel Klein.

'Jon?'

'Right here, sir. We were wondering when you'd call.'

'We had a . . . a situation here. The president just ordered your flight cleared for touchdown. For the purpose of this mission, you and your people will be considered attached to his party.'

'Yes, sir. You mentioned a situation, sir.'

There was a slight hesitation. 'Mission control reports

talking to Reed just before the orbiter entered the black zone. The last thing Landon heard was an explosion, which the computers later confirmed.'

'Is the craft intact?' Smith demanded.

'According to the instrument readings, *Discovery* is still on its designated flight path. The explosion took place in an air lock. For a reason we don't know, the bolts blew.'

'The air lock . . . Where was Reed at the time?'

'On the flight deck. But Landon can't be sure about the extent of the damage or even if Reed's still alive. No one's answering up there, Jon.'

29

The last thing Megan had heard over her headset was the exchange between Reed and Harry Landon, seconds before the bolts on the air-lock doors had blown. After she got up to the mid-deck, she realized that Reed would come down to investigate. He had to make sure that she was dead or injured – either would suit his purpose. When he didn't find her in the air lock or the lower deck, he would start looking elsewhere.

Megan knew she couldn't hide from him for long. The orbiter was simply too small. There was only one escape. Making her way to the mid-deck, she floated to the door that opened up on the tunnel to the Spacelab. She gripped the arms of the wheel on the door and began turning.

But Megan never forgot that she had her back to the ladder that connected the three levels. She would never hear Reed if he spotted her and came up behind her. The small mirror she had placed at the foot of the tunnel door would now save her life.

In the reflection, she had seen Reed descend the ladder, hesitate, then spot her and start floating to her. She watched him stop by a tool kit, retrieve a type of keyhole saw, then keep on coming.

Megan had the wheel on the door turned as far as it would go, but she kept her hands on the grips and pretended that the wheel was stuck. Looking down, she saw Reed drift closer, his right arm stretched out to her.

In his hand, the saw looked like the pointed nose of a marlin.

Megan let her left hand slip from the wheel. Set into the door was a release button that pulled the door open once the wheel had been fully turned. Her eyes riveted on the mirror, she judged the distance between her and Reed. Her timing would have to be perfect.

Reed watched Megan jerk as she tried to force the wheel. Raising the saw, he floated closer. Since she was standing, he chose a spot between her neck and her shoulder. The teeth of the saw would slice through her plastic suit. The result would be instant depressurization. The air inside the suit would rush out . . . and the contaminated air around her would stream into the rent. Two, three breaths and the variola would be in her lungs.

In microgravity, it is impossible to move with any real speed. When Reed started his downward swing, he appeared to be moving in slow motion. But Megan *pushed* off, propelling herself sideways from the door. As she did, she jabbed the release button. With a nearly inaudible pneumatic hiss, the door swung open as Reed drifted into the space Megan had occupied just a second ago. The heavy door caught him square on the helmet, whipping back his neck, then dragging him as it opened fully. His fingers lost their grip on the saw, which floated away.

Stunned and reeling, Reed made a feeble grab for Megan as she floated around him into the tunnel. Inside, she found another button, punched it, and watched the door begin to close.

Come on, come on!

The door seemed to inch its way towards her. As soon as Megan could reach the grips on the wheel, she began pulling.

She saw the flash of the saw as it sliced through the opening, only inches from her suit sleeve. As Reed drew back for another strike, she managed to close the door and spin the wheel. The locks set and Megan pulled the emergency lever to freeze them in place.

His rasping voice made her heart jump into her throat. 'What a clever girl you are, Megan. Can you hear me? Did you fix your intercom too?'

Megan pressed a button on her unit and heard a faint crackle.

'I can hear you breathing,' Reed said. 'Or more accurately, hyperventilating.'

'And I can hear you, but not too well,' she said. 'You'll have to speak up.'

'I'm glad you haven't lost your sense of humour,' Reed said. 'Very slippery, what you did back there. You were playing possum, weren't you? Waiting for me . . .'

'Dylan . . .' She didn't know where to begin.

'You think you're safe, don't you?' he said. 'As long as the emergency locks are set, I can't get in. But if you think about it, Megan, put aside your panic and really think, that's not true.'

Megan struggled to understand what he was referring to but nothing came to mind.

'No matter what you think you can do, you'll never leave this craft alive,' Reed continued.

Suppressing a shudder, she replied: 'You won't win either, Dylan. I'm going to destroy the horror you made here.'

'Really? You have no idea *what* I did in there.'

Oh, yes, I do! 'I'll find it!'

'With less than sixty minutes from touchdown? I don't think so. It'll be all you can do to stay alive when we go through the last stages of reentry. And Megan?

Even if you found it, what would you do – dispose of it through the waste portals? Not a bad idea – if we were still in space. But since you have no idea what I was working on, how can you be sure that it would die once we're in the earth's atmosphere? To jettison it would mean running the risk of possibly *spreading* it.'

He paused. 'You didn't see the bodies, did you? Just as well, really. But if you had, you wouldn't even *think* of dispersing a virus.'

Reed chuckled. 'Now you're asking yourself, where would I have put it? How would it be disguised? So many questions, and no time to find the answers. Because we've just about reached our next bumpy ride. If I were you, I'd find something to hang on to – fast.'

Megan heard the click of the microphone as Reed signed off. Then she felt a tremor race through the ship as the orbiter cut through another layer of the earth's atmosphere. Without looking back, she began pulling herself down the tunnel towards the Spacelab.

Reed climbed back up to the flight deck and managed to strap himself into the commander's chair as waves of turbulence hit the shuttle. The orbiter shuddered, then yawed. Checking the instrument panel, Reed noted that the orbital manoeuvring system engine had fired, slowing the craft just enough so that gravity could take effect. If all went well, gravity would pull *Discovery* out of orbit and into a gentle glide to earth.

The shudders became a series of vibrations as the craft's speed dropped from twenty-five times to two times the speed of sound. Then the buffeting ceased altogether and *Discovery* turned into its glide path. The communications blackout had ended and Reed heard Landon's urgent voice.

'*Discovery*, do you read? Dylan, can you hear me?' After a pause: 'Our instruments registered an onboard explosion. Can you confirm? Are you all right?'

I don't have time for this right now, Harry.

Reed closed the communications channel and glanced over the instrument panel until he found what he was looking for. He'd told Megan that she was mistaken in thinking that he couldn't get past the locks on the door to the tunnel. He wondered if she'd figured out how. Probably not. As bright and as capable as Megan was, she was still a novice. She couldn't have known that a switch on the flight deck could override the locks on the tunnel door.

There wasn't much to hang on to inside the Spacelab, so Megan improvised. In the centre of the lab was a metallic object that looked like something between a modern-day torture rack and a high-tech recliner. Its technical name was a Space Physiology Experiment. The crew called it the sled chair. There, crew members, lying on their backs and strapped in securely, underwent tests on joints and muscles, the effects of gravity on the inner ear and on the eyeball, and various other experiments.

Having strapped herself into the sled chair, Megan managed to ride out the turbulence. Now she undid the straps and, with substantial effort, got to her feet. Light-headedness, caused by decreased blood volume, hit her immediately. Megan knew it would take at least a few minutes for the volume to increase as the orbiter approached earth. The process would have been faster if she'd had some water and salt tablets.

But you don't. And you're running out of time!

She looked at the dozen racks that served as stations for Spacelab experiments.

Think! Where would he have put it?

Megan's gaze travelled to the space accelerator measurement system, then to the critical point facility. *No.* She started to move to the microgravity vestibular investigator module, then stopped.

A virus ... Reed rearranged the order of the experiments. He put himself first, taking my place! He needed the Biorack!

Megan stepped over to the Biorack and fired up its systems. The LCD was blank.

Whatever he did, he erased the records.

Looking into the Glovebox, she discovered it was empty.

This is where you did your work, you son of a bitch. But where did you put the results?

Megan checked both incubator units, the access and control panels, and the power panel. The latter had been on even before she'd touched the Biorack's operating system ...

... because the cooler is on!

Megan opened the cooler and checked the contents. Everything was in place. Nothing had been taken out or added. That left the freezer.

Pulling down the panel, she quickly inventoried the contents. At first glance, everything could be accounted for. Not satisfied, she pulled out one rack of standard test tubes, checked their markings, and set the rack back. She repeated the process with two more racks. In the third, she found a tube with no markings.

As soon as the shuttle's flight had stabilized, Reed unbuckled himself from the commander's chair. He entered an override programme into the computer, set the timer, and activated the sequence. If his judgment was correct, he should reach the door to the tunnel just as the programme released the emergency locks.

Climbing down the ladder, Reed entered mid-deck and plodded his way to the door. He had only a few seconds to wait before the locks popped open. Working the wheel, he pushed open the door and began crawling through the tunnel. Reaching the end, he pulled open the door to the Spacelab. There was Megan, standing by the Biorack, searching the cooler.

Reed came up behind her. His right arm caught her across the chest while his foot swept her legs out from under her. Gravity did the rest. Megan fell back, landing heavily on her shoulder and rolling over.

'Don't bother getting up,' Reed said into his microphone. 'Can you hear me?'

He saw her nod, then opened the freezer and pulled out a rack of test tubes. He knew exactly where he'd placed the one containing the variola and there it was. Tucking it into a pocket with a secure Velcro flap, he stepped back. Megan had rolled over so that she could look at him.

'You can still stop this, Dylan.'

He shook his head. 'You can't put the genie back into the bottle. But at least you'll die knowing that it's *our* genie.'

Reed never took his eyes off her as he backed away towards the door. Stepping into the tunnel, he closed the door and locked it.

The overhead clock read twenty minutes to touchdown.

30

A little over an hour had passed since Air Force One had landed at Groome Lake, Nevada. Escorted by a pair of F-15 Eagle interceptors, it had come in on the same runway that, a decade earlier, had been built to flight-test the B-2 bomber. As soon as the presidential platfrom was on the ground, a contingent of air force security accompanied the chief executive and his working group to the shuttle landing facility a mile and a half away.

In spite of the heat, the president insisted on walking along the runway with his group and then down the ramp into the holding area. He glanced around at the interior of the bunker. With its smooth concrete walls, broken only by outlets for the gas jets, it reminded him of a giant crematorium.

Which is really what it is . . .

The president pointed to a cocoonlike tube, eight feet high, five feet wide, that ran from one of the walls into the middle of the bunker like a gigantic umbilical cord.

'What's that?' he asked an air police lieutenant.

Castilla turned when he heard the soft whir of an electric golf cart. Seated beside an air force security guard was Dr Karl Bauer. When the cart pulled up alongside the group, Bauer got out and, nodding at members of the entourage, walked directly to the president.

'Mr President,' he said gravely. 'It is good to see you

again. Although I wish it were under more pleasant circumstances.'

The president knew that his eyes were his weakness. They always gave away his moods and emotions. Trying not to recall what Smith and Klein had told him, he forced himself to smile and to shake the hand of a man he'd once respected, who had been honoured at the White House. *Who's a fucking monster.*

But what he said was, 'The pleasure is mine, Dr Bauer. Believe me, I'm grateful that you're here.' He gestured towards the cocoon. 'Maybe you could explain this.'

'Certainly.'

Bauer led the way to the end of the cocoon. Looking inside, the president saw that the last six feet of the chamber were sealed off from the rest, creating a kind of vault or air lock.

'This portable cocoon is my own design and manufacture,' Bauer said. 'It can be flown anywhere in the world, set up in a matter of hours, then coupled by remote control to the target. Its sole purpose is to extract an individual from a hot zone that may be difficult or impossible to enter – which is the situation we are faced with.'

'Why not go directly into the shuttle, Doctor? Surely with protective suits that's possible.'

'Possible, yes, Mr President. Advisable? No. We have no idea what is loose on board the orbiter. Right now, we have one survivor, Dr Reed, who is not contaminated. It would be best to bring him off the ship and put him through the decontamination process rather than risk sending someone to get him. There's less chance of an accident, and we'd be able to find out very quickly what happened.'

'But Dr Reed doesn't know what happened,' the president objected. 'Or what we're dealing with.'

'We can't be sure,' Bauer replied. 'Under the circumstances, it's not unusual for people to have observed or remembered more than they think they do. In any event, we then send in a robot probe to take samples. There are full lab facilities here. I will be able to tell you within the hour what it is we're dealing with.'

'In the meantime, the shuttle sits here, hot, as you would say.'

'Certainly you can give the order to have it destroyed immediately,' Bauer replied. 'However, there are the bodies of the other crew members. If there is any chance of bringing them out, giving them a decent burial, I believe we should hold out for it.'

The president fought to keep his rage in check. The butcher's concern for his victims was almost more than he could bear.

'I agree. Please, continue.'

'Once the cocoon is mated to the shuttle, I will enter from the other end – behind the wall,' Bauer explained. 'I will walk into this small decontamination chamber, check it, and seal it. Only then will Dr Reed be instructed to open *Discovery*'s hatch and step directly into the decontamination area.'

Bauer pointed to PVC pipes running along the ceiling the length of the cocoon. 'These supply electricity and decontamination detergents. The chamber is equipped with ultraviolet light, which is deadly to all known forms of bacteria. The detergent is an added precaution. Dr Reed will undress. Both he and his suit – except for the sample we need – will be cleaned at the same time.'

'Why clean the suit?'

'Because we have no practical way to dispose of it in the chamber, Mr President.'

The president remembered the question Klein had asked him to raise. Bauer's response was vital, but it had to be elicited in such a way so as not to arouse the slightest suspicion.

'If the suit needs to be sterilized,' he asked, 'then how does the sample come out?'

'The chamber has a pass-through facility,' Bauer explained. 'Dr Reed will deposit the sample into a carrier tray. On the other side, I will roll the tray through into the Glovebox. This way the sample will always remain in a secure environment. Using the Glovebox, I will deposit the sample into a secure container, then bring that out.'

'And you'll be doing this yourself.'

'As you can see, Mr President, the space inside the cocoon is somewhat restricted. Yes, I will be working alone.'

So nobody can see what you're really doing.

The president stepped back from the cocoon. 'This is all very impressive, Dr Bauer. Let's hope it works as advertised.'

'It will, Mr President. At the very least, we know we can save one of those brave souls.'

The president turned to the group. 'I guess we're as ready as we'll ever be.'

'I recommend we go to the observation bunker,' CIA director Bill Dodge suggested. 'The shuttle is fifteen minutes out. We can watch the touchdown on the monitors.'

'Has there been any contact with Dr Reed?' the president asked.

'No, sir. Communications are still out.'

'What about that explosion?'

'I'm still waiting for more details, Mr President,' Marti Nesbitt replied. 'But whatever it was, it didn't affect *Discovery*'s flight path.'

As the group followed the president to the entrance of the bunker, Castilla looked back. 'Aren't you coming with us, Dr Bauer?'

Bauer's expression was suitably grim. 'Oh, no, Mr President. My place is here.'

Grabbing hold of the space acceleration system, Megan managed to pull herself up. Her chest throbbed where Reed had hit her, and there was a shooting pain in her lower back where she'd fallen.

You're running out of time. Move!

Megan staggered to the sled chair. She had no doubt that Reed would use *Discovery*'s autodestruct system to vaporize all evidence of his diabolical handiwork. That would be the only way to ensure his safety. That was why he hadn't killed her before leaving the Spacelab. Megan glanced at the sled chair and knew it was her only hope.

There was no communications equipment as such in the Spacelab. But during medical tests, crew members had been wired not only into the recording instruments onboard *Discovery* but also to a communications feed that relayed the results directly to physicians at mission control. Settling herself in the chair, Megan strapped down her ankles and one wrist. With her free hand, she plugged a microphone jack into the communications unit on her suit. As far as she knew, the feed sent back digital, not voice, data back to mission control. But then again, no one had ever told her that voice communication was impossible.

Just let someone on the other end hear me, she prayed, and activated the sled's instrument panel.

'RAID One to Looking Glass, come in.'

The voice of the pilot in the lead Commanche crackled in Smith's headset. A second later, he heard the Groome Lake tower's response.

'RAID One, this is Looking Glass. You are in restricted air space. Immediate authorization is requested.'

'Authorization is Brass Hat,' the pilot replied calmly. 'Repeat, Brass Hat.'

Brass Hat was the Secret Service code name for the president.

'RAID flight, this is Looking Glass,' the controller replied. 'We have positive ID on you. You are cleared to land on runway R twenty-seven, L left.'

'R twenty-seven L left, roger,' the pilot said. 'Touchdown in two minutes.'

'Where's the shuttle?' Smith asked.

The pilot keyed into the NASA frequency. 'Thirteen minutes out.'

At mission control, Harry Landon was tracking the shuttle's progress through the atmosphere on a giant plotting board, where she appeared as a gently descending red dot. In a few minutes, low altitude satellites would be able to transmit pictures. As *Discovery* got closer, air force reconnaissance planes would roll their cameras.

'Landon?'

Landon glanced up at the commo tech. 'What is it?'

'I'm not sure, sir,' the tech replied, obviously confused. He handed Landon a printout. 'This just came in.'

Landon glanced at the sheet. 'It's the medical feed from the sled chair.' He shook his head. 'It must be a malfunction. Reed is on the flight deck. For the feed to be accurate would mean that someone else is in the sled chair.'

'Yes, sir,' the tech agreed. He didn't have to be reminded that that someone would have to be *alive*. 'But look at this. The chair's instruments are on. The heart monitor shows signs of activity – very faint, but activity nonetheless.'

Landon slipped his reading glasses down his nose. The tech was right: the heart monitor was registering a living organism.

'What the hell?'

'Listen to this, sir,' the tech said. 'It's the last few minutes of commo tape. We kept it rolling even though . . .'

Landon grabbed the headphones. 'Play it for me!'

Since the beginning of the emergency, Landon had listened to so many hours of transmission that he could tune out the hiss and crackle that filled his ears. Behind the static he heard something, barely discernible but distinctly human . . . a voice calling from the ethers.

'This is . . . *Discovery* . . . Spacelab . . . am alive . . . Repeat, alive . . . Help me . . .'

Jack Riley and his RAID team began jumping out even before the Commanches' rotors wound down. Smith glanced at the enormous hangars lined up like prehistoric turtles, their roofs painted dull brown to blend in with the desolate landscape. To the south and west were mountain ranges; to the northeast, nothing but desert. Even through the din of men and machinery, there was an eerie stillness to the base.

The team arranged their equipment in a flatbed truck that had pulled up, then jumped aboard for the short ride. Smith and Riley followed in the Humvee.

The hangar's interior was partitioned to allow the team privacy – and, Smith suspected, to prevent them from seeing what else was stored there. As Riley had promised, a commo console was up and running, manned by a young female officer.

'Colonel,' she said. 'You have flash traffic from Blue-bird.'

Smith was adjusting his headset when Klein came on. 'What's your status, Jon?'

'We're getting into our Level Four suits right now. How about the shuttle?'

'It'll be in the chamber by the time you get there.'

'Bauer?'

'Doesn't suspect a thing. He's already suited up and ready to mate the cocoon with the shuttle.'

Smith had seen the blueprints and photos of Bauer's creation, but he had never been inside it.

'Jon, there's something you need to know – and hear,' Klein said. 'A few minutes ago, Landon received communications from inside the Spacelab. It was a distress signal. We're running tests right now. I don't want to raise your hopes, but the voice sounded like Megan's.'

Sheer joy surged through Smith. Yet at the same time, he was aware of the possibly deadly consequences of this development.

'Has Landon told Reed about this?'

'Not that I know of. Communications are still down.

But I should have told Landon to keep quiet in case contact was reestablished. Wait one.'

Smith tried to rein in his clashing emotions. The idea that Megan was alive brought him hope. At the same time, if Reed somehow discovered this, he would still have a chance to kill her before he left the shuttle.

'Jon? It's all right. Landon says the link is still down. I confused the hell out of him by ordering him not to talk in case it comes back up, but I have his word that he won't tell Reed a thing.'

'Anything on those voice tests?' Smith demanded.

'So far they're inconclusive.'

'Can you play me the tape?'

'It's pretty scratched up.'

Smith closed his eyes and listened. After a few moments, he said, 'That's her, sir. Megan's alive.'

31

'Looking Glass, this is Eyeball. Do you copy?'

'Eyeball, we read you five by five. What do you see?'

'*Discovery* has just broken cloud cover. Trim is good. Angle of descent good. Speed good. She looks to make a pinpoint landing.'

'Roger that, Eyeball. Maintain surveillance. Looking Glass out.'

The exchange between Eyeball, the lead air force chase plane that would escort the shuttle, and the control tower at Groome Lake was listened to intently by a number of people.

In the observation bunker, the president glanced briefly around the room. All eyes were on the monitors that showed *Discovery* cutting through the air. On another screen he saw Dr Karl Bauer about to leave the decontamination area, called the prep room. The president took a deep breath. Soon . . . very soon.

Wearing a Level Four biohazard suit, Bauer entered the short corridor between the prep room and the massive, vaultlike door that would allow him to enter the cocoon. Reaching it, he glanced up at the wall-mounted camera and nodded. Slowly the door began to open, revealing a cavity cut into the concrete wall. One end of the cocoon was attached to the wall of the cavity, the edges sealed to the concrete. Bauer stepped into the cocoon and immediately the door began to close.

Ahead, he saw a long, blue-lighted tunnel. When the door was firmly closed and locked, he walked along a rubber-padded runway. The walls of the cocoon were constructed of heavy gauge, semitransparent plastic. Looking through them, Bauer could see the vague outlines of the vast holding area, lit up by giant floodlights. As he moved towards the cocoon's decontamination chamber, he heard a low rumble. More light poured into the bunker as the runway ramp was lowered.

'This is Bauer,' he said into his headset. 'Do you copy?'

'We read you, sir,' a tech in the observation bunker replied.

'Has the shuttle landed?'

'It's almost on the ground, sir.'

'Good,' Bauer replied, and continued walking to the cocoon's decontamination chamber.

On the other side of the base, Smith was listening in on this exchange. He turned to Jack Riley. 'Let's mount up.'

The team scrambled into two double deuces with canvas covers. Smith would have preferred to use the more nimble and speedy Humvees instead of the trucks, but given the team's bulky biohazard suits, space was a problem.

The hangar doors opened and the small convoy, with Riley in the lead Humvee, pulled out into the desert night. Rocking back and forth on a bench in the back of the truck, Smith tried to keep a small, Palm Pilot-type monitor as steady as he could. The shuttle was just three thousand feet above the desert floor. Its nose was angled up slightly and the landing gear was locked down. As hard as he tried, Smith couldn't keep his thoughts away from Megan. He knew that his first instinct would be to rush into the orbiter and search for her. But doing so would only jeopardize her life. He had to get to Reed first and neutralize him. Only then could he go after her.

Smith recalled Klein's objections when he had told him what he intended to do. The head of Covert-One shared Smith's concern for Megan, but he also knew the danger that Smith would be exposing himself to.

'There's no guarantee that you'll find her alive, Jon,' he'd said. 'We need to know what we're dealing with before I send you in.'

'We'll know,' Smith had promised him grimly.

Riley's voice crackled over his headset. 'Jon, look to the southeast.'

Smith glanced over the truck's tailgate and saw bright lights descending quickly. On either side were the winking collision lights of the shuttle's escort aircraft. He listened as Riley counted off the descent: 'Five hundred feet . . . two hundred . . . touchdown.'

The convoy was on a runway parallel to the one the shuttle used. Smith saw the orbiter dip as the nose gear absorbed the weight. Then the parachutes popped open, slowing the craft.

'Here comes the cavalry,' he heard Riley say.

Three fire trucks and a HazMat vehicle fanned out behind the shuttle, staying fifty yards back.

Smith watched them roll by, then said, 'Okay, Jack. Let's fall in.'

The double deuces slipped into gear and followed Riley's Humvee as it turned onto the taxiway, then the main runway.

'Step on it, Jack!' Smith said as he watched the shuttle reach the ramp that descended into the bunker.

Riley obliged. Gunning the deuce, he pulled up to the ramp just as the shuttle disappeared.

'Jon!'

But Smith had already jumped out and was running into the bunker. Two-thirds of the way down, he felt the ramp shudder and slowly rise. Moving as fast as he could, he reached the end only to discover that he was ten feet above the bunker floor. Smith took a deep breath and jumped, landing hard, then ducking and rolling. Lying on his back, he watched the ramp slowly rise, blot out the sky, then lock and seal.

Getting to his feet, he turned and saw the cocoon, a monstrous, white worm beneath the overhead lights. Inside it, a shadow paused in its movement and slowly turned towards him.

Dr Karl Bauer had been watching the shuttle park, then turned his attention to the ramp. For an instant, he thought he saw something drop from the ramp, but dismissed the thought when he felt the ramp close with a shudder. The cavern was sealed.

'Control, this is Bauer.'

'This is control, Doctor,' a technician replied. 'Is everything all right?'

'Yes. I am proceeding to mate the cocoon with the orbiter. When Dr Reed is safely out, I will reseal the hatch. Is that understood?'

'We copy, Doctor. Good luck.'

Staring through the plastic, Smith saw Bauer's form become more and more vague as the scientist moved through the cocoon. Careful not to allow Bauer to see

383

him, he started to make his way to the shuttle when he noticed a perfectly round break in the concrete. Then he picked out another one. Then many more. Places where the cement had been cored for the gas lines that would feed the flames.

On the flight deck, Dylan Reed had remained strapped in the pilot's chair until a light on the console indicated that the orbiter's systems had shut down completely. The descent had been nerve-racking. At the Cape, Reed had been shown computer simulations of how, in the event of an emergency, NASA computers would bring down the craft – and park it on a dime if need be. He recalled smiling and saying how wonderful that was. Privately, he'd thought: *Right. A few hundred gallons of residual, high-octane fuel onboard a hurtling, ten-year-old craft built by the lowest bidder.* Yet by some miracle, both the computers and the orbiter had done their job.

Reed unstrapped himself, got out of the chair, and made his way down the ladder to mid-deck. He glanced briefly at the door that opened on the tunnel to the Spacelab. He wondered if Megan Olson had somehow survived. It didn't matter. She would never see anything familiar again.

During reentry, Reed had kept the communications channels switched off. He didn't think he could bear listening to Harry Landon's whiny questions and expressions of concern. Nor did he want to be distracted from what lay ahead. Positioning himself in front of the exit hatch, he punched in the alphanumeric code that shot back the bolts. But the hatch still had to be opened from the outside.

Reed glanced down at the pants pocket in which he'd placed the vial of variola. Suddenly, he wanted very much to be rid of it.

Come on! he thought impatiently.

He felt the orbiter shift slightly. Then a second time. He imagined he could hear the hiss of air as the cocoon mated itself to the shuttle. Anxiously he looked at the overhead display panel. A green light appeared, indicating that the mating was complete.

Reed was changing frequencies on his suit radio when, without warning, the hatch opened and retracted and he found himself looking straight at the masked face of Dr Karl Bauer.

'You!' he cried.

The original plan had called for Bauer to wait for Reed on the quarantine side of the decontamination chamber. But with Richardson and Price out of the picture, Bauer had decided to improve upon his scheme. Working the levers on the pedestal-mounted control panel, he raised the cocoon so that its open end mated with the shuttle. Once the seals were in place, he took a moment to slip into his new role, then opened the hatch. He almost smiled when he saw Reed's startled expression.

'What are you doing here?' Reed demanded. 'What's wrong?'

Bauer motioned him to step back so that he could enter.

'Richardson is dead,' he said bluntly. 'So is Price.'

'Dead? But how could –?'

Bauer began to mix in the lies. 'The president knows about the virus.'

385

Even through his protective faceplate, Bauer saw how badly Reed paled. 'That's impossible!'

'It's true,' Bauer replied. 'Now listen to me. There's still a way out for us. Are you listening?'

Reed's helmet bobbed as he nodded.

'Good. Now give me the sample.'

'But how will we –?'

'Get it out? Me. Listen, Dylan. I haven't a clue as to how much Castilla and his people really know about Richardson and Price. Maybe they've already connected you to them. But we can't afford to take the chance that they have. If you're searched, it's all over. But they wouldn't dare lay a finger on me.'

'What's going to happen to me?' Reed demanded, his voice panicky.

'Nothing. You have my word on that. By the time this is over, you'll be the hero, the only survivor of a mission gone tragically wrong. Now give me the sample.'

Carefully Reed reached into his pocket and handed over the vial. He jumped back as Bauer calmly opened it and poured out the fatal contents on a stainless-steel counter.

'Are you crazy?' he screamed. 'That's all we have!'

'I didn't say that we wouldn't take a sample,' Bauer replied.

He pulled out a swab and a tiny, ceramic capsule, the size of a vitamin capsule. Bending over the puddle he had just created, he brushed the swab in the fluids, broke off the tip, and sealed it in the capsule. Reed watched, puzzled. He couldn't quite snare the purpose of the capsule.

'You're going to carry it out like that?' he asked. 'What about the decontamination process?'

'The ceramic will protect the sample,' Bauer replied.

'After all, that's what the plates on the underbelly of this craft are made of, to preserve the shuttle from the heat of reentry. Don't worry, Dylan. It's all part of my new plan.'

Something didn't sound quite right to Reed. 'So what do I –'

Out of the corner of his eye, he saw a flash of the scalpel that cut open his suit, slicing all the way to flesh.

'No!' he cried, staggering back.

'Witnesses aren't part of the new plan,' Bauer said. 'If I let you come out, the interrogators would tear you apart. And because you are fundamentally a weak man, you would talk. But if you don't survive, then I get to write the final chapter of *Discovery*'s history, sad as it will be.'

Bauer simply sidestepped when Reed made a desperate attempt to grab him. Reed fell and rolled over, then began shaking violently. His body was seized by convulsions that made his spine bend like a bow. Keeping a safe distance, Bauer watched, fascinated, as his creation went about its deadly business. He couldn't take his eyes off Reed for more than a few seconds, not even when he began to arm the autodestruct sequence.

32

It won't be the gas jets. Something else . . . What?

The question echoed in Smith's mind as he hurried under the shuttle's left wing towards the landing gear. Either Bauer didn't know or he had overlooked the fact that there was another way into the craft other than through the cocoon. Smith stepped up on the tyres, then moved onto the landing assembly. He popped open a small hatch, reached inside, and pulled down a handcrank. Fitting one end into a slot, he began turning. Little by little, the much larger hatch detached itself from the orbiter.

Pushing the hatch to one side, Smith climbed into the belly of the payload bay located behind the Spacelab. He found himself crouching next to the get-away canisters where unattended experiments and supplies were stored. In front of them was an oval, submarine-type door – the back entry to the Spacelab.

Inside the Spacelab, Megan Olson stared in horror as the wheel on the rear door spun faster and faster. Leaning against the sled chair, she felt dizzy and nauseated. Even though she'd been strapped in as securely as possible, the buffeting reentry had been extremely jarring. She felt as though her entire body had been pummelled.

It's not too late. I can still get out of here.

Seizing that thought, she'd climbed out of the sled

chair and staggered to the door that connected the lab to the tunnel. But after a few minutes of trying, she realized that either she was too weak or the door was locked from the outside.

Fighting back tears, she had tried desperately to think of another way out. Then she had heard the sounds coming from the get-away section of the pay-load bay.

Why is Reed coming back? And why that way?

Frantically Megan looked around for something that might serve as a weapon, but found nothing. She heard the hiss of a seal breaking. As the door swung back, she moved to the side, raising both arms over her head. Surprise would be her only defence against Reed.

First a leg appeared, then a pair of arms. As soon as Megan saw the helmet, she started to bring down her arms. Then, in that split second, she realized that it wasn't a space suit, but one designed for biohazard work. She managed to stop her swing just as the figure looked up at her.

'Megan!'

She tried to grab Smith but her gloved hands slipped off his suit. The next instant he was holding her by the shoulders, his helmet bumping hers, their faceplates touching. She couldn't take her eyes off his. She leaned against his shoulder and wept for everything that, only moments ago, seemed to have been snatched away, and was now restored. She pulled back a little so that she could look at him.

'How did you know?'

'They heard you in mission control. Not much got through, but enough so they knew you were alive.'

'So you came for me . . .'

They stared at each other, then Smith said, 'Come on. We've got to get out of here.'

'But Reed –'

'I know about him,' Smith told her. 'He was working for Karl Bauer.'

'*Bauer?*'

'He was the man you saw with Reed the night before the launch. Bauer's onboard right now. He came to take the smallpox mutation Reed had created in microgravity. But he's not going to just walk out of here, Megan. He has to destroy all evidence of what happened on this flight.'

Then he told her exactly where the shuttle was parked and why, about the holding chamber that was really a giant crematorium.

Megan shook her head. 'No, Jon,' she said. 'He's doing it another way.'

'What do you mean?'

Megan pointed to an overhead readout she had noticed a moment ago. 'That's the autodestruct sequence, armed and counting down. Once it's been set, it can't be turned off or extended. We have less than four minutes before the shuttle explodes.'

Seventy seconds later, Smith and Megan Olson were climbing out of the craft the way Smith had gone in.

Megan shuddered when she looked around the cavernous death chamber. She turned to Smith, who was locking the hatch they had passed through.

'What are you doing?'

'Making sure that no one follows us.' He stepped on a tyre, then to the ground. 'Let's go.'

Moving as quickly as their bulky suits permitted, they

came around the wing. Megan gasped when she saw the cocoon mated to the shuttle's lower escape hatch and to the cavity in the far wall.

'Is that how we're supposed to get out?'

'It's the only way.'

As they approached the cocoon, Smith could see that the hatch to the shuttle was closed. There was no sign of Bauer inside the plastic tunnel or in the pass-through decontamination area. From his RAID suit he brought out a knife with a retractable blade, and with a few bold strokes, cut an opening in the cocoon.

'Go through,' he told Megan, then followed her into the cocoon.

Once inside, Megan turned when she no longer felt Smith's hand on her shoulder. She found him staring at the hatch.

'Jon, we're running out of time!'

Then she saw the cold, pitiless expression behind his faceplate, the grief in his eyes. His anger spilled into her as she pictured the bodies of her crewmates, the terrible way they had died. She understood exactly what he intended to do.

'Go down the tunnel,' Smith said. 'Don't stop. Don't look back. There's a decontamination chamber right behind the blast door.'

'Jon –?'

'Go, Megan.'

Smith didn't think of the time that he had left, of the odds of making it out of the chamber alive. He knew that men like Bauer, rich and powerful, seldom if ever paid for their crimes – especially since those who could have condemned them were already dead. Worse, Bauer would try again. Somewhere, sometime, there would be another Cassandra Compact.

Smith hurried through the small decontamination pass-through – the size of a shower stall – and came up to the hatch. Through the rectangular porthole he saw the mutilated body of Dylan Reed and Bauer, holding a ceramic capsule in the palm of his hand.

He wasn't going to bring out the entire sample. He didn't need to. A drop would be more than enough. A drop he could hide in his suit; that would be enough to re-create the monstrosity.

Crouching, Smith opened a panel at the bottom of the hatch and engaged the manual override. He rose just as Bauer turned, his expression one of total disbelief.

It can't be . . . !

Smith saw Bauer's lips move but didn't hear his words until he had changed the frequency on his helmet radio.

'. . . are you doing here?'

Silently he watched as Bauer punched the keypad, watched as his incredulity dissolved to horror when the hatch didn't open.

'What are you doing here?' Bauer screamed. 'Open this hatch!'

'No, Doctor,' Smith replied. 'I think I'll leave you with your creation.'

Bauer's face was contorted with fear. 'Listen to me –!'

Smith changed the frequency and began walking away. He thought he heard fists falling on the hatch, but knew that that was just his imagination.

'Control, this is Smith. Where's Olson?'

Static crackled in his ear, then a familiar voice came through. 'Jon, this is Klein. Megan is safe. She's in the decontamination area. She told me that the autodestruct was armed.'

'Bauer did that.'

'Where is he?'

'Still inside.'

After a moment's hesitation, Klein replied, 'Understood. We're opening the blast door, Jon. But you only have a few seconds. Hurry!'

At the end of the cocoon Smith saw the huge door start to swing open. With sweat pouring off him, he forced himself to move even faster. There it was, the cavity cut into the wall at the end of the cocoon.

Then the door stopped and began closing. He was still at least fifteen steps away.

'What's happening?' he demanded.

'The door closes automatically,' Klein shouted back. 'It will seal five seconds before the blast. Jon, get *out* of there.'

Smith forced his screaming muscles to move even faster. One step, one second, one step, one second . . .

The blast door moved relentlessly, reducing the size of the opening. With a final desperate effort Smith hurled himself forward, hitting the leading edge of the door, squeezing himself through as it brushed by him and locked.

Seconds later, he was thrown to the ground as the earth seemed to rear up and something like a giant's fist slammed into the blast door.

He opened his eyes to white: ceiling, walls, sheets. With a soldier's instincts he lay perfectly still, then slowly, carefully moved his neck, hands, feet, arms, and legs. His body felt as though it had gone over Niagara Falls in a barrel.

The door opened and Klein walked in.

'Where am I?' Smith asked, his voice weak.

'In the land of the living, I'm happy to say,' Klein replied. 'The doctor tells me that you'll be just fine.'

'How –?'

'After the shuttle exploded, Jack Riley and his team went into the decontamination chamber, put you through the process, then got you out.'

'Megan?'

'She's fine. You both are.'

Smith felt his limbs turn to jelly. 'It's over,' he whispered.

Somewhere far away he heard Klein reply, 'Yes. The compact has been broken.'

Epilogue

According to the media reports, General Frank Richardson and NSA Deputy-Director Anthony Price were killed in a tragic crash due to faulty brake lines. Richardson was given a warrior's burial at Arlington National Cemetery while Price was interred in his family's plot in New Hampshire. The president, citing overseas commitments, was absent on both occasions.

Subsequent reports dealt with the crash of a private jet over the Pacific Ocean. The plane, belonging to the Bauer-Zermatt pharmaceutical company, went down six hundred miles west of Los Angeles on its way to the Big Island of Hawaii. There was only one passenger onboard: Dr Karl Bauer.

President Castilla led the nation in mourning its greatest space tragedy since the *Challenger* disaster. Investigators determined that the explosion onboard the shuttle *Discovery* was linked to fuel-pump problems during the craft's descent into Edwards Air Force Base.

'What will happen to Megan?' Randi Russell asked.

She stood beside Smith in a small cemetery called Tsarsoye, overlooking Moscow and the river.

'She's not Megan anymore,' Smith replied. 'She has a new name, a new face, new identity.' He paused. 'She survived, but in the end she was counted among the dead. There was no choice. She had to give up her old life if the secret of what really happened was to remain intact.'

Randi nodded. Through the CIA grapevine she had heard rumours that one or more of the shuttle astronauts had survived. But after a while, the whispers died away. When Smith had arrived in Moscow, she turned to him for the truth. Megan Olson had been a longtime friend of Sophia's . . . and of hers as well. Randi felt she had a right to know if Megan was still alive somewhere.

'Thank you for telling me about her,' she said.

Smith looked over the rows of headstones. 'Without your help, everything would have ended differently,' he said softly.

Smith stepped forward and laid flowers on Yuri Danko's grave.

'Without the brave, where would any of us be?'

All Orion/Phoenix titles are available at your local bookshop or from the following address:

Mail Order Department
Littlehampton Book Services
FREEPOST BR535
Worthing, West Sussex, BN13 3BR
telephone 01903 828503, *facsimile* 01903 828802
e-mail MailOrders@lbsltd.co.uk
(Please ensure that you include full postal address details)

Payment can be made either by credit/debit card (Visa, Mastercard, Access and Switch accepted) or by sending a £ Sterling cheque or postal order made payable to *Littlehampton Book Services*.
DO NOT SEND CASH OR CURRENCY

Please add the following to cover postage and packing

UK and BFPO:
£1.50 for the first book, and 50p for each additional book to a maximum of £3.50

Overseas and Eire:
£2.50 for the first book plus £1.00 for the second book and 50p for each additional book ordered

---

BLOCK CAPITALS PLEASE

name of cardholder ....

address of cardholder ....

delivery address
(if different from cardholder)
....
....
....

postcode ....

postcode ....

☐ I enclose my remittance for £............................

☐ please debit my Mastercard/Visa/Access/Switch (delete as appropriate)

card number ☐☐☐☐☐☐☐☐☐☐☐☐☐☐☐☐

expiry date ☐☐☐☐   Switch issue no. ☐☐

signature ....

prices and availability are subject to change without notice